P9-BJO-694

Scribner Reprint Editions

THE NOVELS AND TALES OF HENRY JAMES

New York Edition

VOLUME III

THE PORTRAIT OF A LADY

VOLUME I

HENRY JAMES

AUGUSTUS M. KELLEY • PUBLISHERS

FAIRFIELD 1976

Re-issued 1976 by
Augustus M. Kelley, Publishers
Fairfield, New Jersey 07006
By arrangement with CHARLES SCRIBNER'S SONS

Library of Congress Cataloging in Publication Data

James, Henry, 1843-1916.
The portrait of a lady.

(Scribner reprint editions)
Reprint of the ed. published by Scribner, New York, which was issued as v. 3-4 of The novels and tales of Henry James.
I. Title.
PZ3.J234No7 vol.3 [PS2116.P6] 813'.4 72-158782
ISBN 0-678-02803-6 (v. 3)
ISBN 0-678-02804-4 (v. 4)

PRINTED IN THE UNITED STATES OF AMERICA
by SENTRY PRESS, NEW YORK, N. Y. 10013
Bound by A. HOROWITZ & SON, FAIRFIELD, N. J.

PREFACE

"THE PORTRAIT OF A LADY" was, like "Roderick Hudson," begun in Florence, during three months spent there in the spring of 1879. Like "Roderick" and like "The American," it had been designed for publication in "The Atlantic Monthly," where it began to appear in 1880. It differed from its two predecessors, however, in finding a course also open to it, from month to month, in "Macmillan's Magazine"; which was to be for me one of the last occasions of simultaneous "serialisation" in the two countries that the changing conditions of literary intercourse between England and the United States had up to then left unaltered. It is a long novel, and I was long in writing it; I remember being again much occupied with it, the following year, during a stay of several weeks made in Venice. I had rooms on Riva Schiavoni, at the top of a house near the passage leading off to San Zaccaria; the waterside life, the wondrous lagoon spread before me, and the ceaseless human chatter of Venice came in at my windows, to which I seem to myself to have been constantly driven, in the fruitless fidget of composition, as if to see whether, out in the blue channel, the ship of some right suggestion, of some better phrase, of the next happy twist of my subject, the next true touch for my canvas, might n't come into sight. But I recall vividly enough that the response most elicited, in general, to these restless appeals was the rather grim admonition that romantic and historic sites, such as the land of Italy abounds in, offer the artist a questionable aid to concentration when they themselves are not to be the subject of it. They are too rich in their own life and too charged with their own meanings merely to help him out with a lame phrase; they draw him away from his small question to their own greater ones; so that, after a little, he feels, while thus yearning toward them in his difficulty, as if he were asking an army of glorious veterans to help him to arrest a peddler who has given him the wrong change.

There are pages of the book which, in the reading over, have seemed to make me see again the bristling curve of the wide Riva, the large colour-spots of the balconied houses and the repeated undulation of the little hunchbacked bridges, marked by the rise and drop again, with the wave, of foreshortened clicking pedestrians. The Venetian foot-fall and the Venetian cry — all talk there, wherever uttered, having the pitch of a call across the water — come in once more at the window, renewing one's old impression of the delighted senses and the divided, frustrated mind. How can places that speak *in general* so to the imagination not give it, at the moment, the particular thing it wants? I recollect again and again, in beautiful places, dropping into that wonderment. The real truth is, I think, that they express, under this appeal, only too much — more than, in the given case, one has use for; so that one finds one's self working less congruously, after all, so far as the surrounding picture is concerned, than in presence of the moderate and the neutral, to which we may lend something of the light of our vision. Such a place as Venice is too proud for such charities; Venice does n't borrow, she but all magnificently gives. We profit by that enormously, but to do so we must either be quite off duty or be on it in her service alone. Such, and so rueful, are these reminiscences; though on the whole, no doubt, one's book, and one's "literary effort" at large, were to be the better for them. Strangely fertilising, in the long run, does a wasted effort of attention often prove. It all depends on *how* the attention has been cheated, has been squandered. There are high-handed insolent frauds, and there are insidious sneaking ones. And there is, I fear, even on the most designing artist's part, always witless enough good faith, always anxious enough desire, to fail to guard him against their deceits.

Trying to recover here, for recognition, the germ of my idea, I see that it must have consisted not at all in any conceit of a "plot," nefarious name, in any flash, upon the fancy, of a set of relations, or in any one of those situations that, by a logic of their own, immediately fall, for the fabulist, into movement, into a march or a rush, a patter of quick steps; but altogether in the sense of a single character, the character and aspect of a particular engaging young woman, to which all the usual elements of a "subject," certainly of a setting, were to need to be superadded. Quite as interesting as the young woman herself, at her best, do I find, I must again repeat, this projection of memory upon the whole matter of the growth, in one's imagination, of some such apology for a motive. These are the fascinations of the fabulist's art, these lurking forces of expansion, these necessities of upspringing in the seed, these beautiful determinations, on the part of the idea entertained, to grow as tall as possible, to push into the light and the air and thickly flower there; and, quite as much, these fine possibilities of recovering, from some good standpoint on the ground gained, the intimate history of the business — of retracing and reconstructing its steps and stages. I have always fondly remembered a remark that I heard fall years ago from the lips of Ivan Turgenieff in regard to his own experience of the usual origin of the fictive picture. It began for him almost always with the vision of some person or persons, who hovered before him, soliciting him, as the active or passive figure, interesting him and appealing to him just as they were and by what they were. He saw them, in that fashion, as *disponibles*, saw them subject to the chances, the complications of existence, and saw them vividly, but then had to find for them the right relations, those that would most bring them out; to imagine, to invent and select and piece together the situations most useful and favourable to the sense of the creatures themselves, the complications they would be most likely to produce and to feel.

"To arrive at these things is to arrive at my 'story,'" he said, "and that 's the way I look for it. The result is that I 'm often accused of not having 'story' enough. I seem to myself to have as much as I need — to show my people, to exhibit their relations with each other; for that is all my measure. If I watch them long enough I see them come together, I see them *placed*, I see them engaged in this or that act and in this or that difficulty. How they look and move and speak and behave, always in the setting I have found for them, is my account of them — of which I dare say, alas, *que cela manque souvent d'architecture*. But I would rather, I think, have too little architecture than too much — when there 's danger of its interfering with my measure of the truth. The French of course like more of it than I give — having by their own genius such a hand for it; and indeed one must give all one can. As for the origin of one's wind-blown germs themselves, who shall say, as you ask, where *they* come from? We have to go too far back, too far behind, to say. Is n't it all we can say that they come from every quarter of heaven, that they are *there* at almost any turn of the road? They accumulate, and we are always picking them over, selecting among them. They are the breath of life — by which I mean that life, in its own way, breathes them upon us. They are so, in a manner prescribed and imposed — floated into our minds by the current of life. That reduces to imbecility the vain critic's quarrel, so often, with one's subject, when he has n't the wit to accept it. Will he point out then which other it should properly have been? — his office being, essentially *to* point out. *Il en serait bien embarrassé*. Ah, when he points out what I 've done or failed to do with it, that 's another matter: there he 's on his ground. I give him up my 'architecture,'" my distinguished friend concluded, "as much as he will."

So this beautiful genius, and I recall with comfort the gratitude I drew from his reference to the intensity of suggestion that may reside in the stray figure, the unattached character, the image *en disponibilité*. It gave me higher warrant than I seemed then to have met for just that blest habit of one's own imagination, the trick of investing some conceived or encountered individual, some brace or group of individuals, with the germinal property and authority.

PREFACE

I was myself so much more antecedently conscious of my figures than of their setting — a too preliminary, a preferential interest in which struck me as in general such a putting of the cart before the horse. I might envy, though I could n't emulate, the imaginative writer so constituted as to see his fable first and to make out its agents afterwards: I could think so little of any fable that did n't need its agents positively to launch it; I could think so little of any situation that did n't depend for its interest on the nature of the persons situated, and thereby on their way of taking it. There are methods of so-called presentation, I believe — among novelists who have appeared to flourish — that offer the situation as indifferent to that support; but I have not lost the sense of the value for me, at the time, of the admirable Russian's testimony to my not needing, all superstitiously, to try and perform any such gymnastic. Other echoes from the same source linger with me, I confess, as unfadingly — if it be not all indeed one much-embracing echo. It was impossible after that not to read, for one's uses, high lucidity into the tormented and disfigured and bemuddled question of the objective value, and even quite into that of the critical appreciation, of "subject" in the novel.

One had had from an early time, for that matter, the instinct of the right estimate of such values and of its reducing to the inane the dull dispute over the "immoral" subject and the moral. Recognising so promptly the one measure of the worth of a given subject, the question about it that, rightly answered, disposes of all others — is it valid, in a word, is it genuine, is it sincere, the result of some direct impression or perception of life? — I had found small edification, mostly, in a critical pretension that had neglected from the first all delimitation of ground and all definition of terms. The air of my earlier time shows, to memory, as darkened, all round, with that vanity — unless the difference to-day be just in one's own final impatience, the lapse of one's attention. There is, I think, no more nutritive or suggestive truth in this connexion than that of the perfect dependence of the "moral" sense of a work of art on the amount of felt life concerned in producing it. The question comes back thus, obviously, to the kind and the degree of the artist's prime sensibility, which is the soil out of which his subject springs. The quality and capacity of that soil, its ability to "grow" with due freshness and straightness any vision of life, represents, strongly or weakly, the projected morality. That element is but another name for the more or less close connexion of the subject with some mark made on the intelligence, with some sincere experience. By which, at the same time, of course, one is far from contending that this enveloping air of the artist's humanity — which gives the last touch to the worth of the work — is not a widely and wondrously varying element; being on one occasion a rich and magnificent medium and on another a comparatively poor and ungenerous one. Here we get exactly the high price of the novel as a literary form — its power not only, while preserving that form with closeness, to range through all the differences of the individual relation to its general subject-matter, all the varieties of outlook on life, of disposition to reflect and project, created by conditions that are never the same from man to man (or, so far as that goes, from man to woman), but positively to appear more true to its character in proportion as it strains, or tends to burst, with a latent extravagance, its mould.

The house of fiction has in short not one window, but a million — a number of possible windows not to be reckoned, rather; every one of which has been pierced, or is still pierceable, in its vast front, by the need of the individual vision and by the pressure of the individual will. These apertures, of dissimilar shape and size, hang so, all together, over the human scene that we might have expected of them a greater sameness of report than we find. They are but windows at the best, mere holes in a dead wall, disconnected, perched aloft; they are not hinged doors opening straight upon life. But they have this mark of their own that at each of them stands a figure with a pair of eyes, or at least with a field-glass, which forms, again and again, for observation, a unique instrument, insuring to the person making use of it an impression distinct from every other. He and his neighbours are watching the same show, but one seeing more where the other sees less, one seeing black where the other sees white, one seeing big where the other sees small, one seeing coarse where the other sees fine. And so on, and so on; there is fortunately no saying on what, for the particular pair of eyes, the window may *not* open; "fortunately" by reason, precisely, of this incalculability of range. The spreading field, the human scene, is the "choice of subject"; the pierced aperture, either broad or balconied or slit-like and low-browed, is the "literary form"; but they are, singly or together, as nothing without the posted presence of the watcher — without, in other words, the consciousness of the artist. Tell me what the artist is, and I will tell you of what he has *been* conscious. Thereby I shall express to you at once his boundless freedom and his "moral" reference.

All this is a long way round, however, for my word about my dim first move toward "The Portrait," which was exactly my grasp of a single character — an acquisition I had made, moreover, after a fashion not here to be retraced. Enough that I was, as seemed to me, in complete possession of it, that I had been so for a long time, that this had made it familiar and yet had not blurred its charm, and that, all urgently, all tormentingly, I saw it in motion and, so to speak, in transit. This amounts to saying that I saw it as bent upon its fate — some fate or other; *which*, among the possibilities, being precisely the question. Thus I had my vivid individual — vivid, so strangely, in spite of being still at large, not confined by the conditions, not engaged in the tangle, to which we look for much of the impress that constitutes an identity. If the apparition was still all to be placed how came it to be vivid? — since we puzzle such quantities out, mostly, just by the business of placing them. One could answer such a question beautifully, doubtless, if one could do so subtle, if not so monstrous, a thing as to write the history of the growth of one's imagination. One would describe then what, at a given time, had extraordinarily happened to it, and one would so, for instance, be in a position to tell, with an approach to clearness, how, under favour of occasion, it had been able to take over (take over straight from life) such and such a constituted, animated figure or form. The figure has to that extent, as you see, *been* placed — placed in the imagination that detains it, preserves, protects, enjoys it, conscious of its presence in the dusky, crowded, heterogeneous back-shop of the mind very much as a wary dealer in precious odds and ends, competent to make an "advance" on rare objects confided to him, is conscious of the rare little "piece" left in deposit by the reduced, mysterious lady of title or the speculative amateur, and which is already there to disclose its merit afresh as soon as a key shall have clicked in a cupboard-door.

That may be, I recognise, a somewhat superfine analogy for the particular "value" I here speak of, the image of the young feminine nature that I had had for so considerable a time all curiously at my disposal; but it appears to fond memory quite to fit the fact — with the recall, in addition, of my pious desire but to place my treasure right. I quite remind myself thus of the dealer resigned not to "realise," resigned to keeping the precious object locked up indefinitely rather than commit it, at no matter what price, to vulgar hands. For there *are* dealers in these forms and figures and treasures capable of that refinement. The point is, however, that this single small corner-stone, the conception of a certain young woman affronting her destiny, had begun with being all my outfit for the large building of "The Portrait of a Lady." It came to be a square and spacious house — or has at least seemed so to me in this going over it again; but, such as it is, it had to be put up round my young woman while she stood there in perfect isolation. That is to me, artistically speaking, the circumstance of interest; for I have lost myself once more, I confess, in the curiosity of analysing the structure. By what process of logical accretion was this slight "personality," the mere slim shade of an intelligent but presumptuous girl, to find itself endowed with the high attributes of a Subject? —and indeed by what thinness, at the best, would such a subject not be vitiated? Millions of presumptuous girls, intelligent or not intelligent, daily affront their destiny, and what is it open to their destiny to *be*, at the most, that we should make an ado about it? The novel is of its very nature an "ado," an ado about something, and the larger the form it takes the greater of course the ado. Therefore, consciously, that was what one was in for — for positively organising an ado about Isabel Archer.

One looked it well in the face, I seem to remember, this extravagance; and with the effect precisely of recognising the charm of the problem. Challenge any such problem with any intelligence, and you immediately see how full it is of substance; the wonder being, all the while, as we look at the world, how absolutely, how inordinately, the Isabel Archers, and even much smaller female fry, insist on mattering. George Eliot has admirably noted it — "In these frail vessels is borne onward through the ages the treasure of human affection." In "Romeo and Juliet" Juliet has to be important, just as, in "Adam Bede" and "The Mill on the Floss" and "Middlemarch" and "Daniel Deronda," Hetty Sorrel and Maggie Tulliver and Rosamond Vincy and Gwendolen Harleth have to be; with that much of firm ground, that much of bracing air, at the disposal all the while of their feet and their lungs. They are typical, none the less, of a class difficult, in the individual case, to make a centre of interest; so difficult in fact that many an expert painter, as for instance Dickens and Walter Scott, as for instance even, in the main, so subtle a hand as that of R. L. Stevenson, has preferred to leave the task unattempted. There are in fact writers as to whom we make out that their refuge from this is to assume it to be not worth their attempting; by which pusillanimity in truth their honour is scantly saved. It is never an attestation of a value, or even of our imperfect sense of one, it is never a tribute to any truth at all, that we shall represent that value badly. It never makes up, artistically, for an artist's dim feeling about a thing that he shall "do" the thing as ill as possible. There are better ways than that, the best of all of which is to begin with less stupidity.

It may be answered meanwhile, in regard to Shakespeare's and to George Eliot's testimony, that their concession to the "importance" of their Juliets and Cleopatras and Portias (even with Portia as the very type and model of the young person intelligent and presumptuous) and to that of their Hettys and Maggies and Rosamonds and Gwendolens, suffers the abatement that these slimnesses are, when figuring as the main props of the theme, never suffered to be sole ministers of its appeal, but have their inadequacy eked out with comic relief and underplots, as the playwrights say, when not with murders and battles and the great mutations of the world. If they are shown as "mattering" as much as they could possibly pretend to, the proof of it is in a hundred other persons, made of much stouter stuff, and each involved moreover in a hundred relations which matter to *them* concomitantly with that one. Cleopatra matters, beyond bounds, to Antony, but his colleagues, his antagonists, the state of Rome and the impending battle also prodigiously matter; Portia matters to Antonio, and to Shylock, and to the Prince of Morocco, to the fifty aspiring princes, but for these gentry there are other lively concerns; for Antonio, notably, there are Shylock and Bassanio and his lost ventures and the extremity of his predicament. This extremity indeed, by the same token, matters to Portia — though its doing so becomes of interest all by the fact that Portia matters to *us*. That she does so, at any rate, and that almost everything comes round to it again, supports my contention as to this fine example of the value recognised in the mere young thing. (I say "mere" young thing because I guess that even Shakespeare, preoccupied mainly though he may have been with the passions of princes, would scarce have pretended to found the best of his appeal for her on her high social position.) It is an example exactly of the deep difficulty braved — the difficulty of making George Eliot's "frail vessel," if not the all-in-all for our attention, at least the clearest of the call.

Now to see deep difficulty braved is at any time, for the really addicted artist, to feel almost even as a pang the beautiful incentive, and to feel it verily in such sort as to wish the danger intensified. The difficulty most worth tackling can only be for him, in these conditions, the greatest the case permits of. So I remember feeling here (in presence, always, that is, of the particular uncertainty of my ground), that there would be one way better than another — oh, ever so much better than any other! — of making it fight out its battle. The frail vessel, that charged with George Eliot's "treasure," and thereby of such importance to those who curiously approach it, has likewise possibilities of importance to itself, possibilities which permit of treatment and in fact peculiarly require it from the moment they are considered at all. There is always the escape from any close account of the weak agent of such spells by using as a bridge for evasion, for retreat and flight, the view of her relation to those surrounding her. Make it predominantly a view of *their* relation and the trick is played: you give the general sense of her effect, and you give it, so far as the raising on it of a superstructure goes, with the maximum of ease. Well, I recall perfectly how little, in my now quite established connexion, the maximum of ease appealed to me, and how I seemed to get rid of it by an honest transposition of the weights in the two scales. "Place the centre of the subject in the young woman's own consciousness," I said to myself, "and you get as interesting and as beautiful a difficulty as you could wish. Stick to *that* — for the centre; put the heaviest weight into *that* scale, which will be so largely the scale of her relation to herself. Make her only interested enough, at the same time, in the things that are not herself, and this relation need n't fear to be too limited. Place meanwhile in the other scale the lighter weight (which is usually the one that tips the balance of interest): press least hard, in short, on the consciousness of your heroine's satellites, especially the male; make it an interest contributive only to the greater one. See, at all events, what can be done in this way. What better field could there be for a due ingenuity? The girl hovers, inextinguishable, as a charming creature, and the job will be to translate her into the highest terms of that formula, and as nearly as possible moreover into *all* of them. To depend upon her and her little concerns wholly to see you through will necessitate, remember, your really 'doing' her."

So far I reasoned, and it took nothing less than that technical rigour, I now easily see, to inspire me with the right confidence for erecting on such a plot of ground the neat and careful and proportioned pile of bricks that arches over it and that was thus to form, constructionally speaking, a literary monument. Such is the aspect that to-day "The Portrait" wears for me: a structure reared with an "architectural" competence, as Turgenieff would have said, that makes it, to the author's own sense, the most proportioned of his productions after "The Ambassadors"— which was to follow it so many years later and which has, no doubt, a superior roundness. On one thing I was determined; that, though I should clearly have to pile brick upon brick for the creation of an interest, I would leave no pretext for saying that anything is out of line, scale or perspective. I would build large—in fine embossed vaults and painted arches, as who should say, and yet never let it appear that the chequered pavement, the ground under the reader's feet, fails to stretch at every point to the base of the walls. That precautionary spirit, on re-perusal of the book, is the old note that most touches me: it testifies so, for my own ear, to the anxiety of my provision for the reader's amusement. I felt, in view of the possible limitations of my subject, that no such provision could be excessive, and the development of the latter was simply the general form of that earnest quest. And I find indeed that this is the only account I can give myself of the evolution of the fable: it is all under the head thus named that I conceive the needful accretion as having taken place, the right complications as having started. It was naturally of the essence that the young woman should be herself complex; that was rudimentary — or was at any rate the light in which Isabel Archer had originally dawned. It went, however, but a certain way, and other lights, contending, conflicting lights, and of as many different colours, if possible, as the rockets, the Roman candles and Catherine-wheels of a "pyrotechnic display," would be employable to attest that she was. I had, no doubt, a groping instinct for the right complications, since I am quite unable to track the footsteps of those that constitute, as the case stands, the general situation exhibited. They are there, for what they are worth, and as numerous as might be; but my memory, I confess, is a blank as to how and whence they came.

I seem to myself to have waked up one morning in possession of them — of Ralph Touchett and his parents, of Madame Merle, of Gilbert Osmond and his daughter and his sister, of Lord Warburton, Caspar Goodwood and Miss Stackpole, the definite array of contributions to Isabel Archer's history. I recognised them, I knew them, they were the numbered pieces of my puzzle, the concrete terms of my "plot." It was as if they had simply, by an impulse of their own, floated into my ken, and all in response to my primary question: "Well, what will she *do?*" Their answer seemed to be that if I would trust them they would show me; on which, with an urgent appeal to them to make it at least as interesting as they could, I trusted them. They were like the group of attendants and entertainers who come down by train when people in the country give a party; they represented the contract for carrying the party on. That was an excellent relation with them — a possible one even with so broken a reed (from her slightness of cohesion) as Henrietta Stackpole. It is a familiar truth to the novelist, at the strenuous hour, that, as certain elements in any work are of the essence, so others are only of the form; that as this or that character, this or that disposition of the material, belongs to the subject directly, so to speak, so this or that other belongs to it but indirectly — belongs intimately to the treatment. This is a truth, however, of which he rarely gets the benefit — since it could be assured to him, really, but by criticism based upon perception, criticism which is too little of this world. He must not think of benefits, moreover, I freely recognise, for that way dishonour lies: he has, that is, but one to think of — the benefit, whatever it may be, involved in his having cast a spell upon the simpler, the very simplest, forms of attention. This is all he is entitled to; he is entitled to nothing, he is bound to admit, that can come to him, from the reader, as a result on the latter's part of any act of reflexion or discrimination. He may *enjoy* this finer tribute — that is another affair, but on condition only of taking it as a gratuity "thrown in," a mere miraculous windfall, the fruit of a tree he may not pretend to have shaken. Against reflexion, against discrimination, in his interest, all earth and air conspire; wherefore it is that, as I say, he must in many a case have schooled himself, from the first, to work but for a "living wage." The living wage is the reader's grant of the least possible quantity of attention required for consciousness of a "spell." The occasional charming "tip" is an act of his intelligence over and beyond this, a golden apple, for the writer's lap, straight from the wind-stirred tree. The artist may of course, in wanton moods, dream of some Paradise (for art) where the direct appeal to the intelligence might be legalised; for to such extravagances as these his yearning mind can scarce hope ever completely to close itself. The most he can do is to remember they *are* extravagances.

All of which is perhaps but a gracefully devious way of saying that Henrietta Stackpole was a good example, in "The Portrait," of the truth to which I just adverted — as good an example as I could name were it not that Maria Gostrey, in "The Ambassadors," then in the bosom of time, may be mentioned as a better. Each of these persons is but wheels to the coach; neither belongs to the body of that vehicle, or is for a moment accommodated with a seat inside. There the subject alone is ensconced, in the form of its "hero and heroine," and of the privileged high officials, say, who ride with the king and queen. There are reasons why one would have liked this to be felt, as in general one would like almost anything to be felt, in one's work, that one has one's self contributively felt. We have seen, however, how idle is that pretension, which I should be sorry to make too much of. Maria Gostrey and Miss Stackpole then are cases, each, of the light *ficelle*, not of the true agent; they may run beside the coach "for all they are worth," they may cling to it till they are out of breath (as poor Miss Stackpole all so visibly does), but neither, all the while, so much as gets her foot on the step, neither ceases for a moment to tread the dusty road. Put it even that they are like the fishwives who helped to bring back to Paris from Versailles, on that most ominous day of the first half of the French Revolution, the carriage of the royal family. The only thing is that I may well be asked, I acknowledge, why then, in the present fiction, I have suffered Henrietta (of whom we have indubitably too much) so officiously, so strangely, so almost inexplicably, to pervade. I will presently say what I can for that anomaly — and in the most conciliatory fashion.

A point I wish still more to make is that if my relation of confidence with the actors in my drama who *were*, unlike Miss Stackpole, true agents, was an excellent one to have arrived at, there still remained my relation with the reader, which was another affair altogether and as to which I felt no one to be trusted but myself. That solicitude was to be accordingly expressed in the artful patience with which, as I have said, I piled brick upon brick. The bricks, for the whole counting-over — putting for bricks little touches and inventions and enhancements by the way — affect me in truth as well-nigh innumerable and as ever so scrupulously fitted together and packed-in. It is an effect of detail, of the minutest; though, if one were in this connexion to say all, one would express the hope that the general, the ampler air of the modest monument still survives. I do at least seem to catch the key to a part of this abundance of small anxious, ingenious illustration as I recollect putting my finger, in my young woman's interest, on the most obvious of her predicates. "What will she 'do'? Why, the first thing she'll do will be to come to Europe; which in fact will form, and all inevitably, no small part of her principal adventure. Coming to Europe is even for the 'frail vessels,' in this wonderful age, a mild adventure; but what is truer than that on one side — the side of their independence of flood and field, of the moving accident, of battle and murder and sudden death — her adventures are to be mild? Without her sense of them, her sense *for* them, as one may say, they are next to nothing at all; but isn't the beauty and the difficulty just in showing their mystic conversion by that sense, conversion into the stuff of drama or, even more delightful word still, of 'story'?" It was all as clear, my contention, as a silver bell. Two very good instances, I think, of this effect of conversion, two cases of the rare chemistry, are the pages in which Isabel, coming into the drawing-room at Gardencourt, coming in from a wet walk or whatever, that rainy afternoon, finds Madame Merle in possession of the place, Madame Merle seated, all absorbed but all serene, at the piano, and deeply recognises, in the striking of such an hour, in the presence there, among the gathering shades, of this personage, of whom a moment before she had never so much as heard, a turning-point in her life. It is dreadful to have too much, for any artistic demonstration, to dot one's i's and insist on one's intentions, and I am not eager to do it now; but the question here was that of producing the maximum of intensity with the minimum of strain.

The interest was to be raised to its pitch and yet the elements to be kept in their key; so that, should the whole thing duly impress, I might show what an "exciting" inward life may do for the person leading it even while it remains perfectly normal. And I cannot think of a more consistent application of that ideal unless it be in the long statement, just beyond the middle of the book, of my young woman's extraordinary meditative vigil on the occasion that was to become for her such a landmark. Reduced to its essence, it is but the vigil of searching criticism; but it throws the action further forward than twenty "incidents" might have done. It was designed to have all the vivacity of incident and all the economy of picture. She sits up, by her dying fire, far into the night, under the spell of recognitions on which she finds the last sharpness suddenly wait. It is a representation simply of her motionlessly *seeing*, and an attempt withal to make the mere still lucidity of her act as "interesting" as the surprise of a caravan or the identification of a pirate. It represents, for that matter, one of the identifications dear to the novelist, and even indispensable to him; but it all goes on without her being approached by another person and without her leaving her chair. It is obviously the best thing in the book, but it is only a supreme illustration of the general plan. As to Henrietta, my apology for whom I just left incomplete, she exemplifies, I fear, in her superabundance, not an element of my plan, but only an excess of my zeal. So early was to begin my tendency to *overtreat*, rather than undertreat (when there was choice or danger) my subject. (Many members of my craft, I gather, are far from agreeing with me, but I have always held overtreating the minor disservice.) "Treating" that of "The Portrait" amounted to never forgetting, by any lapse, that the thing was under a special obligation to be amusing. There was the danger of the noted "thinness"—which was to be averted, tooth and nail, by cultivation of the lively. That is at least how I see it to-day. Henrietta must have been at that time a part of my wonderful notion of the lively. And then there was another matter. I had, within the few preceding years, come to live in London, and the "international" light lay, in those days, to my sense, thick and rich upon the scene. It was the light in which so much of the picture hung. But that *is* another matter. There is really too much to say.

HENRY JAMES.

THE PORTRAIT OF A LADY

VOLUME I

THE PORTRAIT OF A LADY

I

UNDER certain circumstances there are few hours in life more agreeable than the hour dedicated to the ceremony known as afternoon tea. There are circumstances in which, whether you partake of the tea or not — some people of course never do, — the situation is in itself delightful. Those that I have in mind in beginning to unfold this simple history offered an admirable setting to an innocent pastime. The implements of the little feast had been disposed upon the lawn of an old English country-house, in what I should call the perfect middle of a splendid summer afternoon. Part of the afternoon had waned, but much of it was left, and what was left was of the finest and rarest quality. Real dusk would not arrive for many hours; but the flood of summer light had begun to ebb, the air had grown mellow, the shadows were long upon the smooth, dense turf. They lengthened slowly, however, and the scene expressed that sense of leisure still to come which is perhaps the chief source of one's enjoyment of such a scene at such an hour. From five o'clock to eight is on certain occasions a little eternity; but on such an occasion as this the interval could be only an eternity of pleasure. The persons concerned in it were taking their pleasure quietly, and they were not of the sex which is supposed to furnish the regular votaries of the ceremony I have mentioned. The shadows on the perfect lawn were straight and angular; they were the shadows of an old man sitting in a deep wicker-chair near the low table on which the tea had been served, and of two younger men strolling to and fro, in desultory talk, in front of him. The old man had his cup in his hand; it was an unusually large cup, of a different pattern from the rest of the set and painted in brilliant colours. He disposed of its contents with much circumspection, holding it for a long time close to his chin, with his face turned to the house. His companions had either finished their tea or were indifferent to their privilege; they smoked cigarettes as they continued to stroll. One of them, from time to time, as he passed, looked with a certain attention at the elder man, who, unconscious of observation, rested his eyes upon the rich red front of his dwelling. The house that rose beyond the lawn was a structure to repay such consideration and was the most characteristic object in the peculiarly English picture I have attempted to sketch.

It stood upon a low hill, above the river — the river being the Thames at some forty miles from London. A long gabled front of red brick, with the complexion of which time and the weather had played all sorts of pictorial tricks, only, however, to improve and refine it, presented to the lawn its patches of ivy, its clustered chimneys, its windows smothered in creepers. The house had a name and a history; the old gentleman taking his tea would have been delighted to tell you these things: how it had been built under

Edward the Sixth, had offered a night's hospitality to the great Elizabeth (whose august person had extended itself upon a huge, magnificent and terribly angular bed which still formed the principal honour of the sleeping apartments), had been a good deal bruised and defaced in Cromwell's wars, and then, under the Restoration, repaired and much enlarged; and how, finally, after having been remodelled and disfigured in the eighteenth century, it had passed into the careful keeping of a shrewd American banker, who had bought it originally because (owing to circumstances too complicated to set forth) it was offered at a great bargain: bought it with much grumbling at its ugliness, its antiquity, its incommodity, and who now, at the end of twenty years, had become conscious of a real æsthetic passion for it, so that he knew all its points and would tell you just where to stand to see them in combination and just the hour when the shadows of its various protuberances — which fell so softly upon the warm, weary brickwork — were of the right measure. Besides this, as I have said, he could have counted off most of the successive owners and occupants, several of whom were known to general fame; doing so, however, with an undemonstrative conviction that the latest phase of its destiny was not the least honourable. The front of the house overlooking that portion of the lawn with which we are concerned was not the entrance-front; this was in quite another quarter. Privacy here reigned supreme, and the wide carpet of turf that covered the level hill-top seemed but the extension of a luxurious interior. The great still oaks and beeches flung down a shade as dense as that of velvet curtains; and the place was furnished, like a room, with cushioned seats, with rich-coloured rugs, with the books and papers that lay upon the grass. The river was at some distance; where the ground began to slope the lawn, properly speaking, ceased. But it was none the less a charming walk down to the water.

The old gentleman at the tea-table, who had come from America thirty years before, had brought with him, at the top of his baggage, his American physiognomy; and he had not only brought it with him, but he had kept it in the best order, so that, if necessary, he might have taken it back to his own country with perfect confidence. At present, obviously, nevertheless, he was not likely to displace himself; his journeys were over and he was taking the rest that precedes the great rest. He had a narrow, clean-shaven face, with features evenly distributed and an expression of placid acuteness. It was evidently a face in which the range of representation was not large, so that the air of contented shrewdness was all the more of a merit. It seemed to tell that he had been successful in life, yet it seemed to tell also that his success had not been exclusive and invidious, but had had much of the inoffensiveness of failure. He had certainly had a great experience of men, but there was an almost rustic simplicity in the faint smile that played upon his lean, spacious cheek and lighted up his humorous eye as he at last slowly and carefully deposited his big tea-cup upon the table. He was neatly dressed, in well-brushed black; but a shawl was folded upon his knees, and his feet were encased in thick, embroidered slippers. A beautiful collie dog lay upon the grass near his chair, watching the master's face almost as tenderly as the master took in the still more magisterial physiognomy of the house; and a little bristling, bustling terrier bestowed a desultory attendance upon the other gentlemen.

One of these was a remarkably well-made man of five-and-thirty, with a face as English as that of the old gentleman I have just sketched was something else; a noticeably handsome face, fresh-coloured, fair and frank, with firm, straight features, a lively grey eye and the rich adornment of a chestnut beard. This person had a certain fortunate, brilliant exceptional look — the air of a happy temperament fertilised by a high civilisation — which would have made almost any observer envy him at a venture. He was booted and spurred, as if he had dismounted from a long ride; he wore a white hat, which looked too large for him; he held his two hands behind him, and in one of them — a large, white, well-shaped fist — was crumpled a pair of soiled dog-skin gloves.

His companion, measuring the length of the lawn beside him, was a person of quite a different pattern, who, although he might have excited grave curiosity, would not, like the other, have provoked you to wish yourself, almost blindly, in his place. Tall, lean, loosely and feebly put together, he had an ugly, sickly, witty, charming face, furnished, but by no means decorated, with a straggling moustache and whisker. He looked clever and ill — a combination by no means felicitous; and he wore a brown velvet jacket. He carried his hands in his pockets, and there was something in the way he did it that showed the habit was inveterate. His gait had a shambling, wandering quality; he was not very firm on his legs. As I have said, whenever he passed the old man in the chair he rested his eyes upon him; and at this moment, with their faces brought into relation, you would easily have seen they were father and son. The father caught his son's eye at last and gave him a mild, responsive smile.

"I 'm getting on very well," he said.

"Have you drunk your tea?" asked the son.

"Yes, and enjoyed it."

"Shall I give you some more?"

The old man considered, placidly. "Well, I guess I 'll wait and see." He had, in speaking, the American tone.

"Are you cold?" the son enquired.

The father slowly rubbed his legs. "Well, I don't know. I can't tell till I feel."

"Perhaps some one might feel for you," said the younger man, laughing.

"Oh, I hope some one will always feel for me! Don't you feel for me, Lord Warburton?"

"Oh yes, immensely," said the gentleman addressed as Lord Warburton, promptly. "I 'm bound to say you look wonderfully comfortable."

"Well, I suppose I am, in most respects." And the old man looked down at his green shawl and smoothed it over his knees. "The fact is I 've been comfortable so many years that I suppose I 've got so used to it I don't know it."

"Yes, that 's the bore of comfort," said Lord Warburton. "We only know when we 're uncomfortable."

"It strikes me we 're rather particular," his companion remarked.

"Oh yes, there 's no doubt we 're particular," Lord Warburton murmured. And then the three men remained silent a while; the two younger ones standing looking down at the other, who presently asked for more tea. "I should think you would be very unhappy with that shawl," Lord Warburton resumed while his companion filled the old man's cup again.

"Oh no, he must have the shawl!" cried the gentleman in the velvet coat. "Don't put such ideas as that into his head."

"It belongs to my wife," said the old man simply.

"Oh, if it's for sentimental reasons —" And Lord Warburton made a gesture of apology.

"I suppose I must give it to her when she comes," the old man went on.

"You 'll please to do nothing of the kind. You 'll keep it to cover your poor old legs."

"Well, you must n't abuse my legs," said the old man. "I guess they are as good as yours."

"Oh, you 're perfectly free to abuse mine," his son replied, giving him his tea.

"Well, we're two lame ducks; I don't think there's much difference."

"I 'm much obliged to you for calling me a duck. How 's your tea?"

"Well, it 's rather hot."

"That 's intended to be a merit."

"Ah, there 's a great deal of merit," murmured the

old man, kindly. "He 's a very good nurse, Lord Warburton."

"Is n't he a bit clumsy?" asked his lordship.

"Oh no, he 's not clumsy — considering that he 's an invalid himself. He 's a very good nurse — for a sick-nurse. I call him my sick-nurse because he 's sick himself."

"Oh, come, daddy!" the ugly young man exclaimed.

"Well, you are; I wish you were n't. But I suppose you can't help it."

"I might try: that's an idea," said the young man.

"Were you ever sick, Lord Warburton?" his father asked.

Lord Warburton considered a moment. "Yes, sir, once, in the Persian Gulf."

"He's making light of you, daddy," said the other young man. "That 's a sort of joke."

"Well, there seem to be so many sorts now," daddy replied, serenely. "You don't look as if you had been sick, any way, Lord Warburton."

"He's sick of life; he was just telling me so; going on fearfully about it," said Lord Warburton's friend.

"Is that true, sir?" asked the old man gravely.

"If it is, your son gave me no consolation. He 's a wretched fellow to talk to — a regular cynic. He does n't seem to believe in anything."

"That 's another sort of joke," said the person accused of cynicism.

"It 's because his health is so poor," his father explained to Lord Warburton. "It affects his mind and colours his way of looking at things; he seems to feel as if he had never had a chance. But it's almost entirely theoretical, you know; it does n't seem to affect his spirits. I've hardly ever seen him when he was n't cheerful — about as he is at present. He often cheers me up."

The young man so described looked at Lord Warburton and laughed. "Is it a glowing eulogy or an accusation of levity? Should you like me to carry out my theories, daddy?"

"By Jove, we should see some queer things!" cried Lord Warburton.

"I hope you have n't taken up that sort of tone," said the old man.

"Warburton's tone is worse than mine; he pretends to be bored. I 'm not in the least bored; I find life only too interesting."

"Ah, *too* interesting; you should n't allow it to be that, you know!"

"I 'm never bored when I come here," said Lord Warburton. "One gets such uncommonly good talk."

"Is that another sort of joke?" asked the old man. "You've no excuse for being bored anywhere. When I was your age I had never heard of such a thing."

"You must have developed very late."

"No, I developed very quick; that was just the reason. When I was twenty years old I was very highly developed indeed. I was working tooth and nail. You would n't be bored if you had something to do; but all you young men are too idle. You think too much of your pleasure. You're too fastidious, and too indolent, and too rich."

"Oh, I say," cried Lord Warburton, "you 're hardly the person to accuse a fellow-creature of being too rich!"

"Do you mean because I'm a banker?" asked the old man.

"Because of that, if you like; and because you have — have n't you? — such unlimited means."

"He is n't very rich," the other young man mercifully pleaded. "He has given away an immense deal of money."

"Well, I suppose it was his own," said Lord Warburton; "and in that case could there be a better proof of wealth? Let not a public benefactor talk of one's being too fond of pleasure."

"Daddy 's very fond of pleasure — of other people's."

The old man shook his head. "I don't pretend to have contributed anything to the amusement of my contemporaries."

"My dear father, you're too modest!"

"That's a kind of joke, sir," said Lord Warburton.

"You young men have too many jokes. When there are no jokes you've nothing left."

"Fortunately there are always more jokes," the ugly young man remarked.

"I don't believe it — I believe things are getting more serious. You young men will find that out."

"The increasing seriousness of things, then — that's the great opportunity of jokes."

"They'll have to be grim jokes," said the old man. "I'm convinced there will be great changes; and not all for the better."

"I quite agree with you, sir," Lord Warburton declared. "I 'm very sure there will be great changes, and that all sorts of queer things will happen. That's why I find so much difficulty in applying your advice; you know you told me the other day that I ought to 'take hold' of something. One hesitates to take hold of a thing that may the next moment be knocked sky-high."

"You ought to take hold of a pretty woman," said his companion. "He 's trying hard to fall in love," he added, by way of explanation, to his father.

"The pretty women themselves may be sent flying!" Lord Warburton exclaimed.

"No, no, they 'll be firm," the old man rejoined; "they 'll not be affected by the social and political changes I just referred to."

"You mean they won't be abolished? Very well, then, I 'll lay hands on one as soon as possible and tie her round my neck as a life-preserver."

"The ladies will save us," said the old man; "that is the best of them will — for I make a difference between them. Make up to a good one and marry her, and your life will become much more interesting."

A momentary silence marked perhaps on the part of his auditors a sense of the magnanimity of this speech, for it was a secret neither for his son nor for his visitor that his own experiment in matrimony had not been a happy one. As he said, however, he made a difference; and these words may have been intended as a confession of personal error; though of course it was not in place for either of his companions to remark that apparently the lady of his choice had not been one of the best.

"If I marry an interesting woman I shall be interested: is that what you say?" Lord Warburton asked. "I'm not at all keen about marrying — your son misrepresented me; but there's no knowing what an interesting woman might do with me."

"I should like to see your idea of an interesting woman," said his friend.

"My dear fellow, you can't see ideas — especially such highly ethereal ones as mine. If I could only see it myself — that would be a great step in advance."

"Well, you may fall in love with whomsoever you please; but you must n't fall in love with my niece," said the old man.

His son broke into a laugh. "He'll think you mean that as a provocation! My dear father, you've lived with the English for thirty years, and you've picked up a good many of the things they say. But you've never learned the things they don't say!"

"I say what I please," the old man returned with all his serenity.

"I have n't the honour of knowing your niece," Lord Warburton said. "I think it 's the first time I 've heard of her."

"She's a niece of my wife's; Mrs. Touchett brings her to England."

Then young Mr. Touchett explained. "My mother, you know, has been spending the winter in America, and we 're expecting her back. She writes that she has discovered a niece and that she has invited her to come out with her."

"I see — very kind of her," said Lord Warburton. "Is the young lady interesting?"

"We hardly know more about her than you; my mother has not gone into details. She chiefly communicates with us by means of telegrams, and her telegrams are rather inscrutable. They say women don't know how to write them, but my mother has thoroughly mastered the art of condensation. 'Tired America, hot weather awful, return England with niece, first steamer decent cabin.' That's the sort of message we get from her — that was the last that came. But there had been another before, which I think contained the first mention of the niece. 'Changed hotel, very bad, impudent clerk, address here. Taken sister's girl, died last year, go to Europe, two sisters, quite independent.' Over that my father and I have scarcely stopped puzzling; it seems to admit of so many interpretations."

"There's one thing very clear in it," said the old man; "she has given the hotel-clerk a dressing."

"I'm not sure even of that, since he has driven her from the field. We thought at first that the sister mentioned might be the sister of the clerk; but the subsequent mention of a niece seems to prove that the allusion is to one of my aunts. Then there was a question as to whose the two other sisters were; they are probably two of my late aunt's daughters. But who 's 'quite independent,' and in what sense is the term used? — that point 's not yet settled. Does the expression apply more particularly to the young lady my mother has adopted, or does it characterise her sisters equally? — and is it used in a moral or in a financial sense? Does it mean that they 've been left well off, or that they wish to be under no obligations? or does it simply mean that they 're fond of their own way?"

"Whatever else it means, it 's pretty sure to mean that," Mr. Touchett remarked.

"You 'll see for yourself," said Lord Warburton. "When does Mrs. Touchett arrive?"

"We 're quite in the dark; as soon as she can find a decent cabin. She may be waiting for it yet; on the other hand she may already have disembarked in England."

"In that case she would probably have telegraphed to you."

"She never telegraphs when you would expect it — only when you don't," said the old man. "She likes to drop on me suddenly; she thinks she'll find me doing something wrong. She has never done so yet, but she 's not discouraged."

"It 's her share in the family trait, the independence she speaks of." Her son's appreciation of the matter was more favourable. "Whatever the high spirit of those young ladies may be, her own is a match for it. She likes to do everything for herself and has no belief in any one's power to help her. She thinks me of no more use than a postage-stamp without gum, and she would never forgive me if I should presume to go to Liverpool to meet her."

"Will you at least let me know when your cousin arrives?" Lord Warburton asked.

"Only on the condition I 've mentioned — that you don't fall in love with her!" Mr. Touchett replied.

"That strikes me as hard. Don't you think me good enough?"

"I think you too good — because I should n't like her to marry you. She has n't come here to look for a husband, I hope; so many young ladies are doing that, as if there were no good ones at home. Then she's probably engaged; American girls are usually engaged, I believe. Moreover I'm not sure, after all, that you'd be a remarkable husband."

"Very likely she 's engaged; I 've known a good many American girls, and they always were; but I could never see that it made any difference, upon my word! As for my being a good husband," Mr. Touchett's visitor pursued, "I 'm not sure of that either. One can but try!"

"Try as much as you please, but don't try on my niece," smiled the old man, whose opposition to the idea was broadly humorous.

"Ah, well," said Lord Warburton with a humour broader still, "perhaps, after all, she 's not worth trying on!"

II

WHILE this exchange of pleasantries took place between the two Ralph Touchett wandered away a little, with his usual slouching gait, his hands in his pockets and his little rowdyish terrier at his heels. His face was turned toward the house, but his eyes were bent musingly on the lawn; so that he had been an object of observation to a person who had just made her appearance in the ample doorway for some moments before he perceived her. His attention was called to her by the conduct of his dog, who had suddenly darted forward with a little volley of shrill barks, in which the note of welcome, however, was more sensible than that of defiance. The person in question was a young lady, who seemed immediately to interpret the greeting of the small beast. He advanced with great rapidity and stood at her feet, looking up and barking hard; whereupon, without hesitation, she stooped and caught him in her hands, holding him face to face while he continued his quick chatter. His master now had had time to follow and to see that Bunchie's new friend was a tall girl in a black dress, who at first sight looked pretty. She was bareheaded, as if she were staying in the house — a fact which conveyed perplexity to the son of its master, conscious of that immunity from visitors which had for some time been rendered necessary by the latter's ill-health. Meantime the two other gentlemen had also taken note of the new-comer.

"Dear me, who 's that strange woman?" Mr. Touchett had asked.

"Perhaps it 's Mrs. Touchett's niece — the independent young lady," Lord Warburton suggested. "I think she must be, from the way she handles the dog."

The collie, too, had now allowed his attention to be diverted, and he trotted toward the young lady in the doorway, slowly setting his tail in motion as he went.

"But where 's my wife then?" murmured the old man.

"I suppose the young lady has left her somewhere: that 's a part of the independence."

The girl spoke to Ralph, smiling, while she still held up the terrier. "Is this your little dog, sir?"

"He was mine a moment ago; but you 've suddenly acquired a remarkable air of property in him."

"Could n't we share him?" asked the girl. "He 's such a perfect little darling."

Ralph looked at her a moment; she was unexpectedly pretty. "You may have him altogether," he then replied.

The young lady seemed to have a great deal of confidence, both in herself and in others; but this abrupt generosity made her blush. "I ought to tell you that I'm probably your cousin," she brought out, putting down the dog. "And here 's another!" she added quickly, as the collie came up.

"Probably?" the young man exclaimed, laughing. "I supposed it was quite settled! Have you arrived with my mother?"

"Yes, half an hour ago."

"And has she deposited you and departed again?"

"No, she went straight to her room, and she told me that, if I should see you, I was to say to you that you must come to her there at a quarter to seven."

The young man looked at his watch. "Thank you very much; I shall be punctual." And then he looked at his cousin. "You 're very welcome here. I 'm delighted to see you."

She was looking at everything, with an eye that denoted clear perception — at her companion, at the two dogs, at the two gentlemen under the trees, at the beautiful scene that surrounded her. "I 've never seen anything so lovely as this place. I 've been all over the house; it 's too enchanting."

"I 'm sorry you should have been here so long without our knowing it."

"Your mother told me that in England people arrived very quietly; so I thought it was all right. Is one of those gentlemen your father?"

"Yes, the elder one — the one sitting down," said Ralph.

The girl gave a laugh. "I don't suppose it 's the other. Who 's the other?"

"He 's a friend of ours — Lord Warburton."

"Oh, I hoped there would be a lord; it's just like a novel!" And then, "Oh you adorable creature!" she suddenly cried, stooping down and picking up the small dog again.

She remained standing where they had met, making no offer to advance or to speak to Mr. Touchett, and while she lingered so near the threshold, slim and charming, her interlocutor wondered if she expected the old man to come and pay her his respects. American girls were used to a great deal of deference, and it had been intimated that this one had a high spirit. Indeed Ralph could see that in her face.

"Won't you come and make acquaintance with my father?" he nevertheless ventured to ask. "He 's old and infirm — he does n't leave his chair."

"Ah, poor man, I 'm very sorry!" the girl exclaimed, immediately moving forward. "I got the impression from your mother that he was rather — rather intensely active."

Ralph Touchett was silent a moment. "She has n't seen him for a year."

"Well, he has a lovely place to sit. Come along, little hound."

"It's a dear old place," said the young man, looking sidewise at his neighbour.

"What 's his name?" she asked, her attention having again reverted to the terrier.

"My father's name?"

"Yes," said the young lady with amusement; "but don't tell him I asked you."

They had come by this time to where old Mr. Touchett was sitting, and he slowly got up from his chair to introduce himself.

"My mother has arrived," said Ralph, "and this is Miss Archer."

The old man placed his two hands on her shoulders, looked at her a moment with extreme benevolence and then gallantly kissed her. "It's a great pleasure to me to see you here; but I wish you had given us a chance to receive you."

"Oh, we were received," said the girl. "There were about a dozen servants in the hall. And there was an old woman curtseying at the gate."

"We can do better than that — if we have notice!" And the old man stood there smiling, rubbing his hands and slowly shaking his head at her. "But Mrs. Touchett does n't like receptions."

"She went straight to her room."

"Yes — and locked herself in. She always does that. Well, I suppose I shall see her next week." And Mrs. Touchett's husband slowly resumed his former posture.

"Before that," said Miss Archer. "She's coming down to dinner — at eight o'clock. Don't you forget a quarter to seven," she added, turning with a smile to Ralph.

"What 's to happen at a quarter to seven?"

"I 'm to see my mother," said Ralph.

"Ah, happy boy!" the old man commented. "You must sit down — you must have some tea," he observed to his wife's niece.

"They gave me some tea in my room the moment I got there," this young lady answered. "I'm sorry you 're out of health," she added, resting her eyes upon her venerable host.

"Oh, I 'm an old man, my dear; it 's time for me to be old. But I shall be the better for having you here."

She had been looking all round her again — at the lawn, the great trees, the reedy, silvery Thames, the beautiful old house; and while engaged in this survey she had made room in it for her companions; a comprehensiveness of observation easily conceivable on the part of a young woman who was evidently both intelligent and excited. She had seated herself and had put away the little dog; her white hands, in her lap, were folded upon her black dress; her head was erect, her eye lighted, her flexible figure turned itself easily this way and that, in sympathy with the alertness with which she evidently caught impressions. Her impressions were numerous, and they were all reflected in a clear, still smile. "I 've never seen anything so beautiful as this."

"It 's looking very well," said Mr. Touchett. "I know the way it strikes you. I 've been through all that. But you 're very beautiful yourself," he added with a politeness by no means crudely jocular and with the happy consciousness that his advanced age gave him the privilege of saying such things — even to young persons who might possibly take alarm at them.

What degree of alarm this young person took need not be exactly measured; she instantly rose, however, with a blush which was not a refutation. "Oh yes, of course I'm lovely!" she returned with a quick laugh. "How old is your house? Is it Elizabethan?"

"It 's early Tudor," said Ralph Touchett.

She turned toward him, watching his face. "Early Tudor? How very delightful! And I suppose there are a great many others."

"There are many much better ones."

"Don't say that, my son!" the old man protested. "There 's nothing better than this."

"I've got a very good one; I think in some respects it 's rather better," said Lord Warburton, who as yet had not spoken, but who had kept an attentive eye upon Miss Archer. He slightly inclined himself, smiling; he had an excellent manner with women. The girl appreciated it in an instant; she had not forgotten that this was Lord Warburton. "I should like very much to show it to you," he added.

"Don't believe him," cried the old man; "don't look at it! It 's a wretched old barrack — not to be compared with this."

"I don't know — I can't judge," said the girl, smiling at Lord Warburton.

In this discussion Ralph Touchett took no interest whatever; he stood with his hands in his pockets, looking greatly as if he should like to renew his conversation with his new-found cousin. "Are you very fond of dogs?" he enquired by way of beginning. He seemed to recognise that it was an awkward beginning for a clever man.

"Very fond of them indeed."

"You must keep the terrier, you know," he went on, still awkwardly.

"I 'll keep him while I 'm here, with pleasure."

"That will be for a long time, I hope."

"You're very kind. I hardly know. My aunt must settle that."

"I 'll settle it with her — at a quarter to seven." And Ralph looked at his watch again.

"I 'm glad to be here at all," said the girl.

"I don't believe you allow things to be settled for you."

"Oh yes; if they 're settled as I like them."

"I shall settle this as I like it," said Ralph. "It's most unaccountable that we should never have known you."

"I was there — you had only to come and see me."

"There? Where do you mean?"

"In the United States: in New York and Albany and other American places."

"I 've been there — all over, but I never saw you. I can't make it out."

Miss Archer just hesitated. "It was because there had been some disagreement between your mother and my father, after my mother's death, which took place when I was a child. In consequence of it we never expected to see you."

"Ah, but I don't embrace all my mother's quarrels — heaven forbid!" the young man cried. "You 've lately lost your father?" he went on more gravely.

"Yes; more than a year ago. After that my aunt was very kind to me; she came to see me and proposed that I should come with her to Europe."

"I see," said Ralph. "She has adopted you."

"Adopted me?" The girl stared, and her blush came back to her, together with a momentary look of pain which gave her interlocutor some alarm. He had underestimated the effect of his words. Lord Warburton, who appeared constantly desirous of a nearer view of Miss Archer, strolled toward the two cousins at the moment, and as he did so she rested her wider eyes on him. "Oh no; she has not adopted me. I 'm not a candidate for adoption."

"I beg a thousand pardons," Ralph murmured. "I meant — I meant —" He hardly knew what he meant.

"You meant she has taken me up. Yes; she likes to take people up. She has been very kind to me; but," she added with a certain visible eagerness of desire to be explicit, "I 'm very fond of my liberty."

"Are you talking about Mrs. Touchett?" the old man called out from his chair. "Come here, my dear, and tell me about her. I 'm always thankful for information."

The girl hesitated again, smiling. "She 's really very benevolent," she answered; after which she went over to her uncle, whose mirth was excited by her words.

Lord Warburton was left standing with Ralph Touchett, to whom in a moment he said: "You wished a while ago to see my idea of an interesting woman. There it is!"

III

Mrs. Touchett was certainly a person of many oddities, of which her behaviour on returning to her husband's house after many months was a noticeable specimen. She had her own way of doing all that she did, and this is the simplest description of a character which, although by no means without liberal motions, rarely succeeded in giving an impression of suavity. Mrs. Touchett might do a great deal of good, but she never pleased. This way of her own, of which she was so fond, was not intrinsically offensive—it was just unmistakeably distinguished from the ways of others. The edges of her conduct were so very clear-cut that for susceptible persons it sometimes had a knife-like effect. That hard fineness came out in her deportment during the first hours of her return from America, under circumstances in which it might have seemed that her first act would have been to exchange greetings with her husband and son. Mrs. Touchett, for reasons which she deemed excellent, always retired on such occasions into impenetrable seclusion, postponing the more sentimental ceremony until she had repaired the disorder of dress with a completeness which had the less reason to be of high importance as neither beauty nor vanity were concerned in it. She was a plain-faced old woman, without graces and without any great elegance, but with an extreme respect for her own motives. She was usually prepared to explain these—when the explanation was asked as a favour; and in such a case they proved totally different from those that had been attributed to her. She was virtually separated from her husband, but she appeared to perceive nothing irregular in the situation. It had become clear, at an early stage of their community, that they should never desire the same thing at the same moment, and this appearance had prompted her to rescue disagreement from the vulgar realm of accident. She did what she could to erect it into a law—a much more edifying aspect of it — by going to live in Florence, where she bought a house and established herself; and by leaving her husband to take care of the English branch of his bank. This arrangement greatly pleased her; it was so felicitously definite. It struck her husband in the same light, in a foggy square in London, where it was at times the most definite fact he discerned; but he would have preferred that such unnatural things should have a greater vagueness. To agree to disagree had cost him an effort; he was ready to agree to almost anything but that, and saw no reason why either assent or dissent should be so terribly consistent. Mrs. Touchett indulged in no regrets nor speculations, and usually came once a year to spend a month with her husband, a period during which she apparently took pains to convince him that she had adopted the right system. She was not fond of the English style of life, and had three or four reasons for it to which she currently alluded; they bore upon minor points of that ancient order, but for Mrs. Touchett they amply justified non-residence. She detested bread-sauce, which, as she said, looked like a poultice and tasted like soap; she objected to the consumption of beer by her maid-servants; and she affirmed that the British laundress (Mrs. Touchett was very particular about the appearance of her linen) was not a mistress of her art. At fixed intervals she paid a visit to her own country; but this last had been longer than any of its predecessors.

She had taken up her niece — there was little doubt of that. One wet afternoon, some four months earlier than the occurrence lately narrated, this young lady had been seated alone with a book. To say she was so occupied is to say that her solitude did not press upon her; for her love of knowledge had a fertilising quality and her imagination was strong. There was at this time, however, a want of fresh taste in her situation which the arrival of an unexpected visitor did much to correct. The visitor had not been announced; the girl heard her at last walking about the adjoining room. It was in an old house at Albany, a large, square, double house, with a notice of sale in the windows of one of the lower apartments. There were two entrances, one of which had long been out of use but had never been removed. They were exactly alike — large white doors, with an arched frame and wide side-lights, perched upon little "stoops" of red stone, which descended sidewise to the brick pavement of the street. The two houses together formed a single dwelling, the party-wall having been removed and the rooms placed in communication. These rooms, above-stairs, were extremely numerous, and were painted all over exactly alike, in a yellowish white which had grown sallow with time. On the third floor there was a sort of arched passage, connecting the two sides of the house, which Isabel and her sisters used in their childhood to call the tunnel and which, though it was short and well-lighted, always seemed to the girl to be strange and lonely, especially on winter afternoons. She had been in the house, at different periods, as a child; in those days her grandmother lived there. Then there had been an absence of ten years, followed by a return to Albany before her father's death. Her grandmother, old Mrs. Archer, had exercised, chiefly within the limits of the family, a large hospitality in the early period, and the little girls often spent weeks under her roof — weeks of which Isabel had the happiest memory. The manner of life was different from that of her own home — larger, more plentiful, practically more festal; the discipline of the nursery was delightfully vague and the opportunity of listening to the conversation of one's elders (which with Isabel was a highly-valued pleasure) almost unbounded. There was a constant coming and going; her grandmother's sons and daughters and their children appeared to be in the enjoyment of standing invitations to arrive and remain, so that the house offered to a certain extent the appearance of a bustling provincial inn kept by a gentle old landlady who sighed a great deal and never presented a bill. Isabel of course knew nothing about bills; but even as a child she thought her grandmother's home romantic. There was a covered piazza behind it, furnished with a swing which was a source of tremulous interest; and beyond this was a long garden, sloping down to the stable and containing peach-trees of barely credible familiarity. Isabel had stayed with her grandmother at various seasons, but somehow all her visits had a flavour of peaches. On the other side, across the street, was an old house that was called the Dutch House — a peculiar structure dating from the earliest colonial time, composed of bricks that had been painted yellow, crowned with a gable that was pointed out to strangers, defended by a rickety wooden paling and standing sidewise to the street. It was occupied by a primary school for children of both sexes, kept or rather let go, by a demonstrative lady of whom Isabel's chief recollection was that her hair was fastened with strange bedroomy combs at the temples and that she was the widow of some one of consequence. The little girl had been offered the opportunity of laying a foundation of knowledge in this establishment; but having spent a single day in it, she had protested against its laws and had been allowed to stay at home, where, in the September days, when the windows of the Dutch House were open, she used to hear the hum of childish voices repeating the multiplication-table — an incident in which the elation of liberty and the pain of exclusion were indistinguishably mingled. The foundation of her knowledge was really laid in the idleness of her grandmother's house, where, as most of the other inmates were not reading people, she had uncontrolled use of a library full of books with frontispieces, which she used to climb upon a chair to take down. When she had found one to her taste — she was guided in the selection chiefly by the frontispiece — she carried it into a mysterious apartment which lay beyond the library and which was called, traditionally, no one knew why, the office. Whose office it had been and at what period it had flourished, she never learned; it was enough for her that it contained an echo and a pleasant musty smell and that it was a chamber of disgrace for old pieces of furniture whose infirmities were not always apparent (so that the disgrace seemed unmerited and rendered them victims of injustice) and with which, in the manner of children, she had established relations almost human, certainly dramatic. There was an old haircloth sofa in especial, to which she had confided a hundred childish sorrows. The place owed much of its mysterious melancholy to the fact that it was properly entered from the second door of the house, the door that had been condemned, and that it was secured by bolts which a particularly slender little girl found it impossible to slide. She knew that this silent, motionless portal opened into the street; if the sidelights had not been filled with green paper she might have looked out upon the little brown stoop and the well-worn brick pavement. But she had no wish to look out, for this would have interfered with her theory that there was a strange, unseen place on the other side — a place which became to the child's imagination, according to its different moods, a region of delight or of terror.

It was in the "office" still that Isabel was sitting on that melancholy afternoon of early spring which I have just mentioned. At this time she might have had the whole house to choose from, and the room she had selected was the most depressed of its scenes. She had never opened the bolted door nor removed the green paper (renewed by other hands) from its side-lights; she had never assured herself that the vulgar street lay beyond. A crude, cold rain fell heavily; the spring-time was indeed an appeal — and it seemed a cynical, insincere appeal — to patience. Isabel, however, gave as little heed as possible to cosmic treacheries; she kept her eyes on her book and tried to fix her mind. It had lately occurred to her that her mind was a good deal of a vagabond, and she had spent much ingenuity in training it to a military step and teaching it to advance, to halt, to retreat, to perform even more complicated manœuvres, at the word of command. Just now she had given it marching orders and it had been trudging over the sandy plains of a history of German Thought. Suddenly she became aware of a step very different from her own intellectual pace; she listened a little and perceived that some one was moving in the library, which communicated with the office. It struck her first as the step of a person from whom she was looking for a visit, then almost immediately announced itself as the tread of a woman and a stranger — her possible visitor being neither. It had an inquisitive, experimental quality which suggested that it would not stop short of the threshold of the office; and in fact the doorway of this apartment was presently occupied by a lady who paused there and looked very hard at our heroine. She was a plain, elderly woman, dressed in a comprehensive waterproof mantle; she had a face with a good deal of rather violent point.

"Oh," she began, "is that where you usually sit?" She looked about at the heterogeneous chairs and tables.

"Not when I have visitors," said Isabel, getting up to receive the intruder.

She directed their course back to the library while the visitor continued to look about her. "You seem to have plenty of other rooms; they 're in rather better condition. But everything 's immensely worn."

"Have you come to look at the house?" Isabel asked. "The servant will show it to you."

"Send her away; I don't want to buy it. She has probably gone to look for you and is wandering about upstairs; she did n't seem at all intelligent. You had better tell her it 's no matter." And then, since the girl stood there hesitating and wondering, this unexpected critic said to her abruptly: "I suppose you 're one of the daughters?"

Isabel thought she had very strange manners. "It depends upon whose daughters you mean."

"The late Mr. Archer's — and my poor sister's."

"Ah," said Isabel slowly, "you must be our crazy Aunt Lydia!"

"Is that what your father told you to call me? I'm your Aunt Lydia, but I'm not at all crazy: I have n't a delusion! And which of the daughters are you?"

"I 'm the youngest of the three, and my name 's Isabel."

"Yes; the others are Lilian and Edith. And are you the prettiest?"

"I have n't the least idea," said the girl.

"I think you must be." And in this way the aunt

and the niece made friends. The aunt had quarrelled years before with her brother-in-law, after the death of her sister, taking him to task for the manner in which he brought up his three girls. Being a high-tempered man he had requested her to mind her own business, and she had taken him at his word. For many years she held no communication with him and after his death had addressed not a word to his daughters, who had been bred in that disrespectful view of her which we have just seen Isabel betray. Mrs. Touchett's behaviour was, as usual, perfectly deliberate. She intended to go to America to look after her investments (with which her husband, in spite of his great financial position, had nothing to do) and would take advantage of this opportunity to enquire into the condition of her nieces. There was no need of writing, for she should attach no importance to any account of them she should elicit by letter; she believed, always, in seeing for one's self. Isabel found, however, that she knew a good deal about them, and knew about the marriage of the two elder girls; knew that their poor father had left very little money, but that the house in Albany, which had passed into his hands, was to be sold for their benefit; knew, finally, that Edmund Ludlow, Lilian's husband, had taken upon himself to attend to this matter, in consideration of which the young couple, who had come to Albany during Mr. Archer's illness, were remaining there for the present and, as well as Isabel herself, occupying the old place.

"How much money do you expect for it?" Mrs. Touchett asked of her companion, who had brought her to sit in the front parlour, which she had inspected without enthusiasm.

"I have n't the least idea," said the girl.

"That's the second time you have said that to me," her aunt rejoined. "And yet you don't look at all stupid."

"I'm not stupid; but I don't know anything about money."

"Yes, that 's the way you were brought up — as if you were to inherit a million. What have you in point of fact inherited ?"

"I really can't tell you. You must ask Edmund and Lilian; they 'll be back in half an hour."

"In Florence we should call it a very bad house," said Mrs. Touchett; "but here, I dare say, it will bring a high price. It ought to make a considerable sum for each of you. In addition to that you *must* have something else; it 's most extraordinary your not knowing. The position 's of value, and they 'll probably pull it down and make a row of shops. I wonder you don't do that yourself; you might let the shops to great advantage."

Isabel stared; the idea of letting shops was new to her. "I hope they won't pull it down," she said; "I'm extremely fond of it."

"I don't see what makes you fond of it; your father died here."

"Yes; but I don't dislike it for that," the girl rather strangely returned. "I like places in which things have happened — even if they 're sad things. A great many people have died here; the place has been full of life."

"Is that what you call being full of life?"

"I mean full of experience — of people's feelings and sorrows. And not of their sorrows only, for I've been very happy here as a child."

"You should go to Florence if you like houses in which things have happened — especially deaths. I live in an old palace in which three people have been murdered; three that were known and I don't know how many more besides."

"In an old palace?" Isabel repeated.

"Yes, my dear; a very different affair from this. This is very bourgeois."

Isabel felt some emotion, for she had always thought highly of her grandmother's house. But the emotion was of a kind which led her to say: "I should like very much to go to Florence."

"Well, if you'll be very good, and do everything I tell you I'll take you there," Mrs. Touchett declared.

Our young woman's emotion deepened; she flushed a little and smiled at her aunt in silence. "Do everything you tell me? I don't think I can promise that."

"No, you don't look like a person of that sort. You're fond of your own way; but it's not for me to blame you."

"And yet, to go to Florence," the girl exclaimed in a moment, "I'd promise almost anything!"

Edmund and Lilian were slow to return, and Mrs. Touchett had an hour's uninterrupted talk with her niece, who found her a strange and interesting figure: a figure essentially — almost the first she had ever met. She was as eccentric as Isabel had always supposed; and hitherto, whenever the girl had heard people described as eccentric, she had thought of them as offensive or alarming. The term had always suggested to her something grotesque and even sinister. But her aunt made it a matter of high but easy irony, or comedy, and led her to ask herself if the common tone, which was all she had known, had ever been as interesting. No one certainly had on any occasion so held her as this little thin-lipped, bright-eyed, foreign-looking woman, who retrieved an insignificant appearance by a distinguished manner and, sitting there in a well-worn waterproof, talked with striking familiarity of the courts of Europe. There was nothing flighty about Mrs. Touchett, but she recognised no social superiors, and, judging the great ones of the earth in a way that spoke of this, enjoyed the consciousness of making an impression on a candid and susceptible mind. Isabel at first had answered a good many questions, and it was from her answers apparently that Mrs. Touchett derived a high opinion of her intelligence. But after this she had asked a good many, and her aunt's answers, whatever turn they took, struck her as food for deep reflexion. Mrs. Touchett waited for the return of her other niece as long as she thought reasonable, but as at six o'clock Mrs. Ludlow had not come in she prepared to take her departure.

"Your sister must be a great gossip. Is she accustomed to staying out so many hours?"

"You 've been out almost as long as she," Isabel replied; "she can have left the house but a short time before you came in."

Mrs. Touchett looked at the girl without resentment; she appeared to enjoy a bold retort and to be disposed to be gracious. "Perhaps she has n't had so good an excuse as I. Tell her at any rate that she must come and see me this evening at that horrid hotel. She may bring her husband if she likes, but she need n't bring you. I shall see plenty of you later."

IV

Mrs. Ludlow was the eldest of the three sisters, and was usually thought the most sensible; the classification being in general that Lilian was the practical one, Edith the beauty and Isabel the "intellectual" superior. Mrs. Keyes, the second of the group, was the wife of an officer of the United States Engineers, and as our history is not further concerned with her it will suffice that she was indeed very pretty and that she formed the ornament of those various military stations, chiefly in the unfashionable West, to which, to her deep chagrin, her husband was successively relegated. Lilian had married a New York lawyer, a young man with a loud voice and an enthusiasm for his profession; the match was not brilliant, any more than Edith's, but Lilian had occasionally been spoken of as a young woman who might be thankful to marry at all — she was so much plainer than her sisters. She was, however, very happy, and now, as the mother of two peremptory little boys and the mistress of a wedge of brown stone violently driven into Fifty-third Street, seemed to exult in her condition as in a bold escape. She was short and solid, and her claim to figure was questioned, but she was conceded presence, though not majesty; she had moreover, as people said, improved since her marriage, and the two things in life of which she was most distinctly conscious were her husband's force in argument and her sister Isabel's originality. "I 've never kept up with Isabel — it would have taken *all* my time," she had often remarked; in spite of which, however, she held her rather wistfully in sight; watching her as a motherly spaniel might watch a free greyhound. "I want to see her safely married — that's what I want to see," she frequently noted to her husband.

"Well, I must say I should have no particular desire to marry her," Edmund Ludlow was accustomed to answer in an extremely audible tone.

"I know you say that for argument; you always take the opposite ground. I don't see what you've against her except that she 's so original."

"Well, I don't like originals; I like translations," Mr. Ludlow had more than once replied. "Isabel 's written in a foreign tongue. I can't make her out. She ought to marry an Armenian or a Portuguese."

"That 's just what I 'm afraid she 'll do!" cried Lilian, who thought Isabel capable of anything.

She listened with great interest to the girl's account of Mrs. Touchett's appearance and in the evening prepared to comply with their aunt's commands. Of what Isabel then said no report has remained, but her sister's words had doubtless prompted a word spoken to her husband as the two were making ready for their visit. "I do hope immensely she'll do something handsome for Isabel; she has evidently taken a great fancy to her."

"What is it you wish her to do?" Edmund Ludlow asked. "Make her a big present?"

"No indeed; nothing of the sort. But take an interest in her — sympathise with her. She 's evidently just the sort of person to appreciate her. She has lived so much in foreign society; she told Isabel all about it. You know you 've always thought Isabel rather foreign."

"You want her to give her a little foreign sympathy, eh? Don't you think she gets enough at home?"

"Well, she ought to go abroad," said Mrs. Ludlow. "She 's just the person to go abroad."

"And you want the old lady to take her, is that it?"

"She has offered to take her — she's dying to have Isabel go. But what I want her to do when she gets her there is to give her all the advantages. I 'm sure all we 've got to do," said Mrs. Ludlow, "is to give her a chance."

"A chance for what?"

"A chance to develop."

"Oh Moses!" Edmund Ludlow exclaimed. "I hope she is n't going to develop any more!"

"If I were not sure you only said that for argument I should feel very badly," his wife replied. "But you know you love her."

"*Do* you know I love you?" the young man said, jocosely, to Isabel a little later, while he brushed his hat.

"I 'm sure I don't care whether you do or not!" exclaimed the girl; whose voice and smile, however, were less haughty than her words.

"Oh, she feels so grand since Mrs. Touchett's visit," said her sister.

But Isabel challenged this assertion with a good

deal of seriousness. "You must not say that, Lily. I don't feel grand at all."

"I'm sure there 's no harm," said the conciliatory Lily.

"Ah, but there 's nothing in Mrs. Touchett's visit to make one feel grand."

"Oh," exclaimed Ludlow, "she 's grander than ever!"

"Whenever I feel grand," said the girl, "it will be for a better reason."

Whether she felt grand or no, she at any rate felt different, felt as if something had happened to her. Left to herself for the evening she sat a while under the lamp, her hands empty, her usual avocations unheeded. Then she rose and moved about the room, and from one room to another, preferring the places where the vague lamplight expired. She was restless and even agitated; at moments she trembled a little. The importance of what had happened was out of proportion to its appearance; there had really been a change in her life. What it would bring with it was as yet extremely indefinite; but Isabel was in a situation that gave a value to any change. She had a desire to leave the past behind her and, as she said to herself, to begin afresh. This desire indeed was not a birth of the present occasion; it was as familiar as the sound of the rain upon the window and it had led to her beginning afresh a great many times. She closed her eyes as she sat in one of the dusky corners of the quiet parlour; but it was not with a desire for dozing forgetfulness. It was on the contrary because she felt too wide-eyed and wished to check the sense of seeing too many things at once. Her imagination was by habit ridiculously active; when the door was not open it jumped out of the window. She was not accustomed indeed to keep it behind bolts; and at important moments, when she would have been thankful to make use of her judgement alone, she paid the penalty of having given undue encouragement to the faculty of seeing without judging. At present, with her sense that the note of change had been struck, came gradually a host of images of the things she was leaving behind her. The years and hours of her life came back to her, and for a long time, in a stillness broken only by the ticking of the big bronze clock, she passed them in review. It had been a very happy life and she had been a very fortunate person — this was the truth that seemed to emerge most vividly. She had had the best of everything, and in a world in which the circumstances of so many people made them unenviable it was an advantage never to have known anything particularly unpleasant. It appeared to Isabel that the unpleasant had been even too absent from her knowledge, for she had gathered from her acquaintance with literature that it was often a source of interest and even of instruction. Her father had kept it away from her — her handsome, much-loved father, who always had such an aversion to it. It was a great felicity to have been his daughter; Isabel rose even to pride in her parentage. Since his death she had seemed to see him as turning his braver side to his children and as not having managed to ignore the ugly quite so much in practice as in aspiration. But this only made her tenderness for him greater; it was scarcely even painful to have to suppose him too generous, too good-natured, too indifferent to sordid considerations. Many persons had held that he carried this indifference too far, especially the large number of those to whom he owed money. Of their opinions Isabel was never very definitely informed; but it may interest the reader to know that, while they had recognised in the late Mr. Archer a remarkably handsome head and a very taking manner (indeed, as one of them had said, he was always taking something), they had declared that he was making a very poor use of his life. He had squandered a substantial fortune, he had been deplorably convivial, he was known to have gambled freely. A few very harsh critics went so far as to say that he had not even brought up his daughters. They had had no regular education and no permanent home; they had been at once spoiled and neglected; they had lived with nursemaids and governesses (usually very bad ones) or had been sent to superficial schools, kept by the French, from which, at the end of a month, they had been removed in tears. This view of the matter would have excited Isabel's indignation, for to her own sense her opportunities had been large. Even when her father had left his daughters for three months at Neufchatel with a French *bonne* who had eloped with a Russian nobleman staying at the same hotel — even in this irregular situation (an incident of the girl's eleventh year) she had been neither frightened nor ashamed, but had thought it a romantic episode in a liberal education. Her father had a large way of looking at life, of which his restlessness and even his occasional incoherency of conduct had been only a proof. He wished his daughters, even as children, to see as much of the world as possible; and it was for this purpose that, before Isabel was fourteen, he had transported them three times across the Atlantic, giving them on each occasion, however, but a few months' view of the subject proposed: a course which had whetted our heroine's curiosity without enabling her to satisfy it. She ought to have been a partisan of her father, for she was the member of his trio who most "made up" to him for the disagreeables he did n't mention. In his last days his general willingness to take leave of a world in which the difficulty of doing as one liked appeared to increase as one grew older had been sensibly modified by the pain of separation from his clever, his superior, his remarkable girl. Later, when the journeys to Europe ceased, he still had shown his children all sorts of indulgence, and if he had been troubled about money-matters nothing ever disturbed their irreflective consciousness of many possessions. Isabel, though she danced very well, had not the recollection of having been in New York a successful member of the choregraphic circle; her sister Edith was, as every one said, so very much more fetching. Edith was so striking an example of success that Isabel could have no illusions as to what constituted this advantage, or as to the limits of her own power to frisk and jump and shriek—above all with rightness of effect. Nineteen persons out of twenty (including the younger sister herself) pronounced Edith infinitely the prettier of the two; but the twentieth, besides reversing this judgement, had the entertainment of thinking all the others æsthetic vulgarians. Isabel had in the depths of her nature an even more unquenchable desire to please than Edith; but the depths of this young lady's nature were a very out-of-the-way place, between which and the surface communication was interrupted by a dozen capricious forces. She saw the young men who came in large numbers to see her sister; but as a general thing they were afraid of her; they had a belief that some special preparation was required for talking with her. Her reputation of reading a great deal hung about her like the cloudy envelope of a goddess in an epic; it was supposed to engender difficult questions and to keep the conversation at a low temperature. The poor girl liked to be thought clever, but she hated to be thought bookish; she used to read in secret and, though her memory was excellent, to abstain from showy reference. She had a great desire for knowledge, but she really preferred almost any source of information to the printed page; she had an immense curiosity about life and was constantly staring and wondering. She carried within herself a great fund of life, and her deepest enjoyment was to feel the continuity between the movements of her own soul and the agitations of the world. For this reason she was fond of seeing great crowds and large stretches of country, of reading about revolutions and wars, of looking at historical pictures — a class of efforts as to which she had often committed the conscious solecism of forgiving them much bad painting for the sake of the subject. While the Civil War went on she was still a very young girl; but she passed months of this long period in a state of almost passionate excitement, in which she felt herself at times (to her extreme confusion) stirred almost indiscriminately by the valour of either army. Of course the circumspection of suspicious swains had never gone the length of making her a social proscript; for the number of those whose hearts, as they approached her, beat only just fast enough to remind them they had heads as well, had kept her unacquainted with the supreme disciplines of her sex and age. She had had everything a girl could have: kindness, admiration, bonbons, bouquets, the sense of exclusion from none of the privileges of the world she lived in, abundant opportunity for dancing, plenty of new dresses, the London *Spectator*, the latest publications, the music of Gounod, the poetry of Browning, the prose of George Eliot.

These things now, as memory played over them, resolved themselves into a multitude of scenes and figures. Forgotten things came back to her; many others, which she had lately thought of great moment, dropped out of sight. The result was kaleidoscopic, but the movement of the instrument was checked at last by the servant's coming in with the name of a gentleman. The name of the gentleman was Caspar Goodwood; he was a straight young man from Boston, who had known Miss Archer for the last twelvemonth and who, thinking her the most beautiful young woman of her time, had pronounced the time, according to the rule I have hinted at, a foolish period of history. He sometimes wrote to her and had within a week or two written from New York. She had thought it very possible he would come in — had indeed all the rainy day been vaguely expecting him. Now that she learned he was there, nevertheless, she felt no eagerness to receive him. He was the finest young man she had ever seen, was indeed quite a splendid young man; he inspired her with a sentiment of high, of rare respect. She had never felt equally moved to it by any other person. He was supposed by the world in general to wish to marry her, but this of course was between themselves. It at least may be affirmed that he had travelled from New York to Albany expressly to see her; having learned in the former city, where he was spending a few days and where he had hoped to find her, that she was still at the State capital. Isabel delayed for some minutes to go to him; she moved about the room with a new sense of complications. But at last she presented herself and found him standing near the lamp. He was tall, strong and somewhat stiff; he was also lean and brown. He was not romantically, he was much rather obscurely, handsome; but his physiognomy had an air of requesting your attention, which it rewarded according to the charm you found in blue eyes of remarkable fixedness, the eyes of a complexion other than his own, and a jaw of the somewhat angular mould which is supposed to bespeak resolution. Isabel said to herself that it bespoke resolution to-night; in spite of which, in half an hour, Caspar Goodwood, who had arrived hopeful as well as resolute, took his way back to his lodging with the feeling of a man defeated. He was not, it may be added, a man weakly to accept defeat.

V

Ralph Touchett was a philosopher, but nevertheless he knocked at his mother's door (at a quarter to seven) with a good deal of eagerness. Even philosophers have their preferences, and it must be admitted that of his progenitors his father ministered most to his sense of the sweetness of filial dependence. His father, as he had often said to himself, was the more motherly; his mother, on the other hand, was paternal, and even, according to the slang of the day, gubernatorial. She was nevertheless very fond of her only child and had always insisted on his spending three months of the year with her. Ralph rendered perfect justice to her affection and knew that in her thoughts and her thoroughly arranged and servanted life his turn always came after the other nearest subjects of her solicitude, the various punctualities of performance of the workers of her will. He found her completely dressed for dinner, but she embraced her boy with her gloved hands and made him sit on the sofa beside her. She enquired scrupulously about her husband's health and about the young man's own, and, receiving no very brilliant account of either, remarked that she was more than ever convinced of her wisdom in not exposing herself to the English climate. In this case she also might have given way. Ralph smiled at the idea of his mother's giving way, but made no point of reminding her that his own infirmity was not the result of the English climate, from which he absented himself for a considerable part of each year.

He had been a very small boy when his father, Daniel Tracy Touchett, a native of Rutland, in the State of Vermont, came to England as subordinate partner in a banking-house where some ten years later he gained preponderant control. Daniel Touchett saw before him a life-long residence in his adopted country, of which, from the first, he took a simple, sane and accommodating view. But, as he said to himself, he had no intention of disamericanising, nor had he a desire to teach his only son any such subtle art. It had been for himself so very soluble a problem to live in England assimilated yet unconverted that it seemed to him equally simple his lawful heir should after his death carry on the grey old bank in the white American light. He was at pains to intensify this light, however, by sending the boy home for his education. Ralph spent several terms at an American school and took a degree at an American university, after which, as he struck his father on his return as even redundantly native, he was placed for some three years in residence at Oxford. Oxford swallowed up Harvard, and Ralph became at last English enough. His outward conformity to the manners that surrounded him was none the less the mask of a mind that greatly enjoyed its independence, on which nothing long imposed itself, and which, naturally inclined to adventure and irony, indulged in a boundless liberty of appreciation. He began with being a young man of promise; at Oxford he distinguished himself, to his father's ineffable satisfaction, and the people about him said it was a thousand pities so clever a fellow should be shut out from a career. He might have had a career by returning to his own country (though this point is shrouded in uncertainty) and even if Mr. Touchett had been willing to part with him (which was not the case) it would have gone hard with him to put a watery waste permanently between himself and the old man whom he regarded as his best friend. Ralph was not only fond of his father, he admired him — he enjoyed the opportunity of observing him. Daniel Touchett, to his perception, was a man of genius, and though he himself had no aptitude for the banking mystery he made a point of learning enough of it to measure the great figure his father had played. It was not this, however, he mainly relished; it was the fine ivory surface, polished as by the English air, that the old man had opposed to possibilities of penetration. Daniel Touchett had been neither at Harvard nor at Oxford, and it was his own fault if he had placed in his son's hands the key to modern criticism. Ralph, whose head was full of ideas which his father had never guessed, had a high esteem for the latter's originality. Americans, rightly or wrongly, are commended for the ease with which they adapt themselves to foreign conditions; but Mr. Touchett had made of the very limits of his pliancy half the ground of his general success. He had retained in their freshness most of his marks of primary pressure; his tone, as his son always noted with pleasure, was that of the more luxuriant parts of New England. At the end of his life he had become, on his own ground, as mellow as he was rich; he combined consummate shrewdness with the disposition superficially to fraternise, and his "social position," on which he had never wasted a care, had the firm perfection of an unthumbed fruit. It was perhaps his want of imagination and of what is called the historic consciousness; but to many of the impressions usually made by English life upon the cultivated stranger his sense was completely closed. There were certain differences he had never perceived, certain habits he had never formed, certain obscurities he had never sounded. As regards these latter, on the day he *had* sounded them his son would have thought less well of him.

Ralph, on leaving Oxford, had spent a couple of years in travelling; after which he had found himself perched on a high stool in his father's bank. The responsibility and honour of such positions is not, I believe, measured by the height of the stool, which depends upon other considerations: Ralph, indeed, who had very long legs, was fond of standing, and even of walking about, at his work. To this exercise, however, he was obliged to devote but a limited period, for at the end of some eighteen months he had become aware of his being seriously out of health. He had caught a violent cold, which fixed itself on his lungs and threw them into dire confusion. He had to give up work and apply, to the letter, the sorry injunction to take care of himself. At first he slighted the task; it appeared to him it was not himself in the least he was taking care of, but an uninteresting and uninterested person with whom he had nothing in common. This person, however, improved on acquaintance, and Ralph grew at last to have a certain grudging tolerance, even an undemonstrative respect, for him. Misfortune makes strange bedfellows, and our young man, feeling that he had something at stake in the matter — it usually struck him as his reputation for ordinary wit — devoted to his graceless charge an amount of attention of which note was duly taken and which had at least the effect of keeping the poor fellow alive. One of his lungs began to heal, the other promised to follow its example, and he was assured he might outweather a dozen winters if he would betake himself to those climates in which consumptives chiefly congregate. As he had grown extremely fond of London, he cursed the flatness of exile: but at the same time that he cursed he conformed, and gradually, when he found his sensitive organ grateful even for grim favours, he conferred them with a lighter hand. He wintered abroad, as the phrase is; basked in the sun, stopped at home when the wind blew, went to bed when it rained, and once or twice, when it had snowed overnight, almost never got up again.

A secret hoard of indifference — like a thick cake a fond old nurse might have slipped into his first school outfit — came to his aid and helped to reconcile him to sacrifice; since at the best he was too ill for aught but that arduous game. As he said to himself, there was really nothing he had wanted very much to do, so that he had at least not renounced the field of valour. At present, however, the fragrance of forbidden fruit seemed occasionally to float past him and remind him that the finest of pleasures is the rush of action. Living as he now lived was like reading a good book in a poor translation — a meagre entertainment for a young man who felt that he might have been an excellent linguist. He had good winters and poor winters, and while the former lasted he was sometimes the sport of a vision of virtual recovery. But this vision was dispelled some three years before the occurrence of the incidents with which this history opens: he had on that occasion remained later than usual in England and had been overtaken by bad weather before reaching Algiers. He arrived more dead than alive and lay there for several weeks between life and death. His convalescence was a miracle, but the first use he made of it was to assure himself that such miracles happen but once. He said to himself that his hour was in sight and that it behoved him to keep his eyes upon it, yet that it was also open to him to spend the interval as agreeably as might be consistent with such a preoccupation. With the prospect of losing them the simple use of his faculties became an exquisite pleasure; it seemed to him the joys of contemplation had never been sounded. He was far from the time when he had found it hard that he should be obliged to give up the idea of distinguishing himself; an idea none the less importunate for being vague and none the less delightful for having had to struggle in the same breast with bursts of inspiring self-criticism. His friends at present judged him more cheerful, and attributed it to a theory, over which they shook their heads knowingly, that he would recover his health. His serenity was but the array of wild flowers niched in his ruin.

It was very probably this sweet-tasting property of the observed thing in itself that was mainly concerned in Ralph's quickly-stirred interest in the advent of a young lady who was evidently not insipid. If he was consideringly disposed, something told him, here was occupation enough for a succession of days. It may be added, in summary fashion, that the imagination of loving — as distinguished from that of being loved — had still a place in his reduced sketch. He had only forbidden himself the riot of expression. However, he should n't inspire his cousin with a passion, nor would she be able, even should she try, to help him to one. "And now tell me about the young lady," he said to his mother. "What do you mean to do with her?"

Mrs. Touchett was prompt. "I mean to ask your father to invite her to stay three or four weeks at Gardencourt."

"You need n't stand on any such ceremony as that," said Ralph. "My father will ask her as a matter of course."

"I don't know about that. She 's my niece; she 's not his."

"Good Lord, dear mother; what a sense of property! That 's all the more reason for his asking her. But after that — I mean after three months (for it 's absurd asking the poor girl to remain but for three or four paltry weeks) — what do you mean to do with her?"

"I mean to take her to Paris. I mean to get her clothing."

"Ah yes, that 's of course. But independently of that?"

"I shall invite her to spend the autumn with me in Florence."

"You don't rise above detail, dear mother," said Ralph. "I should like to know what you mean to do with her in a general way."

"My duty!" Mrs. Touchett declared. "I suppose you pity her very much," she added.

"No, I don't think I pity her. She does n't strike me as inviting compassion. I think I envy her. Before being sure, however, give me a hint of where you see your duty."

"In showing her four European countries — I shall leave her the choice of two of them — and in giving her the opportunity of perfecting herself in French, which she already knows very well."

Ralph frowned a little. "That sounds rather dry — even allowing her the choice of two of the countries."

"If it 's dry," said his mother with a laugh, "you can leave Isabel alone to water it! She is as good as a summer rain, any day."

"Do you mean she 's a gifted being?"

"I don't know whether she 's a gifted being, but she 's a clever girl — with a strong will and a high temper. She has no idea of being bored."

"I can imagine that," said Ralph; and then he added abruptly: "How do you two get on?"

"Do you mean by that that I 'm a bore? I don't think she finds me one. Some girls might, I know;

but Isabel 's too clever for that. I think I greatly amuse her. We get on because I understand her; I know the sort of girl she is. She 's very frank, and I 'm very frank: we know just what to expect of each other."

"Ah, dear mother," Ralph exclaimed, "one always knows what to expect of *you!* You 've never surprised me but once, and that 's to-day — in presenting me with a pretty cousin whose existence I had never suspected."

"Do you think her so very pretty?"

"Very pretty indeed; but I don't insist upon that. It 's her general air of being some one in particular that strikes me. Who is this rare creature, and what is she? Where did you find her, and how did you make her acquaintance?"

"I found her in an old house at Albany, sitting in a dreary room on a rainy day, reading a heavy book and boring herself to death. She did n't know she was bored, but when I left her no doubt of it she seemed very grateful for the service. You may say I should n't have enlightened her — I should have let her alone. There 's a good deal in that, but I acted conscientiously; I thought she was meant for something better. It occurred to me that it would be a kindness to take her about and introduce her to the world. She thinks she knows a great deal of it — like most American girls; but like most American girls she 's ridiculously mistaken. If you want to know, I thought she would do me credit. I like to be well thought of, and for a woman of my age there 's no greater convenience, in some ways, than an attractive niece. You know I had seen nothing of my sister's children for years; I disapproved entirely of the father. But I always meant to do something for them when he should have gone to his reward. I ascertained where they were to be found and, without any preliminaries, went and introduced myself. There are two others of them, both of whom are married; but I saw only the elder, who has, by the way, a very uncivil husband. The wife, whose name is Lily, jumped at the idea of my taking an interest in Isabel; she said it was just what her sister needed — that some one should take an interest in her. She spoke of her as you might speak of some young person of genius — in want of encouragement and patronage. It may be that Isabel 's a genius; but in that case I 've not yet learned her special line. Mrs. Ludlow was especially keen about my taking her to Europe; they all regard Europe over there as a land of emigration, of rescue, a refuge for their superfluous population. Isabel herself seemed very glad to come, and the thing was easily arranged. There was a little difficulty about the money-question, as she seemed averse to being under pecuniary obligations. But she has a small income and she supposes herself to be travelling at her own expense."

Ralph had listened attentively to this judicious report, by which his interest in the subject of it was not impaired. "Ah, if she 's a genius," he said, "we must find out her special line. Is it by chance for flirting?"

"I don't think so. You may suspect that at first,

but you 'll be wrong. You won't, I think, in anyway, be easily right about her."

"Warburton 's wrong then!" Ralph rejoicingly exclaimed. "He flatters himself he has made that discovery."

His mother shook her head. "Lord Warburton won't understand her. He need n't try."

"He 's very intelligent," said Ralph; "but it 's right he should be puzzled once in a while."

"Isabel will enjoy puzzling a lord," Mrs. Touchett remarked.

Her son frowned a little. "What does she know about lords?"

"Nothing at all: that will puzzle him all the more."

Ralph greeted these words with a laugh and looked out of the window. Then, "Are you not going down to see my father?" he asked.

"At a quarter to eight," said Mrs. Touchett.

Her son looked at his watch. "You 've another quarter of an hour then. Tell me some more about Isabel." After which, as Mrs. Touchett declined his invitation, declaring that he must find out for himself, "Well," he pursued, "she 'll certainly do you credit. But won't she also give you trouble?"

"I hope not; but if she does I shall not shrink from it. I never do that."

"She strikes me as very natural," said Ralph.

"Natural people are not the most trouble."

"No," said Ralph; "you yourself are a proof of that. You 're extremely natural, and I 'm sure you have never troubled any one. It *takes* trouble to do that. But tell me this; it just occurs to me. Is Isabel capable of making herself disagreeable?"

"Ah," cried his mother, "you ask too many questions! Find that out for yourself."

His questions, however, were not exhausted. "All this time," he said, "you 've not told me what you intend to do with her."

"Do with her? You talk as if she were a yard of calico. I shall do absolutely nothing with her, and she herself will do everything she chooses. She gave me notice of that."

"What you meant then, in your telegram, was that her character 's independent."

"I never know what I mean in my telegrams — especially those I send from America. Clearness is too expensive. Come down to your father."

"It 's not yet a quarter to eight," said Ralph.

"I must allow for his impatience," Mrs. Touchett answered.

Ralph knew what to think of his father's impatience; but, making no rejoinder, he offered his mother his arm. This put it in his power, as they descended together, to stop her a moment on the middle landing of the staircase — the broad, low, wide-armed staircase of time-blackened oak which was one of the most striking features of Gardencourt. "You 've no plan of marrying her?" he smiled.

"Marrying her? I should be sorry to play her such a trick! But apart from that, she 's perfectly able to marry herself. She has every facility."

"Do you mean to say she has a husband picked out?"

"I don't know about a husband, but there 's a young man in Boston —!"

Ralph went on; he had no desire to hear about the young man in Boston. "As my father says, they 're always engaged!"

His mother had told him that he must satisfy his curiosity at the source, and it soon became evident he should not want for occasion. He had a good deal of talk with his young kinswoman when the two had been left together in the drawing-room. Lord Warburton, who had ridden over from his own house, some ten miles distant, remounted and took his departure before dinner; and an hour after this meal was ended Mr. and Mrs. Touchett, who appeared to have quite emptied the measure of their forms, withdrew, under the valid pretext of fatigue, to their respective apartments. The young man spent an hour with his cousin; though she had been travelling half the day she appeared in no degree spent. She was really tired; she knew it, and knew she should pay for it on the morrow; but it was her habit at this period to carry exhaustion to the furthest point and confess to it only when dissimulation broke down. A fine hypocrisy was for the present possible; she was interested; she was, as she said to herself, floated. She asked Ralph to show her the pictures; there were a great many in the house, most of them of his own choosing. The best were arranged in an oaken gallery, of charming proportions, which had a sitting-room at either end of it and which in the evening was usually lighted. The light was insufficient to show the pictures to advantage, and the visit might have stood over to the morrow. This suggestion Ralph had ventured to make; but Isabel looked disappointed — smiling still, however — and said: "If you please I should like to see them just a little." She was eager, she knew she was eager and now seemed so; she could n't help it. "She does n't take suggestions," Ralph said to himself; but he said it without irritation; her pressure amused and even pleased him. The lamps were on brackets, at intervals, and if the light was imperfect it was genial. It fell upon the vague squares of rich colour and on the faded gilding of heavy frames; it made a sheen on the polished floor of the gallery. Ralph took a candlestick and moved about, pointing out the things he liked; Isabel, inclining to one picture after another, indulged in little exclamations and murmurs. She was evidently a judge; she had a natural taste; he was struck with that. She took a candlestick herself and held it slowly here and there; she lifted it high, and as she did so he found himself pausing in the middle of the place and bending his eyes much less upon the pictures than on her presence. He lost nothing, in truth, by these wandering glances, for she was better worth looking at than most works of art. She was undeniably spare, and ponderably light, and proveably tall; when people had wished to distinguish her from the other two Miss Archers they had always called her the willowy one. Her hair, which was dark even to blackness, had been an object of envy to many women; her light grey eyes, a little too firm perhaps in her graver moments, had an enchanting range of concession. They walked slowly up one side of the gallery and down the other, and then she said: "Well, now I know more than I did when I began!"

"You apparently have a great passion for knowledge," her cousin returned.

"I think I have; most girls are horridly ignorant."

"You strike me as different from most girls."

"Ah, some of them *would* — but the way they 're talked to!" murmured Isabel, who preferred not to dilate just yet on herself. Then in a moment, to change the subject, "Please tell me — is n't there a ghost?" she went on.

"A ghost?"

"A castle-spectre, a thing that appears. We call them ghosts in America."

"So we do here, when we see them."

"You do see them then? You ought to, in this romantic old house."

"It 's not a romantic old house," said Ralph. "You 'll be disappointed if you count on that. It 's a dismally prosaic one; there 's no romance here but what you may have brought with you."

"I 've brought a great deal; but it seems to me I 've brought it to the right place."

"To keep it out of harm, certainly; nothing will ever happen to it here, between my father and me."

Isabel looked at him a moment. "Is there never any one here but your father and you?"

"My mother, of course."

"Oh, I know your mother; she 's not romantic. Have n't you other people?"

"Very few."

"I 'm sorry for that; I like so much to see people."

"Oh, we 'll invite all the county to amuse you," said Ralph.

"Now you 're making fun of me," the girl answered rather gravely. "Who was the gentleman on the lawn when I arrived?"

"A county neighbour; he does n't come very often."

"I 'm sorry for that; I liked him," said Isabel.

"Why, it seemed to me that you barely spoke to him," Ralph objected.

"Never mind, I like him all the same. I like your father too, immensely."

"You can't do better than that. He 's the dearest of the dear."

"I 'm so sorry he is ill," said Isabel.

"You must help me to nurse him; you ought to be a good nurse."

"I don't think I am; I 've been told I 'm not; I 'm said to have too many theories. But you have n't told me about the ghost," she added.

Ralph, however, gave no heed to this observation. "You like my father and you like Lord Warburton. I infer also that you like my mother."

"I like your mother very much, because — because —" And Isabel found herself attempting to assign a reason for her affection for Mrs. Touchett.

"Ah, we never know why!" said her companion, laughing.

"I always know why," the girl answered. "It 's because she does n't expect one to like her. She does n't care whether one does or not."

"So you adore her — out of perversity? Well, I take greatly after my mother," said Ralph.

"I don't believe you do at all. You wish people to like you, and you try to make them do it."

"Good heavens, how you see through one!" he cried with a dismay that was not altogether jocular.

"But I like you all the same," his cousin went on. "The way to clinch the matter will be to show me the ghost."

Ralph shook his head sadly. "I might show it to you, but you 'd never see it. The privilege is n't given to every one; it 's not enviable. It has never been seen by a young, happy, innocent person like you. You must have suffered first, have suffered greatly, have gained some miserable knowledge. In that way your eyes are opened to it. I saw it long ago," said Ralph.

"I told you just now I 'm very fond of knowledge," Isabel answered.

"Yes, of happy knowledge — of pleasant knowledge. But you have n't suffered, and you 're not made to suffer. I hope you 'll never see the ghost!"

She had listened to him attentively, with a smile on her lips, but with a certain gravity in her eyes. Charming as he found her, she had struck him as rather presumptuous — indeed it was a part of her charm; and he wondered what she would say. "I'm not afraid, you know," she said: which seemed quite presumptuous enough.

"You 're not afraid of suffering?"

"Yes, I 'm afraid of suffering. But I 'm not afraid

of ghosts. And I think people suffer too easily," she added.

"I don't believe *you* do," said Ralph, looking at her with his hands in his pockets.

"I don't think that's a fault," she answered. "It's not absolutely necessary to suffer; we were not made for that."

"You were not, certainly."

"I'm not speaking of myself." And she wandered off a little.

"No, it is n't a fault," said her cousin. "It 's a merit to be strong."

"Only, if you don't suffer they call you hard," Isabel remarked.

They passed out of the smaller drawing-room, into which they had returned from the gallery, and paused in the hall, at the foot of the staircase. Here Ralph presented his companion with her bedroom candle, which he had taken from a niche. "Never mind what they call you. When you do suffer they call you an idiot. The great point's to be as happy as possible."

She looked at him a little; she had taken her candle and placed her foot on the oaken stair. "Well," she said, "that 's what I came to Europe for, to be as happy as possible. Good-night."

"Good-night! I wish you all success, and shall be very glad to contribute to it!"

She turned away, and he watched her as she slowly ascended. Then, with his hands always in his pockets, he went back to the empty drawing-room.

VI

Isabel Archer was a young person of many theories; her imagination was remarkably active. It had been her fortune to possess a finer mind than most of the persons among whom her lot was cast; to have a larger perception of surrounding facts and to care for knowledge that was tinged with the unfamiliar. It is true that among her contemporaries she passed for a young woman of extraordinary profundity; for these excellent people never withheld their admiration from a reach of intellect of which they themselves were not conscious, and spoke of Isabel as a prodigy of learning, a creature reported to have read the classic authors — in translations. Her paternal aunt, Mrs. Varian, once spread the rumour that Isabel was writing a book — Mrs. Varian having a reverence for books, and averred that the girl would distinguish herself in print. Mrs. Varian thought highly of literature, for which she entertained that esteem that is connected with a sense of privation. Her own large house, remarkable for its assortment of mosaic tables and decorated ceilings, was unfurnished with a library, and in the way of printed volumes contained nothing but half a dozen novels in paper on a shelf in the apartment of one of the Miss Varians. Practically, Mrs. Varian's acquaintance with literature was confined to *The New York Interviewer;* as she very justly said, after you had read the *Interviewer* you had lost all faith in culture. Her tendency, with this, was rather to keep the *Interviewer* out of the way of her daughters; she was determined to bring them up properly, and they read nothing at all. Her impression with regard to Isabel's labours was quite illusory; the girl had never attempted to write a book and had no desire for the laurels of authorship. She had no talent for expression and too little of the consciousness of genius; she only had a general idea that people were right when they treated her as if she were rather superior. Whether or no she were superior, people were right in admiring her if they thought her so; for it seemed to her often that her mind moved more quickly than theirs, and this encouraged an impatience that might easily be confounded with superiority. It may be affirmed without delay that Isabel was probably very liable to the sin of self-esteem; she often surveyed with complacency the field of her own nature; she was in the habit of taking for granted, on scanty evidence, that she was right; she treated herself to occasions of homage. Meanwhile her errors and delusions were frequently such as a biographer interested in preserving the dignity of his subject must shrink from specifying. Her thoughts were a tangle of vague outlines which had never been corrected by the judgement of people speaking with authority. In matters of opinion she had had her own way, and it had led her into a thousand ridiculous zigzags. At moments she discovered she was grotesquely wrong, and then she treated herself to a week of passionate humility. After this she held her head higher than ever again; for it was of no use, she had an unquenchable desire to think well of herself. She had a theory that it was only under this provision life was worth living; that one should be one of the best, should be conscious of a fine organisation (she could n't help knowing her organisation was fine), should move in a realm of light, of natural wisdom, of happy impulse, of inspiration gracefully chronic. It was almost as unnecessary to cultivate doubt of one's self as to cultivate doubt of one's best friend: one should try to be one's own best friend and to give one's self, in this manner, distinguished company. The girl had a certain nobleness of imagination which rendered her a good many services and played her a great many tricks. She spent half her time in thinking of beauty and bravery and magnanimity; she had a fixed determination to regard the world as a place of brightness, of free expansion, of irresistible action: she held it must be detestable to be afraid or ashamed. She had an infinite hope that she should never do anything wrong. She had resented so strongly, after discovering them, her mere errors of feeling (the discovery always made her tremble as if she had escaped from a trap which might have caught her and smothered her) that the chance of inflicting a sensible injury upon another person, presented only as a contingency, caused her at moments to hold her breath. That always struck her as the worst thing that could happen to her. On the whole, reflectively, she was in no uncertainty about the things that were wrong. She had no love of their look, but when she fixed them hard she recognised them. It was wrong to be mean, to be jealous, to be false, to be cruel; she had seen very little of the evil of the world, but she had seen women who lied and who tried to hurt each other. Seeing such things had quickened her high spirit; it seemed indecent not to scorn them. Of course the danger of a high spirit was the danger of inconsistency — the danger of keeping up the flag after the place has surrendered; a sort of behaviour so crooked as to be almost a dishonour to the flag. But Isabel, who knew little of the sorts of artillery to which young women are exposed, flattered herself that such contradictions would never be noted in her own conduct. Her life should always be in harmony with the most pleasing impression she should produce; she would be what she appeared, and she would appear what she was. Sometimes she went so far as to wish that she might find herself some day in a difficult position, so that she should have the pleasure of being as heroic as the occasion demanded. Altogether, with her meagre knowledge, her inflated ideals, her confidence at once innocent and dogmatic, her temper at once exacting and indulgent, her mixture of curiosity and fastidiousness, of vivacity and indifference, her desire to look very well and to be if possible even better, her determination to see, to try, to know, her combination of the delicate, desultory, flame-like spirit and the eager and personal creature of conditions: she would be an easy victim of scientific criticism if she were not intended to awaken on the reader's part an impulse more tender and more purely expectant.

It was one of her theories that Isabel Archer was very fortunate in being independent, and that she ought to make some very enlightened use of that state. She never called it the state of solitude, much less of singleness; she thought such descriptions weak, and, besides, her sister Lily constantly urged her to come and abide. She had a friend whose acquaintance she had made shortly before her father's death, who offered so high an example of useful activity that Isabel always thought of her as a model. Henrietta Stackpole had the advantage of an admired ability; she was thoroughly launched in journalism, and her letters to the *Interviewer*, from Washington, Newport, the White Mountains and other places, were universally quoted. Isabel pronounced them with confidence "ephemeral," but she esteemed the courage, energy and good-humour of the writer, who, without parents and without property, had adopted three of the children of an infirm and widowed sister and was paying their school-bills out of the proceeds of her literary labour. Henrietta was in the van of progress and had clear-cut views on most subjects; her cherished desire had long been to come to Europe and write a series of letters to the *Interviewer* from the radical point of view — an enterprise the less difficult as she knew perfectly in advance what her opinions would be and to how many objections most European institutions lay open. When she heard that Isabel was coming she wished to start at once; thinking, naturally, that it would be delightful the two should travel together. She had been obliged, however, to postpone this enterprise. She thought Isabel a glorious creature, and had spoken of her covertly in some of her letters, though she never mentioned the fact to her friend, who would not have taken pleasure in it and was not a regular student of the *Interviewer*. Henrietta, for Isabel, was chiefly a proof that a woman might suffice to herself and be happy. Her resources were of the obvious kind; but even if one had not the journalistic talent and a genius for guessing, as Henrietta said, what the public was going to want, one was not therefore to conclude that one had no vocation, no beneficent aptitude of any sort, and resign one's self to being frivolous and hollow. Isabel was stoutly determined not to be hollow. If one should wait with the right patience one would find some happy work to one's hand. Of course, among her theories, this young lady was not without a collection of views on the subject of marriage. The first on the list was a conviction of the vulgarity of thinking too much of it. From lapsing into eagerness on this point she earnestly prayed she might be delivered; she held that a woman ought to be able to live to herself, in the absence of exceptional flimsiness, and that it was perfectly possible to be happy without the society of a more or less coarse-minded person of another sex. The girl's prayer was very sufficiently answered; something pure and proud that there was in her — something cold and dry an unappreciated suitor with a taste for analysis might have called it — had hitherto kept her from any great vanity of conjecture on the article of possible husbands. Few of the men she saw seemed worth a ruinous expenditure, and it made her smile to think that one of them should present himself as an incentive to hope and a reward of patience. Deep in her soul — it was the deepest thing there — lay a belief that if a certain light should dawn she could give herself completely; but this image, on the whole, was too formidable to be attractive. Isabel's thoughts hovered about it, but they seldom rested on it long; after a little it ended in alarms. It often seemed to her that she thought too much about herself; you could have made her colour, any day in the year, by calling her a rank egoist. She was always planning out her development, desiring her perfection, observing her progress. Her nature had, in her conceit, a certain garden-like quality, a suggestion of perfume and murmuring boughs, of shady bowers and lengthening vistas, which made her feel that introspection was, after all, an exercise in the open air, and that a visit to the recesses of one's spirit was harmless when one returned from it with a lapful of roses. But she was often reminded that there were other gardens in the world than those of her remarkable soul, and that there were moreover a great many places which were not gardens at all — only dusky pestiferous tracts, planted thick with ugliness and misery. In the current of that repaid curiosity on which she had lately been floating, which had conveyed her to this beautiful old England and might carry her much further still, she often checked herself with the thought of the thousands of people who were less happy than herself — a thought which for the moment made her fine, full consciousness appear a kind of immodesty. What should one do with the misery of the world in a scheme of the agreeable for one's self? It must be confessed that this question never held her long. She was too young, too impatient to live, too unacquainted with pain. She always returned to her theory that a young woman whom after all every one thought clever should begin by getting a general impression of life. This impression was necessary to prevent mistakes, and after it should be secured she might make the unfortunate condition of others a subject of special attention.

England was a revelation to her, and she found herself as diverted as a child at a pantomime. In her infantine excursions to Europe she had seen only the Continent, and seen it from the nursery window; Paris, not London, was her father's Mecca, and into many of his interests there his children had naturally not entered. The images of that time moreover had grown faint and remote, and the old-world quality in everything that she now saw had all the charm of strangeness. Her uncle's house seemed a picture made real; no refinement of the agreeable was lost upon Isabel; the rich perfection of Gardencourt at once revealed a world and gratified a need. The large, low rooms, with brown ceilings and dusky corners, the deep embrasures and curious casements, the quiet light on dark, polished panels, the deep greenness outside, that seemed always peeping in, the sense of well-ordered privacy in the centre of a "property" — a place where sounds were felicitously accidental, where the tread was muffled by the earth itself and in the thick mild air all friction dropped out of contact and all shrillness out of talk — these things were much to the taste of our young lady, whose taste played a considerable part in her emotions. She formed a fast friendship with her uncle, and often sat by his chair when he had had it moved out to the lawn. He passed hours in the open air, sitting with folded hands like a placid, homely household god, a god of service, who had done his work and received his wages and was trying to grow used to weeks and months made up only of off-days. Isabel amused him more than she suspected — the effect she produced upon people was often different from what she supposed — and he frequently gave himself the pleasure of making her chatter. It was by this term that he qualified her conversation, which had much of the "point" observable in that of the young ladies of her country, to whom the ear of the world is more directly presented than to their sisters in other lands. Like the mass of American girls Isabel had been encouraged to express herself; her remarks had been attended to; she had been expected to have emotions and opinions. Many of her opinions had doubtless but a slender value, many of her emotions passed away in the utterance; but they had left a trace in giving her the habit of seeming at least to feel and think, and in imparting moreover to her words when she was really moved that prompt vividness which so many people had regarded as a sign of superiority. Mr. Touchett used to think that she reminded him of his wife when his wife was in her teens. It was because she was fresh and natural and quick to understand, to speak — so many characteristics of her niece — that he had fallen in love with Mrs. Touchett. He never expressed this analogy to the girl herself, however; for if Mrs. Touchett had once been like Isabel, Isabel was not at all like Mrs. Touchett. The old man was full of kindness for her; it was a long time, as he said, since they had had any young life in the house; and our rustling, quickly-moving, clear-voiced heroine was as agreeable to his sense as the sound of flowing water. He wanted to do something for her and wished she would ask it of him. She would ask nothing but questions; it is true that of these she asked a quantity. Her uncle had a great fund of answers, though her pressure sometimes came in forms that puzzled him. She questioned him immensely about England, about the British constitution, the English character, the state of politics, the manners and customs of the royal family, the peculiarities of the aristocracy, the way of living and thinking of his neighbours; and in begging to be enlightened on these points she usually enquired whether they corresponded with the descriptions in the books. The old man always looked at her a little with his fine dry smile while he smoothed down the shawl spread across his legs.

"The books?" he once said; "well, I don't know much about the books. You must ask Ralph about that. I 've always ascertained for myself — got my information in the natural form. I never asked many questions even; I just kept quiet and took notice. Of course I've had very good opportunities — better than what a young lady would naturally have. I'm of an inquisitive disposition, though you might n't think it if you were to watch me: however much you might watch me I should be watching you more. I 've been watching these people for upwards of thirty-five years, and I don't hesitate to say that I 've acquired considerable information. It 's a very fine country on the whole — finer perhaps than what we give it credit for on the other side. There are several improvements I should like to see introduced; but the necessity of them does n't seem to be generally felt as yet. When the necessity of a thing is generally felt they usually manage to accomplish it; but they seem to feel pretty comfortable about waiting till then. I certainly feel more at home among them than I expected to when I first came over; I suppose it 's because I 've had a considerable degree of success. When you 're successful you naturally feel more at home."

"Do you suppose that if I'm successful I shall feel at home?" Isabel asked.

"I should think it very probable, and you certainly will be successful. They like American young ladies very much over here; they show them a great deal of kindness. But you must n't feel too much at home, you know."

"Oh, I 'm by no means sure it will *satisfy* me," Isabel judicially emphasised. "I like the place very much, but I 'm not sure I shall like the people."

"The people are very good people; especially if you like them."

"I 've no doubt they 're good," Isabel rejoined; "but are they pleasant in society? They won't rob me nor beat me; but will they make themselves agreeable to me? That's what I like people to do. I don't hesitate to say so, because I always appreciate it. I don't believe they 're very nice to girls; they 're not nice to them in the novels."

"I don't know about the novels," said Mr. Touchett. "I believe the novels have a great deal of ability, but I don't suppose they 're very accurate. We once had a lady who wrote novels staying here; she was a friend of Ralph's and he asked her down. She was very positive, quite up to everything; but she was not the sort of person you could depend on for evidence. Too free a fancy — I suppose that was it. She afterwards published a work of fiction in which she was understood to have given a representation — something in the nature of a caricature, as you might say — of my unworthy self. I did n't read it, but Ralph just handed me the book with the principal passages marked. It was understood to be a description of my conversation; American peculiarities, nasal twang, Yankee notions, stars and stripes. Well, it was not at all accurate; she could n't have listened very attentively. I had no objection to her giving a report of my conversation, if she liked; but I did n't like the idea that she had n't taken the trouble to listen to it. Of course I talk like an American — I can't talk like a Hottentot. However I talk, I 've made them understand me pretty well over here. But I don't talk like the old gentleman in that lady's novel. He was n't an American; we would n't have him over there at any price. I just mention that fact to show you that they 're not always accurate. Of course, as I 've no daughters, and as Mrs. Touchett resides in Florence, I have n't had much chance to notice about the young ladies. It sometimes appears as if the young women in the lower class were not very well treated; but I guess their position is better in the upper and even to some extent in the middle."

"Gracious," Isabel exclaimed; "how many classes have they? About fifty, I suppose."

"Well, I don't know that I ever counted them. I never took much notice of the classes. That 's the advantage of being an American here; you don't belong to any class."

"I hope so," said Isabel. "Imagine one's belonging to an English class!"

"Well, I guess some of them are pretty comfortable — especially towards the top. But for me there are only two classes: the people I trust and the people I don't. Of those two, my dear Isabel, you belong to the first."

"I 'm much obliged to you," said the girl quickly. Her way of taking compliments seemed sometimes rather dry; she got rid of them as rapidly as possible. But as regards this she was sometimes misjudged; she was thought insensible to them, whereas in fact she was simply unwilling to show how infinitely they pleased her. To show that was to show too much. "I 'm sure the English are very conventional," she added.

"They 've got everything pretty well fixed," Mr. Touchett admitted. "It 's all settled beforehand — they don't leave it to the last moment."

"I don't like to have everything settled beforehand," said the girl. "I like more unexpectedness."

Her uncle seemed amused at her distinctness of preference. "Well, it 's settled beforehand that you 'll have great success," he rejoined. "I suppose you 'll like that."

"I shall not have success if they 're too stupidly

conventional. I 'm not in the least stupidly conventional. I 'm just the contrary. That 's what they won't like."

"No, no, you 're all wrong," said the old man. "You can't tell what they 'll like. They 're very inconsistent; that 's their principal interest."

"Ah well," said Isabel, standing before her uncle with her hands clasped about the belt of her black dress and looking up and down the lawn — "that will suit me perfectly!"

VII

THE two amused themselves, time and again, with talking of the attitude of the British public as if the young lady had been in a position to appeal to it; but in fact the British public remained for the present profoundly indifferent to Miss Isabel Archer, whose fortune had dropped her, as her cousin said, into the dullest house in England. Her gouty uncle received very little company, and Mrs. Touchett, not having cultivated relations with her husband's neighbours, was not warranted in expecting visits from them. She had, however, a peculiar taste; she liked to receive cards. For what is usually called social intercourse she had very little relish; but nothing pleased her more than to find her hall-table whitened with oblong morsels of symbolic pasteboard. She flattered herself that she was a very just woman, and had mastered the sovereign truth that nothing in this world is got for nothing. She had played no social part as mistress of Gardencourt, and it was not to be supposed that, in the surrounding country, a minute account should be kept of her comings and goings. But it is by no means certain that she did not feel it to be wrong that so little notice was taken of them and that her failure (really very gratuitous) to make herself important in the neighbourhood had not much to do with the acrimony of her allusions to her husband's adopted country. Isabel presently found herself in the singular situation of defending the British constitution against her aunt; Mrs. Touchett having formed the habit of sticking pins into this venerable instrument. Isabel always felt an impulse to pull out the pins; not that she imagined they inflicted any damage on the tough old parchment, but because it seemed to her her aunt might make better use of her sharpness. She was very critical herself — it was incidental to her age, her sex and her nationality; but she was very sentimental as well, and there was something in Mrs. Touchett's dryness that set her own moral fountains flowing.

"Now what 's your point of view?" she asked of her aunt. "When you criticise everything here you should have a point of view. Yours does n't seem to be American — you thought everything over there so disagreeable. When I criticise I have mine; it 's thoroughly American!"

"My dear young lady," said Mrs. Touchett, "there are as many points of view in the world as there are people of sense to take them. You may say that does n't make them very numerous! American? Never in the world; that 's shockingly narrow. My point of view, thank God, is personal!"

Isabel thought this a better answer than she admitted; it was a tolerable description of her own manner of judging, but it would not have sounded well for her to say so. On the lips of a person less advanced in life and less enlightened by experience than Mrs. Touchett such a declaration would savour of immodesty, even of arrogance. She risked it nevertheless in talking with Ralph, with whom she talked a great deal and with whom her conversation was of a sort that gave a large licence to extravagance. Her cousin used, as the phrase is, to chaff her; he very soon established with her a reputation for treating everything as a joke, and he was not a man to neglect the privileges such a reputation conferred. She accused him of an odious want of seriousness, of laughing at all things, beginning with himself. Such slender faculty of reverence as he possessed centred wholly upon his father; for the rest, he exercised his wit indifferently upon his father's son, this gentleman's weak lungs, his useless life, his fantastic mother, his friends (Lord Warburton in especial), his adopted, and his native country, his charming new-found cousin. "I keep a band of music in my ante-room," he said once to her. "It has orders to play without stopping; it renders me two excellent services. It keeps the sounds of the world from reaching the private apartments, and it makes the world think that dancing 's going on within." It was dance-music indeed that you usually heard when you came within ear-shot of Ralph's band; the liveliest waltzes seemed to float upon the air. Isabel often found herself irritated by this perpetual fiddling; she would have liked to pass through the ante-room, as her cousin called it, and enter the private apartments. It mattered little that he had assured her they were a very dismal place; she would have been glad to undertake to sweep them and set them in order. It was but half-hospitality to let her remain outside; to punish him for which Isabel administered innumerable taps with the ferule of her straight young wit. It must be said that her wit was exercised to a large extent in self-defence, for her cousin amused himself with calling her "Columbia" and accusing her of a patriotism so heated that it scorched. He drew a caricature of her in which she was represented as a very pretty young woman dressed, on the lines of the prevailing fashion, in the folds of the national banner. Isabel's chief dread in life at this period of her development was that she should appear narrow-minded; what she feared next afterwards was that she should really be so. But she nevertheless made no scruple of abounding in her cousin's sense and pretending to sigh for the charms of her native land. She would be as American as it pleased him to regard her, and if he chose to laugh at her she would give him plenty of occupation. She defended England against his mother, but when Ralph sang its praises on purpose, as she said, to work her up, she found herself able to differ from him on a variety of points. In fact, the quality of this small ripe country seemed as sweet to her as the taste of an October pear; and her satisfaction was at the root of the good spirits which enabled her to take her cousin's chaff and return it in kind. If her good-humour flagged at moments it was not because she thought herself ill-used, but because she suddenly felt sorry for Ralph. It seemed to her he was talking as a blind and had little heart in what he said.

"I don't know what 's the matter with you," she observed to him once; "but I suspect you 're a great humbug."

"That 's your privilege," Ralph answered, who had not been used to being so crudely addressed.

"I don't know what you care for; I don't think you care for anything. You don't really care for England when you praise it; you don't care for America even when you pretend to abuse it."

"I care for nothing but you, dear cousin," said Ralph.

"If I could believe even that, I should be very glad."

"Ah well, I should hope so!" the young man exclaimed.

Isabel might have believed it and not have been far from the truth. He thought a great deal about her; she was constantly present to his mind. At a time when his thoughts had been a good deal of a burden to him her sudden arrival, which promised nothing and was an open-handed gift of fate, had refreshed and quickened them, given them wings and something to fly for. Poor Ralph had been for many weeks steeped in melancholy; his outlook, habitually sombre, lay under the shadow of a deeper cloud. He had grown anxious about his father, whose gout, hitherto confined to his legs, had begun to ascend into regions more vital. The old man had been gravely ill in the spring, and the doctors had whispered to Ralph that another attack would be less easy to deal with. Just now he appeared disburdened of pain, but Ralph could not rid himself of a suspicion that this was a subterfuge of the enemy, who was waiting to take him off his guard. If the manœuvre should succeed there would be little hope of any great resistance. Ralph had always taken for granted that his father would survive him — that his own name would be the first grimly called. The father and son had been close companions, and the idea of being left alone with the remnant of a tasteless life on his hands was not gratifying to the young man, who had always and tacitly counted upon his elder's help in making the best of a poor business. At the prospect of losing his great motive Ralph lost indeed his one inspiration. If they might die at the same time it would be all very well; but without the encouragement of his father's society he should barely have patience to await his own turn. He had not the incentive of feeling that he was indispensable to his mother; it was a rule with his mother to have no regrets. He bethought himself of course that it had been a small kindness to his father to wish that, of the two, the active rather than the passive party should know the felt wound; he remembered that the old man had always treated his own forecast of an early end as a clever fallacy, which he should be delighted to discredit so far as he might by dying first. But of the two triumphs, that of refuting a sophistical son and that of holding on a while longer to a state of being which, with all abatements, he enjoyed, Ralph deemed it no sin to hope the latter might be vouchsafed to Mr. Touchett.

These were nice questions, but Isabel's arrival put a stop to his puzzling over them. It even suggested there might be a compensation for the intolerable ennui of surviving his genial sire. He wondered whether he were harbouring "love" for this spontaneous young woman from Albany; but he judged that on the whole he was not. After he had known her for a week he quite made up his mind to this, and every day he felt a little more sure. Lord Warburton had been right about her; she was a really interesting little figure. Ralph wondered how their neighbour had found it out so soon; and then he said it was only another proof of his friend's high abilities, which he had always greatly admired. If his cousin were to be nothing more than an entertainment to him, Ralph was conscious she was an entertainment of a high order. "A character like that," he said to himself — "a real little passionate force to see at play is the finest thing in nature. It 's finer than the finest work of art — than a Greek bas-relief, than a great Titian, than a Gothic cathedral. It 's very pleasant to be so well treated where one had least looked for it. I had never been more blue, more bored, than for a week before she came; I had never expected less that anything pleasant would happen. Suddenly I receive a Titian, by the post, to hang on my wall — a Greek bas-relief to stick over my chimney-piece. The key of a beautiful edifice is thrust into my hand, and I 'm told to walk in and admire. My poor boy, you 've been sadly ungrateful, and now you had better keep very quiet and never grumble again." The sentiment of these reflexions was very just; but it was not exactly true that Ralph Touchett had had a key put into his hand. His cousin was a very brilliant girl, who would take, as he said, a good deal of knowing; but she needed the knowing, and his attitude with regard to her, though it was contemplative and critical, was not judicial. He surveyed the edifice from the outside and admired it greatly; he looked in at the windows and received an impression of proportions equally fair. But he felt that he saw it only by glimpses and that he had not yet stood under the roof. The door was fastened, and though he had keys in his pocket he had a conviction that none of them would fit. She was intelligent and generous; it was a fine free nature; but what was she going to do with herself? This question was irregular, for with most women one had no occasion to ask it. Most women did with themselves nothing at all; they waited, in attitudes more or less gracefully passive, for a man to come that way and furnish them with a destiny. Isabel's originality was that she gave one an impression of having intentions of her own. "Whenever she executes them," said Ralph, "may I be there to see!"

It devolved upon him of course to do the honours of the place. Mr. Touchett was confined to his chair, and his wife's position was that of rather a grim visitor; so that in the line of conduct that opened itself to Ralph duty and inclination were harmoniously mixed. He was not a great walker, but he strolled about the grounds with his cousin — a pastime for which the weather remained favourable with a persistency not allowed for in Isabel's somewhat lugubrious prevision of the climate; and in the long afternoons, of which the length was but the measure of her gratified eagerness, they took a boat on the river, the dear little river, as Isabel called it, where the opposite shore seemed still a part of the foreground of the landscape; or drove over the country in a phaeton — a low, capacious, thick-wheeled phaeton formerly much used by Mr. Touchett, but which he had now ceased to enjoy. Isabel enjoyed it largely and, handling the reins in a manner which approved itself to the groom as "knowing," was never weary of driving her uncle's capital horses through winding lanes and byways full of the rural incidents she had confidently expected to find; past cottages thatched and timbered, past ale-houses latticed and sanded, past patches of ancient common and glimpses of empty parks, between hedgerows made thick by midsummer. When they reached home they usually found tea had been served on the lawn and that Mrs. Touchett had not shrunk from the extremity of handing her husband his cup. But the two for the most part sat silent; the old man with his head back and his eyes closed, his wife occupied with her knitting and wearing that appearance of rare profundity with which some ladies consider the movement of their needles.

One day, however, a visitor had arrived. The two young persons, after spending an hour on the river, strolled back to the house and perceived Lord Warburton sitting under the trees and engaged in conversation, of which even at a distance the desultory character was appreciable, with Mrs. Touchett. He had driven over from his own place with a portmanteau and had asked, as the father and son often invited him to do, for a dinner and a lodging. Isabel, seeing him for half an hour on the day of her arrival, had discovered in this brief space that she liked him; he had indeed rather sharply registered himself on her fine sense and she had thought of him several times. She had hoped she should see him again -- hoped too that she should see a few others. Gardencourt was not dull; the place itself was sovereign, her uncle was more and more a sort of golden grandfather, and Ralph was unlike any cousin she had ever encountered — her idea of cousins having tended to gloom. Then her impressions were still so fresh and so quickly renewed that there was as yet hardly a hint of vacancy in the view. But Isabel had need to remind herself that she was interested in human nature and that her foremost hope in coming abroad had been that she should see a great many people. When Ralph said to her, as he had done several times, "I wonder you find this endurable; you ought to see some of the neighbours and some of our friends, because we have really got a few, though you would never suppose it" — when he offered to invite what he called a "lot of people" and make her acquainted with English society, she encouraged the hospitable impulse and promised in advance to hurl herself into the fray. Little, however, for the present, had come of his offers, and it may be confided to the reader that if the young man delayed to carry them out it was because he found the labour of providing for his companion by no means so severe as to require extraneous help. Isabel had spoken to him very often about "specimens;" it was a word that played a considerable part in her vocabulary; she had given him to understand that she wished to see English society illustrated by eminent cases.

"Well now, there 's a specimen," he said to her

as they walked up from the riverside and he recognised Lord Warburton.

"A specimen of what?" asked the girl.

"A specimen of an English gentleman."

"Do you mean they 're all like him?"

"Oh no; they 're not all like him."

"He 's a favourable specimen then," said Isabel; "because I 'm sure he 's nice."

"Yes, he 's very nice. And he 's very fortunate."

The fortunate Lord Warburton exchanged a handshake with our heroine and hoped she was very well. "But I need n't ask that," he said, "since you 've been handling the oars."

"I 've been rowing a little," Isabel answered; "but how should you know it?"

"Oh, I know *he* does n't row; he 's too lazy," said his lordship, indicating Ralph Touchett with a laugh.

"He has a good excuse for his laziness," Isabel rejoined, lowering her voice a little.

"Ah, he has a good excuse for everything!" cried Lord Warburton, still with his sonorous mirth.

"My excuse for not rowing is that my cousin rows so well," said Ralph. "She does everything well. She touches nothing that she does n't adorn!"

"It makes one want to be touched, Miss Archer," Lord Warburton declared.

"Be touched in the right sense and you 'll never look the worse for it," said Isabel, who, if it pleased her to hear it said that her accomplishments were numerous, was happily able to reflect that such complacency was not the indication of a feeble mind, inasmuch as there were several things in which she excelled. Her desire to think well of herself had at least the element of humility that it always needed to be supported by proof.

Lord Warburton not only spent the night at Gardencourt, but he was persuaded to remain over the second day; and when the second day was ended he determined to postpone his departure till the morrow. During this period he addressed many of his remarks to Isabel, who accepted this evidence of his esteem with a very good grace. She found herself liking him extremely; the first impression he had made on her had had weight, but at the end of an evening spent in his society she scarce fell short of seeing him — though quite without luridity — as a hero of romance. She retired to rest with a sense of good fortune, with a quickened consciousness of possible felicities. "It 's very nice to know two such charming people as those," she said, meaning by "those" her cousin and her cousin's friend. It must be added moreover that an incident had occurred which might have seemed to put her good-humour to the test. Mr. Touchett went to bed at half-past nine o'clock, but his wife remained in the drawing-room with the other members of the party. She prolonged her vigil for something less than an hour, and then, rising, observed to Isabel that it was time they should bid the gentlemen good-night. Isabel had as yet no desire to go to bed; the occasion wore, to her sense, a festive character, and feasts were not in the habit of terminating so early. So, without further thought, she replied, very simply —

"Need I go, dear aunt? I 'll come up in half an hour."

"It 's impossible I should wait for you," Mrs. Touchett answered.

"Ah, you need n't wait! Ralph will light my candle," Isabel gaily engaged.

"I 'll light your candle; do let me light your candle, Miss Archer!" Lord Warburton exclaimed. "Only I beg it shall not be before midnight."

Mrs. Touchett fixed her bright little eyes upon him a moment and transferred them coldly to her niece. "You can't stay alone with the gentlemen. You 're not — you 're not at your blest Albany, my dear."

Isabel rose, blushing. "I wish I were," she said.

"Oh, I say, mother!" Ralph broke out.

"My dear Mrs. Touchett!" Lord Warburton murmured.

"I did n't make your country, my lord," Mrs. Touchett said majestically. "I must take it as I find it."

"Can't I stay with my own cousin?" Isabel enquired.

"I 'm not aware that Lord Warburton is your cousin."

"Perhaps *I* had better go to bed!" the visitor suggested. "That will arrange it."

Mrs. Touchett gave a little look of despair and sat down again. "Oh, if it 's necessary I 'll stay up till midnight."

Ralph meanwhile handed Isabel her candlestick. He had been watching her; it had seemed to him her temper was involved — an accident that might be interesting. But if he had expected anything of a flare he was disappointed, for the girl simply laughed a little, nodded good-night and withdrew accompanied by her aunt. For himself he was annoyed at his mother, though he thought she was right. Above-stairs the two ladies separated at Mrs. Touchett's door. Isabel had said nothing on her way up.

"Of course you're vexed at my interfering with you," said Mrs. Touchett.

Isabel considered. "I 'm not vexed, but I 'm surprised — and a good deal mystified. Was n't it proper I should remain in the drawing-room?"

"Not in the least. Young girls here — in decent houses — don't sit alone with the gentlemen late at night."

"You were very right to tell me then," said Isabel. "I don't understand it, but I 'm very glad to know it."

"I shall always tell you," her aunt answered, "whenever I see you taking what seems to me too much liberty."

"Pray do; but I don't say I shall always think your remonstrance just."

"Very likely not. You 're too fond of your own ways."

"Yes, I think I'm very fond of them. But I always want to know the things one should n't do."

"So as to do them?" asked her aunt.

"So as to choose," said Isabel.

VIII

As she was devoted to romantic effects Lord Warburton ventured to express a hope that she would come some day and see his house, a very curious old place. He extracted from Mrs. Touchett a promise that she would bring her niece to Lockleigh, and Ralph signified his willingness to attend the ladies if his father should be able to spare him. Lord Warburton assured our heroine that in the mean time his sisters would come and see her. She knew something about his sisters, having sounded him, during the hours they spent together while he was at Gardencourt, on many points connected with his family. When Isabel was interested she asked a great many questions, and as her companion was a copious talker she urged him on this occasion by no means in vain. He told her he had four sisters and two brothers and had lost both his parents. The brothers and sisters were very good people — "not particularly clever, you know," he said, "but very decent and pleasant;" and he was so good as to hope Miss Archer might know them well. One of the brothers was in the Church, settled in the family living, that of Lockleigh, which was a heavy, sprawling parish, and was an excellent fellow in spite of his thinking differently from himself on every conceivable topic. And then Lord Warburton mentioned some of the opinions held by his brother, which were opinions Isabel had often heard expressed and that she supposed to be entertained by a considerable portion of the human family. Many of them indeed she supposed she had held herself, till he assured her she was quite mistaken, that it was really impossible, that she had doubtless imagined she entertained them, but that she might depend that, if she thought them over a little, she would find there was nothing in them. When she answered that she had already thought several of the questions involved over very attentively he declared that she was only another example of what he had often been struck with — the fact that, of all the people in the world, the Americans were the most grossly superstitious. They were rank Tories and bigots, every one of them; there were no conservatives like American conservatives. Her uncle and her cousin were there to prove it; nothing could be more mediæval than many of their views; they had ideas that people in England nowadays were ashamed to confess to; and they had the impudence moreover, said his lordship, laughing, to pretend they knew more about the needs and dangers of this poor dear stupid old England than he who was born in it and owned a considerable slice of it — the more shame to him! From all of which Isabel gathered that Lord Warburton was a nobleman of the newest pattern, a reformer, a radical, a contemner of ancient ways. His other brother, who was in the army in India, was rather wild and pig-headed and had not been of much use as yet but to make debts for Warburton to pay — one of the most precious privileges of an elder brother. "I don't think I shall pay any more," said her friend; "he lives a monstrous deal better than I do, enjoys unheard-of luxuries and thinks himself a much finer gentleman than I. As I'm a consistent radical I go in only for equality; I don't go in for the superiority of the younger brothers." Two of his four sisters, the second and fourth, were married, one of them having done very well, as they said, the other only so-so. The husband of the elder, Lord Haycock, was a very good fellow, but unfortunately a horrid Tory; and his wife, like all good English wives, was worse than her husband. The other had espoused a smallish squire in Norfolk and, though married but the other day, had already five children. This information and much more Lord Warburton imparted to his young American listener, taking pains to make many things clear and to lay bare to her apprehension the peculiarities of English life. Isabel was often amused at his explicitness and at the small allowance he seemed to make either for her own experience or for her imagination. "He thinks I'm a barbarian," she said, "and that I've never seen forks and spoons;" and she used to ask him artless questions for the pleasure of hearing him answer seriously. Then when he had fallen into the trap, "It's a pity you can't see me in my war-paint and feathers," she remarked; "if I had known how kind you are to the poor savages I would have brought over my native costume!" Lord Warburton had travelled through the United States and knew much more about them than Isabel; he was so good as to say that America was the most charming country in the world, but his recollections of it appeared to encourage the idea that Americans in England would need to have a great many things explained to them. "If I had only had you to explain things to me in America!" he said. "I was rather puzzled in your country; in fact I was quite bewildered, and the trouble was that the explanations only puzzled me more. You know I think they often gave me the wrong ones on purpose; they're rather clever about that over there. But when I explain you can trust me; about what I tell you there 's no mistake." There was no mistake at least about his being very intelligent and cultivated and knowing almost everything in the world. Although he gave the most interesting and thrilling glimpses Isabel felt he never did it to exhibit himself, and though he had had rare chances and had tumbled in, as she put it, for high prizes, he was as far as possible from making a merit of it. He had enjoyed the best things of life, but they had not spoiled his sense of proportion. His quality was a mixture of the effect of rich experience — oh, so easily come by! — with a modesty at times almost boyish; the sweet and wholesome savour of which — it was as agreeable as something tasted — lost nothing from the addition of a tone of responsible kindness.

"I like your specimen English gentleman very much," Isabel said to Ralph after Lord Warburton had gone.

"I like him too — I love him well," Ralph returned. "But I pity him more."

Isabel looked at him askance. "Why, that seems to me his only fault — that one can't pity him a little. He appears to have everything, to know everything, to *be* everything."

"Oh, he 's in a bad way!" Ralph insisted.

"I suppose you don't mean in health?"

"No, as to that he 's detestably sound. What I mean is that he 's a man with a great position who 's playing all sorts of tricks with it. He does n't take himself seriously."

"Does he regard himself as a joke?"

"Much worse; he regards himself as an imposition — as an abuse."

"Well, perhaps he is," said Isabel.

"Perhaps he is — though on the whole I don't think so. But in that case what 's more pitiable than a sentient, self-conscious abuse planted by other hands, deeply rooted but aching with a sense of its injustice? For me, in his place, I could be as solemn as a statue of Buddha. He occupies a position that appeals to my imagination. Great responsibilities, great opportunities, great consideration, great wealth, great power, a natural share in the public affairs of a great country. But he 's all in a muddle about himself, his position, his power, and indeed about everything in the world. He 's the victim of a critical age; he has ceased to believe in himself and he does n't know what to believe in. When I attempt to tell him (because if I were he I know very well what I should believe in) he calls me a pampered bigot. I believe he seriously thinks me an awful Philistine; he says I don't understand my time. I understand it certainly better than he, who can neither abolish himself as a nuisance nor maintain himself as an institution."

"He does n't look very wretched," Isabel observed.

"Possibly not; though, being a man of a good deal

of charming taste, I think he often has uncomfortable hours. But what is it to say of a being of his opportunities that he 's not miserable? Besides, I believe he is."

"I don't," said Isabel.

"Well," her cousin rejoined, "if he is n't he ought to be!"

In the afternoon she spent an hour with her uncle on the lawn, where the old man sat, as usual, with his shawl over his legs and his large cup of diluted tea in his hands. In the course of conversation he asked her what she thought of their late visitor.

Isabel was prompt. "I think he 's charming."

"He 's a nice person," said Mr. Touchett, "but I don't recommend you to fall in love with him."

"I shall not do it then; I shall never fall in love but on your recommendation. Moreover," Isabel added, "my cousin gives me rather a sad account of Lord Warburton."

"Oh, indeed? I don't know what there may be to say, but you must remember that Ralph *must* talk."

"He thinks your friend 's too subversive — or not subversive enough! I don't quite understand which," said Isabel.

The old man shook his head slowly, smiled and put down his cup. "I don't know which either. He goes very far, but it 's quite possible he does n't go far enough. He seems to want to do away with a good many things, but he seems to want to remain himself. I suppose that 's natural, but it 's rather inconsistent."

"Oh, I hope he 'll remain himself," said Isabel.

"If he were to be done away with his friends would miss him sadly."

"Well," said the old man, "I guess he 'll stay and amuse his friends. I should certainly miss him very much here at Gardencourt. He always amuses me when he comes over, and I think he amuses himself as well. There's a considerable number like him, round in society; they 're very fashionable just now. I don't know what they 're trying to do — whether they 're trying to get up a revolution. I hope at any rate they'll put it off till after I 'm gone. You see they want to disestablish everything; but I 'm a pretty big landowner here, and I don't want to be disestablished. I would n't have come over if I had thought they were going to behave like that," Mr. Touchett went on with expanding hilarity. "I came over because I thought England was a safe country. I call it a regular fraud if they are going to introduce any considerable changes; there 'll be a large number disappointed in that case."

"Oh, I do hope they'll make a revolution!" Isabel exclaimed. "I should delight in seeing a revolution."

"Let me see," said her uncle, with a humorous intention; "I forget whether you 're on the side of the old or on the side of the new. I 've heard you take such opposite views."

"I 'm on the side of both. I guess I 'm a little on the side of everything. In a revolution — after it was well begun — I think I should be a high, proud loyalist. One sympathises more with them, and they've a chance to behave so exquisitely. I mean so picturesquely."

"I don't know that I understand what you mean by behaving picturesquely, but it seems to me that you do that always, my dear."

"Oh, you lovely man, if I could believe that!" the girl interrupted.

"I'm afraid, after all, you won't have the pleasure of going gracefully to the guillotine here just now," Mr. Touchett went on. "If you want to see a big outbreak you must pay us a long visit. You see, when you come to the point it would n't suit them to be taken at their word."

"Of whom are you speaking?"

"Well, I mean Lord Warburton and his friends — the radicals of the upper class. Of course I only know the way it strikes me. They talk about the changes, but I don't think they quite realise. You and I, you know, we know what it is to have lived under democratic institutions: I always thought them very comfortable, but I was used to them from the first. And then I ain't a lord; you're a lady, my dear, but I ain't a lord. Now over here I don't think it quite comes home to them. It's a matter of every day and every hour, and I don't think many of them would find it as pleasant as what they've got. Of course if they want to try, it 's their own business; but I expect they won't try very hard."

"Don't you think they 're sincere?" Isabel asked.

"Well, they want to *feel* earnest," Mr. Touchett allowed; "but it seems as if they took it out in theories mostly. Their radical views are a kind of amusement; they've got to have some amusement, and they might have coarser tastes than that. You see they're very luxurious, and these progressive ideas are about their biggest luxury. They make them feel moral and yet don't damage their position. They think a great deal of their position; don't let one of them ever persuade you he does n't, for if you were to proceed on that basis you 'd be pulled up very short."

Isabel followed her uncle's argument, which he unfolded with his quaint distinctness, most attentively, and though she was unacquainted with the British aristocracy she found it in harmony with her general impressions of human nature. But she felt moved to put in a protest on Lord Warburton's behalf. "I don't believe Lord Warburton 's a humbug; I don't care what the others are. I should like to see Lord Warburton put to the test."

"Heaven deliver me from my friends!" Mr. Touchett answered. "Lord Warburton 's a very amiable young man — a very fine young man. He has a hundred thousand a year. He owns fifty thousand acres of the soil of this little island and ever so many other things besides. He has half a dozen houses to live in. He has a seat in Parliament as I have one at my own dinner-table. He has elegant tastes — cares for literature, for art, for science, for charming young ladies. The most elegant is his taste for the new views. It affords him a great deal of pleasure — more perhaps than anything else, except the young ladies. His old house over there — what does he call it, Lockleigh? — is very attractive; but I don't think it 's as pleasant as this. That does n't matter, however — he has so many others. His views don't hurt any one as far as I can see; they certainly don't hurt himself.

And if there were to be a revolution he would come off very easily. They would n't touch him, they 'd leave him as he is: he 's too much liked."

"Ah, he could n't be a martyr even if he wished!" Isabel sighed. "That 's a very poor position."

"He 'll never be a martyr unless you make him one," said the old man.

Isabel shook her head; there might have been something laughable in the fact that she did it with a touch of melancholy. "I shall never make any one a martyr."

"You 'll never be one, I hope."

"I hope not. But you don't pity Lord Warburton then as Ralph does?"

Her uncle looked at her a while with genial acuteness. "Yes, I do, after all!"

IX

THE two Misses Molyneux, this nobleman's sisters, came presently to call upon her, and Isabel took a fancy to the young ladies, who appeared to her to show a most original stamp. It is true that when she described them to her cousin by that term he declared that no epithet could be less applicable than this to the two Misses Molyneux, since there were fifty thousand young women in England who exactly resembled them. Deprived of this advantage, however, Isabel's visitors retained that of an extreme sweetness and shyness of demeanour, and of having, as she thought, eyes like the balanced basins, the circles of "ornamental water," set, in parterres, among the geraniums.

"They 're not morbid, at any rate, whatever they are," our heroine said to herself; and she deemed this a great charm, for two or three of the friends of her girlhood had been regrettably open to the charge (they would have been so nice without it), to say nothing of Isabel's having occasionally suspected it as a tendency of her own. The Misses Molyneux were not in their first youth, but they had bright, fresh complexions and something of the smile of childhood. Yes, their eyes, which Isabel admired, were round, quiet and contented, and their figures, also of a generous roundness, were encased in sealskin jackets. Their friendliness was great, so great that they were almost embarrassed to show it; they seemed somewhat afraid of the young lady from the other side of the world and rather looked than spoke their good wishes. But they made it clear to her that they hoped she would come to luncheon at Lockleigh, where they lived with their brother, and then they might see her very, very often. They wondered if she would n't come over some day and sleep: they were expecting some people on the twenty-ninth, so perhaps she would come while the people were there.

"I 'm afraid it is n't any one very remarkable," said the elder sister; "but I dare say you 'll take us as you find us."

"I shall find you delightful; I think you 're enchanting just as you are," replied Isabel, who often praised profusely.

Her visitors flushed, and her cousin told her, after they were gone, that if she said such things to those poor girls they would think she was in some wild, free manner practising on them: he was sure it was the first time they had been called enchanting.

"I can't help it," Isabel answered. "I think it 's lovely to be so quiet and reasonable and satisfied. I should like to be like that."

"Heaven forbid!" cried Ralph with ardour.

"I mean to try and imitate them," said Isabel. "I want very much to see them at home."

She had this pleasure a few days later, when, with Ralph and his mother, she drove over to Lockleigh. She found the Misses Molyneux sitting in a vast drawing-room (she perceived afterwards it was one of several) in a wilderness of faded chintz; they were dressed on this occasion in black velveteen. Isabel liked them even better at home than she had done at Gardencourt, and was more than ever struck with the fact that they were not morbid. It had seemed to her before that if they had a fault it was a want of play of mind; but she presently saw they were capable of deep emotion. Before luncheon she was alone with them for some time, on one side of the room, while Lord Warburton, at a distance, talked to Mrs. Touchett.

"Is it true your brother 's such a great radical?" Isabel asked. She knew it was true, but we have seen that her interest in human nature was keen, and she had a desire to draw the Misses Molyneux out.

"Oh dear, yes; he 's immensely advanced," said Mildred, the younger sister.

"At the same time Warburton 's very reasonable," Miss Molyneux observed.

Isabel watched him a moment at the other side of the room; he was clearly trying hard to make himself agreeable to Mrs. Touchett. Ralph had met the frank advances of one of the dogs before the fire that the temperature of an English August, in the ancient expanses, had not made an impertinence. "Do you suppose your brother 's sincere?" Isabel enquired with a smile.

"Oh, he must be, you know!" Mildred exclaimed quickly, while the elder sister gazed at our heroine in silence.

"Do you think he would stand the test?"

"The test?"

"I mean for instance having to give up all this."

"Having to give up Lockleigh?" said Miss Molyneux, finding her voice.

"Yes, and the other places; what are they called?"

The two sisters exchanged an almost frightened glance. "Do you mean — do you mean on account of the expense?" the younger one asked.

"I dare say he might let one or two of his houses," said the other.

"Let them for nothing?" Isabel demanded.

"I can't fancy his giving up his property," said Miss Molyneux.

"Ah, I'm afraid he is an impostor!" Isabel returned. "Don't you think it's a false position?"

Her companions, evidently, had lost themselves. "My brother's position?" Miss Molyneux enquired.

"It's thought a very good position," said the younger sister. "It's the first position in this part of the county."

"I dare say you think me very irreverent," Isabel took occasion to remark. "I suppose you revere your brother and are rather afraid of him."

"Of course one looks up to one's brother," said Miss Molyneux simply.

"If you do that he must be very good — because you, evidently, are beautifully good."

"He's most kind. It will never be known, the good he does."

"His ability is known," Mildred added; "every one thinks it's immense."

"Oh, I can see that," said Isabel. "But if I were he I should wish to fight to the death: I mean for the heritage of the past. I should hold it tight."

"I think one ought to be liberal," Mildred argued gently. "We've always been so, even from the earliest times."

"Ah well," said Isabel, "you 've made a great success of it; I don't wonder you like it. I see you're very fond of crewels."

When Lord Warburton showed her the house, after luncheon, it seemed to her a matter of course that it should be a noble picture. Within, it had been a good deal modernised — some of its best points had lost their purity; but as they saw it from the gardens, a stout grey pile, of the softest, deepest, most weather-fretted hue, rising from a broad, still moat, it affected the young visitor as a castle in a legend. The day was cool and rather lustreless; the first note of autumn had been struck, and the watery sunshine rested on the walls in blurred and desultory gleams, washing them, as it were, in places tenderly chosen, where the ache of antiquity was keenest. Her host's brother, the Vicar, had come to luncheon, and Isabel had had five minutes' talk with him — time enough to institute a search for a rich ecclesiasticism and give it up as vain. The marks of the Vicar of Lockleigh were a big, athletic figure, a candid, natural countenance, a capacious appetite and a tendency to indiscriminate laughter. Isabel learned afterwards from her cousin that before taking orders he had been a mighty wrestler and that he was still, on occasion — in the privacy of the family circle as it were — quite capable of flooring his man. Isabel liked him — she was in the mood for liking everything; but her imagination was a good deal taxed to think of him as a source of spiritual aid. The whole party, on leaving lunch, went to walk in the grounds; but Lord Warburton exercised some ingenuity in engaging his least familiar guest in a stroll apart from the others.

"I wish you to see the place properly, seriously," he said. "You can't do so if your attention is distracted by irrelevant gossip." His own conversation (though he told Isabel a good deal about the house, which had a very curious history) was not purely archæological; he reverted at intervals to matters more personal — matters personal to the young lady as well as to himself. But at last, after a pause of some duration, returning for a moment to their ostensible theme, "Ah, well," he said, "I 'm very glad indeed you like the old barrack. I wish you could see more of it — that you could stay here a while. My sisters have taken an immense fancy to you — if that would be any inducement."

"There 's no want of inducements," Isabel answered; "but I 'm afraid I can't make engagements. I 'm quite in my aunt's hands."

"Ah, pardon me if I say I don't exactly believe that. I 'm pretty sure you can do whatever you want."

"I 'm sorry if I make that impression on you; I don't think it 's a nice impression to make."

"It has the merit of permitting me to hope." And Lord Warburton paused a moment.

"To hope what?"

"That in future I may see you often."

"Ah," said Isabel, "to enjoy that pleasure I need n't be so terribly emancipated."

"Doubtless not; and yet, at the same time, I don't think your uncle likes me."

"You 're very much mistaken. I 've heard him speak very highly of you."

"I 'm glad you have talked about me," said Lord Warburton. "But, I nevertheless don't think he 'd like me to keep coming to Gardencourt."

"I can't answer for my uncle's tastes," the girl rejoined, "though I ought as far as possible to take them into account. But for myself I shall be very glad to see you."

"Now that 's what I like to hear you say. I 'm charmed when you say that."

"You 're easily charmed, my lord," said Isabel.

"No, I 'm not easily charmed!" And then he stopped a moment. "But you 've charmed me, Miss Archer."

These words were uttered with an indefinable sound which startled the girl; it struck her as the prelude to something grave: she had heard the sound before and she recognised it. She had no wish, however, that for the moment such a prelude should have a sequel, and she said as gaily as possible and as quickly as an appreciable degree of agitation would allow her: "I 'm afraid there 's no prospect of my being able to come here again."

"Never?" said Lord Warburton.

"I won't say 'never'; I should feel very melodramatic."

"May I come and see you then some day next week?"

"Most assuredly. What is there to prevent it?"

"Nothing tangible. But with you I never feel safe. I 've a sort of sense that you 're always summing people up."

"You don't of necessity lose by that."

"It 's very kind of you to say so; but, even if I gain, stern justice is not what I most love. Is Mrs. Touchett going to take you abroad?"

"I hope so."

"Is England not good enough for you?"

"That 's a very Machiavellian speech; it does n't deserve an answer. I want to see as many countries as I can."

"Then you 'll go on judging, I suppose."

"Enjoying, I hope, too."

"Yes, that 's what you enjoy most; I can't make out what you 're up to," said Lord Warburton. "You strike me as having mysterious purposes — vast designs."

"You 're so good as to have a theory about me which I don't at all fill out. Is there anything mysterious in a purpose entertained and executed every year, in the most public manner, by fifty thousand of my fellow-countrymen — the purpose of improving one's mind by foreign travel?"

"You can't improve your mind, Miss Archer," her companion declared. "It 's already a most formidable instrument. It looks down on us all; it despises us."

"Despises you? You 're making fun of me," said Isabel seriously.

"Well, you think us 'quaint' — that 's the same

thing. I won't be thought 'quaint,' to begin with; I 'm not so in the least. I protest."

"That protest is one of the quaintest things I 've ever heard," Isabel answered with a smile.

Lord Warburton was briefly silent. "You judge only from the outside — you don't care," he said presently. "You only care to amuse yourself." The note she had heard in his voice a moment before reappeared, and mixed with it now was an audible strain of bitterness — a bitterness so abrupt and inconsequent that the girl was afraid she had hurt him. She had often heard that the English are a highly eccentric people, and she had even read in some ingenious author that they are at bottom the most romantic of races. Was Lord Warburton suddenly turning romantic — was he going to make her a scene, in his own house, only the third time they had met? She was reassured quickly enough by her sense of his great good manners, which was not impaired by the fact that he had already touched the furthest limit of good taste in expressing his admiration of a young lady who had confided in his hospitality. She was right in trusting to his good manners, for he presently went on, laughing a little and without a trace of the accent that had discomposed her: "I don't mean of course that you amuse yourself with trifles. You select great materials; the foibles, the afflictions of human nature, the peculiarities of nations!"

"As regards that," said Isabel, "I should find in my own nation entertainment for a lifetime. But we 've a long drive, and my aunt will soon wish to start." She turned back toward the others and Lord Warburton walked beside her in silence. But before they reached the others, "I shall come and see you next week," he said.

She had received an appreciable shock, but as it died away she felt that she could n't pretend to herself that it was altogether a painful one. Nevertheless she made answer to his declaration, coldly enough, "Just as you please." And her coldness was not the calculation of her effect — a game she played in a much smaller degree than would have seemed probable to many critics. It came from a certain fear.

X

THE day after her visit to Lockleigh she received a note from her friend Miss Stackpole — a note of which the envelope, exhibiting in conjunction the postmark of Liverpool and the neat calligraphy of the quick-fingered Henrietta, caused her some liveliness of emotion. "Here I am, my lovely friend," Miss Stackpole wrote; "I managed to get off at last. I decided only the night before I left New York — the *Interviewer* having come round to my figure. I put a few things into a bag, like a veteran journalist, and came down to the steamer in a street-car. Where are you and where can we meet? I suppose you 're visiting at some castle or other and have already acquired the correct accent. Perhaps even you have married a lord; I almost hope you have, for I want some introductions to the first people and shall count on you for a few. The *Interviewer* wants some light on the nobility. My first impressions (of the people at large) are not rose-coloured; but I wish to talk them over with you, and you know that, whatever I am, at least I 'm not superficial. I 've also something very particular to tell you. Do appoint a meeting as quickly as you can; come to London (I should like so much to visit the sights with you) or else let me come to you, *wherever you are.* I will do so with pleasure; for you know everything interests me and I wish to see as much as possible of the inner life."

Isabel judged best not to show this letter to her uncle; but she acquainted him with its purport, and, as she expected, he begged her instantly to assure Miss Stackpole, in his name, that he should be delighted to receive her at Gardencourt. "Though she 's a literary lady," he said, "I suppose that, being an American, she won't show me up, as that other one did. She has seen others like me."

"She has seen no other so delightful!" Isabel answered; but she was not altogether at ease about Henrietta's reproductive instincts, which belonged to that side of her friend's character which she regarded with least complacency. She wrote to Miss Stackpole, however, that she would be very welcome under Mr. Touchett's roof; and this alert young woman lost no time in announcing her prompt approach. She had gone up to London, and it was from that centre that she took the train for the station nearest to Gardencourt, where Isabel and Ralph were in waiting to receive her.

"Shall I love her or shall I hate her?" Ralph asked while they moved along the platform.

"Whichever you do will matter very little to her," said Isabel. "She does n't care a straw what men think of her."

"As a man I 'm bound to dislike her then. She must be a kind of monster. Is she very ugly?"

"No, she 's decidedly pretty."

"A female interviewer — a reporter in petticoats? I 'm very curious to see her," Ralph conceded.

"It 's very easy to laugh at her but it is not easy to be as brave as she."

"I should think not; crimes of violence and attacks on the person require more or less pluck. Do you suppose she 'll interview *me?*"

"Never in the world. She 'll not think you of enough importance."

"You 'll see," said Ralph. "She 'll send a description of us all, including Bunchie, to her newspaper."

"I shall ask her not to," Isabel answered.

"You think she 's capable of it then?"

"Perfectly."

"And yet you 've made her your bosom-friend?"

"I 've not made her my bosom-friend; but I like her in spite of her faults."

"Ah well," said Ralph, "I 'm afraid I shall dislike her in spite of her merits."

"You 'll probably fall in love with her at the end of three days."

"And have my love-letters published in the *Interviewer?* Never!" cried the young man.

The train presently arrived, and Miss Stackpole, promptly descending, proved, as Isabel had promised, quite delicately, even though rather provincially, fair. She was a neat, plump person, of medium stature, with a round face, a small mouth, a delicate complexion, a bunch of light brown ringlets at the back of her head and a peculiarly open, surprised-looking eye. The most striking point in her appearance was the remarkable fixedness of this organ, which rested without impudence or defiance, but as if in conscientious exercise of a natural right, upon every object it happened to encounter. It rested in this manner upon Ralph himself, a little arrested by Miss Stackpole's gracious and comfortable aspect, which hinted that it would n't be so easy as he had assumed to disapprove of her. She rustled, she shimmered, in fresh, dove-coloured draperies, and Ralph saw at a glance that she was as crisp and new and comprehensive as a first issue before the folding. From top to toe she had probably no misprint. She spoke in a clear, high voice — a voice not rich but loud; yet after she had taken her place with her companions in Mr. Touchett's carriage she struck him as not all in the large type, the type of horrid "headings," that he had expected. She answered the enquiries made of her by Isabel, however, and in which the young man ventured to join, with copious lucidity; and later, in the library at Gardencourt, when she had made the acquaintance of Mr. Touchett (his wife not having thought it necessary to appear) did more to give the measure of her confidence in her powers.

"Well, I should like to know whether you consider yourselves American or English," she broke out. "If once I knew I could talk to you accordingly."

"Talk to us anyhow and we shall be thankful," Ralph liberally answered.

She fixed her eyes on him, and there was something in their character that reminded him of large polished buttons — buttons that might have fixed the elastic loops of some tense receptacle: he seemed to see the reflection of surrounding objects on the pupil. The expression of a button is not usually deemed human, but there was something in Miss Stackpole's gaze that made him, as a very modest man, feel vaguely embarrassed — less inviolate, more dishonoured, than he liked. This sensation, it must be added, after he had spent a day or two in her company, sensibly diminished, though it never wholly lapsed. "I don't suppose that you 're going to undertake to persuade me that *you 're* an American," she said.

"To please you I 'll be an Englishman, I 'll be a Turk!"

"Well, if you can change about that way you 're very welcome," Miss Stackpole returned.

"I 'm sure you understand everything and that differences of nationality are no barrier to you," Ralph went on.

Miss Stackpole gazed at him still. "Do you mean the foreign languages?"

"The languages are nothing. I mean the spirit — the genius."

"I 'm not sure that I understand you," said the correspondent of the *Interviewer;* "but I expect I shall before I leave."

"He 's what 's called a cosmopolite," Isabel suggested.

"That means he 's a little of everything and not much of any. I must say I think patriotism is like charity — it begins at home."

"Ah, but where does home begin, Miss Stackpole?" Ralph enquired.

"I don't know where it begins, but I know where it ends. It ended a long time before I got here."

"Don't you like it over here?" asked Mr. Touchett with his aged, innocent voice.

"Well, sir, I have n't quite made up my mind what ground I shall take. I feel a good deal cramped. I felt it on the journey from Liverpool to London."

"Perhaps you were in a crowded carriage," Ralph suggested.

"Yes, but it was crowded with friends — a party of Americans whose acquaintance I had made upon the steamer; a lovely group from Little Rock, Arkansas. In spite of that I felt cramped — I felt something pressing upon me; I could n't tell what it was. I felt at the very commencement as if I were not going to accord with the atmosphere. But I suppose I shall make my own atmosphere. That 's the true way — then you can breathe. Your surroundings seem very attractive."

"Ah, we too are a lovely group!" said Ralph. "Wait a little and you 'll see."

Miss Stackpole showed every disposition to wait and evidently was prepared to make a considerable stay at Gardencourt. She occupied herself in the mornings with literary labour; but in spite of this Isabel spent many hours with her friend, who, once her daily task performed, deprecated, in fact defied, isolation. Isabel speedily found occasion to desire her to desist from celebrating the charms of their common sojourn in print, having discovered, on the second morning of Miss Stackpole's visit, that she was engaged on a letter to the *Interviewer*, of which the title, in her exquisitely neat and legible hand (exactly that of the copybooks which our heroine remembered at school) was "Americans and Tudors — Glimpses of Gardencourt." Miss Stackpole, with the best conscience in the world, offered to read her letter to Isabel, who immediately put in her protest.

"I don't think you ought to do that. I don't think you ought to describe the place."

Henrietta gazed at her as usual. "Why, it 's just what the people want, and it 's a lovely place."

"It 's too lovely to be put in the newspapers, and it 's not what my uncle wants."

"Don't you believe that!" cried Henrietta. "They 're always delighted afterwards."

"My uncle won't be delighted — nor my cousin either. They 'll consider it a breach of hospitality."

Miss Stackpole showed no sense of confusion; she simply wiped her pen, very neatly, upon an elegant little implement which she kept for the purpose, and put away her manuscript. "Of course if you don't approve I won't do it; but I sacrifice a beautiful subject."

"There are plenty of other subjects, there are subjects all round you. We 'll take some drives; I 'll show you some charming scenery."

"Scenery 's not my department; I always need a human interest. You know I 'm deeply human, Isabel; I always was," Miss Stackpole rejoined. "I was going to bring in your cousin — the alienated American. There 's a great demand just now for the alienated American, and your cousin 's a beautiful specimen. I should have handled him severely."

"He would have died of it!" Isabel exclaimed. "Not of the severity, but of the publicity."

"Well, I should have liked to kill him a little. And I should have delighted to do your uncle, who seems to me a much nobler type — the American faithful still. He 's a grand old man; I don't see how he can object to my paying him honour."

Isabel looked at her companion in much wonderment; it struck her as strange that a nature in which she found so much to esteem should break down so in spots. "My poor Henrietta," she said, "you 've no sense of privacy."

Henrietta coloured deeply, and for a moment her brilliant eyes were suffused, while Isabel found her more than ever inconsequent. "You do me great injustice," said Miss Stackpole with dignity. "I 've never written a word about myself!"

"I 'm very sure of that; but it seems to me one should be modest for others also!"

"Ah, that 's very good!" cried Henrietta, seizing her pen again. "Just let me make a note of it and I'll put it in somewhere." She was a thoroughly good-natured woman, and half an hour later she was in as cheerful a mood as should have been looked for in a newspaper-lady in want of matter. "I 've promised to do the social side," she said to Isabel; "and how can I do it unless I get ideas? If I can't describe this place don't you know some place I *can* describe?" Isabel promised she would bethink herself, and the next day, in conversation with her friend, she happened to mention her visit to Lord Warburton's ancient house. "Ah, you must take me there — that's just the place for me!" Miss Stackpole cried. "I must get a glimpse of the nobility."

"I can't take you," said Isabel; "but Lord Warburton 's coming here, and you 'll have a chance to see him and observe him. Only if you intend to repeat his conversation I shall certainly give him warning."

"Don't do that," her companion pleaded; "I want him to be natural."

"An Englishman 's never so natural as when he 's holding his tongue," Isabel declared.

It was not apparent, at the end of three days, that her cousin had, according to her prophecy, lost his heart to their visitor, though he had spent a good deal of time in her society. They strolled about the park together and sat under the trees, and in the afternoon, when it was delightful to float along the Thames, Miss Stackpole occupied a place in the boat in which hitherto Ralph had had but a single companion. Her presence proved somehow less irreducible to soft particles than Ralph had expected in the natural perturbation of his sense of the perfect solubility of that of his cousin; for the correspondent of the *Interviewer* prompted mirth in him, and he had long since decided that the *crescendo* of mirth should be the flower of his declining days. Henrietta, on her side, failed a little to justify Isabel's declaration with regard to her indifference to masculine opinion; for poor Ralph appeared to have presented himself to her as an irritating problem, which it would be almost immoral not to work out.

"What does he do for a living?" she asked of Isabel the evening of her arrival. "Does he go round all day with his hands in his pockets?"

"He does nothing," smiled Isabel; "he's a gentleman of large leisure."

"Well, I call that a shame — when I have to work like a car-conductor," Miss Stackpole replied. "I should like to show him up."

"He 's in wretched health; he 's quite unfit for work," Isabel urged.

"Pshaw! don't you believe it. I work when I 'm sick," cried her friend. Later, when she stepped into the boat on joining the water-party, she remarked to Ralph that she supposed he hated her and would like to drown her.

"Ah no," said Ralph, "I keep my victims for a slower torture. And you 'd be such an interesting one!"

"Well, you do torture me; I may say that. But I shock all your prejudices; that 's one comfort."

"My prejudices? I have n't a prejudice to bless myself with. There 's intellectual poverty for you."

"The more shame to you; I 've some delicious ones. Of course I spoil your flirtation, or whatever it is you call it, with your cousin; but I don't care for that, as I render her the service of drawing you out. She 'll see how thin you are."

"Ah, do draw me out!" Ralph exclaimed. "So few people will take the trouble."

Miss Stackpole, in this undertaking, appeared to shrink from no effort; resorting largely, whenever the opportunity offered, to the natural expedient of interrogation. On the following day the weather was bad, and in the afternoon the young man, by way of providing indoor amusement, offered to show her the pictures. Henrietta strolled through the long gallery in his society, while he pointed out its principal ornaments and mentioned the painters and subjects. Miss Stackpole looked at the pictures in perfect silence, committing herself to no opinion, and Ralph was gratified by the fact that she delivered herself of none of the little ready-made ejaculations of delight of which the visitors to Gardencourt were so frequently lavish. This young lady indeed, to do her justice, was but little addicted to the use of conventional terms; there was something earnest and inventive in her tone, which at times, in its strained deliberation, suggested a person of high culture speaking a foreign language. Ralph Touchett subsequently learned that she had at one time officiated as art-critic to a journal of the other world; but she appeared, in spite of this fact, to carry in her pocket none of the small change of admiration. Suddenly, just after he had called her attention to a charming Constable, she turned and looked at him as if he himself had been a picture.

"Do you always spend your time like this?" she demanded.

"I seldom spend it so agreeably."

"Well, you know what I mean — without any regular occupation."

"Ah," said Ralph, "I 'm the idlest man living."

Miss Stackpole directed her gaze to the Constable again, and Ralph bespoke her attention for a small Lancret hanging near it, which represented a gentleman in a pink doublet and hose and a ruff, leaning against the pedestal of the statue of a nymph in a garden and playing the guitar to two ladies seated on the grass. "That 's my ideal of a regular occupation," he said.

Miss Stackpole turned to him again, and, though her eyes had rested upon the picture, he saw she had missed the subject. She was thinking of something much more serious. "I don't see how you can reconcile it to your conscience."

"My dear lady, I *have* no conscience!"

"Well, I advise you to cultivate one. You 'll need it the next time you go to America."

"I shall probably never go again."

"Are you ashamed to show yourself?"

Ralph meditated with a mild smile. "I suppose that if one has no conscience one has no shame."

"Well, you 've got plenty of assurance," Henrietta declared. "Do you consider it right to give up your country?"

"Ah, one does n't give up one's country any more than one gives up one's grandmother. They 're both antecedent to choice—elements of one's composition that are not to be eliminated."

"I suppose that means that you 've tried and been worsted. What do they think of you over here?"

"They delight in me."

"That 's because you truckle to them."

"Ah, set it down a little to my natural charm!" Ralph sighed.

"I don't know anything about your natural charm. If you 've got any charm it 's quite unnatural. It 's wholly acquired—or at least you 've tried hard to acquire it, living over here. I don't say you 've succeeded. It 's a charm that I don't appreciate, anyway. Make yourself useful in some way, and then we 'll talk about it."

"Well, now, tell me what I shall do," said Ralph.

"Go right home, to begin with."

"Yes, I see. And then?"

"Take right hold of something."

"Well, now, what sort of thing?"

"Anything you please, so long as you take hold. Some new idea, some big work."

"Is it very difficult to take hold?" Ralph enquired.

"Not if you put your heart into it."

"Ah, my heart," said Ralph. "If it depends upon my heart —!"

"Have n't you got a heart?"

"I had one a few days ago, but I 've lost it since."

"You 're not serious," Miss Stackpole remarked; "that 's what 's the matter with you." But for all this, in a day or two, she again permitted him to fix her attention and on the later occasion assigned a different cause to her mysterious perversity. "I know what 's the matter with you, Mr. Touchett," she said. "You think you 're too good to get married."

"I thought so till I knew you, Miss Stackpole," Ralph answered; "and then I suddenly changed my mind."

"Oh pshaw!" Henrietta groaned.

"Then it seemed to me," said Ralph, "that I was not good enough."

"It would improve you. Besides, it 's your duty."

"Ah," cried the young man, "one has so many duties! Is that a duty too?"

"Of course it is — did you never know that before? It 's every one's duty to get married."

Ralph meditated a moment; he was disappointed. There was something in Miss Stackpole he had begun to like; it seemed to him that if she was not a charming woman she was at least a very good "sort." She was wanting in distinction, but, as Isabel had said, she was brave: she went into cages, she flourished lashes, like a spangled lion-tamer. He had not supposed her to be capable of vulgar arts, but these last words struck him as a false note. When a marriageable young woman urges matrimony on an unencumbered young man the most obvious explanation of her conduct is not the altruistic impulse.

"Ah, well now, there 's a good deal to be said about that," Ralph rejoined.

"There may be, but that 's the principal thing. I must say I think it looks very exclusive, going round all alone, as if you thought no woman was good enough for you. Do you think you 're better than any one else in the world? In America it 's usual for people to marry."

"If it 's my duty," Ralph asked, "is it not, by analogy, yours as well?"

Miss Stackpole's ocular surfaces unwinkingly caught the sun. "Have you the fond hope of finding a flaw in my reasoning? Of course I 've as good a right to marry as any one else."

"Well then," said Ralph, "I won't say it vexes me to see you single. It delights me rather."

"You 're not serious yet. You never will be."

"Shall you not believe me to be so on the day I tell

you I desire to give up the practice of going round alone?"

Miss Stackpole looked at him for a moment in a manner which seemed to announce a reply that might technically be called encouraging. But to his great surprise this expression suddenly resolved itself into an appearance of alarm and even of resentment. "No, not even then," she answered dryly. After which she walked away.

"I 've not conceived a passion for your friend," Ralph said that evening to Isabel, "though we talked some time this morning about it."

"And you said something she did n't like," the girl replied.

Ralph stared. "Has she complained of me?"

"She told me she thinks there 's something very low in the tone of Europeans towards women."

"Does she call me a European?"

"One of the worst. She told me you had said to her something that an American never would have said. But she did n't repeat it."

Ralph treated himself to a luxury of laughter. "She 's an extraordinary combination. Did she think I was making love to her?"

"No; I believe even Americans do that. But she apparently thought you mistook the intention of something she had said, and put an unkind construction on it."

"I thought she was proposing marriage to me and I accepted her. Was that unkind?"

Isabel smiled. "It was unkind to *me*. I don't want you to marry."

"My dear cousin, what 's one to do among you all?" Ralph demanded. "Miss Stackpole tells me it 's my bounden duty, and that it 's hers, in general, to see I do mine!"

"She has a great sense of duty," said Isabel gravely. "She has indeed, and it 's the motive of everything she says. That 's what I like her for. She thinks it 's unworthy of you to keep so many things to yourself. That 's what she wanted to express. If you thought she was trying to — to attract you, you were very wrong."

"It 's true it was an odd way, but I did think she was trying to attract me. Forgive my depravity."

"You 're very conceited. She had no interested views, and never supposed you would think she had."

"One must be very modest then to talk with such women," Ralph said humbly. "But it 's a very strange type. She 's too personal — considering that she expects other people not to be. She walks in without knocking at the door."

"Yes," Isabel admitted, "she does n't sufficiently recognise the existence of knockers; and indeed I 'm not sure that she does n't think them rather a pretentious ornament. She thinks one's door should stand ajar. But I persist in liking her."

"I persist in thinking her too familiar," Ralph rejoined, naturally somewhat uncomfortable under the sense of having been doubly deceived in Miss Stackpole.

"Well," said Isabel, smiling, "I 'm afraid it 's because she 's rather vulgar that I like her."

"She would be flattered by your reason!"

"If I should tell her I would n't express it in that way. I should say it 's because there 's something of the 'people' in her."

"What do you know about the people? and what does she, for that matter?"

"She knows a great deal, and I know enough to feel that she 's a kind of emanation of the great democracy — of the continent, the country, the nation. I don't say that she sums it all up, that would be too much to ask of her. But she suggests it; she vividly figures it."

"You like her then for patriotic reasons. I 'm afraid it is on those very grounds I object to her."

"Ah," said Isabel with a kind of joyous sigh, "I like so many things! If a thing strikes me with a certain intensity I accept it. I don't want to swagger, but I suppose I 'm rather versatile. I like people to be totally different from Henrietta — in the style of Lord Warburton's sisters for instance. So long as I look at the Misses Molyneux they seem to me to answer a kind of ideal. Then Henrietta presents herself, and I 'm straightway convinced by *her;* not so much in respect to herself as in respect to what masses behind her."

"Ah, you mean the back view of her," Ralph suggested.

"What she says is true," his cousin answered; "you 'll never be serious. I like the great country stretching away beyond the rivers and across the prairies, blooming and smiling and spreading till it stops at the green Pacific! A strong, sweet, fresh odour seems to rise from it, and Henrietta — pardon my simile — has something of that odour in her garments."

Isabel blushed a little as she concluded this speech, and the blush, together with the momentary ardour she had thrown into it, was so becoming to her that Ralph stood smiling at her for a moment after she had ceased speaking. "I 'm not sure the Pacific 's so green as that," he said; "but you 're a young woman of imagination. Henrietta, however, does smell of the Future — it almost knocks one down!"

XI

He took a resolve after this not to misinterpret her words even when Miss Stackpole appeared to strike the personal note most strongly. He bethought himself that persons, in her view, were simple and homogeneous organisms, and that he, for his own part, was too perverted a representative of the nature of man to have a right to deal with her in strict reciprocity. He carried out his resolve with a great deal of tact, and the young lady found in renewed contact with him no obstacle to the exercise of her genius for unshrinking enquiry, the general application of her confidence. Her situation at Gardencourt therefore, appreciated as we have seen her to be by Isabel and full of appreciation herself of that free play of intelligence which, to her sense, rendered Isabel's character a sister-spirit, and of the easy venerableness of Mr. Touchett, whose noble tone, as she said, met with her full approval — her situation at Gardencourt would have been perfectly comfortable had she not conceived an irresistible mistrust of the little lady for whom she had at first supposed herself obliged to "allow" as mistress of the house. She presently discovered, in truth, that this obligation was of the lightest and that Mrs. Touchett cared very little how Miss Stackpole behaved. Mrs. Touchett had defined her to Isabel as both an adventuress and a bore — adventuresses usually giving one more of a thrill; she had expressed some surprise at her niece's having selected such a friend, yet had immediately added that she knew Isabel's friends were her own affair and that she had never undertaken to like them all or to restrict the girl to those she liked.

"If you could see none but the people I like, my dear, you'd have a very small society," Mrs. Touchett frankly admitted; "and I don't think I like any man or woman well enough to recommend them to you. When it comes to recommending it's a serious affair. I don't like Miss Stackpole — everything about her displeases me; she talks so much too loud and looks at one as if one wanted to look at *her* — which one does n't. I'm sure she has lived all her life in a boarding-house, and I detest the manners and the liberties of such places. If you ask me if I prefer my own manners, which you doubtless think very bad, I'll tell you that I prefer them immensely. Miss Stackpole knows I detest boarding-house civilisation, and she detests me for detesting it, because she thinks it the highest in the world. She 'd like Gardencourt a great deal better if it were a boarding-house. For me, I find it almost too much of one! We shall never get on together therefore, and there 's no use trying."

Mrs. Touchett was right in guessing that Henrietta disapproved of her, but she had not quite put her finger on the reason. A day or two after Miss Stackpole's arrival she had made some invidious reflexions on American hotels, which excited a vein of counter-argument on the part of the correspondent of the *Interviewer*, who in the exercise of her profession had acquainted herself, in the western world, with every form of caravansary. Henrietta expressed the opinion that American hotels were the best in the world, and Mrs. Touchett, fresh from a renewed struggle with them, recorded a conviction that they were the worst. Ralph, with his experimental geniality, suggested, by way of healing the breach, that the truth lay between the two extremes and that the establishments in question ought to be described as fair middling. This contribution to the discussion, however, Miss Stackpole rejected with scorn. Middling indeed! If they were not the best in the world they were the worst, but there was nothing middling about an American hotel.

"We judge from different points of view, evidently," said Mrs. Touchett. "I like to be treated as an individual; you like to be treated as a 'party.'"

"I don't know what you mean," Henrietta replied. "I like to be treated as an American lady."

"Poor American ladies!" cried Mrs. Touchett with a laugh. "They 're the slaves of slaves."

"They 're the companions of freemen," Henrietta retorted.

"They 're the companions of their servants—the Irish chambermaid and the negro waiter. They share their work."

"Do you call the domestics in an American household 'slaves'?" Miss Stackpole enquired. "If that's the way you desire to treat them, no wonder you don't like America."

"If you 've not good servants you 're miserable," Mrs. Touchett serenely said. "They 're very bad in America, but I 've five perfect ones in Florence."

"I don't see what you want with five," Henrietta could n't help observing. "I don't think I should like to see five persons surrounding me in that menial position."

"I like them in that position better than in some others," proclaimed Mrs. Touchett with much meaning.

"Should you like me better if I were your butler, dear?" her husband asked.

"I don't think I should: you would n't at all have the *tenue*."

"The companions of freemen — I like that, Miss Stackpole," said Ralph. "It 's a beautiful description."

"When I said freemen I did n't mean you, sir!"

And this was the only reward that Ralph got for his compliment. Miss Stackpole was baffled; she evidently thought there was something treasonable in Mrs. Touchett's appreciation of a class which she privately judged to be a mysterious survival of feudalism. It was perhaps because her mind was oppressed with this image that she suffered some days to elapse before she took occasion to say to Isabel: "My dear friend, I wonder if you 're growing faithless."

"Faithless? Faithless to you, Henrietta?"

"No, that would be a great pain; but it 's not that."

"Faithless to my country then?"

"Ah, that I hope will never be. When I wrote to you from Liverpool I said I had something particular to tell you. You 've never asked me what it is. Is it because you 've suspected?"

"Suspected what? As a rule I don't think I suspect," said Isabel. "I remember now that phrase in your letter, but I confess I had forgotten it. What have you to tell me?"

Henrietta looked disappointed, and her steady gaze betrayed it. "You don't ask that right—as if you thought it important. You 're changed—you 're thinking of other things."

"Tell me what you mean, and I'll think of that."

"Will you really think of it? That 's what I wish to be sure of."

"I 've not much control of my thoughts, but I 'll do my best," said Isabel. Henrietta gazed at her, in silence, for a period which tried Isabel's patience, so that our heroine added at last: "Do you mean that you 're going to be married?"

"Not till I 've seen Europe!" said Miss Stackpole. "What are you laughing at?" she went on. "What I mean is that Mr. Goodwood came out in the steamer with me."

"Ah!" Isabel responded.

"You say *that* right. I had a good deal of talk with him; he has come after you."

"Did he tell you so?"

"No, he told me nothing; that 's how I knew it," said Henrietta cleverly. "He said very little about you, but I spoke of you a good deal."

Isabel waited. At the mention of Mr. Goodwood's name she had turned a little pale. "I 'm very sorry you did that," she observed at last.

"It was a pleasure to me, and I liked the way he listened. I could have talked a long time to such a listener; he was so quiet, so intense; he drank it all in."

"What did you say about me?" Isabel asked.

"I said you were on the whole the finest creature I know."

"I 'm very sorry for that. He thinks too well of me already; he ought n't to be encouraged."

"He 's dying for a little encouragement. I see his face now, and his earnest absorbed look while I talked. I never saw an ugly man look so handsome."

"He 's very simple-minded," said Isabel. "And he 's not so ugly."

"There 's nothing so simplifying as a grand passion."

"It 's not a grand passion; I 'm very sure it 's not that."

"You don't say that as if you were sure."

Isabel gave rather a cold smile. "I shall say it better to Mr. Goodwood himself."

"He 'll soon give you a chance," said Henrietta. Isabel offered no answer to this assertion, which her companion made with an air of great confidence. "He 'll find you changed," the latter pursued. "You 've been affected by your new surroundings."

"Very likely. I 'm affected by everything."

"By everything but Mr. Goodwood!" Miss Stackpole exclaimed with a slightly harsh hilarity.

Isabel failed even to smile back and in a moment she said: "Did he ask you to speak to me?"

"Not in so many words. But his eyes asked it — and his handshake, when he bade me good-bye."

"Thank you for doing so." And Isabel turned away.

"Yes, you 're changed; you 've got new ideas over here," her friend continued.

"I hope so," said Isabel; "one should get as many new ideas as possible."

"Yes; but they should n't interfere with the old ones when the old ones have been the right ones."

Isabel turned about again. "If you mean that I had any idea with regard to Mr. Goodwood—!" But she faltered before her friend's implacable glitter.

"My dear child, you certainly encouraged him."

Isabel made for the moment as if to deny this charge; instead of which, however, she presently answered: "It 's very true. I did encourage him." And then she asked if her companion had learned from Mr. Goodwood what he intended to do. It was a concession to her curiosity, for she disliked discussing the subject and found Henrietta wanting in delicacy.

"I asked him, and he said he meant to do nothing," Miss Stackpole answered. "But I don't believe that; he 's not a man to do nothing. He is a man of high, bold action. Whatever happens to him he 'll always do something, and whatever he does will always be right."

"I quite believe that." Henrietta might be wanting in delicacy, but it touched the girl, all the same, to hear this declaration.

"Ah, you *do* care for him!" her visitor rang out.

"Whatever he does will always be right," Isabel

repeated. "When a man 's of that infallible mould what does it matter to him what one feels?"

"It may not matter to him, but it matters to one's self."

"Ah, what it matters to me — that 's not what we 're discussing," said Isabel with a cold smile.

This time her companion was grave. "Well, I don't care; you *have* changed. You 're not the girl you were a few short weeks ago, and Mr. Goodwood will see it. I expect him here any day."

"I hope he 'll hate me then," said Isabel.

"I believe you hope it about as much as I believe him capable of it."

To this observation our heroine made no return; she was absorbed in the alarm given her by Henrietta's intimation that Caspar Goodwood would present himself at Gardencourt. She pretended to herself, however, that she thought the event impossible, and, later, she communicated her disbelief to her friend. For the next forty-eight hours, nevertheless, she stood prepared to hear the young man's name announced. The feeling pressed upon her; it made the air sultry, as if there were to be a change of weather; and the weather, socially speaking, had been so agreeable during Isabel's stay at Gardencourt that any change would be for the worse. Her suspense indeed was dissipated the second day. She had walked into the park in company with the sociable Bunchie, and after strolling about for some time, in a manner at once listless and restless, had seated herself on a garden-bench, within sight of the house, beneath a spreading beech, where, in a white dress ornamented with black ribbons, she formed among the flickering shadows a graceful and harmonious image. She entertained herself for some moments with talking to the little terrier, as to whom the proposal of an ownership divided with her cousin had been applied as impartially as possible — as impartially as Bunchie's own somewhat fickle and inconstant sympathies would allow. But she was notified for the first time, on this occasion, of the finite character of Bunchie's intellect; hitherto she had been mainly struck with its extent. It seemed to her at last that she would do well to take a book; formerly, when heavy-hearted, she had been able, with the help of some well-chosen volume, to transfer the seat of consciousness to the organ of pure reason. Of late, it was not to be denied, literature had seemed a fading light, and even after she had reminded herself that her uncle's library was provided with a complete set of those authors which no gentleman's collection should be without, she sat motionless and empty-handed, her eyes bent on the cool green turf of the lawn. Her meditations were presently interrupted by the arrival of a servant who handed her a letter. The letter bore the London postmark and was addressed in a hand she knew — that came into her vision, already so held by him, with the vividness of the writer's voice or his face. This document proved short and may be given entire.

My dear Miss Archer — I don't know whether you will have heard of my coming to England, but even if you have not it will scarcely be a surprise to you. You will remember that when you gave me my dismissal at Albany, three months ago, I did not accept it. I protested against it. You in fact appeared to accept my protest and to admit that I had the right on my side. I had come to see you with the hope that you would let me bring you over to my conviction; my reasons for entertaining this hope had been of the best. But you disappointed it; I found you changed, and you were able to give me no reason for the change. You admitted that you were unreasonable, and it was the only concession you would make; but it was a very cheap one, because that 's not your character. No, you are not, and you never will be, arbitrary or capricious. Therefore it is that I believe you will let me see you again. You told me that I 'm not disagreeable to you, and I believe it; for I don't see why that should be. I shall always think of you; I shall never think of any one else. I came to England simply because you are here; I could n't stay at home after you had gone: I hated the country because you were not in it. If I like this country at present it is only because it holds you. I have been to England before, but have never enjoyed it much. May I not come and see you for half an hour? This at present is the dearest wish of yours faithfully

CASPAR GOODWOOD.

Isabel read this missive with such deep attention that she had not perceived an approaching tread on the soft grass. Looking up, however, as she mechanically folded it she saw Lord Warburton standing before her.

XII

SHE put the letter into her pocket and offered her visitor a smile of welcome, exhibiting no trace of discomposure and half surprised at her coolness.

"They told me you were out here," said Lord Warburton; "and as there was no one in the drawing-room and it 's really you that I wish to see, I came out with no more ado."

Isabel had got up; she felt a wish, for the moment, that he should not sit down beside her. "I was just going indoors."

"Please don't do that; it 's much jollier here; I 've ridden over from Lockleigh; it 's a lovely day." His smile was peculiarly friendly and pleasing, and his whole person seemed to emit that radiance of good-feeling and good fare which had formed the charm of the girl's first impression of him. It surrounded him like a zone of fine June weather.

"We 'll walk about a little then," said Isabel, who could not divest herself of the sense of an intention on the part of her visitor and who wished both to elude the intention and to satisfy her curiosity about it. It had flashed upon her vision once before, and it had given her on that occasion, as we know, a certain alarm. This alarm was composed of several elements, not all of which were disagreeable; she had indeed spent some days in analysing them and had succeeded in separating the pleasant part of the idea of Lord Warburton's "making up" to her from the painful. It may appear to some readers that the young lady was both precipitate and unduly fastidious; but the latter of these facts, if the charge be true, may serve to exonerate her from the discredit of the former. She was not eager to convince herself that a territorial magnate, as she had heard Lord Warburton called, was smitten with her charms; the fact of a declaration from such a source carrying with it really more questions than it would answer. She had received a strong impression of his being a "personage," and she had occupied herself in examining the image so conveyed. At the risk of adding to the evidence of her self-sufficiency it must be said that there had been moments when this possibility of admiration by a personage represented to her an aggression almost to the degree of an affront, quite to the degree of an inconvenience. She had never yet known a personage; there had been no personages, in this sense, in her life; there were probably none such at all in her native land. When she had thought of individual eminence she had thought of it on the basis of character and wit — of what one might like in a gentleman's mind and in his talk. She herself was a character — she could n't help being aware of that; and hitherto her visions of a completed consciousness had concerned themselves largely with moral images — things as to which the question would be whether they pleased her sublime soul. Lord Warburton loomed up before her, largely and brightly, as a collection of attributes and powers which were not to be measured by this simple rule, but which demanded a different sort of appreciation — an appreciation that the girl, with her habit of judging quickly and freely, felt she lacked patience to bestow. He appeared to demand of her something that no one else, as it were, had presumed to do. What she felt was that a territorial, a political, a social magnate had conceived the design of drawing her into the system in which he rather invidiously lived and moved. A certain instinct, not imperious, but persuasive, told her to resist — murmured to her that virtually she had a system and an orbit of her own. It told her other things besides — things which both contradicted and confirmed each other; that a girl might do much worse than trust herself to such a man and that it would be very interesting to see something of his system from his own point of view; that on the other hand, however, there was evidently a great deal of it which she should regard only as a complication of every hour, and that even in the whole there was something stiff and stupid which would make it a burden. Furthermore there was a young man lately come from America who had no system at all, but who had a character of which it was useless for her to try to persuade herself that the impression on her mind had been light. The letter she carried in her pocket all sufficiently reminded her of the contrary. Smile not, however, I venture to repeat, at this simple young woman from Albany who debated whether she should accept an English peer before he had offered himself and who was disposed to believe that on the whole she could do better. She was a person of great good faith, and if there was a great deal of folly in her wisdom those who judge her severely may have the satisfaction of finding that, later, she became consistently wise only at the cost of an amount of folly which will constitute almost a direct appeal to charity.

Lord Warburton seemed quite ready to walk, to sit or to do anything that Isabel should propose, and he gave her this assurance with his usual air of being particularly pleased to exercise a social virtue. But he was, nevertheless, not in command of his emotions, and as he strolled beside her for a moment, in silence, looking at her without letting her know it, there was something embarrassed in his glance and his misdirected laughter. Yes, assuredly — as we have touched on the point, we may return to it for a moment again — the English are the most romantic people in the world and Lord Warburton was about to give an example of it. He was about to take a step which would astonish all his friends and displease a great many of them, and which had superficially nothing to recommend it. The young lady who trod the turf beside him had come from a queer country across the sea which he knew a good deal about; her antecedents, her associations were very vague to his mind except in so far as they were generic, and in this sense they showed as distinct and unimportant. Miss Archer had neither a fortune nor the sort of beauty that justifies a man to the multitude, and he calculated that he had spent about twenty-six hours in her company. He had summed up all this — the perversity of the impulse, which had declined to avail itself of the most liberal opportunities to subside, and the judgement of mankind, as exemplified particularly in the more quickly-judging half of it: he had looked these things well in the face and then had dismissed them from his thoughts. He cared no more for them than for the rosebud in his buttonhole. It is the good fortune of a man who for the greater part of a lifetime has abstained without effort from making himself disagreeable to his friends, that when the need comes for such a course it is not discredited by irritating associations.

"I hope you had a pleasant ride," said Isabel, who observed her companion's hesitancy.

"It would have been pleasant if for nothing else than that it brought me here."

"Are you so fond of Gardencourt?" the girl asked, more and more sure that he meant to make some appeal to her; wishing not to challenge him if he hesitated, and yet to keep all the quietness of her reason if he proceeded. It suddenly came upon her that her situation was one which a few weeks ago she would have deemed deeply romantic: the park of an old English country-house, with the foreground embellished by a "great" (as she supposed) nobleman in the act of making love to a young lady who, on careful inspection, should be found to present remarkable analogies with herself. But if she was now the heroine of the situation she succeeded scarcely the less in looking at it from the outside.

"I care nothing for Gardencourt," said her companion. "I care only for you."

"You 've known me too short a time to have a right to say that, and I can't believe you 're serious."

These words of Isabel's were not perfectly sincere, for she had no doubt whatever that he himself was. They were simply a tribute to the fact, of which she was perfectly aware, that those he had just uttered would have excited surprise on the part of a vulgar world. And, moreover, if anything beside the sense she had already acquired that Lord Warburton was not a loose thinker had been needed to convince her, the tone in which he replied would quite have served the purpose.

"One's right in such a matter is not measured by the time, Miss Archer; it 's measured by the feeling itself. If I were to wait three months it would make no difference; I shall not be more sure of what I mean than I am to-day. Of course I've seen you very little, but my impression dates from the very first hour we met. I lost no time, I fell in love with you then. It was at first sight, as the novels say; I know now that 's not a fancy-phrase, and I shall think better of novels for evermore. Those two days I spent here settled it; I don't know whether you suspected I was doing so, but I paid — mentally speaking I mean — the greatest possible attention to you. Nothing you said, nothing you did, was lost upon me. When you came to Lockleigh the other day — or rather when you went away — I was perfectly sure. Nevertheless I made up my mind to think it over and to question myself narrowly. I 've done so; all these days I 've done nothing else. I don't make mistakes about such things; I 'm a very judicious animal. I don't go off easily, but when I'm touched, it's for life. It's for life, Miss Archer, it's for life," Lord Warburton repeated in the kindest, tenderest, pleasantest voice Isabel had ever heard, and looking at her with eyes charged with the light of a passion that had sifted itself clear of the baser parts of emotion — the heat, the violence, the unreason — and that burned as steadily as a lamp in a windless place.

By tacit consent, as he talked, they had walked more and more slowly, and at last they stopped and he took her hand. "Ah, Lord Warburton, how little you know me!" Isabel said very gently. Gently too she drew her hand away.

"Don't taunt me with that; that I don't know you better makes me unhappy enough already; it 's all my loss. But that 's what I want, and it seems to me I 'm taking the best way. If you 'll be my wife, then I shall know you, and when I tell you all the good I think of you you 'll not be able to say it 's from ignorance."

"If you know me little I know you even less," said Isabel.

"You mean that, unlike yourself, I may not improve on acquaintance? Ah, of course that 's very possible. But think, to speak to you as I do, how determined I must be to try and give satisfaction! You do like me rather, don't you?"

"I like you very much, Lord Warburton," she answered; and at this moment she liked him immensely.

"I thank you for saying that; it shows you don't regard me as a stranger. I really believe I 've filled all the other relations of life very creditably, and I don't see why I should n't fill this one — in which I offer myself to you — seeing that I care so much more about it. Ask the people who know me well; I 've friends who 'll speak for me."

"I don't need the recommendation of your friends," said Isabel.

"Ah now, that 's delightful of you. You believe in me yourself."

"Completely," Isabel declared. She quite glowed there, inwardly, with the pleasure of feeling she did.

The light in her companion's eyes turned into a smile, and he gave a long exhalation of joy. "If you're mistaken, Miss Archer, let me lose all I possess!"

She wondered whether he meant this for a reminder that he was rich, and, on the instant, felt sure that he did n't. He was sinking that, as he would have said himself; and indeed he might safely leave it to the memory of any interlocutor, especially of one to whom he was offering his hand. Isabel had prayed that she might not be agitated, and her mind was tranquil enough, even while she listened and asked herself what it was best she should say, to indulge in this incidental criticism. What she should say, had she asked herself? Her foremost wish was to say something if possible not less kind than what he had said to her. His words had carried perfect conviction with them; she felt she did, all so mysteriously, matter to him. "I thank you more than I can say for your offer," she returned at last. "It does me great honour."

"Ah, don't say that!" he broke out. "I was afraid you'd say something like that. I don't see what you've to do with that sort of thing. I don't see why you should thank me — it's I who ought to thank you for listening to me: a man you know so little coming down on you with such a thumper! Of course it's a great question; I must tell you that I'd rather ask it than have it to answer myself. But the way you've listened — or at least your having listened at all — gives me some hope."

"Don't hope too much," Isabel said.

"Oh Miss Archer!" her companion murmured, smiling again, in his seriousness, as if such a warning might perhaps be taken but as the play of high spirits, the exuberance of elation.

"Should you be greatly surprised if I were to beg you not to hope at all?" Isabel asked.

"Surprised? I don't know what you mean by surprise. It would n't be that; it would be a feeling very much worse."

Isabel walked on again; she was silent for some minutes. "I 'm very sure that, highly as I already think of you, my opinion of you, if I should know you well, would only rise. But I 'm by no means sure that you would n't be disappointed. And I say that not in the least out of conventional modesty; it 's perfectly sincere."

"I 'm willing to risk it, Miss Archer," her companion replied.

"It 's a great question, as you say. It 's a very difficult question."

"I don't expect you of course to answer it outright. Think it over as long as may be necessary. If I can gain by waiting I 'll gladly wait a long time. Only remember that in the end my dearest happiness depends on your answer."

"I should be very sorry to keep you in suspense," said Isabel.

"Oh, don't mind. I 'd much rather have a good answer six months hence than a bad one to-day."

"But it's very probable that even six months hence I should n't be able to give you one that you 'd think good."

"Why not, since you really like me?"

"Ah, you must never doubt that," said Isabel.

"Well then, I don't see what more you ask!"

"It's not what I ask; it's what I can give. I don't think I should suit you; I really don't think I should."

"You need n't worry about that. That's my affair. You need n't be a better royalist than the king."

"It 's not only that," said Isabel; "but I 'm not sure I wish to marry any one."

"Very likely you don't. I've no doubt a great many women begin that way," said his lordship, who, be it averred, did not in the least believe in the axiom he thus beguiled his anxiety by uttering. "But they're frequently persuaded."

"Ah, that's because they want to be!" And Isabel lightly laughed.

Her suitor's countenance fell, and he looked at her for a while in silence. "I 'm afraid it 's my being an Englishman that makes you hesitate," he said presently. "I know your uncle thinks you ought to marry in your own country."

Isabel listened to this assertion with some interest; it had never occurred to her that Mr. Touchett was likely to discuss her matrimonial prospects with Lord Warburton. "Has he told you that?"

"I remember his making the remark. He spoke perhaps of Americans generally."

"He appears himself to have found it very pleasant to live in England." Isabel spoke in a manner that might have seemed a little perverse, but which expressed both her constant perception of her uncle's outward felicity and her general disposition to elude any obligation to take a restricted view.

It gave her companion hope, and he immediately cried with warmth: "Ah, my dear Miss Archer, old England 's a very good sort of country, you know! And it will be still better when we 've furbished it up a little."

"Oh, don't furbish it, Lord Warburton; leave it alone. I like it this way."

"Well then, if you like it, I 'm more and more unable to see your objection to what I propose."

"I 'm afraid I can't make you understand."

"You ought at least to try. I've a fair intelligence. Are you afraid — afraid of the climate? We can easily live elsewhere, you know. You can pick out your climate, the whole world over."

These words were uttered with a breadth of candour that was like the embrace of strong arms — that was like the fragrance straight in her face, and by his clean, breathing lips, of she knew not what strange gardens, what charged airs. She would have given her little finger at that moment to feel strongly and simply the impulse to answer: "Lord Warburton, it 's impossible for me to do better in this wonderful world, I think, than commit myself, very gratefully, to your loyalty." But though she was lost in admiration of her opportunity she managed to move back into the deepest shade of it, even as some wild, caught creature in a vast cage. The "splendid" security so offered her was *not* the greatest she could conceive. What she finally bethought herself of saying was something very different — something that deferred the need of really facing her crisis. "Don't think me unkind if I ask you to say no more about this to-day."

"Certainly, certainly!" her companion cried. "I would n't bore you for the world."

"You've given me a great deal to think about, and I promise you to do it justice."

"That 's all I ask of you, of course — and that you 'll remember how absolutely my happiness is in your hands."

Isabel listened with extreme respect to this admonition, but she said after a minute: "I must tell you that what I shall think about is some way of letting you know that what you ask is impossible — letting you know it without making you miserable."

"There's no way to do that, Miss Archer. I won't say that if you refuse me you'll kill me; I shall not die of it. But I shall do worse; I shall live to no purpose."

"You'll live to marry a better woman than I."

"Don't say that, please," said Lord Warburton very gravely. "That's fair to neither of us."

"To marry a worse one then."

"If there are better women than you I prefer the bad ones. That's all I can say," he went on with the same earnestness. "There's no accounting for tastes."

His gravity made her feel equally grave, and she showed it by again requesting him to drop the subject for the present. "I'll speak to you myself — very soon. Perhaps I shall write to you."

"At your convenience, yes," he replied. "Whatever time you take, it must seem to me long, and I suppose I must make the best of that."

"I shall not keep you in suspense; I only want to collect my mind a little."

He gave a melancholy sigh and stood looking at her a moment, with his hands behind him, giving short nervous shakes to his hunting-crop. "Do you know I'm very much afraid of it — of that remarkable mind of yours?"

Our heroine's biographer can scarcely tell why, but the question made her start and brought a conscious blush to her cheek. She returned his look a moment, and then with a note in her voice that might almost have appealed to his compassion, "So am I, my lord!" she oddly exclaimed.

His compassion was not stirred, however; all he possessed of the faculty of pity was needed at home. "Ah! be merciful, be merciful," he murmured.

"I think you had better go," said Isabel. "I'll write to you."

"Very good; but whatever you write I'll come and see you, you know." And then he stood reflecting, his eyes fixed on the observant countenance of Bunchie, who had the air of having understood all that had been said and of pretending to carry off the indiscretion by a simulated fit of curiosity as to the roots of an ancient oak. "There's one thing more," he went on. "You know, if you don't like Lockleigh — if you think it's damp or anything of that sort — you need never go within fifty miles of it. It's not damp, by the way; I've had the house thoroughly examined; it's perfectly safe and right. But if you should n't fancy it you need n't dream of living in it. There's no difficulty whatever about that; there are plenty of houses. I thought I'd just mention it; some people don't like a moat, you know. Good-bye."

"I adore a moat," said Isabel. "Good-bye."

He held out his hand, and she gave him hers a moment — a moment long enough for him to bend his handsome bared head and kiss it. Then, still agitating, in his mastered emotion, his implement of the chase, he walked rapidly away. He was evidently much upset.

Isabel herself was upset, but she had not been affected as she would have imagined. What she felt was not a great responsibility, a great difficulty of choice; it appeared to her there had been no choice in the question. She could n't marry Lord Warburton; the idea failed to support any enlightened prejudice in favour of the free exploration of life that she had hitherto entertained or was now capable of entertaining. She must write this to him, she must convince him, and that duty was comparatively simple. But what disturbed her, in the sense that it struck her with wonderment, was this very fact that it cost her so little to refuse a magnificent "chance." With whatever qualifications one would, Lord Warburton had offered her a great opportunity; the situation might have discomforts, might contain oppressive, might contain narrowing elements, might prove really but a stupefying anodyne; but she did her sex no injustice in believing that nineteen women out of twenty would have accommodated themselves to it without a pang. Why then upon her also should it not irresistibly impose itself? Who was she, what was she, that she should hold herself superior? What view of life, what design upon fate, what conception of happiness, had she that pretended to be larger than these large, these fabulous occasions? If she would n't do such a thing as that then she must do great things, she must do something greater. Poor Isabel found ground to remind herself from time to time that she must not be too proud, and nothing could be more sincere than her prayer to be delivered from such a danger: the isolation and loneliness of pride had for her mind the horror of a desert place. If it had been pride that interfered with her accepting Lord Warburton such a *bêtise* was singularly misplaced; and she was so conscious of liking him that she ventured to assure herself it was the very softness, and the fine intelligence, of sympathy. She liked him too much to marry him, that was the truth; something assured her there was a fallacy somewhere in the glowing logic of the proposition — as *he* saw it — even though she might n't put her very finest finger-point on it; and to inflict upon a man who offered so much a wife with a tendency to criticise would be a peculiarly discreditable act. She had promised him she would consider his question, and when, after he had left her, she wandered back to the bench where he had found her and lost herself in meditation, it might have seemed that she was keeping her vow. But this was not the case; she was wondering if she were not a cold, hard, priggish person, and, on her at last getting up and going rather quickly back to the house, felt, as she had said to her friend, really frightened at herself.

XIII

It was this feeling and not the wish to ask advice — she had no desire whatever for that — that led her to speak to her uncle of what had taken place. She wished to speak to some one; she should feel more natural, more human, and her uncle, for this purpose, presented himself in a more attractive light than either her aunt or her friend Henrietta. Her cousin of course was a possible confidant; but she would have had to do herself violence to air this special secret to Ralph. So the next day, after breakfast, she sought her occasion. Her uncle never left his apartment till the afternoon, but he received his cronies, as he said, in his dressing-room. Isabel had quite taken her place in the class so designated, which, for the rest, included the old man's son, his physician, his personal servant, and even Miss Stackpole. Mrs. Touchett did not figure in the list, and this was an obstacle the less to Isabel's finding her host alone. He sat in a complicated mechanical chair, at the open window of his room, looking westward over the park and the river, with his newspapers and letters piled up beside him, his toilet freshly and minutely made, and his smooth, speculative face composed to benevolent expectation.

She approached her point directly. "I think I ought to let you know that Lord Warburton has asked me to marry him. I suppose I ought to tell my aunt; but it seems best to tell you first."

The old man expressed no surprise, but thanked her for the confidence she showed him. "Do you mind telling me whether you accepted him?" he then enquired.

"I've not answered him definitely yet; I've taken a little time to think of it, because that seems more respectful. But I shall not accept him."

Mr. Touchett made no comment upon this; he had the air of thinking that, whatever interest he might take in the matter from the point of view of sociability, he had no active voice in it. "Well, I told you you'd be a success over here. Americans are highly appreciated."

"Very highly indeed," said Isabel. "But at the cost of seeming both tasteless and ungrateful, I don't think I can marry Lord Warburton."

"Well," her uncle went on, "of course an old man can't judge for a young lady. I'm glad you did n't ask me before you made up your mind. I suppose I ought to tell you," he added slowly, but as if it were not of much consequence, "that I've known all about it these three days."

"About Lord Warburton's state of mind?"

"About his intentions, as they say here. He wrote me a very pleasant letter, telling me all about them. Should you like to see his letter?" the old man obligingly asked.

"Thank you; I don't think I care about that. But I'm glad he wrote to you; it was right that he should, and he would be certain to do what was right."

"Ah well, I guess you do like him!" Mr. Touchett declared. "You need n't pretend you don't."

"I like him extremely; I 'm very free to admit that. But I don't wish to marry any one just now."

"You think some one may come along whom you may like better. Well, that 's very likely," said Mr. Touchett, who appeared to wish to show his kindness to the girl by easing off her decision, as it were, and finding cheerful reasons for it.

"I don't care if I don't meet any one else. I like Lord Warburton quite well enough." She fell into that appearance of a sudden change of point of view with which she sometimes startled and even displeased her interlocutors.

Her uncle, however, seemed proof against either of these impressions. "He 's a very fine man," he resumed in a tone which might have passed for that of encouragement. "His letter was one of the pleasantest I 've received for some weeks. I suppose one of the reasons I liked it was that it was all about you; that is all except the part that was about himself. I suppose he told you all that."

"He would have told me everything I wished to ask him," Isabel said.

"But you did n't feel curious?"

"My curiosity would have been idle — once I had determined to decline his offer."

"You did n't find it sufficiently attractive?" Mr. Touchett enquired.

She was silent a little. "I suppose it was that," she presently admitted. "But I don't know why."

"Fortunately ladies are not obliged to give reasons," said her uncle. "There 's a great deal that 's attractive about such an idea; but I don't see why the

English should want to entice us away from our native land. I know that we try to attract them over there, but that 's because our population is insufficient. Here, you know, they 're rather crowded. However, I presume there 's room for charming young ladies everywhere."

"There seems to have been room here for you," said Isabel, whose eyes had been wandering over the large pleasure-spaces of the park.

Mr. Touchett gave a shrewd, conscious smile. "There 's room everywhere, my dear, if you 'll pay for it. I sometimes think I 've paid too much for this. Perhaps you also might have to pay too much."

"Perhaps I might," the girl replied.

That suggestion gave her something more definite to rest on than she had found in her own thoughts, and the fact of this association of her uncle's mild acuteness with her dilemma seemed to prove that she was concerned with the natural and reasonable emotions of life and not altogether a victim to intellectual eagerness and vague ambitions — ambitions reaching beyond Lord Warburton's beautiful appeal, reaching to something indefinable and possibly not commendable. In so far as the indefinable had an influence upon Isabel's behaviour at this juncture, it was not the conception, even unformulated, of a union with Caspar Goodwood; for however she might have resisted conquest at her English suitor's large quiet hands she was at least as far removed from the disposition to let the young man from Boston take positive possession of her. The sentiment in which she sought refuge after reading his letter was a critical view of his having come abroad; for it was part of the influence he had upon her that he seemed to deprive her of the sense of freedom. There was a disagreeably strong push, a kind of hardness of presence, in his way of rising before her. She had been haunted at moments by the image, by the danger, of his disapproval and had wondered — a consideration she had never paid in equal degree to any one else — whether he would like what she did. The difficulty was that more than any man she had ever known, more than poor Lord Warburton (she had begun now to give his lordship the benefit of this epithet), Caspar Goodwood expressed for her an energy — and she had already felt it as a power — that was of his very nature. It was in no degree a matter of his "advantages" — it was a matter of the spirit that sat in his clear-burning eyes like some tireless watcher at a window. She might like it or not, but he insisted, ever, with his whole weight and force: even in one's usual contact with him one had to reckon with that. The idea of a diminished liberty was particularly disagreeable to her at present, since she had just given a sort of personal accent to her independence by looking so straight at Lord Warburton's big bribe and yet turning away from it. Sometimes Caspar Goodwood had seemed to range himself on the side of her destiny, to be the stubbornest fact she knew; she said to herself at such moments that she might evade him for a time, but that she must make terms with him at last — terms which would be certain to be favourable to himself. Her impulse had been to avail herself of the things that helped her to resist such an obligation; and this impulse had been much concerned in her eager acceptance of her aunt's invitation, which had come to her at an hour when she expected from day to day to see Mr. Goodwood and when she was glad to have an answer ready for something she was sure he would say to her. When she had told him at Albany, on the evening of Mrs. Touchett's visit, that she could n't then discuss difficult questions, dazzled as she was by the great immediate opening of her aunt's offer of "Europe," he declared that this was no answer at all; and it was now to obtain a better one that he was following her across the sea. To say to herself that he was a kind of grim fate was well enough for a fanciful young woman who was able to take much for granted in him; but the reader has a right to a nearer and a clearer view.

He was the son of a proprietor of well-known cotton-mills in Massachusetts — a gentleman who had accumulated a considerable fortune in the exercise of this industry. Caspar at present managed the works, and with a judgement and a temper which, in spite of keen competition and languid years, had kept their prosperity from dwindling. He had received the better part of his education at Harvard College, where, however, he had gained renown rather as a gymnast and an oarsman than as a gleaner of more dispersed knowledge. Later on he had learned that the finer intelligence too could vault and pull and strain — might even, breaking the record, treat itself to rare exploits. He had thus discovered in himself a sharp eye for the mystery of mechanics, and had invented an improvement in the cotton-spinning process which was now largely used and was known by his name. You might have seen it in the newspapers in connection with this fruitful contrivance; assurance of which he had given to Isabel by showing her in the columns of the New York *Interviewer* an exhaustive article on the Goodwood patent — an article not prepared by Miss Stackpole, friendly as she had proved herself to his more sentimental interests. There were intricate, bristling things he rejoiced in; he liked to organise, to contend, to administer; he could make people work his will, believe in him, march before him and justify him. This was the art, as they said, of managing men — which rested, in him, further, on a bold though brooding ambition. It struck those who knew him well that he might do greater things than carry on a cotton-factory; there was nothing cottony about Caspar Goodwood, and his friends took for granted that he would somehow and somewhere write himself in bigger letters. But it was as if something large and confused, something dark and ugly, would have to call upon him: he was not after all in harmony with mere smug peace and greed and gain, an order of things of which the vital breath was ubiquitous advertisement. It pleased Isabel to believe that he might have ridden, on a plunging steed, the whirlwind of a great war — a war like the Civil strife that had overdarkened her conscious childhood and his ripening youth.

She liked at any rate this idea of his being by character and in fact a mover of men — liked it much better than some other points in his nature and aspect. She cared nothing for his cotton-mill — the Goodwood patent left her imagination absolutely cold. She wished him no ounce less of his manhood, but she sometimes thought he would be rather nicer if he looked, for instance, a little differently. His jaw was too square and set and his figure too straight and stiff: these things suggested a want of easy consonance with the deeper rhythms of life. Then she viewed with reserve a habit he had of dressing always in the same manner; it was not apparently that he wore the same clothes continually, for, on the contrary, his garments had a way of looking rather too new. But they all seemed of the same piece; the figure, the stuff, was so drearily usual. She had reminded herself more than once that this was a frivolous objection to a person of his importance; and then she had amended the rebuke by saying that it would be a frivolous objection only if she were in love with him. She was not in love with him and therefore might criticise his small defects as well as his great — which latter consisted in the collective reproach of his being too serious, or, rather, not of his being so, since one could never be, but certainly of his seeming so. He showed his appetites and designs too simply and artlessly; when one was alone with him he talked too much about the same subject, and when other people were present he talked too little about anything. And yet he was of supremely strong, clean make — which was so much: she saw the different fitted parts of him as she had seen, in museums and portraits, the different fitted parts of armoured warriors — in plates of steel handsomely inlaid with gold. It was very strange: where, ever, was any tangible link between her impression and her act? Caspar Goodwood had never corresponded to her idea of a delightful person, and she supposed that this was why he left her so harshly critical. When, however, Lord Warburton, who not only did correspond with it, but gave an extension to the term, appealed to her approval, she found herself still unsatisfied. It was certainly strange.

The sense of her incoherence was not a help to answering Mr. Goodwood's letter, and Isabel determined to leave it a while unhonoured. If he had determined to persecute her he must take the consequences; foremost among which was his being left to perceive how little it charmed her that he should come down to Gardencourt. She was already liable to the incursions of one suitor at this place, and though it might be pleasant to be appreciated in opposite quarters there was a kind of grossness in entertaining two such passionate pleaders at once, even in a case where the entertainment should consist of dismissing them. She made no reply to Mr. Goodwood; but at the end of three days she wrote to Lord Warburton, and the letter belongs to our history.

DEAR LORD WARBURTON—A great deal of earnest thought has not led me to change my mind about the suggestion you were so kind as to make me the other day. I am not, I am really and truly not, able to regard you in the light of a companion for life; or to think of your home — your various homes — as the settled seat of my existence. These things cannot be reasoned about, and I very earnestly entreat you not to return to the subject we discussed so exhaustively. We see our lives from our own point of view; that is the privilege of the weakest and humblest of us; and I shall never be able to see mine in the manner you proposed. Kindly let this suffice you, and do me the justice to believe that I have given your proposal the deeply respectful consideration it deserves. It is with this very great regard that I remain sincerely yours,

ISABEL ARCHER.

While the author of this missive was making up her mind to despatch it Henrietta Stackpole formed a resolve which was accompanied by no demur. She invited Ralph Touchett to take a walk with her in the garden, and when he had assented with that alacrity which seemed constantly to testify to his high expectations, she informed him that she had a favour to ask of him. It may be admitted that at this information the young man flinched; for we know that Miss Stackpole had struck him as apt to push an advantage. The alarm was unreasoned, however; for he was clear about the area of her indiscretion as little as advised of its vertical depth, and he made a very civil profession of the desire to serve her. He was afraid of her and presently told her so. "When you look at me in a certain way my knees knock together, my faculties desert me; I'm filled with trepidation and I ask only for strength to execute your commands. You've an address that I've never encountered in any woman."

"Well," Henrietta replied good-humouredly, "if I

had not known before that you were trying somehow to abash me I should know it now. Of course I'm easy game — I was brought up with such different customs and ideas. I'm not used to your arbitrary standards, and I've never been spoken to in America as you have spoken to me. If a gentleman conversing with me over there were to speak to me like that I should n't know what to make of it. We take everything more naturally over there, and, after all, we're a great deal more simple. I admit that; I'm very simple myself. Of course if you choose to laugh at me for it you're very welcome; but I think on the whole I would rather be myself than you. I'm quite content to be myself; I don't want to change. There are plenty of people that appreciate me just as I am. It's true they're nice fresh free-born Americans!" Henrietta had lately taken up the tone of helpless innocence and large concession. "I want you to assist me a little," she went on. "I don't care in the least whether I amuse you while you do so; or, rather, I'm perfectly willing your amusement should be your reward. I want you to help me about Isabel."

"Has she injured you?" Ralph asked.

"If she had I should n't mind, and I should never tell you. What I'm afraid of is that she'll injure herself."

"I think that's very possible," said Ralph.

His companion stopped in the garden-walk, fixing on him perhaps the very gaze that unnerved him. "That too would amuse you, I suppose. The way you do say things! I never heard any one so indifferent."

"To Isabel? Ah, not that!"

"Well, you're not in love with her, I hope."

"How can that be, when I'm in love with Another?"

"You're in love with yourself, that's the Other!" Miss Stackpole declared. "Much good may it do you! But if you wish to be serious once in your life here's a chance; and if you really care for your cousin here's an opportunity to prove it. I don't expect you to understand her; that's too much to ask. But you need n't do that to grant my favour. I'll supply the necessary intelligence."

"I shall enjoy that immensely!" Ralph exclaimed. "I'll be Caliban and you shall be Ariel."

"You're not at all like Caliban, because you're sophisticated, and Caliban was not. But I'm not talking about imaginary characters; I'm talking about Isabel. Isabel's intensely real. What I wish to tell you is that I find her fearfully changed."

"Since you came, do you mean?"

"Since I came and before I came. She's not the same as she once so beautifully was."

"As she was in America?"

"Yes, in America. I suppose you know she comes from there. She can't help it, but she does."

"Do you want to change her back again?"

"Of course I do, and I want you to help me."

"Ah," said Ralph, "I'm only Caliban; I'm not Prospero."

"You were Prospero enough to make her what she has become. You've acted on Isabel Archer since she came here, Mr. Touchett."

"I, my dear Miss Stackpole? Never in the world. Isabel Archer has acted on me — yes; she acts on every one. But I 've been absolutely passive."

"You're too passive then. You had better stir yourself and be careful. Isabel 's changing every day; she's drifting away — right out to sea. I've watched her and I can see it. She's not the bright American girl she was. She's taking different views, a different colour, and turning away from her old ideals. I want to save those ideals, Mr. Touchett, and that's where you come in."

"Not surely as an ideal?"

"Well, I hope not," Henrietta replied promptly. "I've got a fear in my heart that she's going to marry one of these fell Europeans, and I want to prevent it."

"Ah, I see," cried Ralph; "and to prevent it you want me to step in and marry her?"

"Not quite; that remedy would be as bad as the disease, for you're the typical, the fell European from whom I wish to rescue her. No; I wish you to take an interest in another person — a young man to whom she once gave great encouragement and whom she now does n't seem to think good enough. He 's a thoroughly grand man and a very dear friend of mine, and I wish very much you would invite him to pay a visit here."

Ralph was much puzzled by this appeal, and it is perhaps not to the credit of his purity of mind that he failed to look at it at first in the simplest light. It wore, to his eyes, a tortuous air, and his fault was that he was not quite sure that anything in the world could really be as candid as this request of Miss Stackpole's appeared. That a young woman should demand that a gentleman whom she described as her very dear friend should be furnished with an opportunity to make himself agreeable to another young woman, a young woman whose attention had wandered and whose charms were greater — this was an anomaly which for the moment challenged all his ingenuity of interpretation. To read between the lines was easier than to follow the text, and to suppose that Miss Stackpole wished the gentleman invited to Gardencourt on her own account was the sign not so much of a vulgar as of an embarrassed mind. Even from this venial act of vulgarity, however, Ralph was saved, and saved by a force that I can only speak of as inspiration. With no more outward light on the subject than he already possessed he suddenly acquired the conviction that it would be a sovereign injustice to the correspondent of the *Interviewer* to assign a dishonourable motive to any act of hers. This conviction passed into his mind with extreme rapidity; it was perhaps kindled by the pure radiance of the young lady's imperturbable gaze. He returned this challenge a moment, consciously, resisting an inclination to frown as one frowns in the presence of larger luminaries. "Who's the gentleman you speak of?"

"Mr. Caspar Goodwood — of Boston. He has been extremely attentive to Isabel — just as devoted to her as he can live. He has followed her out here and he's at present in London. I don't know his address, but I guess I can obtain it."

"I've never heard of him," said Ralph.

"Well, I suppose you have n't heard of every one. I don't believe he has ever heard of you; but that's no reason why Isabel should n't marry him."

Ralph gave a mild ambiguous laugh. "What a rage you have for marrying people! Do you remember how you wanted to marry *me* the other day?"

"I've got over that. You don't know how to take such ideas. Mr. Goodwood does, however; and that's what I like about him. He's a splendid man and a perfect gentleman, and Isabel knows it."

"Is she very fond of him?"

"If she is n't she ought to be. He 's simply wrapped up in her."

"And you wish me to ask him here," said Ralph reflectively.

"It would be an act of true hospitality."

"Caspar Goodwood," Ralph continued—"it's rather a striking name."

"I don't care anything about his name. It might be Ezekiel Jenkins, and I should say the same. He's the only man I have ever seen whom I think worthy of Isabel."

"You're a very devoted friend," said Ralph.

"Of course I am. If you say that to pour scorn on me I don't care."

"I don't say it to pour scorn on you; I'm very much struck with it."

"You 're more satiric than ever, but I advise you not to laugh at Mr. Goodwood."

"I assure you I'm very serious; you ought to understand that," said Ralph.

In a moment his companion understood it. "I believe you are; now you're too serious."

"You're difficult to please."

"Oh, you're very serious indeed. You won't invite Mr. Goodwood."

"I don't know," said Ralph. "I'm capable of strange things. Tell me a little about Mr. Goodwood. What 's he like?"

"He's just the opposite of you. He's at the head of a cotton-factory; a very fine one."

"Has he pleasant manners?" asked Ralph.

"Splendid manners — in the American style."

"Would he be an agreeable member of our little circle?"

"I don't think he'd care much about our little circle. He'd concentrate on Isabel."

"And how would my cousin like that?"

"Very possibly not at all. But it will be good for her. It will call back her thoughts."

"Call them back — from where?"

"From foreign parts and other unnatural places. Three months ago she gave Mr. Goodwood every reason to suppose he was acceptable to her, and it's not worthy of Isabel to go back on a real friend simply because she has changed the scene. I've changed the scene too, and the effect of it has been to make me care more for my old associations than ever. It's my belief that the sooner Isabel changes it back again the better. I know her well enough to know that she would never be truly happy over here, and I wish her to form some strong American tie that will act as a preservative."

"Are n't you perhaps a little too much in a hurry?" Ralph enquired. "Don't you think you ought to give her more of a chance in poor old England?"

"A chance to ruin her bright young life? One's never too much in a hurry to save a precious human creature from drowning."

"As I understand it then," said Ralph, "you wish me to push Mr. Goodwood overboard after her. Do you know," he added, "that I've never heard her mention his name?"

Henrietta gave a brilliant smile. "I'm delighted to hear that; it proves how much she thinks of him."

Ralph appeared to allow that there was a good deal in this, and he surrendered to thought while his companion watched him askance. "If I should invite Mr. Goodwood," he finally said, "it would be to quarrel with him."

"Don't do that; he'd prove the better man."

"You certainly are doing your best to make me hate him! I really don't think I can ask him. I should be afraid of being rude to him."

"It's just as you please," Henrietta returned. "I had no idea you were in love with her yourself."

"Do you really believe that?" the young man asked with lifted eyebrows.

"That's the most natural speech I've ever heard you make! Of course I believe it," Miss Stackpole ingeniously said.

"Well," Ralph concluded, "to prove to you that you're wrong I'll invite him. It must be of course as a friend of yours."

"It will not be as a friend of mine that he'll come;

and it will not be to prove to me that I'm wrong that you'll ask him — but to prove it to yourself!"

These last words of Miss Stackpole's (on which the two presently separated) contained an amount of truth which Ralph Touchett was obliged to recognise; but it so far took the edge from too sharp a recognition that, in spite of his suspecting it would be rather more indiscreet to keep than to break his promise, he wrote Mr. Goodwood a note of six lines, expressing the pleasure it would give Mr. Touchett the elder that he should join a little party at Gardencourt, of which Miss Stackpole was a valued member. Having sent his letter (to the care of a banker whom Henrietta suggested) he waited in some suspense. He had heard this fresh formidable figure named for the first time; for when his mother had mentioned on her arrival that there was a story about the girl's having an "admirer" at home, the idea had seemed deficient in reality and he had taken no pains to ask questions the answers to which would involve only the vague or the disagreeable. Now, however, the native admiration of which his cousin was the object had become more concrete; it took the form of a young man who had followed her to London, who was interested in a cotton-mill and had manners in the most splendid of the American styles. Ralph had two theories about this intervener. Either his passion was a sentimental fiction of Miss Stackpole's (there was always a sort of tacit understanding among women, born of the solidarity of the sex, that they should discover or invent lovers for each other), in which case he was not to be feared and would probably not accept the invitation; or else he would accept the invitation and in this event prove himself a creature too irrational to demand further consideration. The latter clause of Ralph's argument might have seemed incoherent; but it embodied his conviction that if Mr. Goodwood were interested in Isabel in the serious manner described by Miss Stackpole he would not care to present himself at Gardencourt on a summons from the latter lady. "On this supposition," said Ralph, "he must regard her as a thorn on the stem of his rose; as an intercessor he must find her wanting in tact."

Two days after he had sent his invitation he received a very short note from Caspar Goodwood, thanking him for it, regretting that other engagements made a visit to Gardencourt impossible and presenting many compliments to Miss Stackpole. Ralph handed the note to Henrietta, who, when she had read it, exclaimed: "Well, I never have heard of anything so stiff!"

"I'm afraid he does n't care so much about my cousin as you suppose," Ralph observed.

"No, it's not that; it's some subtler motive. His nature's very deep. But I'm determined to fathom it, and I shall write to him to know what he means."

His refusal of Ralph's overtures was vaguely disconcerting; from the moment he declined to come to Gardencourt our friend began to think him of importance. He asked himself what it signified to him whether Isabel's admirers should be desperadoes or laggards; they were not rivals of his and were perfectly welcome to act out their genius. Nevertheless he felt much curiosity as to the result of Miss Stackpole's promised enquiry into the causes of Mr. Goodwood's stiffness — a curiosity for the present ungratified, inasmuch as when he asked her three days later if she had written to London she was obliged to confess she had written in vain. Mr. Goodwood had not replied.

"I suppose he's thinking it over," she said; "he thinks everything over; he 's not *really* at all impetuous. But I'm accustomed to having my letters answered the same day." She presently proposed to Isabel, at all events, that they should make an excursion to London together. "If I must tell the truth," she observed, "I'm not seeing much at this place, and I should n't think you were either. I've not even seen that aristocrat — what's his name? — Lord Washburton. He seems to let you severely alone."

"Lord Warburton 's coming to-morrow, I happen to know," replied her friend, who had received a note from the master of Lockleigh in answer to her own letter. "You'll have every opportunity of turning him inside out."

"Well, he may do for one letter, but what's one letter when you want to write fifty? I've described all the scenery in this vicinity and raved about all the old women and donkeys. You may say what you please, scenery does n't make a vital letter. I must go back to London and get some impressions of real life. I was there but three days before I came away, and that's hardly time to get in touch."

As Isabel, on her journey from New York to Gardencourt, had seen even less of the British capital than this, it appeared a happy suggestion of Henrietta's that the two should go thither on a visit of pleasure. The idea struck Isabel as charming; she was curious of the thick detail of London, which had always loomed large and rich to her. They turned over their schemes together and indulged in visions of romantic hours. They would stay at some picturesque old inn — one of the inns described by Dickens — and drive over the town in those delightful hansoms. Henrietta was a literary woman, and the great advantage of being a literary woman was that you could go everywhere and do everything. They would dine at a coffee-house and go afterwards to the play; they would frequent the Abbey and the British Museum and find out where Doctor Johnson had lived, and Goldsmith and Addison. Isabel grew eager and presently unveiled the bright vision to Ralph, who burst into a fit of laughter which scarce expressed the sympathy she had desired.

"It's a delightful plan," he said. "I advise you to go to the Duke's Head in Covent Garden, an easy, informal, old-fashioned place, and I'll have you put down at my club."

"Do you mean it's improper?" Isabel asked. "Dear me, is n't anything proper here? With Henrietta surely I may go anywhere; she is n't hampered in that way. She has travelled over the whole American continent and can at least find her way about this minute island."

"Ah then," said Ralph, "let me take advantage of her protection to go up to town as well. I may never have a chance to travel so safely!"

XIV

Miss Stackpole would have prepared to start immediately; but Isabel, as we have seen, had been notified that Lord Warburton would come again to Gardencourt, and she believed it her duty to remain there and see him. For four or five days he had made no response to her letter; then he had written, very briefly, to say he would come to luncheon two days later. There was something in these delays and postponements that touched the girl and renewed her sense of his desire to be considerate and patient, not to appear to urge her too grossly; a consideration the more studied that she was so sure he "really liked" her. Isabel told her uncle she had written to him, mentioning also his intention of coming; and the old man, in consequence, left his room earlier than usual and made his appearance at the two o'clock repast. This was by no means an act of vigilance on his part, but the fruit of a benevolent belief that his being of the company might help to cover any conjoined straying away in case Isabel should give their noble visitor another hearing. That personage drove over from Lockleigh and brought the elder of his sisters with him, a measure presumably dictated by reflexions of the same order as Mr. Touchett's. The two visitors were introduced to Miss Stackpole, who, at luncheon, occupied a seat adjoining Lord Warburton's. Isabel, who was nervous and had no relish for the prospect of again arguing the question he had so prematurely opened, could not help admiring his good-humoured self-possession, which quite disguised the symptoms of that preoccupation with her presence it was natural she should suppose him to feel. He neither looked at her nor spoke to her, and the only sign of his emotion was that he avoided meeting her eyes. He had plenty of talk for the others, however, and he appeared to eat his luncheon with discrimination and appetite. Miss Molyneux, who had a smooth, nun-like forehead and wore a large silver cross suspended from her neck, was evidently preoccupied with Henrietta Stackpole, upon whom her eyes constantly rested in a manner suggesting a conflict between deep alienation and yearning wonder. Of the two ladies from Lockleigh she was the one Isabel had liked best; there was such a world of hereditary quiet in her. Isabel was sure moreover that her mild forehead and silver cross referred to some weird Anglican mystery — some delightful reinstitution perhaps of the quaint office of the canoness. She wondered what Miss Molyneux would think of her if she knew Miss Archer had refused her brother; and then she felt sure that Miss Molyneux would never know — that Lord Warburton never told her such things. He was fond of her and kind to her, but on the whole he told her little. Such, at least, was Isabel's theory; when, at table, she was not occupied in conversation she was usually occupied in forming theories about her neighbours. According to Isabel, if Miss Molyneux should ever learn what had passed between Miss Archer and Lord Warburton she would probably be shocked at such a girl's failure to rise; or no, rather (this was our heroine's last position) she would impute to the young American but a due consciousness of inequality.

Whatever Isabel might have made of her opportunities, at all events, Henrietta Stackpole was by no means disposed to neglect those in which she now found herself immersed. "Do you know you're the first lord I've ever seen?" she said very promptly to her neighbour. "I suppose you think I'm awfully benighted."

"You've escaped seeing some very ugly men," Lord Warburton answered, looking a trifle absently about the table.

"Are they very ugly? They try to make us believe in America that they're all handsome and magnificent and that they wear wonderful robes and crowns."

"Ah, the robes and crowns are gone out of fashion," said Lord Warburton, "like your tomahawks and revolvers."

"I'm sorry for that; I think an aristocracy ought to be splendid," Henrietta declared. "If it's not that, what is it?"

"Oh, you know, it isn't much, at the best," her neighbour allowed. "Won't you have a potato?"

"I don't care much for these European potatoes. I shouldn't know you from an ordinary American gentleman."

"Do talk to me as if I *were* one," said Lord Warburton. "I don't see how you manage to get on without potatoes; you must find so few things to eat over here."

Henrietta was silent a little; there was a chance he was not sincere. "I've had hardly any appetite since I've been here," she went on at last; "so it does n't much matter. I don't approve of *you*, you know; I feel as if I ought to tell you that."

"Don't approve of me?"

"Yes; I don't suppose any one ever said such a thing to you before, did they? I don't approve of lords as an institution. I think the world has got beyond them — far beyond."

"Oh, so do I. I don't approve of myself in the least. Sometimes it comes over me — how I should object to myself if I were not myself, don't you know? But that's rather good, by the way — not to be vainglorious."

"Why don't you give it up then?" Miss Stackpole enquired.

"Give up — a — ?" asked Lord Warburton, meeting her harsh inflexion with a very mellow one.

"Give up being a lord."

"Oh, I'm so little of one! One would really forget all about it if you wretched Americans were not constantly reminding one. However, I do think of giving it up, the little there is left of it, one of these days."

"I should like to see you do it!" Henrietta exclaimed rather grimly.

"I 'll invite you to the ceremony; we 'll have a supper and a dance."

"Well," said Miss Stackpole, "I like to see all sides. I don't approve of a privileged class, but I like to hear what they have to say for themselves."

"Mighty little, as you see!"

"I should like to draw you out a little more," Henrietta continued. "But you're always looking away. You're afraid of meeting my eye. I see you want to escape me."

"No, I 'm only looking for those despised potatoes."

"Please explain about that young lady — your sister — then. I don't understand about her. Is she a Lady?"

"She's a capital good girl."

"I don't like the way you say that — as if you wanted to change the subject. Is her position inferior to yours?"

"We neither of us have any position to speak of; but she 's better off than I, because she has none of the bother."

"Yes, she does n't look as if she had much bother. I wish I had as little bother as that. You do produce quiet people over here, whatever else you may do."

"Ah, you see one takes life easily, on the whole," said Lord Warburton. "And then you know we're very dull. Ah, we can be dull when we try!"

"I should advise you to try something else. I should n't know what to talk to your sister about; she looks so different. Is that silver cross a badge?"

"A badge?"

"A sign of rank."

Lord Warburton's glance had wandered a good deal, but at this it met the gaze of his neighbour. "Oh yes," he answered in a moment; "the women go in for those things. The silver cross is worn by the eldest daughters of Viscounts." Which was his harmless revenge for having occasionally had his credulity too easily engaged in America. After luncheon he proposed to Isabel to come into the gallery and look at the pictures; and though she knew he had seen the pictures twenty times she complied without criticising this pretext. Her conscience now was very easy; ever since she sent him her letter she had felt particularly light of spirit. He walked slowly to the end of the gallery, staring at its contents and saying nothing; and then he suddenly broke out: "I hoped you would n't write to me that way."

"It was the only way, Lord Warburton," said the girl. "Do try and believe that."

"If I could believe it of course I should let you alone. But we can't believe by willing it; and I confess I don't understand. I could understand your disliking me; that I could understand well. But that you should admit you do —"

"What have I admitted?" Isabel interrupted, turning slightly pale.

"That you think me a good fellow; is n't that it?" She said nothing, and he went on: "You don't seem to have any reason, and that gives me a sense of injustice."

"I have a reason, Lord Warburton." She said it in a tone that made his heart contract.

"I should like very much to know it."

"I'll tell you some day when there's more to show for it."

"Excuse my saying that in the mean time I must doubt of it."

"You make me very unhappy," said Isabel.

"I'm not sorry for that; it may help you to know how I feel. Will you kindly answer me a question?" Isabel made no audible assent, but he apparently saw in her eyes something that gave him courage to go on. "Do you prefer some one else?"

"That's a question I'd rather not answer."

"Ah, you *do* then!" her suitor murmured with bitterness.

The bitterness touched her, and she cried out: "You're mistaken! I don't."

He sat down on a bench, unceremoniously, doggedly, like a man in trouble; leaning his elbows on his knees and staring at the floor. "I can't even be glad of that," he said at last, throwing himself back against the wall; "for that would be an excuse."

She raised her eyebrows in surprise. "An excuse? Must I excuse myself?"

He paid, however, no answer to the question. Another idea had come into his head. "Is it my political opinions? Do you think I go too far?"

"I can't object to your political opinions, because I don't understand them."

"You don't care what I think!" he cried, getting up. "It's all the same to you."

Isabel walked to the other side of the gallery and stood there showing him her charming back, her light slim figure, the length of her white neck as she bent her head, and the density of her dark braids. She stopped in front of a small picture as if for the purpose of examining it; and there was something so young and free in her movement that her very pliancy seemed to mock at him. Her eyes, however, saw nothing; they had suddenly been suffused with tears. In a moment he followed her, and by this time she had brushed her tears away; but when she turned round her face was pale and the expression of her eyes strange. "That reason that I would n't tell you — I'll tell it you after all. It's that I can't escape my fate."

"Your fate?"

"I should try to escape it if I were to marry you."

"I don't understand. Why should not *that* be your fate as well as anything else?"

"Because it's not," said Isabel femininely. "I know it's not. It's not my fate to give up — I know it can't be."

Poor Lord Warburton stared, an interrogative point in either eye. "Do you call marrying *me* giving up?"

"Not in the usual sense. It's getting — getting — getting a great deal. But it's giving up other chances."

"Other chances for what?"

"I don't mean chances to marry," said Isabel, her colour quickly coming back to her. And then she stopped, looking down with a deep frown, as if it were hopeless to attempt to make her meaning clear.

"I don't think it presumptuous in me to suggest that you'll gain more than you'll lose," her companion observed.

"I can't escape unhappiness," said Isabel. "In marrying you I shall be trying to."

"I don't know whether you'd try to, but you certainly would: that I must in candour admit!" he exclaimed with an anxious laugh.

"I must n't — I can't!" cried the girl.

"Well, if you're bent on being miserable I don't see why you should make *me* so. Whatever charms a life of misery may have for you, it has none for me."

"I'm not bent on a life of misery," said Isabel. "I've always been intensely determined to be happy, and I've often believed I should be. I've told people that; you can ask them. But it comes over me every now and then that I can never be happy in any extraordinary way; not by turning away, by separating myself."

"By separating yourself from what?"

"From life. From the usual chances and dangers, from what most people know and suffer."

Lord Warburton broke into a smile that almost denoted hope. "Why, my dear Miss Archer," he began to explain with the most considerate eagerness, "I don't offer you any exoneration from life or from any chances or dangers whatever. I wish I could; depend upon it I would! For what do you take me, pray? Heaven help me, I'm not the Emperor of China! All I offer you is the chance of taking the common lot in a comfortable sort of way. The common lot? Why, I'm devoted to the common lot! Strike an alliance with me, and I promise you that you shall have plenty of it. You shall separate from nothing whatever — not even from your friend Miss Stackpole."

"She'd never approve of it," said Isabel, trying to smile and take advantage of this side-issue; despising herself too, not a little, for doing so.

"Are we speaking of Miss Stackpole?" his lordship asked impatiently. "I never saw a person judge things on such theoretic grounds."

"Now I suppose you're speaking of me," said Isabel with humility; and she turned away again, for she saw Miss Molyneux enter the gallery, accompanied by Henrietta and by Ralph.

Lord Warburton's sister addressed him with a certain timidity and reminded him she ought to return home in time for tea, as she was expecting company to partake of it. He made no answer — apparently not having heard her; he was preoccupied, and with good reason. Miss Molyneux — as if he had been Royalty — stood like a lady-in-waiting.

"Well, I never, Miss Molyneux!" said Henrietta Stackpole. "If I wanted to go he'd have to go. If I wanted my brother to do a thing he'd have to do it."

"Oh, Warburton does everything one wants," Miss Molyneux answered with a quick, shy laugh. "How very many pictures you have!" she went on, turning to Ralph.

"They look a good many, because they're all put together," said Ralph. "But it's really a bad way."

"Oh, I think it's so nice. I wish we had a gallery at Lockleigh. I'm so very fond of pictures," Miss Molyneux went on, persistently, to Ralph, as if she were afraid Miss Stackpole would address her again. Henrietta appeared at once to fascinate and to frighten her.

"Ah yes, pictures are very convenient," said Ralph, who appeared to know better what style of reflexion was acceptable to her.

"They're so very pleasant when it rains," the young lady continued. "It has rained of late so very often."

"I'm sorry you're going away, Lord Warburton," said Henrietta. "I wanted to get a great deal more out of you."

"I'm not going away," Lord Warburton answered.

"Your sister says you must. In America the gentlemen obey the ladies."

"I'm afraid we have some people to tea," said Miss Molyneux, looking at her brother.

"Very good, my dear. We'll go."

"I hoped you would resist!" Henrietta exclaimed. "I wanted to see what Miss Molyneux would do."

"I never do anything," said this young lady.

"I suppose in your position it's sufficient for you to exist!" Miss Stackpole returned. "I should like very much to see you at home."

"You must come to Lockleigh again," said Miss Molyneux, very sweetly, to Isabel, ignoring this remark of Isabel's friend.

Isabel looked into her quiet eyes a moment, and for that moment seemed to see in their grey depths the reflexion of everything she had rejected in rejecting Lord Warburton — the peace, the kindness, the honour, the possessions, a deep security and a great exclusion. She kissed Miss Molyneux and then she said: "I'm afraid I can never come again."

"Never again?"

"I'm afraid I'm going away."

"Oh, I'm so very sorry," said Miss Molyneux. "I think that's so very wrong of you."

Lord Warburton watched this little passage; then

he turned away and stared at a picture. Ralph, leaning against the rail before the picture with his hands in his pockets, had for the moment been watching him.

"I should like to see you at home," said Henrietta, whom Lord Warburton found beside him. "I should like an hour's talk with you; there are a great many questions I wish to ask you."

"I shall be delighted to see you," the proprietor of Lockleigh answered; "but I'm certain not to be able to answer many of your questions. When will you come?"

"Whenever Miss Archer will take me. We're thinking of going to London, but we'll go and see you first. I'm determined to get some satisfaction out of you."

"If it depends upon Miss Archer I'm afraid you won't get much. She won't come to Lockleigh; she does n't like the place."

"She told me it was lovely!" said Henrietta.

Lord Warburton hesitated. "She won't come, all the same. You had better come alone," he added.

Henrietta straightened herself, and her large eyes expanded. "Would you make that remark to an English lady?" she enquired with soft asperity.

Lord Warburton stared. "Yes, if I liked her enough."

"You'd be careful not to like her enough. If Miss Archer won't visit your place again it's because she does n't want to take me. I know what she thinks of me, and I suppose you think the same — that I ought n't to bring in individuals." Lord Warburton was at a loss; he had not been made acquainted with

Miss Stackpole's professional character and failed to catch her allusion. "Miss Archer has been warning you!" she therefore went on.

"Warning me?"

"Is n't that why she came off alone with you here — to put you on your guard?"

"Oh dear, no," said Lord Warburton brazenly; "our talk had no such solemn character as that."

"Well, you've been on your guard — intensely. I suppose it's natural to you; that's just what I wanted to observe. And so, too, Miss Molyneux — she would n't commit herself. *You* have been warned, anyway," Henrietta continued, addressing this young lady; "but for you it was n't necessary."

"I hope not," said Miss Molyneux vaguely.

"Miss Stackpole takes notes," Ralph soothingly explained. "She's a great satirist; she sees through us all and she works us up."

"Well, I must say I never have had such a collection of bad material!" Henrietta declared, looking from Isabel to Lord Warburton and from this nobleman to his sister and to Ralph. "There's something the matter with you all; you 're as dismal as if you had got a bad cable."

"You do see through us, Miss Stackpole," said Ralph in a low tone, giving her a little intelligent nod as he led the party out of the gallery. "There's something the matter with us all."

Isabel came behind these two; Miss Molyneux, who decidedly liked her immensely, had taken her arm, to walk beside her over the polished floor. Lord Warburton strolled on the other side with his hands behind him and his eyes lowered. For some moments he said nothing; and then, "Is it true you're going to London?" he asked.

"I believe it has been arranged."

"And when shall you come back?"

"In a few days; but probably for a very short time. I'm going to Paris with my aunt."

"When, then, shall I see you again?"

"Not for a good while," said Isabel. "But some day or other, I hope."

"Do you really hope it?"

"Very much."

He went a few steps in silence; then he stopped and put out his hand. "Good-bye."

"Good-bye," said Isabel.

Miss Molyneux kissed her again, and she let the two depart. After it, without rejoining Henrietta and Ralph, she retreated to her own room; in which apartment, before dinner, she was found by Mrs. Touchett, who had stopped on her way to the saloon. "I may as well tell you," said that lady, "that your uncle has informed me of your relations with Lord Warburton."

Isabel considered. "Relations? They're hardly relations. That's the strange part of it: he has seen me but three or four times."

"Why did you tell your uncle rather than me?" Mrs. Touchett dispassionately asked.

Again the girl hesitated. "Because he knows Lord Warburton better."

"Yes, but I know you better."

"I'm not sure of that," said Isabel, smiling.

"Neither am I, after all; especially when you give me that rather conceited look. One would think you were awfully pleased with yourself and had carried off a prize! I suppose that when you refuse an offer like Lord Warburton's it 's because you expect to do something better."

"Ah, my uncle did n't say that!" cried Isabel, smiling still.

XV

IT had been arranged that the two young ladies should proceed to London under Ralph's escort, though Mrs. Touchett looked with little favour on the plan. It was just the sort of plan, she said, that Miss Stackpole would be sure to suggest, and she enquired if the correspondent of the *Interviewer* was to take the party to stay at her favourite boarding-house.

"I don't care where she takes us to stay, so long as there's local colour," said Isabel. "That 's what we're going to London for."

"I suppose that after a girl has refused an English lord she may do anything," her aunt rejoined. "After that one need n't stand on trifles."

"Should you have liked me to marry Lord Warburton ?" Isabel enquired.

"Of course I should."

"I thought you disliked the English so much."

"So I do; but it's all the greater reason for making use of them."

"Is that your idea of marriage ?" And Isabel ventured to add that her aunt appeared to her to have made very little use of Mr. Touchett.

"Your uncle's not an English nobleman," said Mrs. Touchett, "though even if he had been I should still probably have taken up my residence in Florence."

"Do you think Lord Warburton could make me any better than I am ?" the girl asked with some animation. "I don't mean I'm too good to improve. I mean — I mean that I don't love Lord Warburton enough to marry him."

"You did right to refuse him then," said Mrs. Touchett in her smallest, sparest voice. "Only, the next great offer you get, I hope you'll manage to come up to your standard."

"We had better wait till the offer comes before we talk about it. I hope very much I may have no more offers for the present. They upset me completely."

"You probably won't be troubled with them if you adopt permanently the Bohemian manner of life. However, I've promised Ralph not to criticise."

"I'll do whatever Ralph says is right," Isabel returned. "I've unbounded confidence in Ralph."

"His mother's much obliged to you!" this lady dryly laughed.

"It seems to me indeed she ought to feel it!" Isabel irrepressibly answered.

Ralph had assured her that there would be no violation of decency in their paying a visit — the little party of three — to the sights of the metropolis; but Mrs. Touchett took a different view. Like many ladies of her country who had lived a long time in Europe, she had completely lost her native tact on such points, and in her reaction, not in itself deplorable, against the liberty allowed to young persons beyond the seas, had fallen into gratuitous and exaggerated scruples. Ralph accompanied their visitors to town and established them at a quiet inn in a street that ran at right angles to Piccadilly. His first idea had been to take them to his father's house in Winchester Square, a large, dull mansion which at this period of the year was shrouded in silence and brown holland; but he bethought himself that, the cook being at Gardencourt, there was no one in the house to get them their meals, and Pratt's Hotel accordingly became their resting-place. Ralph, on his side, found quarters in Winchester Square, having a "den" there of which he was very fond and being familiar with deeper fears than that of a cold kitchen. He availed himself largely indeed of the resources of Pratt's Hotel, beginning his day with an early visit to his fellow travellers, who had Mr. Pratt in person, in a large bulging white waistcoat, to remove their dish-covers. Ralph turned up, as he said, after breakfast, and the little party made out a scheme of entertainment for the day. As London wears in the month of September a face blank but for its smears of prior service, the young man, who occasionally took an apologetic tone, was obliged to remind his companion, to Miss Stackpole's high derision, that there was n't a creature in town.

"I suppose you mean the aristocracy are absent," Henrietta answered; "but I don't think you could have a better proof that if they were absent altogether they would n't be missed. It seems to me the place is about as full as it can be. There's no one here, of course, but three or four millions of people. What is it you call them — the lower-middle class? They're only the population of London, and that's of no consequence."

Ralph declared that for him the aristocracy left no void that Miss Stackpole herself did n't fill, and that a more contented man was nowhere at that moment to be found. In this he spoke the truth, for the stale September days, in the huge half-empty town, had a charm wrapped in them as a coloured gem might be wrapped in a dusty cloth. When he went home at night to the empty house in Winchester Square, after a chain of hours with his comparatively ardent friends, he wandered into the big dusky dining-room, where the candle he took from the hall-table, after letting himself in, constituted the only illumination. The square was still, the house was still; when he raised one of the windows of the dining-room to let in the air he heard the slow creak of the boots of a lone constable. His own step, in the empty place, seemed loud and sonorous; some of the carpets had been raised, and whenever he moved he roused a melancholy echo. He sat down in one of the armchairs; the big dark dining table twinkled here and there in the small candle-light; the pictures on the wall, all of them very brown, looked vague and incoherent. There was a ghostly presence as of dinners long since digested, of table-talk that had lost its actuality. This hint of the supernatural perhaps had something to do with the fact that his imagination took a flight and that he remained in his chair a long time beyond the hour at which he should have been in bed; doing nothing, not even reading the evening paper. I say he did nothing, and I maintain the phrase in the face of the fact that he thought at these moments of Isabel. To think of Isabel could only be for him an idle pursuit, leading to nothing and profiting little to any one. His cousin had not yet seemed to him so charming as during these days spent in sounding, tourist-fashion, the deeps and shallows of the metropolitan element. Isabel was full of premises, conclusions, emotions; if she had come in search of local colour she found it everywhere. She asked more questions than he could answer, and launched brave theories, as to historic cause and social effect, that he was equally unable to accept or to refute. The party went more than once to the British Museum and to that brighter palace of art which reclaims for antique variety so large an area of a monotonous suburb; they spent a morning in the Abbey and went on a penny-steamer to the Tower; they looked at pictures both in public and private collections and sat on various occasions beneath the great trees in Kensington Gardens. Henrietta proved an indestructible sight-seer and a more lenient judge than Ralph had ventured to hope. She had indeed many disappointments, and London at large suffered from her vivid remembrance of the strong points of the American civic idea; but she made the best of its dingy dignities and only heaved an occasional sigh and uttered a desultory "Well!" which led no further and lost itself in retrospect. The truth was that, as she said herself, she was not in her element. "I've not a sympathy with inanimate objects," she remarked to Isabel at the National Gallery; and she continued to suffer from the meagreness of the glimpse that had as yet been vouchsafed to her of the inner life. Landscapes by Turner and Assyrian bulls were a poor substitute for the literary dinner-parties at which she had hoped to meet the genius and renown of Great Britain.

"Where are your public men, where are your men and women of intellect?" she enquired of Ralph, standing in the middle of Trafalgar Square as if she had supposed this to be a place where she would naturally meet a few. "That's one of them on the top of the column, you say — Lord Nelson? Was he a lord too? Was n't he high enough, that they had to stick him a hundred feet in the air? That's the past — I don't care about the past; I want to see some of the leading minds of the present. I won't say of the future, because I don't believe much in your future." Poor Ralph had few leading minds among his acquaintance and rarely enjoyed the pleasure of buttonholing a celebrity; a state of things which appeared to Miss Stackpole to indicate a deplorable want of enterprise. "If I were on the other side I should call," she said, "and tell the gentleman, whoever he might be, that I had heard a great deal about him and had come to see for myself. But I gather from what you say that this is not the custom here. You seem to have plenty of meaningless customs, but none of those that would help along. We *are* in advance, certainly. I suppose I shall have to give up the social side altogether;" and Henrietta, though she went about with her guidebook and pencil and wrote a letter to the *Interviewer* about the Tower (in which she described the execution of Lady Jane Grey), had a sad sense of falling below her mission.

The incident that had preceded Isabel's departure from Gardencourt left a painful trace in our young woman's mind: when she felt again in her face, as from a recurrent wave, the cold breath of her last suitor's surprise, she could only muffle her head till the air cleared. She could not have done less than what she did; this was certainly true. But her necessity, all the same, had been as graceless as some physical act in a strained attitude, and she felt no desire to take credit for her conduct. Mixed with this imperfect pride, nevertheless, was a feeling of freedom which in itself was sweet and which, as she wandered through the great city with her ill-matched companions, occasionally throbbed into odd demonstrations. When she walked in Kensington Gardens she stopped the children (mainly of the poorer sort) whom she saw playing on the grass; she asked them their names and gave them sixpence and, when they were pretty, kissed them. Ralph noticed these quaint charities; he noticed everything she did. One afternoon, that his companions might pass the time, he invited them to tea in Winchester Square, and he had the house set in order as much as possible for their visit. There was another guest to meet them, an amiable bachelor, an old friend of Ralph's who happened to be in town and for whom prompt commerce with Miss Stackpole appeared to have neither difficulty nor dread. Mr. Bantling, a stout, sleek, smiling man of forty, wonderfully dressed, universally informed and incoherently amused, laughed immoderately at everything Henrietta said, gave her several cups of tea, examined in her society the *bric-à-brac*, of which Ralph had a considerable collection, and afterwards, when the host proposed they should go out into the square and pretend it was a *fête-champêtre*, walked round the limited enclosure several times with her and, at a dozen turns of their talk, bounded responsive — as with a positive passion for argument — to her remarks upon the inner life.

"Oh, I see; I dare say you found it very quiet at Gardencourt. Naturally there's not much going on there when there's such a lot of illness about. Touchett 's very bad, you know; the doctors have forbidden his being in England at all, and he has only come back to take care of his father. The old man, I believe, has half a dozen things the matter with him. They call it gout, but to my certain knowledge he has organic disease so developed that you may depend upon it he'll go, some day soon, quite quickly. Of course that sort of thing makes a dreadfully dull house; I wonder they have people when they can do so little for them. Then I believe Mr. Touchett 's always squabbling with his wife; she lives away from her husband, you know, in that extraordinary American way of yours. If you want a house where there's always something going on, I recommend you to go down and stay with my sister, Lady Pensil, in Bedfordshire. I 'll write to her to-morrow and I 'm sure she'll be delighted to ask you. I know just what you want — you want a house where they go in for theatricals and picnics and that sort of thing. My sister's just that sort of woman; she's always getting up something or other and she 's always glad to have the sort of people who help her. I'm sure she'll ask you down by return of post : she's tremendously fond of distinguished people and writers. She writes herself, you know; but I have n't read everything she has written. It's usually poetry, and I don't go in much for poetry — unless it's Byron. I suppose you think a great deal of Byron in America," Mr. Bantling continued, expanding in the stimulating air of Miss Stackpole's attention, bringing up his sequences promptly and changing his topic with an easy turn of hand. Yet he none the less gracefully kept in sight of the idea, dazzling to Henrietta, of her going to stay with Lady Pensil in Bedfordshire. "I understand what you want; you want to see some genuine English sport. The Touchetts are n't English at all, you know; they have their own habits, their own language, their own food — some odd religion even, I believe, of their own. The old man thinks it's wicked to hunt, I'm told. You must get down to my sister's in time for the theatricals, and I'm sure she'll be glad to give you a part. I'm sure you act well; I know you're very clever. My sister's forty years old and has seven children, but she 's going to play the principal part. Plain as she is she makes up awfully well — I *will* say for her. Of course you need n't act if you don't want to."

In this manner Mr. Bantling delivered himself while they strolled over the grass in Winchester Square, which, although it had been peppered by the London soot, invited the tread to linger. Henrietta thought her blooming, easy-voiced bachelor, with his impressibility to feminine merit and his splendid range of suggestion, a very agreeable man, and she valued the opportunity he offered her. "I don't know but I *would* go, if your sister should ask me. I think it would be my duty. What do you call her name?"

"Pensil. It's an odd name, but it is n't a bad one."

"I think one name's as good as another. But what's her rank?"

"Oh, she's a baron's wife; a convenient sort of rank. You're fine enough and you're not too fine."

"I don't know but what she'd be too fine for me. What do you call the place she lives in — Bedfordshire?"

"She lives away in the northern corner of it. It's a tiresome country, but I dare say you won't mind it. I'll try and run down while you're there."

All this was very pleasant to Miss Stackpole, and she was sorry to be obliged to separate from Lady Pensil's obliging brother. But it happened that she had met the day before, in Piccadilly, some friends whom she had not seen for a year: the Miss Climbers, two ladies from Wilmington, Delaware, who had been travelling on the Continent and were now preparing to re-embark. Henrietta had had a long interview with them on the Piccadilly pavement, and though the three ladies all talked at once they had not exhausted their store. It had been agreed therefore that Henrietta should come and dine with them in their lodgings in Jermyn Street at six o'clock on the morrow, and she now bethought herself of this engagement. She prepared to start for Jermyn Street, taking leave first of Ralph Touchett and Isabel, who, seated on garden chairs in another part of the enclosure, were occupied — if the term may be used — with an exchange of amenities less pointed than the practical colloquy of Miss Stackpole and Mr. Bantling. When it had been settled between Isabel and her friend that they should be reunited at some reputable hour at Pratt's Hotel, Ralph remarked that the latter must have a cab. She could n't walk all the way to Jermyn Street.

"I suppose you mean it's improper for me to walk alone!" Henrietta exclaimed. "Merciful powers, have I come to this?"

"There's not the slightest need of your walking alone," Mr. Bantling gaily interposed. "I should be greatly pleased to go with you."

"I simply meant that you'd be late for dinner," Ralph returned. "Those poor ladies may easily believe that we refuse, at the last, to spare you."

"You had better have a hansom, Henrietta," said Isabel.

"I'll get you a hansom if you'll trust me," Mr. Bantling went on. "We might walk a little till we meet one."

"I don't see why I should n't trust him, do *you?*" Henrietta enquired of Isabel.

"I don't see what Mr. Bantling could do to you," Isabel obligingly answered; "but, if you like, we'll walk with you till you find your cab."

"Never mind; we'll go alone. Come on, Mr. Bantling, and take care you get me a good one."

Mr. Bantling promised to do his best, and the two took their departure, leaving the girl and her cousin together in the square, over which a clear September twilight had now begun to gather. It was perfectly still; the wide quadrangle of dusky houses showed lights in none of the windows, where the shutters and blinds were closed; the pavements were a vacant expanse, and, putting aside two small children from a neighbouring slum, who, attracted by symptoms of abnormal animation in the interior, poked their faces between the rusty rails of the enclosure, the most vivid object within sight was the big red pillar-post on the southeast corner.

"Henrietta will ask him to get into the cab and go with her to Jermyn Street," Ralph observed. He always spoke of Miss Stackpole as Henrietta.

"Very possibly," said his companion.

"Or rather, no, she won't," he went on. "But Bantling will ask leave to get in."

"Very likely again. I 'm glad very they're such good friends."

"She has made a conquest. He thinks her a brilliant woman. It may go far," said Ralph.

Isabel was briefly silent. "I call Henrietta a very brilliant woman, but I don't think it will go far. They would never really know each other. He has not the least idea what she really is, and she has no just comprehension of Mr. Bantling."

"There's no more usual basis of union than a mutual misunderstanding. But it ought not to be so difficult to understand Bob Bantling," Ralph added. "He is a very simple organism."

"Yes, but Henrietta's a simpler one still. And, pray, what am I to do?" Isabel asked, looking about her through the fading light, in which the limited landscape-gardening of the square took on a large and effective appearance. "I don't imagine that you'll propose that you and I, for our amusement, shall drive about London in a hansom."

"There's no reason we should n't stay here — if you don't dislike it. It's very warm; there will be half an hour yet before dark; and if you permit it I'll light a cigarette."

"You may do what you please," said Isabel, "if you'll amuse me till seven o'clock. I propose at that hour to go back and partake of a simple and solitary repast — two poached eggs and a muffin — at Pratt's Hotel."

"May n't I dine with you?" Ralph asked.

"No, you'll dine at your club."

They had wandered back to their chairs in the centre of the square again, and Ralph had lighted his cigarette. It would have given him extreme pleasure to be present in person at the modest little feast she had sketched; but in default of this he liked even being forbidden. For the moment, however, he liked immensely being alone with her, in the thickening dusk, in the centre of the multitudinous town; it made her seem to depend upon him and to be in his power. This power he could exert but vaguely; the best exercise of it was to accept her decisions submissively — which indeed there was already an emotion in doing. "Why won't you let me dine with you?" he demanded after a pause.

"Because I don't care for it."

"I suppose you're tired of me."

"I shall be an hour hence. You see I have the gift of foreknowledge."

"Oh, I shall be delightful meanwhile," said Ralph.

But he said nothing more, and as she made no rejoinder they sat some time in a stillness which seemed to contradict his promise of entertainment. It seemed to him she was preoccupied, and he wondered what she was thinking about; there were two or three very possible subjects. At last he spoke again. "Is your objection to my society this evening caused by your expectation of another visitor?"

She turned her head with a glance of her clear, fair eyes. "Another visitor? What visitor should I have?"

He had none to suggest; which made his question seem to himself silly as well as brutal. "You've a great many friends that I don't know. You've a whole past from which I was perversely excluded."

"You were reserved for my future. You must remember that my past is over there across the water. There's none of it here in London."

"Very good, then, since your future is seated beside you. Capital thing to have your future so handy." And Ralph lighted another cigarette and reflected that Isabel probably meant she had received news that Mr. Caspar Goodwood had crossed to Paris. After he had lighted his cigarette he puffed it a while, and then he resumed. "I promised just now to be very amusing; but you see I don't come up to the mark, and the fact is there's a good deal of temerity in one's undertaking to amuse a person like you. What do you care for my feeble attempts? You've grand ideas — you've a high standard in such matters. I ought at least to bring in a band of music or a company of mountebanks."

"One mountebank 's enough, and you do very well.

Pray go on, and in another ten minutes I shall begin to laugh."

"I assure you I'm very serious," said Ralph. "You do really ask a great deal."

"I don't know what you mean. I ask nothing!"

"You accept nothing," said Ralph. She coloured, and now suddenly it seemed to her that she guessed his meaning. But why should he speak to her of such things? He hesitated a little and then he continued: "There's something I should like very much to say to you. It's a question I wish to ask. It seems to me I've a right to ask it, because I've a kind of interest in the answer."

"Ask what you will," Isabel replied gently, "and I'll try to satisfy you."

"Well then, I hope you won't mind my saying that Warburton has told me of something that has passed between you."

Isabel suppressed a start; she sat looking at her open fan. "Very good; I suppose it was natural he should tell you."

"I have his leave to let you know he has done so. He has some hope still," said Ralph.

"Still?"

"He had it a few days ago."

"I don't believe he has any now," said the girl.

"I'm very sorry for him then; he's such an honest man."

"Pray, did he ask you to talk to me?"

"No, not that. But he told me because he could n't help it. We're old friends, and he was greatly disappointed. He sent me a line asking me to come and see him, and I drove over to Lockleigh the day before he and his sister lunched with us. He was very heavy-hearted; he had just got a letter from you."

"Did he show you the letter?" asked Isabel with momentary loftiness.

"By no means. But he told me it was a neat refusal. I was very sorry for him," Ralph repeated.

For some moments Isabel said nothing; then at last, "Do you know how often he had seen me?" she enquired. "Five or six times."

"That's to your glory."

"It's not for that I say it."

"What then do you say it for? Not to prove that poor Warburton's state of mind's superficial, because I'm pretty sure you don't think that."

Isabel certainly was unable to say she thought it; but presently she said something else. "If you've not been requested by Lord Warburton to argue with me, then you're doing it disinterestedly — or for the love of argument."

"I've no wish to argue with you at all. I only wish to leave you alone. I'm simply greatly interested in your own sentiments."

"I'm greatly obliged to you!" cried Isabel with a slightly nervous laugh.

"Of course you mean that I'm meddling in what does n't concern me. But why should n't I speak to you of this matter without annoying you or embarrassing myself? What's the use of being your cousin if I can't have a few privileges? What's the use of adoring you without hope of a reward if I can't have a few compensations? What's the use of being ill and disabled and restricted to mere spectatorship at the game of life if I really can't see the show when I've paid so much for my ticket? Tell me this," Ralph went on while she listened to him with quickened attention. "What had you in mind when you refused Lord Warburton?"

"What had I in mind?"

"What was the logic — the view of your situation — that dictated so remarkable an act?"

"I did n't wish to marry him — if that's logic."

"No, that's not logic — and I knew that before. It's really nothing, you know. What was it you *said* to yourself? You certainly said more than that."

Isabel reflected a moment, then answered with a question of her own. "Why do you call it a remarkable act? That's what your mother thinks too."

"Warburton's such a thorough good sort; as a man, I consider he has hardly a fault. And then he's what they call here no end of a swell. He has immense possessions, and his wife would be thought a superior being. He unites the intrinsic and the extrinsic advantages."

Isabel watched her cousin as to see how far he would go. "I refused him because he was too perfect then. I'm not perfect myself, and he's too good for me. Besides, his perfection would irritate me."

"That's ingenious rather than candid," said Ralph. "As a fact you think nothing in the world too perfect for you."

"Do you think I'm so good?"

"No, but you're exacting, all the same, without the excuse of thinking yourself good. Nineteen women out of twenty, however, even of the most exacting sort, would have managed to do with Warburton. Perhaps you don't know how he has been stalked."

"I don't wish to know. But it seems to me," said Isabel, "that one day when we talked of him you mentioned odd things in him."

Ralph smokingly considered. "I hope that what I said then had no weight with you; for they were not faults, the things I spoke of: they were simply peculiarities of his position. If I had known he wished to marry you I'd never have alluded to them. I think I said that as regards that position he was rather a sceptic. It would have been in your power to make him a believer."

"I think not. I don't understand the matter, and I'm not conscious of any mission of that sort. You're evidently disappointed," Isabel added, looking at her cousin with rueful gentleness. "You'd have liked me to make such a marriage."

"Not in the least. I'm absolutely without a wish on the subject. I don't pretend to advise you, and I content myself with watching you — with the deepest interest."

She gave rather a conscious sigh. "I wish I could be as interesting to myself as I am to you!"

"There you're not candid again; you 're extremely interesting to yourself. Do you know, however," said Ralph, "that if you've really given Warburton his final answer I'm rather glad it has been what it was. I don't mean I'm glad for you, and still less of course for him. I'm glad for myself."

"Are *you* thinking of proposing to me?"

"By no means. From the point of view I speak of that would be fatal; I should kill the goose that supplies me with the material of my inimitable omelettes. I use that animal as the symbol of my insane illusions. What I mean is that I shall have the thrill of seeing what a young lady does who won't marry Lord Warburton."

"That's what your mother counts upon too," said Isabel.

"Ah, there will be plenty of spectators! We shall hang on the rest of your career. I shall not see all of it, but I shall probably see the most interesting years. Of course if you were to marry our friend you'd still have a career — a very decent, in fact a very brilliant one. But relatively speaking it would be a little prosaic. It would be definitely marked out in advance; it would be wanting in the unexpected. You know I'm extremely fond of the unexpected, and now that you've kept the game in your hands I depend on your giving us some grand example of it."

"I don't understand you very well," said Isabel, "but I do so well enough to be able to say that if you look for grand examples of anything from me I shall disappoint you."

"You'll do so only by disappointing yourself — and that will go hard with you!"

To this she made no direct reply; there was an amount of truth in it that would bear consideration. At last she said abruptly: "I don't see what harm there is in my wishing not to tie myself. I don't want to begin life by marrying. There are other things a woman can do."

"There's nothing she can do so well. But you're of course so many-sided."

"If one's two-sided it's enough," said Isabel.

"You're the most charming of polygons!" her companion broke out. At a glance from his companion, however, he became grave, and to prove it went on: "You want to see life—you 'll be hanged if you don't, as the young men say."

"I don't think I want to see it as the young men want to see it. But I do want to look about me."

"You want to drain the cup of experience."

"No, I don't wish to touch the cup of experience. It's a poisoned drink! I only want to see for myself."

"You want to see, but not to feel," Ralph remarked.

"I don't think that if one's a sentient being one can make the distinction. I'm a good deal like Henrietta. The other day when I asked her if she wished to marry she said: 'Not till I've seen Europe!' I too don't wish to marry till I've seen Europe."

"You evidently expect a crowned head will be struck with you."

"No, that would be worse than marrying Lord Warburton. But it's getting very dark," Isabel continued, "and I must go home." She rose from her place, but Ralph only sat still and looked at her. As he remained there she stopped, and they exchanged a gaze that was full on either side, but especially on Ralph's, of utterances too vague for words.

"You've answered my question," he said at last. "You've told me what I wanted. I'm greatly obliged to you."

"It seems to me I've told you very little."

"You've told me the great thing: that the world interests you and that you want to throw yourself into it."

Her silvery eyes shone a moment in the dusk. "I never said that."

"I think you meant it. Don't repudiate it. It's so fine!"

"I don't know what you're trying to fasten upon me, for I'm not in the least an adventurous spirit. Women are not like men."

Ralph slowly rose from his seat and they walked together to the gate of the square. "No," he said; "women rarely boast of their courage. Men do so with a certain frequency."

"Men have it to boast of!"

"Women have it too. You 've a great deal."

"Enough to go home in a cab to Pratt's Hotel, but not more."

Ralph unlocked the gate, and after they had passed out he fastened it. "We 'll find your cab," he said; and as they turned toward a neighbouring street in which this quest might avail he asked her again if he might n't see her safely to the inn.

"By no means," she answered; "you 're very tired; you must go home and go to bed."

The cab was found, and he helped her into it, standing a moment at the door. "When people forget I 'm a poor creature I 'm often incommoded," he said. "But it 's worse when they remember it!"

XVI

SHE had had no hidden motive in wishing him not to take her home; it simply struck her that for some days past she had consumed an inordinate quantity of his time, and the independent spirit of the American girl whom extravagance of aid places in an attitude that she ends by finding "affected" had made her decide that for these few hours she must suffice to herself. She had moreover a great fondness for intervals of solitude, which since her arrival in England had been but meagrely met. It was a luxury she could always command at home and she had wittingly missed it. That evening, however, an incident occurred which — had there been a critic to note it — would have taken all colour from the theory that the wish to be quite by herself had caused her to dispense with her cousin's attendance. Seated toward nine o'clock in the dim illumination of Pratt's Hotel and trying with the aid of two tall candles to lose herself in a volume she had brought from Gardencourt, she succeeded only to the extent of reading other words than those printed on the page — words that Ralph had spoken to her that afternoon. Suddenly the well-muffled knuckle of the waiter was applied to the door, which presently gave way to his exhibition, even as a glorious trophy, of the card of a visitor. When this memento had offered to her fixed sight the name of Mr. Caspar Goodwood she let the man stand before her without signifying her wishes.

"Shall I show the gentleman up, ma'am?" he asked with a slightly encouraging inflexion.

Isabel hesitated still and while she hesitated glanced at the mirror. "He may come in," she said at last; and waited for him not so much smoothing her hair as girding her spirit.

Caspar Goodwood was accordingly the next moment shaking hands with her, but saying nothing till the servant had left the room. "Why did n't you answer my letter?" he then asked in a quick, full, slightly peremptory tone — the tone of a man whose questions were habitually pointed and who was capable of much insistence.

She answered by a ready question, "How did you know I was here?"

"Miss Stackpole let me know," said Caspar Goodwood. "She told me you would probably be at home alone this evening and would be willing to see me."

"Where did she see you — to tell you that?"

"She did n't see me; she wrote to me."

Isabel was silent; neither had sat down; they stood there with an air of defiance, or at least of contention. "Henrietta never told me she was writing to you," she said at last. "This is not kind of her."

"Is it so disagreeable to you to see me?" asked the young man.

"I did n't expect it. I don't like such surprises."

"But you knew I was in town; it was natural we should meet."

"Do you call this meeting? I hoped I should n't

see you. In so big a place as London it seemed very possible."

"It was apparently repugnant to you even to write to me," her visitor went on.

Isabel made no reply; the sense of Henrietta Stackpole's treachery, as she momentarily qualified it, was strong within her. "Henrietta 's certainly not a model of all the delicacies!" she exclaimed with bitterness. "It was a great liberty to take."

"I suppose I'm not a model either — of those virtues or of any others. The fault 's mine as much as hers."

As Isabel looked at him it seemed to her that his jaw had never been more square. This might have displeased her, but she took a different turn. "No, it 's not your fault so much as hers. What you 've done was inevitable, I suppose, for *you*."

"It was indeed!" cried Caspar Goodwood with a voluntary laugh. "And now that I 've come, at any rate, may n't I stay?"

"You may sit down, certainly."

She went back to her chair again, while her visitor took the first place that offered, in the manner of a man accustomed to pay little thought to that sort of furtherance. "I 've been hoping every day for an answer to my letter. You might have written me a few lines."

"It was n't the trouble of writing that prevented me; I could as easily have written you four pages as one. But my silence was an intention," Isabel said. "I thought it the best thing."

He sat with his eyes fixed on hers while she spoke;

then he lowered them and attached them to a spot in the carpet as if he were making a strong effort to say nothing but what he ought. He was a strong man in the wrong, and he was acute enough to see that an uncompromising exhibition of his strength would only throw the falsity of his position into relief. Isabel was not incapable of tasting any advantage of position over a person of this quality, and though little desirous to flaunt it in his face she could enjoy being able to say "You know you ought n't to have written to me yourself!" and to say it with an air of triumph.

Caspar Goodwood raised his eyes to her own again; they seemed to shine through the vizard of a helmet. He had a strong sense of justice and was ready any day in the year — over and above this — to argue the question of his rights. "You said you hoped never to hear from me again; I know that. But I never accepted any such rule as my own. I warned you that you should hear very soon."

"I did n't say I hoped *never* to hear from you," said Isabel.

"Not for five years then; for ten years; twenty years. It's the same thing."

"Do you find it so? It seems to me there's a great difference. I can imagine that at the end of ten years we might have a very pleasant correspondence. I shall have matured my epistolary style."

She looked away while she spoke these words, knowing them of so much less earnest a cast than the countenance of her listener. Her eyes, however, at last came back to him, just as he said very irrelevantly: "Are you enjoying your visit to your uncle?"

"Very much indeed." She dropped, but then she broke out. "What good do you expect to get by insisting?"

"The good of not losing you."

"You 've no right to talk of losing what 's not yours. And even from your own point of view," Isabel added, "you ought to know when to let one alone."

"I disgust you very much," said Caspar Goodwood gloomily; not as if to provoke her to compassion for a man conscious of this blighting fact, but as if to set it well before himself, so that he might endeavour to act with his eyes on it.

"Yes, you don't at all delight me, you don't fit in, not in any way, just now, and the worst is that your putting it to the proof in this manner is quite unnecessary." It was n't certainly as if his nature had been soft, so that pin-pricks would draw blood from it; and from the first of her acquaintance with him, and of her having to defend herself against a certain air that he had of knowing better what was good for her than she knew herself, she had recognised the fact that perfect frankness was her best weapon. To attempt to spare his sensibility or to escape from him edgewise, as one might do from a man who had barred the way less sturdily — this, in dealing with Caspar Goodwood, who would grasp at everything of every sort that one might give him, was wasted agility. It was not that he had not susceptibilities, but his passive surface, as well as his active, was large and hard, and he might always be trusted to dress his wounds, so far as they required it, himself. She came back, even for her measure of possible pangs and aches in him, to her old sense that he was naturally plated and steeled, armed essentially for aggression.

"I can't reconcile myself to that," he simply said. There was a dangerous liberality about it; for she felt how open it was to him to make the point that he had not always disgusted her.

"I can't reconcile myself to it either, and it's not the state of things that ought to exist between us. If you'd only try to banish me from your mind for a few months we should be on good terms again."

"I see. If I should cease to think of you at all for a prescribed time, I should find I could keep it up indefinitely."

"Indefinitely is more than I ask. It's more even than I should like."

"You know that what you ask is impossible," said the young man, taking his adjective for granted in a manner she found irritating.

"Are n't you capable of making a calculated effort?" she demanded. "You're strong for everything else; why should n't you be strong for that?"

"An effort calculated for what?" And then as she hung fire, "I'm capable of nothing with regard to you," he went on, "but just of being infernally in love with you. If one's strong one loves only the more strongly."

"There's a good deal in that;" and indeed our young lady felt the force of it — felt it thrown off, into the vast of truth and poetry, as practically a bait to her imagination. But she promptly came round. "Think of me or not, as you find most possible; only leave me alone."

"Until when?"

"Well, for a year or two."

"Which do you mean? Between one year and two there's all the difference in the world."

"Call it two then," said Isabel with a studied effect of eagerness.

"And what shall I gain by that?" her friend asked with no sign of wincing.

"You'll have obliged me greatly."

"And what will be my reward?"

"Do you need a reward for an act of generosity?"

"Yes, when it involves a great sacrifice."

"There's no generosity without some sacrifice. Men don't understand such things. If you make the sacrifice you'll have all my admiration."

"I don't care a cent for your admiration — not one straw, with nothing to show for it. When will you marry me? That's the only question."

"Never — if you go on making me feel only as I feel at present."

"What do I gain then by not trying to make you feel otherwise?"

"You'll gain quite as much as by worrying me to death!" Caspar Goodwood bent his eyes again and gazed a while into the crown of his hat. A deep flush overspread his face; she could see her sharpness had at last penetrated. This immediately had a value — classic, romantic, redeeming, what did she know? — for her; "the strong man in pain" was one of the categories of the human appeal, little charm as he might exert in the given case. "Why do you make me say such things to you?" she cried in a trembling voice. "I only want to be gentle — to be thoroughly kind. It's not delightful to me to feel people care for me and yet to have to try and reason them out of it. I think others also ought to be considerate; we have each to judge for ourselves. I know you're considerate, as much as you can be; you've good reasons for what you do. But I really don't want to marry, or to talk about it at all now. I shall probably never do it — no, never. I've a perfect right to feel that way, and it's no kindness to a woman to press her so hard, to urge her against her will. If I give you pain I can only say I'm very sorry. It's not my fault; I can't marry you simply to please you. I won't say that I shall always remain your friend, because when women say that, in these situations, it passes, I believe, for a sort of mockery. But try me some day."

Caspar Goodwood, during this speech, had kept his eyes fixed upon the name of his hatter, and it was not until some time after she had ceased speaking that he raised them. When he did so the sight of a rosy, lovely eagerness in Isabel's face threw some confusion into his attempt to analyse her words. "I'll go home — I'll go to-morrow — I'll leave you alone," he brought out at last. "Only," he heavily said, "I hate to lose sight of you!"

"Never fear. I shall do no harm."

"You'll marry some one else, as sure as I sit here," Caspar Goodwood declared.

"Do you think that a generous charge?"

"Why not? Plenty of men will try to make you."

"I told you just now that I don't wish to marry and that I almost certainly never shall."

"I know you did, and I like your 'almost certainly'! I put no faith in what you say."

"Thank you very much. Do you accuse me of lying to shake you off? You say very delicate things."

"Why should I not say that? You've given me no pledge of anything at all."

"No, that's all that would be wanting!"

"You may perhaps even believe you're safe — from wishing to be. But you're not," the young man went on as if preparing himself for the worst.

"Very well then. We'll put it that I'm not safe. Have it as you please."

"I don't know, however," said Caspar Goodwood, "that my keeping you in sight would prevent it."

"Don't you indeed? I'm after all very much afraid of you. Do you think I'm so very easily pleased?" she asked suddenly, changing her tone.

"No — I don't; I shall try to console myself with that. But there are a certain number of very dazzling men in the world, no doubt; and if there were only one it would be enough. The most dazzling of all will make straight for you. You'll be sure to take no one who is n't dazzling."

"If you mean by dazzling brilliantly clever," Isabel said — "and I can't imagine what else you mean — I don't need the aid of a clever man to teach me how to live. I can find it out for myself."

"Find out how to live alone? I wish that, when you have, you'd teach *me!*"

She looked at him a moment; then with a quick smile, "Oh, *you* ought to marry!" she said.

He might be pardoned if for an instant this exclamation seemed to him to sound the infernal note, and it is not on record that her motive for discharging such a shaft had been of the clearest. He ought n't to stride about lean and hungry, however — she certainly felt *that* for him. "God forgive you!" he murmured between his teeth as he turned away.

Her accent had put her slightly in the wrong, and after a moment she felt the need to right herself. The easiest way to do it was to place him where she had been. "You do me great injustice — you say what you don't know!" she broke out. "I should n't be an easy victim — I 've proved it."

"Oh, to me, perfectly."

"I 've proved it to others as well." And she paused a moment. "I refused a proposal of marriage last week; what they call — no doubt — a dazzling one."

"I'm very glad to hear it," said the young man gravely.

"It was a proposal many girls would have accepted; it had everything to recommend it." Isabel had not proposed to herself to tell this story, but, now she had begun, the satisfaction of speaking it out and doing herself justice took possession of her. "I was offered a great position and a great fortune — by a person whom I like extremely."

Caspar watched her with intense interest. "Is he an Englishman?"

"He's an English nobleman," said Isabel.

Her visitor received this announcement at first in silence, but at last said: "I'm glad he's disappointed."

"Well then, as you have companions in misfortune, make the best of it."

"I don't call him a companion," said Caspar grimly.

"Why not — since I declined his offer absolutely?"

"That does n't make him my companion. Besides, he's an Englishman."

"And pray is n't an Englishman a human being?" Isabel asked.

"Oh, those people? They're not of *my* humanity, and I don't care what becomes of them."

"You're very angry," said the girl. "We've discussed this matter quite enough."

"Oh yes, I'm very angry. I plead guilty to that!"

She turned away from him, walked to the open window and stood a moment looking into the dusky void of the street, where a turbid gaslight alone represented social animation. For some time neither of these young persons spoke; Caspar lingered near the chimney-piece with eyes gloomily attached. She had virtually requested him to go — he knew that; but at the risk of making himself odious he kept his ground. She was too nursed a need to be easily renounced, and he had crossed the sea all to wring from her some scrap of a vow. Presently she left the window and stood again before him. "You do me very little justice — after my telling you what I told you just now. I'm sorry I told you — since it matters so little to you."

"Ah," cried the young man, "if you were thinking of *me* when you did it!" And then he paused with the fear that she might contradict so happy a thought.

"I was thinking of you a little," said Isabel.

"A little? I don't understand. If the knowledge of what I feel for you had any weight with you at all, calling it a 'little' is a poor account of it."

Isabel shook her head as if to carry off a blunder. "I've refused a most kind, noble gentleman. Make the most of that."

"I thank you then," said Caspar Goodwood gravely. "I thank you immensely."

"And now you had better go home."

"May I not see you again?" he asked.

"I think it's better not. You'll be sure to talk of this, and you see it leads to nothing."

"I promise you not to say a word that will annoy you."

Isabel reflected and then answered: "I return in a day or two to my uncle's, and I can't propose to you to come there. It would be too inconsistent."

Caspar Goodwood, on his side, considered. "You must do me justice too. I received an invitation to your uncle's more than a week ago, and I declined it."

She betrayed surprise. "From whom was your invitation?"

"From Mr. Ralph Touchett, whom I suppose to be your cousin. I declined it because I had not your authorisation to accept it. The suggestion that Mr. Touchett should invite me appeared to have come from Miss Stackpole."

"It certainly never did from me. Henrietta really goes very far," Isabel added.

"Don't be too hard on her — that touches *me*."

"No; if you declined you did quite right, and I

thank you for it." And she gave a little shudder of dismay at the thought that Lord Warburton and Mr. Goodwood might have met at Gardencourt: it would have been so awkward for Lord Warburton.

"When you leave your uncle where do you go?" her companion asked.

"I go abroad with my aunt — to Florence and other places."

The serenity of this announcement struck a chill to the young man's heart; he seemed to see her whirled away into circles from which he was inexorably excluded. Nevertheless he went on quickly with his questions. "And when shall you come back to America?"

"Perhaps not for a long time. I'm very happy here."

"Do you mean to give up your country?"

"Don't be an infant!"

"Well, you'll be out of my sight indeed!" said Caspar Goodwood.

"I don't know," she answered rather grandly. "The world — with all these places so arranged and so touching each other — comes to strike one as rather small."

"It's a sight too big for *me!*" Caspar exclaimed with a simplicity our young lady might have found touching if her face had not been set against concessions.

This attitude was part of a system, a theory, that she had lately embraced, and to be thorough she said after a moment: "Don't think me unkind if I say it's just *that* — being out of your sight — that I like.

If you were in the same place I should feel you were watching me, and I don't like that — I like my liberty too much. If there's a thing in the world I'm fond of," she went on with a slight recurrence of grandeur, "it's my personal independence."

But whatever there might be of the too superior in this speech moved Caspar Goodwood's admiration; there was nothing he winced at in the large air of it. He had never supposed she had n't wings and the need of beautiful free movements — he was n't, with his own long arms and strides, afraid of any force in her. Isabel's words, if they had been meant to shock him, failed of the mark and only made him smile with the sense that here was common ground. "Who would wish less to curtail your liberty than I? What can give me greater pleasure than to see you perfectly independent — doing whatever you like? It's to make you independent that I want to marry you."

"That's a beautiful sophism," said the girl with a smile more beautiful still.

"An unmarried woman — a girl of your age — is n't independent. There are all sorts of things she can't do. She's hampered at every step."

"That's as she looks at the question," Isabel answered with much spirit. "I'm not in my first youth — I can do what I choose — I belong quite to the independent class. I've neither father nor mother; I'm poor and of a serious disposition; I'm not pretty. I therefore am not bound to be timid and conventional; indeed I can't afford such luxuries. Besides, I try to judge things for myself; to judge wrong, I think, is more honourable than not to judge at all. I don't wish to be a mere sheep in the flock; I wish to choose my fate and know something of human affairs beyond what other people think it compatible with propriety to tell me." She paused a moment, but not long enough for her companion to reply. He was apparently on the point of doing so when she went on: "Let me say this to you, Mr. Goodwood. You're so kind as to speak of being afraid of my marrying. If you should hear a rumour that I'm on the point of doing so — girls are liable to have such things said about them — remember what I have told you about my love of liberty and venture to doubt it."

There was something passionately positive in the tone in which she gave him this advice, and he saw a shining candour in her eyes that helped him to believe her. On the whole he felt reassured, and you might have perceived it by the manner in which he said, quite eagerly: "You want simply to travel for two years? I'm quite willing to wait two years, and you may do what you like in the interval. If that's all you want, pray say so. I don't want you to be conventional; do I strike you as conventional myself? Do you want to improve your mind? Your mind's quite good enough for me; but if it interests you to wander about a while and see different countries I shall be delighted to help you in any way in my power."

"You're very generous; that's nothing new to me. The best way to help me will be to put as many hundred miles of sea between us as possible."

"One would think you were going to commit some atrocity!" said Caspar Goodwood.

"Perhaps I am. I wish to be free even to do that if the fancy takes me."

"Well then," he said slowly, "I'll go home." And he put out his hand, trying to look contented and confident.

Isabel's confidence in him, however, was greater than any he could feel in her. Not that he thought her capable of committing an atrocity; but, turn it over as he would, there was something ominous in the way she reserved her option. As she took his hand she felt a great respect for him; she knew how much he cared for her and she thought him magnanimous. They stood so for a moment, looking at each other, united by a hand-clasp which was not merely passive on her side. "That's right," she said very kindly, almost tenderly. "You'll lose nothing by being a reasonable man."

"But I'll come back, wherever you are, two years hence," he returned with characteristic grimness.

We have seen that our young lady was inconsequent, and at this she suddenly changed her note. "Ah, remember, I promise nothing — absolutely nothing!" Then more softly, as if to help him to leave her: "And remember too that I shall not be an easy victim!"

"You'll get very sick of your independence."

"Perhaps I shall; it's even very probable. When that day comes I shall be very glad to see you."

She had laid her hand on the knob of the door that led into her room, and she waited a moment to see whether her visitor would not take his departure. But he appeared unable to move; there was still an immense unwillingness in his attitude and a sore remonstrance in his eyes. "I must leave you now," said Isabel; and she opened the door and passed into the other room.

This apartment was dark, but the darkness was tempered by a vague radiance sent up through the window from the court of the hotel, and Isabel could make out the masses of the furniture, the dim shining of the mirror and the looming of the big four-posted bed. She stood still a moment, listening, and at last she heard Caspar Goodwood walk out of the sitting-room and close the door behind him. She stood still a little longer, and then, by an irresistible impulse, dropped on her knees before her bed and hid her face in her arms.

XVII

SHE was not praying; she was trembling — trembling all over. Vibration was easy to her, was in fact too constant with her, and she found herself now humming like a smitten harp. She only asked, however, to put on the cover, to case herself again in brown holland, but she wished to resist her excitement, and the attitude of devotion, which she kept for some time, seemed to help her to be still. She intensely rejoiced that Caspar Goodwood was gone; there was something in having thus got rid of him that was like the payment, for a stamped receipt, of some debt too long on her mind. As she felt the glad relief she bowed her head a little lower; the sense was there, throbbing in her heart; it was part of her emotion, but it was a thing to be ashamed of — it was profane and out of place. It was not for some ten minutes that she rose from her knees, and even when she came back to the sitting-room her tremor had not quite subsided. It had had, verily, two causes: part of it was to be accounted for by her long discussion with Mr. Goodwood, but it might be feared that the rest was simply the enjoyment she found in the exercise of her power. She sat down in the same chair again and took up her book, but without going through the form of opening the volume. She leaned back, with that low, soft, aspiring murmur with which she often uttered her response to accidents of which the brighter side was not superficially obvious, and yielded to the satisfaction of having refused two ardent suitors in a fortnight. That love of liberty of which she had given Caspar Goodwood so bold a sketch was as yet almost exclusively theoretic; she had not been able to indulge it on a large scale. But it appeared to her she had done something; she had tasted of the delight, if not of battle, at least of victory; she had done what was truest to her plan. In the glow of this consciousness the image of Mr. Goodwood taking his sad walk homeward through the dingy town presented itself with a certain reproachful force; so that, as at the same moment the door of the room was opened, she rose with an apprehension that he had come back. But it was only Henrietta Stackpole returning from her dinner.

Miss Stackpole immediately saw that our young lady had been "through" something, and indeed the discovery demanded no great penetration. She went straight up to her friend, who received her without a greeting. Isabel's elation in having sent Caspar Goodwood back to America presupposed her being in a manner glad he had come to see her; but at the same time she perfectly remembered Henrietta had had no right to set a trap for her. "Has he been here, dear?" the latter yearningly asked.

Isabel turned away and for some moments answered nothing. "You acted very wrongly," she declared at last.

"I acted for the best. I only hope you acted as well."

"You're not the judge. I can't trust you," said Isabel.

This declaration was unflattering, but Henrietta was much too unselfish to heed the charge it conveyed; she cared only for what it intimated with regard to her friend. "Isabel Archer," she observed with equal abruptness and solemnity, "if you marry one of these people I'll never speak to you again!"

"Before making so terrible a threat you had better wait till I'm asked," Isabel replied. Never having said a word to Miss Stackpole about Lord Warburton's overtures, she had now no impulse whatever to justify herself to Henrietta by telling her that she had refused that nobleman.

"Oh, you'll be asked quick enough, once you get off on the Continent. Annie Climber was asked three times in Italy — poor plain little Annie."

"Well, if Annie Climber was n't captured why should I be?"

"I don't believe Annie was pressed; but you'll be."

"That's a flattering conviction," said Isabel without alarm.

"I don't flatter you, Isabel, I tell you the truth!" cried her friend. "I hope you don't mean to tell me that you did n't give Mr. Goodwood some hope."

"I don't see why I should tell you anything; as I said to you just now, I can't trust you. But since you're so much interested in Mr. Goodwood I won't conceal from you that he returns immediately to America."

"You don't mean to say you've sent him off?" Henrietta almost shrieked.

"I asked him to leave me alone; and I ask you the same, Henrietta." Miss Stackpole glittered for an instant with dismay, and then passed to the mirror over the chimney-piece and took off her bonnet. "I hope you've enjoyed your dinner," Isabel went on.

But her companion was not to be diverted by frivolous propositions. "Do you know where you're going, Isabel Archer?"

"Just now I'm going to bed," said Isabel with persistent frivolity.

"Do you know where you're drifting?" Henrietta pursued, holding out her bonnet delicately.

"No, I have n't the least idea, and I find it very pleasant not to know. A swift carriage, of a dark night, rattling with four horses over roads that one can't see — that's my idea of happiness."

"Mr. Goodwood certainly did n't teach you to say such things as that — like the heroine of an immoral novel," said Miss Stackpole. "You're drifting to some great mistake."

Isabel was irritated by her friend's interference, yet she still tried to think what truth this declaration could represent. She could think of nothing that diverted her from saying: "You must be very fond of me, Henrietta, to be willing to be so aggressive."

"I love you intensely, Isabel," said Miss Stackpole with feeling.

"Well, if you love me intensely let me as intensely alone. I asked that of Mr. Goodwood, and I must also ask it of you."

"Take care you're not let alone too much."

"That's what Mr. Goodwood said to me. I told him I must take the risks."

"You're a creature of risks — you make me

shudder!" cried Henrietta. "When does Mr. Goodwood return to America?"

"I don't know — he did n't tell me."

"Perhaps you did n't enquire," said Henrietta with the note of righteous irony.

"I gave him too little satisfaction to have the right to ask questions of him."

This assertion seemed to Miss Stackpole for a moment to bid defiance to comment; but at last she exclaimed: "Well, Isabel, if I did n't know you I might think you were heartless!"

"Take care," said Isabel; "you're spoiling me."

"I'm afraid I've done that already. I hope, at least," Miss Stackpole added, "that he may cross with Annie Climber!"

Isabel learned from her the next morning that she had determined not to return to Gardencourt (where old Mr. Touchett had promised her a renewed welcome), but to await in London the arrival of the invitation that Mr. Bantling had promised her from his sister Lady Pensil. Miss Stackpole related very freely her conversation with Ralph Touchett's sociable friend and declared to Isabel that she really believed she had now got hold of something that would lead to something. On the receipt of Lady Pensil's letter — Mr. Bantling had virtually guaranteed the arrival of this document — she would immediately depart for Bedfordshire, and if Isabel cared to look out for her impressions in the *Interviewer* she would certainly find them. Henrietta was evidently going to see something of the inner life this time.

"Do you know where you're drifting, Henrietta

Stackpole?" Isabel asked, imitating the tone in which her friend had spoken the night before.

"I'm drifting to a big position — that of the Queen of American Journalism. If my next letter is n't copied all over the West I'll swallow my pen-wiper!"

She had arranged with her friend Miss Annie Climber, the young lady of the continental offers, that they should go together to make those purchases which were to constitute Miss Climber's farewell to a hemisphere in which she at least had been appreciated; and she presently repaired to Jermyn Street to pick up her companion. Shortly after her departure Ralph Touchett was announced, and as soon as he came in Isabel saw he had something on his mind. He very soon took his cousin into his confidence. He had received from his mother a telegram to the effect that his father had had a sharp attack of his old malady, that she was much alarmed and that she begged he would instantly return to Gardencourt. On this occasion at least Mrs. Touchett's devotion to the electric wire was not open to criticism.

"I've judged it best to see the great doctor, Sir Matthew Hope, first," Ralph said; "by great good luck he's in town. He's to see me at half-past twelve, and I shall make sure of his coming down to Gardencourt — which he will do the more readily as he has already seen my father several times, both there and in London. There's an express at two-forty-five, which I shall take; and you'll come back with me or remain here a few days longer, exactly as you prefer."

"I shall certainly go with you," Isabel returned. "I don't suppose I can be of any use to my uncle, but if he's ill I shall like to be near him."

"I think you're fond of him," said Ralph with a certain shy pleasure in his face. "You appreciate him, which all the world has n't done. The quality's too fine."

"I quite adore him," Isabel after a moment said.

"That's very well. After his son he's your greatest admirer."

She welcomed this assurance, but she gave secretly a small sigh of relief at the thought that Mr. Touchett was one of those admirers who could n't propose to marry her. This, however, was not what she spoke; she went on to inform Ralph that there were other reasons for her not remaining in London. She was tired of it and wished to leave it; and then Henrietta was going away — going to stay in Bedfordshire.

"In Bedfordshire?"

"With Lady Pensil, the sister of Mr. Bantling, who has answered for an invitation."

Ralph was feeling anxious, but at this he broke into a laugh. Suddenly, none the less, his gravity returned. "Bantling's a man of courage. But if the invitation should get lost on the way?"

"I thought the British post-office was impeccable."

"The good Homer sometimes nods," said Ralph. "However," he went on more brightly, "the good Bantling never does, and, whatever happens, he'll take care of Henrietta."

Ralph went to keep his appointment with Sir Matthew Hope, and Isabel made her arrangements for quitting Pratt's Hotel. Her uncle's danger touched her nearly, and while she stood before her open trunk, looking about her vaguely for what she should put into it, the tears suddenly rose to her eyes. It was perhaps for this reason that when Ralph came back at two o'clock to take her to the station she was not yet ready. He found Miss Stackpole, however, in the sitting-room, where she had just risen from her luncheon, and this lady immediately expressed her regret at his father's illness.

"He's a grand old man," she said; "he's faithful to the last. If it's really to be the last — pardon my alluding to it, but you must often have thought of the possibility — I'm sorry that I shall not be at Gardencourt."

"You'll amuse yourself much more in Bedfordshire."

"I shall be sorry to amuse myself at such a time," said Henrietta with much propriety. But she immediately added: "I should like so to commemorate the closing scene."

"My father may live a long time," said Ralph simply. Then, adverting to topics more cheerful, he interrogated Miss Stackpole as to her own future.

Now that Ralph was in trouble she addressed him in a tone of larger allowance and told him that she was much indebted to him for having made her acquainted with Mr. Bantling. "He has told me just the things I want to know," she said; "all the society-items and all about the royal family. I can't make out that what he tells me about the royal family is much to their credit; but he says that's only my peculiar way of looking at it. Well, all I want is that he should give me the facts; I can put them together quick enough, once I've got them." And she added that Mr. Bantling had been so good as to promise to come and take her out that afternoon.

"To take you where?" Ralph ventured to enquire.

"To Buckingham Palace. He's going to show me over it, so that I may get some idea how they live."

"Ah," said Ralph, "we leave you in good hands. The first thing we shall hear is that you're invited to Windsor Castle."

"If they ask me, I shall certainly go. Once I get started I'm not afraid. But for all that," Henrietta added in a moment, "I'm not satisfied; I'm not at peace about Isabel."

"What is her last misdemeanour?"

"Well, I've told you before, and I suppose there's no harm in my going on. I always finish a subject that I take up. Mr. Goodwood was here last night."

Ralph opened his eyes; he even blushed a little — his blush being the sign of an emotion somewhat acute. He remembered that Isabel, in separating from him in Winchester Square, had repudiated his suggestion that her motive in doing so was the expectation of a visitor at Pratt's Hotel, and it was a new pang to him to have to suspect her of duplicity. On the other hand, he quickly said to himself, what concern was it of his that she should have made an appointment with a lover? Had it not been thought graceful in every age that young ladies should make a mystery of such appointments? Ralph gave Miss Stackpole a diplomatic answer. "I should have thought that, with the views you expressed to me the other day, this would satisfy you perfectly."

"That he should come to see her? That was very well, as far as it went. It was a little plot of mine; I let him know that we were in London, and when it had been arranged that I should spend the evening out I sent him a word — the word we just utter to the 'wise.' I hoped he would find her alone; I won't pretend I did n't hope that you 'd be out of the way. He came to see her, but he might as well have stayed away."

"Isabel was cruel?" — and Ralph's face lighted with the relief of his cousin's not having shown duplicity.

"I don't exactly know what passed between them. But she gave him no satisfaction — she sent him back to America."

"Poor Mr. Goodwood!" Ralph sighed.

"Her only idea seems to be to get rid of him," Henrietta went on.

"Poor Mr. Goodwood!" Ralph repeated. The exclamation, it must be confessed, was automatic; it failed exactly to express his thoughts, which were taking another line.

"You don't say that as if you felt it. I don't believe you care."

"Ah," said Ralph, "you must remember that I don't know this interesting young man — that I 've never seen him."

"Well, I shall see him, and I shall tell him not to give up. If I did n't believe Isabel would come round," Miss Stackpole added — "well, I 'd give up myself. I mean I 'd give *her* up!"

XVIII

It had occurred to Ralph that, in the conditions, Isabel's parting with her friend might be of a slightly embarrassed nature, and he went down to the door of the hotel in advance of his cousin, who, after a slight delay, followed with the traces of an unaccepted remonstrance, as he thought, in her eyes. The two made the journey to Gardencourt in almost unbroken silence, and the servant who met them at the station had no better news to give them of Mr. Touchett — a fact which caused Ralph to congratulate himself afresh on Sir Matthew Hope's having promised to come down in the five o'clock train and spend the night. Mrs. Touchett, he learned, on reaching home, had been constantly with the old man and was with him at that moment; and this fact made Ralph say to himself that, after all, what his mother wanted was just easy occasion. The finer natures were those that shone at the larger times. Isabel went to her own room, noting throughout the house that perceptible hush which precedes a crisis. At the end of an hour, however, she came downstairs in search of her aunt, whom she wished to ask about Mr. Touchett. She went into the library, but Mrs. Touchett was not there, and as the weather, which had been damp and chill, was now altogether spoiled, it was not probable she had gone for her usual walk in the grounds. Isabel was on the point of ringing to send a question to her room, when this purpose quickly yielded to an unexpected sound — the sound of low music proceeding apparently from the saloon. She knew her aunt never touched the piano, and the musician was therefore probably Ralph, who played for his own amusement. That he should have resorted to this recreation at the present time indicated apparently that his anxiety about his father had been relieved; so that the girl took her way, almost with restored cheer, toward the source of the harmony. The drawing-room at Gardencourt was an apartment of great distances, and, as the piano was placed at the end of it furthest removed from the door at which she entered, her arrival was not noticed by the person seated before the instrument. This person was neither Ralph nor his mother; it was a lady whom Isabel immediately saw to be a stranger to herself, though her back was presented to the door. This back — an ample and well-dressed one — Isabel viewed for some moments with surprise. The lady was of course a visitor who had arrived during her absence and who had not been mentioned by either of the servants — one of them her aunt's maid — of whom she had had speech since her return. Isabel had already learned, however, with what treasures of reserve the function of receiving orders may be accompanied, and she was particularly conscious of having been treated with dryness by her aunt's maid, through whose hands she had slipped perhaps a little too mistrustfully and with an effect of plumage but the more lustrous. The advent of a guest was in itself far from disconcerting; she had not yet divested herself of a young faith that each new acquaintance would exert some momentous influence on her life. By the time she had made these reflexions she became aware that the lady at the piano played remarkably well. She was playing something of Schubert's—Isabel knew not what, but recognised Schubert — and she touched the piano with a discretion of her own. It showed skill, it showed feeling; Isabel sat down noiselessly on the nearest chair and waited till the end of the piece. When it was finished she felt a strong desire to thank the player, and rose from her seat to do so, while at the same time the stranger turned quickly round, as if but just aware of her presence.

"That's very beautiful, and your playing makes it more beautiful still," said Isabel with all the young radiance with which she usually uttered a truthful rapture.

"You don't think I disturbed Mr. Touchett then?" the musician answered as sweetly as this compliment deserved. "The house is so large and his room so far away that I thought I might venture, especially as I played just — just *du bout des doigts*."

"She's a Frenchwoman," Isabel said to herself; "she says that as if she were French." And this supposition made the visitor more interesting to our speculative heroine. "I hope my uncle's doing well," Isabel added. "I should think that to hear such lovely music as that would really make him feel better."

The lady smiled and discriminated. "I'm afraid there are moments in life when even Schubert has nothing to say to us. We must admit, however, that they are our worst."

"I'm not in that state now then," said Isabel. "On the contrary I should be so glad if you would play something more."

"If it will give you pleasure — delighted." And this obliging person took her place again and struck a few chords, while Isabel sat down nearer the instrument. Suddenly the new-comer stopped with her hands on the keys, half-turning and looking over her shoulder. She was forty years old and not pretty, though her expression charmed. "Pardon me," she said; "but are you the niece — the young American?"

"I'm my aunt's niece," Isabel replied with simplicity.

The lady at the piano sat still a moment longer, casting her air of interest over her shoulder. "That's very well; we're compatriots." And then she began to play.

"Ah then she's not French," Isabel murmured; and as the opposite supposition had made her romantic it might have seemed that this revelation would have marked a drop. But such was not the fact; rarer even than to be French seemed it to be American on such interesting terms.

The lady played in the same manner as before, softly and solemnly, and while she played the shadows deepened in the room. The autumn twilight gathered in, and from her place Isabel could see the rain, which had now begun in earnest, washing the cold-looking lawn and the wind shaking the great trees. At last, when the music had ceased, her companion got up and, coming nearer with a smile, before Isabel had time to thank her again, said: "I'm very glad you've come back; I've heard a great deal about you."

Isabel thought her a very attractive person, but nevertheless spoke with a certain abruptness in reply to this speech. "From whom have you heard about me?"

The stranger hesitated a single moment and then, "From your uncle," she answered. "I've been here three days, and the first day he let me come and pay him a visit in his room. Then he talked constantly of you."

"As you did n't know me that must rather have bored you."

"It made me want to know you. All the more that since then — your aunt being so much with Mr. Touchett — I've been quite alone and have got rather tired of my own society. I've not chosen a good moment for my visit."

A servant had come in with lamps and was presently followed by another bearing the tea-tray. On the appearance of this repast Mrs. Touchett had apparently been notified, for she now arrived and addressed herself to the tea-pot. Her greeting to her niece did not differ materially from her manner of raising the lid of this receptacle in order to glance at the contents: in neither act was it becoming to make a show of avidity. Questioned about her husband she was unable to say he was better; but the local doctor was with him, and much light was expected from this gentleman's consultation with Sir Matthew Hope.

"I suppose you two ladies have made acquaintance," she pursued. "If you have n't I recommend you to do so; for so long as we continue — Ralph and I — to cluster about Mr. Touchett's bed you 're not likely to have much society but each other."

"I know nothing about you but that you 're a great musician," Isabel said to the visitor.

"There 's a good deal more than that to know," Mrs. Touchett affirmed in her little dry tone.

"A very little of it, I am sure, will content Miss Archer!" the lady exclaimed with a light laugh. "I 'm an old friend of your aunt's. I 've lived much in Florence. I 'm Madame Merle." She made this last announcement as if she were referring to a person of tolerably distinct identity. For Isabel, however, it represented little; she could only continue to feel that Madame Merle had as charming a manner as any she had ever encountered.

"She 's not a foreigner in spite of her name," said Mrs. Touchett. "She was born — I always forget where you were born."

"It 's hardly worth while then I should tell you."

"On the contrary," said Mrs. Touchett, who rarely missed a logical point; "if I remembered your telling me would be quite superfluous."

Madame Merle glanced at Isabel with a sort of world-wide smile, a thing that over-reached frontiers. "I was born under the shadow of the national banner."

"She 's too fond of mystery," said Mrs. Touchett; "that 's her great fault."

"Ah," exclaimed Madame Merle, "I 've great faults, but I don't think that 's one of them; it certainly is n't the greatest. I came into the world in the Brooklyn navy-yard. My father was a high officer in the United States Navy, and had a post — a post of responsibility — in that establishment at the time. I suppose I ought to love the sea, but I hate it. That 's why I don't return to America. I love the land; the great thing is to love something."

Isabel, as a dispassionate witness, had not been struck with the force of Mrs. Touchett's characterisation of her visitor, who had an expressive, communicative, responsive face, by no means of the sort which, to Isabel's mind, suggested a secretive disposition. It was a face that told of an amplitude of nature and of quick and free motions and, though it had no regular beauty, was in the highest degree engaging and attaching. Madame Merle was a tall, fair, smooth woman; everything in her person was round and replete, though without those accumulations which suggest heaviness. Her features were thick but in perfect proportion and harmony, and her complexion had a healthy clearness. Her grey eyes were small but full of light and incapable of stupidity — incapable, according to some people, even of tears; she had a liberal, full-rimmed mouth which when she smiled drew itself upward to the left side in a manner that most people thought very odd, some very affected and a few very graceful. Isabel inclined to range herself in the last category. Madame Merle had thick, fair hair, arranged somehow "classically" and as if she were a Bust, Isabel judged — a Juno or a Niobe; and large white hands, of a perfect shape, a shape so perfect that their possessor, preferring to leave them unadorned, wore no jewelled rings. Isabel had taken her at first, as we have seen, for a Frenchwoman; but extended observation might have ranked her as a German — a German of high degree, perhaps an Austrian, a baroness, a countess, a princess. It would never have been supposed she had come into the world in Brooklyn — though one could doubtless not have carried through any argument that the air of distinction marking her in so eminent a degree was inconsistent with such a birth. It was true that the national banner had floated immediately over her cradle, and the breezy freedom of the stars and stripes might have shed an influence upon the attitude she there took towards life. And yet she had evidently nothing of the fluttered, flapping quality of a morsel of bunting in the wind; her manner expressed the repose and confidence which come from a large experience. Experience, however, had not quenched her youth; it had simply made her sympathetic and supple. She was in a word a woman of strong impulses kept in admirable order. This commended itself to Isabel as an ideal combination.

The girl made these reflexions while the three ladies sat at their tea, but that ceremony was interrupted before long by the arrival of the great doctor from London, who had been immediately ushered into the drawing-room. Mrs. Touchett took him off to the library for a private talk; and then Madame Merle and Isabel parted, to meet again at dinner. The idea of seeing more of this interesting woman did much to mitigate Isabel's sense of the sadness now settling on Gardencourt.

When she came into the drawing-room before dinner she found the place empty; but in the course of a moment Ralph arrived. His anxiety about his father had been lightened; Sir Matthew Hope's view of his condition was less depressed than his own had been. The doctor recommended that the nurse alone should remain with the old man for the next three or four hours; so that Ralph, his mother and the great physician himself were free to dine at table. Mrs. Touchett and Sir Matthew appeared; Madame Merle was the last.

Before she came Isabel spoke of her to Ralph, who was standing before the fireplace. "Pray who is this Madame Merle?"

"The cleverest woman I know, not excepting yourself," said Ralph.

"I thought she seemed very pleasant."

"I was sure you'd think her very pleasant."

"Is that why you invited her?"

"I did n't invite her, and when we came back from London I did n't know she was here. No one invited her. She's a friend of my mother's, and just after you and I went to town my mother got a note from her. She had arrived in England (she usually lives abroad, though she has first and last spent a good deal of time here), and asked leave to come down for a few days. She's a woman who can make such proposals with perfect confidence; she's so welcome wherever she goes. And with my mother there could be no question of hesitating; she's the one person in the world whom my mother very much admires. If she were not herself (which she after all much prefers), she would like to be Madame Merle. It would indeed be a great change."

"Well, she's very charming," said Isabel. "And she plays beautifully."

"She does everything beautifully. She's complete."

Isabel looked at her cousin a moment. "You don't like her."

"On the contrary, I was once in love with her."

"And she did n't care for you, and that's why you don't like her."

"How can we have discussed such things? Monsieur Merle was then living."

"Is he dead now?"

"So she says."

"Don't you believe her?"

"Yes, because the statement agrees with the probabilities. The husband of Madame Merle would be likely to pass away."

Isabel gazed at her cousin again. "I don't know what you mean. You mean something — that you don't mean. What was Monsieur Merle?"

"The husband of Madame."

"You're very odious. Has she any children?"

"Not the least little child — fortunately."

"Fortunately?"

"I mean fortunately for the child. She'd be sure to spoil it."

Isabel was apparently on the point of assuring her cousin for the third time that he was odious; but the discussion was interrupted by the arrival of the lady who was the topic of it. She came rustling in quickly, apologising for being late, fastening a bracelet, dressed in dark blue satin, which exposed a white bosom that was ineffectually covered by a curious silver necklace. Ralph offered her his arm with the exaggerated alertness of a man who was no longer a lover.

Even if this had still been his condition, however, Ralph had other things to think about. The great doctor spent the night at Gardencourt and, returning to London on the morrow, after another consultation with Mr. Touchett's own medical adviser, concurred in Ralph's desire that he should see the patient again on the day following. On the day following Sir Matthew Hope reappeared at Gardencourt, and now took a less encouraging view of the old man, who had grown worse in the twenty-four hours. His feebleness was extreme, and to his son, who constantly sat by his bedside, it often seemed that his end must be at hand. The local doctor, a very sagacious man, in whom Ralph had secretly more confidence than in his distinguished colleague, was constantly in attendance, and Sir Matthew Hope came back several times. Mr. Touchett was much of the time unconscious; he slept a great deal; he rarely spoke. Isabel had a great desire to be useful to him and was allowed to watch with him at hours when his other attendants (of whom Mrs. Touchett was not the least regular) went to take rest. He never seemed to know her, and she always said to herself "Suppose he should die while I'm sitting here;" an idea which excited her and kept her awake. Once he opened his eyes for a while and fixed them upon her intelligently, but when she went to him, hoping he would recognise her, he closed them and relapsed into stupor. The day after this, however, he revived for a longer time ; but on this occasion Ralph only was with him. The old man began to talk, much to his son's satisfaction, who assured him that they should presently have him sitting up.

"No, my boy," said Mr. Touchett, "not unless you bury me in a sitting posture, as some of the ancients — was it the ancients ? — used to do."

"Ah, daddy, don't talk about that," Ralph murmured. "You must n't deny that you're getting better."

"There will be no need of my denying it if you don't say it," the old man answered. "Why should we prevaricate just at the last ? We never prevaricated before. I've got to die some time, and it's better to die when one's sick than when one's well. I'm very sick — as sick as I shall ever be. I hope you don't want to prove that I shall ever be worse than this ? That would be too bad. You don't ? Well then."

Having made this excellent point he became quiet; but the next time that Ralph was with him he again addressed himself to conversation. The nurse had gone to her supper and Ralph was alone in charge, having just relieved Mrs. Touchett, who had been on guard since dinner. The room was lighted only by the flickering fire, which of late had become necessary, and Ralph's tall shadow was projected over wall and ceiling with an outline constantly varying but always grotesque.

"Who's that with me — is it my son ?" the old man asked.

"Yes, it's your son, daddy."

"And is there no one else?"

"No one else."

Mr. Touchett said nothing for a while; and then, "I want to talk a little," he went on.

"Won't it tire you?" Ralph demurred.

"It won't matter if it does. I shall have a long rest. I want to talk about *you*."

Ralph had drawn nearer to the bed; he sat leaning forward with his hand on his father's. "You had better select a brighter topic."

"You were always bright; I used to be proud of your brightness. I should like so much to think you'd do something."

"If you leave us," said Ralph, "I shall do nothing but miss you."

"That's just what I don't want; it's what I want to talk about. You must get a new interest.

"I don't want a new interest, daddy. I have more old ones than I know what to do with."

The old man lay there looking at his son; his face was the face of the dying, but his eyes were the eyes of Daniel Touchett. He seemed to be reckoning over Ralph's interests. "Of course you have your mother," he said at last. "You'll take care of her."

"My mother will always take care of herself," Ralph returned.

"Well," said his father, "perhaps as she grows older she'll need a little help."

"I shall not see that. She'll outlive me."

"Very likely she will; but that's no reason —!" Mr. Touchett let his phrase die away in a helpless but not quite querulous sigh and remained silent again.

"Don't trouble yourself about us," said his son. "My mother and I get on very well together, you know."

"You get on by always being apart; that's not natural."

"If you leave us we shall probably see more of each other."

"Well," the old man observed with wandering irrelevance, "it can't be said that my death will make much difference in your mother's life."

"It will probably make more than you think."

"Well, she'll have more money," said Mr. Touchett. "I've left her a good wife's portion, just as if she had been a good wife."

"She has been one, daddy, according to her own theory. She has never troubled you."

"Ah, some troubles are pleasant," Mr. Touchett murmured. "Those you've given me for instance. But your mother has been less — less — what shall I call it? less out of the way since I've been ill. I presume she knows I've noticed it."

"I shall certainly tell her so; I'm so glad you mention it."

"It won't make any difference to her; she does n't do it to please me. She does it to please — to please —" And he lay a while trying to think why she did it. "She does it because it suits her. But that's not what I want to talk about," he added. "It's about *you*. You'll be very well off."

"Yes," said Ralph, "I know that. But I hope

you've not forgotten the talk we had a year ago — when I told you exactly what money I should need and begged you to make some good use of the rest."

"Yes, yes, I remember. I made a new will — in a few days. I suppose it was the first time such a thing had happened — a young man trying to get a will made against him."

"It is not against me," said Ralph. "It would be against me to have a large property to take care of. It's impossible for a man in my state of health to spend much money, and enough is as good as a feast."

"Well, you'll have enough — and something over. There will be more than enough for one — there will be enough for two."

"That's too much," said Ralph.

"Ah, don't say that. The best thing you can do, when I'm gone, will be to marry."

Ralph had foreseen what his father was coming to, and this suggestion was by no means fresh. It had long been Mr. Touchett's most ingenious way of taking the cheerful view of his son's possible duration. Ralph had usually treated it facetiously; but present circumstances proscribed the facetious. He simply fell back in his chair and returned his father's appealing gaze.

"If I, with a wife who has n't been very fond of me, have had a very happy life," said the old man, carrying his ingenuity further still, "what a life might n't you have if you should marry a person different from Mrs. Touchett. There are more different from her than there are like her." Ralph still said nothing; and after a pause his father resumed softly: "What do you think of your cousin?"

At this Ralph started, meeting the question with a strained smile. "Do I understand you to propose that I should marry Isabel?"

"Well, that's what it comes to in the end. Don't you like Isabel?"

"Yes, very much." And Ralph got up from his chair and wandered over to the fire. He stood before it an instant and then he stooped and stirred it mechanically. "I like Isabel very much," he repeated.

"Well," said his father, "I know she likes you. She has told me how much she likes you."

"Did she remark that she would like to marry me?"

"No, but she can't have anything against you. And she's the most charming young lady I've ever seen. And she would be good to you. I have thought a great deal about it."

"So have I," said Ralph, coming back to the bedside again. "I don't mind telling you that."

"You *are* in love with her then? I should think you would be. It's as if she came over on purpose."

"No, I'm not in love with her; but I should be if — if certain things were different."

"Ah, things are always different from what they might be," said the old man. "If you wait for them to change you'll never do anything. I don't know whether you know," he went on; "but I suppose there's no harm in my alluding to it at such an hour as this: there was some one wanted to marry Isabel the other day, and she would n't have him."

"I know she refused Warburton: he told me himself."

"Well, that proves there 's a chance for somebody else."

"Somebody else took his chance the other day in London — and got nothing by it."

"Was it you?" Mr. Touchett eagerly asked.

"No, it was an older friend; a poor gentleman who came over from America to see about it."

"Well, I'm sorry for him, whoever he was. But it only proves what I say — that the way 's open to you."

"If it is, dear father, it 's all the greater pity that I 'm unable to tread it. I have n't many convictions; but I have three or four that I hold strongly. One is that people, on the whole, had better not marry their cousins. Another is that people in an advanced stage of pulmonary disorder had better not marry at all."

The old man raised his weak hand and moved it to and fro before his face. "What do you mean by that? You look at things in a way that would make everything wrong. What sort of a cousin is a cousin that you had never seen for more than twenty years of her life? We 're all each other's cousins, and if we stopped at that the human race would die out. It 's just the same with your bad lung. You 're a great deal better than you used to be. All you want is to lead a natural life. It is a great deal more natural to marry a pretty young lady that you 're in love with than it is to remain single on false principles."

"I 'm not in love with Isabel," said Ralph.

"You said just now that you would be if you did n't

think it wrong. I want to prove to you that it is n't wrong."

"It will only tire you, dear daddy," said Ralph, who marvelled at his father's tenacity and at his finding strength to insist. "Then where shall we all be?"

"Where shall you be if I don't provide for you? You won't have anything to do with the bank, and you won't have me to take care of. You say you 've so many interests; but I can't make them out."

Ralph leaned back in his chair with folded arms; his eyes were fixed for some time in meditation. At last, with the air of a man fairly mustering courage, "I take a great interest in my cousin," he said, "but not the sort of interest you desire. I shall not live many years; but I hope I shall live long enough to see what she does with herself. She 's entirely independent of me; I can exercise very little influence upon her life. But I should like to do something for her."

"What should you like to do?"

"I should like to put a little wind in her sails."

"What do you mean by that?"

"I should like to put it into her power to do some of the things she wants. She wants to see the world for instance. I should like to put money in her purse."

"Ah, I 'm glad you 've thought of that," said the old man. "But I 've thought of it too. I 've left her a legacy — five thousand pounds."

"That 's capital; it 's very kind of you. But I should like to do a little more."

Something of that veiled acuteness with which it had been on Daniel Touchett's part the habit of a lifetime to listen to a financial proposition still lingered in the face in which the invalid had not obliterated the man of business. "I shall be happy to consider it," he said softly.

"Isabel's poor then. My mother tells me that she has but a few hundred dollars a year. I should like to make her rich."

"What do you mean by rich?"

"I call people rich when they're able to meet the requirements of their imagination. Isabel has a great deal of imagination."

"So have you, my son," said Mr. Touchett, listening very attentively but a little confusedly.

"You tell me I shall have money enough for two. What I want is that you should kindly relieve me of my superfluity and make it over to Isabel. Divide my inheritance into two equal halves and give her the second."

"To do what she likes with?"

"Absolutely what she likes."

"And without an equivalent?"

"What equivalent could there be?"

"The one I've already mentioned."

"Her marrying — some one or other? It's just to do away with anything of that sort that I make my suggestion. If she has an easy income she'll never have to marry for a support. That's what I want cannily to prevent. She wishes to be free, and your bequest will make her free."

"Well, you seem to have thought it out," said Mr. Touchett. "But I don't see why you appeal to me. The money will be yours, and you can easily give it to her yourself."

Ralph openly stared. "Ah, dear father, *I* can't offer Isabel money!"

The old man gave a groan. "Don't tell me you're not in love with her! Do you want *me* to have the credit of it?"

"Entirely. I should like it simply to be a clause in your will, without the slightest reference to me."

"Do you want me to make a new will then?"

"A few words will do it; you can attend to it the next time you feel a little lively."

"You must telegraph to Mr. Hilary then. I'll do nothing without my solicitor."

"You shall see Mr. Hilary to-morrow."

"He'll think we've quarrelled, you and I," said the old man.

"Very probably; I shall like him to think it," said Ralph, smiling; "and, to carry out the idea, I give you notice that I shall be very sharp, quite horrid and strange, with you."

The humour of this appeared to touch his father, who lay a little while taking it in. "I'll do anything you like," Mr. Touchett said at last; "but I'm not sure it's right. You say you want to put wind in her sails; but aren't you afraid of putting too much?"

"I should like to see her going before the breeze!" Ralph answered.

"You speak as if it were for your mere amusement."

"So it is, a good deal."

"Well, I don't think I understand," said Mr. Touchett with a sigh. "Young men are very different from what I was. When I cared for a girl — when I was young — I wanted to do more than look at her.

You've scruples that I should n't have had, and you've ideas that I should n't have had either. You say Isabel wants to be free, and that her being rich will keep her from marrying for money. Do you think that she's a girl to do that?"

"By no means. But she has less money than she has ever had before. Her father then gave her everything, because he used to spend his capital. She has nothing but the crumbs of that feast to live on, and she does n't really know how meagre they are — she has yet to learn it. My mother has told me all about it. Isabel will learn it when she's really thrown upon the world, and it would be very painful to me to think of her coming to the consciousness of a lot of wants she should be unable to satisfy."

"I've left her five thousand pounds. She can satisfy a good many wants with that."

"She can indeed. But she would probably spend it in two or three years."

"You think she'd be extravagant then?"

"Most certainly," said Ralph, smiling serenely.

Poor Mr. Touchett's acuteness was rapidly giving place to pure confusion. "It would merely be a question of time then, her spending the larger sum?"

"No — though at first I think she'd plunge into that pretty freely: she'd probably make over a part of it to each of her sisters. But after that she'd come to her senses, remember she has still a lifetime before her, and live within her means."

"Well, you *have* worked it out," said the old man helplessly. "You do take an interest in her, certainly."

"You can't consistently say I go too far. You wished me to go further."

"Well, I don't know," Mr. Touchett answered. "I don't think I enter into your spirit. It seems to me immoral."

"Immoral, dear daddy?"

"Well, I don't know that it's right to make everything so easy for a person."

"It surely depends upon the person. When the person's good, your making things easy is all to the credit of virtue. To facilitate the execution of good impulses, what can be a nobler act?"

This was a little difficult to follow, and Mr. Touchett considered it for a while. At last he said: "Isabel's a sweet young thing; but do you think she's so good as that?"

"She's as good as her best opportunities," Ralph returned.

"Well," Mr. Touchett declared, "she ought to get a great many opportunities for sixty thousand pounds."

"I've no doubt she will."

"Of course I'll do what you want," said the old man. "I only want to understand it a little."

"Well, dear daddy, don't you understand it now?" his son caressingly asked. "If you don't we won't take any more trouble about it. We'll leave it alone."

Mr. Touchett lay a long time still. Ralph supposed he had given up the attempt to follow. But at last, quite lucidly, he began again. "Tell me this first. Does n't it occur to you that a young lady with sixty thousand pounds may fall a victim to the fortune-hunters?"

"She 'll hardly fall a victim to more than one."

"Well, one 's too many."

"Decidedly. That 's a risk, and it has entered into my calculation. I think it 's appreciable, but I think it 's small, and I 'm prepared to take it."

Poor Mr. Touchett's acuteness had passed into perplexity, and his perplexity now passed into admiration. "Well, you *have* gone into it!" he repeated. "But I don't see what good you 're to get of it."

Ralph leaned over his father's pillows and gently smoothed them; he was aware their talk had been unduly prolonged. "I shall get just the good I said a few moments ago I wished to put into Isabel's reach — that of having met the requirements of my imagination. But it 's scandalous, the way I 've taken advantage of you!"

XIX

As Mrs. Touchett had foretold, Isabel and Madame Merle were thrown much together during the illness of their host, so that if they had not become intimate it would have been almost a breach of good manners. Their manners were of the best, but in addition to this they happened to please each other. It is perhaps too much to say that they swore an eternal friendship, but tacitly at least they called the future to witness. Isabel did so with a perfectly good conscience, though she would have hesitated to admit she was intimate with her new friend in the high sense she privately attached to this term. She often wondered indeed if she ever had been, or ever could be, intimate with any one. She had an ideal of friendship as well as of several other sentiments, which it failed to seem to her in this case — it had not seemed to her in other cases — that the actual completely expressed. But she often reminded herself that there were essential reasons why one's ideal could never become concrete. It was a thing to believe in, not to see — a matter of faith, not of experience. Experience, however, might supply us with very creditable imitations of it, and the part of wisdom was to make the best of these. Certainly, on the whole, Isabel had never encountered a more agreeable and interesting figure than Madame Merle; she had never met a person having less of that fault which is the principal obstacle to friendship—the air of reproducing the more tiresome, the stale, the too-familiar parts of one's own character. The gates of the girl's confidence were opened wider than they had ever been; she said things to this amiable auditress that she had not yet said to any one. Sometimes she took alarm at her candour: it was as if she had given to a comparative stranger the key to her cabinet of jewels. These spiritual gems were the only ones of any magnitude that Isabel possessed, but there was all the greater reason for their being carefully guarded. Afterwards, however, she always remembered that one should never regret a generous error and that if Madame Merle had not the merits she attributed to her, so much the worse for Madame Merle. There was no doubt she had great merits — she was charming, sympathetic, intelligent, cultivated. More than this (for it had not been Isabel's ill-fortune to go through life without meeting in her own sex several persons of whom no less could fairly be said), she was rare, superior and preëminent. There are many amiable people in the world, and Madame Merle was far from being vulgarly good-natured and restlessly witty. She knew how to think — an accomplishment rare in women; and she had thought to very good purpose. Of course, too, she knew how to feel; Isabel could n't have spent a week with her without being sure of that. This was indeed Madame Merle's great talent, her most perfect gift. Life had told upon her; she had felt it strongly, and it was part of the satisfaction to be taken in her society that when the girl talked of what she was pleased to call serious matters this lady understood her so easily and quickly. Emotion, it is true, had become with her rather historic; she made no secret of the fact that the fount of passion, thanks to having been rather violently tapped at one period, did n't flow quite so freely as of yore. She proposed moreover, as well as expected, to cease feeling; she freely admitted that of old she had been a little mad, and now she pretended to be perfectly sane.

"I judge more than I used to," she said to Isabel, "but it seems to me one has earned the right. One can't judge till one 's forty; before that we 're too eager, too hard, too cruel, and in addition much too ignorant. I 'm sorry for you; it will be a long time before you 're forty. But every gain 's a loss of some kind; I often think that after forty one *can't* really feel. The freshness, the quickness have certainly gone. You 'll keep them longer than most people; it will be a great satisfaction to me to see you some years hence. I want to see what life makes of you. One thing 's certain — it can't spoil you. It may pull you about horribly, but I defy it to break you up."

Isabel received this assurance as a young soldier, still panting from a slight skirmish in which he has come off with honour, might receive a pat on the shoulder from his colonel. Like such a recognition of merit it seemed to come with authority. How could the lightest word do less on the part of a person who was prepared to say, of almost everything Isabel told her, "Oh, I 've been in that, my dear; it passes, like everything else." On many of her interlocutors Madame Merle might have produced an irritating effect; it was disconcertingly difficult to surprise her. But Isabel, though by no means incapable of desiring to be effective, had not at present this impulse. She was too sincere, too interested in her judicious companion. And then moreover Madame Merle never said such things in the tone of triumph or of boastfulness; they dropped from her like cold confessions.

A period of bad weather had settled upon Gardencourt; the days grew shorter and there was an end to the pretty tea-parties on the lawn. But our young woman had long indoor conversations with her fellow visitor, and in spite of the rain the two ladies often sallied forth for a walk, equipped with the defensive apparatus which the English climate and the English genius have between them brought to such perfection. Madame Merle liked almost everything, including the English rain. "There's always a little of it and never too much at once," she said; "and it never wets you and it always smells good." She declared that in England the pleasures of smell were great — that in this inimitable island there was a certain mixture of fog and beer and soot which, however odd it might sound, was the national aroma, and was most agreeable to the nostril; and she used to lift the sleeve of her British overcoat and bury her nose in it, inhaling the clear, fine scent of the wool. Poor Ralph Touchett, as soon as the autumn had begun to define itself, became almost a prisoner; in bad weather he was unable to step out of the house, and he used sometimes to stand at one of the windows with his hands in his pockets and, from a countenance half-rueful, half-critical, watch Isabel and Madame Merle as they walked down the avenue under a pair of umbrellas. The roads about Gardencourt were so firm, even in the worst weather, that the two ladies always came back with a healthy glow in their cheeks, looking at the soles of their neat, stout boots and declaring that their walk had done them inexpressible good. Before luncheon, always, Madame Merle was engaged; Isabel admired and envied her rigid possession of her morning. Our heroine had always passed for a person of resources and had taken a certain pride in being one; but she wandered, as by the wrong side of the wall of a private garden, round the enclosed talents, accomplishments, aptitudes of Madame Merle. She found herself desiring to emulate them, and in twenty such ways this lady presented herself as a model. "I should like awfully to be *so!*" Isabel secretly exclaimed, more than once, as one after another of her friend's fine aspects caught the light, and before long she knew that she had learned a lesson from a high authority. It took no great time indeed for her to feel herself, as the phrase is, under an influence. "What's the harm," she wondered, "so long as it's a good one? The more one's under a good influence the better. The only thing is to see our steps as we take them — to understand them as we go. That, no doubt, I shall always do. I need n't be afraid of becoming too pliable; is n't it my fault that I'm not pliable enough?" It is said that imitation is the sincerest flattery; and if Isabel was sometimes moved to gape at her friend aspiringly and despairingly it was not so much because she desired herself to shine as because she wished to hold up the lamp for Madame Merle. She liked her extremely, but was even more dazzled than attracted. She sometimes asked herself what Henrietta Stackpole would say to her thinking so much of this perverted product of their common soil, and had a conviction that it would be severely judged. Henrietta would not at all subscribe to Madame Merle; for reasons she could not have defined this truth came home to the girl. On the other hand she was equally sure that, should the occasion offer, her new friend would strike off some happy view of her old: Madame Merle was too humorous, too observant, not to do justice to Henrietta, and on becoming acquainted with her would probably give the measure of a tact which Miss Stackpole could n't hope to emulate. She appeared to have in her experience a touchstone for everything, and somewhere in the capacious pocket of her genial memory she would find the key to Henrietta's value. "That 's the great thing," Isabel solemnly pondered; "that 's the supreme good fortune: to be in a better position for appreciating people than they are for appreciating you." And she added that such, when one considered it, was simply the essence of the aristocratic situation. In this light, if in none other, one should aim at the aristocratic situation.

I may not count over all the links in the chain which led Isabel to think of Madame Merle's situation as aristocratic — a view of it never expressed in any reference made to it by that lady herself. She had known great things and great people, but she had never played a great part. She was one of the small ones of the earth; she had not been born to honours; she knew the world too well to nourish fatuous illusions on the article of her own place in it. She had encountered many of the fortunate few and was perfectly aware of those points at which their fortune differed from hers. But if by her informed measure she was no figure for a high scene, she had yet to Isabel's imagination a sort of greatness. To be so cultivated and civilised, so wise and so easy, and still make so light of it — that was really to be a great lady, especially when one so carried and presented one's self. It was as if somehow she had all society under contribution, and all the arts and graces it practised — or was the effect rather that of charming uses found *for* her, even from a distance, subtle service rendered by her to a clamorous world wherever she might be? After breakfast she wrote a succession of letters, as those arriving for her appeared innumerable: her correspondence was a source of surprise to Isabel when they sometimes walked together to the village post-office to deposit Madame Merle's offering to the mail. She knew more people, as she told Isabel, than she knew what to do with, and something was always turning up to be written about. Of painting she was devotedly fond, and made no more of brushing in a sketch than of pulling off her gloves. At Gardencourt she was perpetually taking advantage of an hour's sunshine to go out with a camp-stool and a box of water-colours. That she was a brave musician we have already perceived, and it was evidence of the fact that when she seated herself at the piano, as she always did in the evening, her listeners resigned themselves without a murmur to losing the grace of her talk. Isabel, since she had known her, felt ashamed of her own facility, which she now looked upon as basely inferior; and indeed, though she had been thought rather a prodigy at home, the loss to society when, in taking her place upon the music-stool, she turned her back to the room, was usually deemed greater than the gain. When Madame Merle was neither writing, nor painting, nor touching the piano, she was usually employed upon wonderful tasks of rich embroidery, cushions, curtains, decorations for the chimney-piece; an art in which her bold, free invention was as noted as the agility of her needle. She was never idle, for when engaged in none of the ways I have mentioned she was either reading (she appeared to Isabel to read "everything important"), or walking out, or playing patience with the cards, or talking with her fellow inmates. And with all this she had always the social quality, was never rudely absent and yet never too seated. She laid down her pastimes as easily as she took them up; she worked and talked at the same time, and appeared to impute scant worth to anything she did. She gave away her sketches and tapestries; she rose from the piano or remained there, according to the convenience of her auditors, which she always unerringly divined. She was in short the most comfortable, profitable, amenable person to live with. If for Isabel she had a fault it was that she was not natural; by which the girl meant, not that she was either affected or pretentious, since from these vulgar vices no woman could have been more exempt, but that her nature had been too much overlaid by custom and her angles too much rubbed away. She had become too flexible, too useful, was too ripe and too final. She was in a word too perfectly the social animal that man and woman are supposed to have been intended to be; and she had rid herself of every remnant of that tonic wildness which we may assume to have belonged even to the most amiable persons in the ages before country-house life was the fashion. Isabel found it difficult to think of her in any detachment or privacy, she existed only in her relations, direct or indirect, with her fellow mortals. One might wonder what commerce she could possibly hold with her own spirit. One always ended, however, by feeling that a charming surface does n't necessarily prove one superficial; this was an illusion in which, in one's youth, one had but just escaped being nourished. Madame Merle was not superficial — not she. She was deep, and her nature spoke none the less in her behaviour because it spoke a conventional tongue. "What's language at all but a convention?" said Isabel. "She has the good taste not to pretend, like some people I've met, to express herself by original signs."

"I'm afraid you've suffered much," she once found occasion to say to her friend in response to some allusion that had appeared to reach far.

"What makes you think that?" Madame Merle asked with the amused smile of a person seated at a game of guesses. "I hope I have n't too much the droop of the misunderstood."

"No; but you sometimes say things that I think people who have always been happy would n't have found out."

"I have n't always been happy," said Madame Merle, smiling still, but with a mock gravity, as if she were telling a child a secret. "Such a wonderful thing!"

But Isabel rose to the irony. "A great many people give me the impression of never having for a moment felt anything."

"It's very true; there are many more iron pots certainly than porcelain. But you may depend on it that every one bears some mark; even the hardest iron pots have a little bruise, a little hole somewhere. I flatter myself that I'm rather stout, but if I must tell you the truth I've been shockingly chipped and cracked. I do very well for service yet, because I've been cleverly mended; and I try to remain in the cupboard — the quiet, dusky cupboard where there's an odour of stale spices — as much as I can. But when I've to come out and into a strong light — then, my dear, I'm a horror!"

I know not whether it was on this occasion or on some other that when the conversation had taken the turn I have just indicated she said to Isabel that she would some day a tale unfold. Isabel assured her she should delight to listen to one, and reminded her more than once of this engagement. Madame Merle, however, begged repeatedly for a respite, and at last frankly told her young companion that they must wait till they knew each other better. This would be sure to happen; a long friendship so visibly lay before them. Isabel assented, but at the same time enquired if she might n't be trusted — if she appeared capable of a betrayal of confidence.

"It's not that I'm afraid of your repeating what I say," her fellow visitor answered; "I'm afraid, on the contrary, of your taking it too much to yourself. You'd judge me too harshly; you're of the cruel age." She preferred for the present to talk to Isabel of Isabel, and exhibited the greatest interest in our heroine's history, sentiments, opinions, prospects. She made her chatter and listened to her chatter with infinite good nature. This flattered and quickened the girl, who was struck with all the distinguished people her friend had known and with her having lived, as Mrs. Touchett said, in the best company in Europe. Isabel thought the better of herself for enjoying the favour of a person who had so large a field of comparison; and it was perhaps partly to gratify the sense of profiting by comparison that she often appealed to these stores of reminiscence. Madame Merle had been a dweller in many lands and had social ties in a dozen different countries. "I don't pretend to be educated," she would say, "but I think I know my Europe;" and she spoke one day of going to Sweden to stay with an old friend, and another of proceeding to Malta to follow up a new acquaintance. With England, where she had often dwelt, she was thoroughly familiar, and for Isabel's benefit threw a great deal of light upon the customs of the country and the character of the people, who "after all," as she was fond of saying, were the most convenient in the world to live with.

"You must n't think it strange her remaining here at such a time as this, when Mr. Touchett 's passing away," that gentleman's wife remarked to her niece.

"She is incapable of a mistake; she's the most tactful woman I know. It's a favour to me that she stays; she's putting off a lot of visits at great houses," said Mrs. Touchett, who never forgot that when she herself was in England her social value sank two or three degrees in the scale. "She has her pick of places; she's not in want of a shelter. But I've asked her to put in this time because I wish you to know her. I think it will be a good thing for you. Serena Merle has n't a fault."

"If I did n't already like her very much that description might alarm me," Isabel returned.

"She's never the least little bit 'off.' I've brought you out here and I wish to do the best for you. Your sister Lily told me she hoped I would give you plenty of opportunities. I give you one in putting you in relation with Madame Merle. She's one of the most brilliant women in Europe."

"I like her better than I like your description of her," Isabel persisted in saying.

"Do you flatter yourself that you'll ever feel her open to criticism? I hope you'll let me know when you do."

"That will be cruel — to you," said Isabel.

"You need n't mind me. You won't discover a fault in her."

"Perhaps not. But I dare say I shan't miss it."

"She knows absolutely everything on earth there is to know," said Mrs. Touchett.

Isabel after this observed to their companion that she hoped she knew Mrs. Touchett considered she had n't a speck on her perfection. On which "I'm obliged to you," Madame Merle replied, "but I'm afraid your aunt imagines, or at least alludes to, no aberrations that the clock-face does n't register."

"So that you mean you've a wild side that's unknown to her?"

"Ah no, I fear my darkest sides are my tamest. I mean that having no faults, for your aunt, means that one's never late for dinner — that is for *her* dinner. I was not late, by the way, the other day, when you came back from London; the clock was just at eight when I came into the drawing-room: it was the rest of you that were before the time. It means that one answers a letter the day one gets it and that when one comes to stay with her one does n't bring too much luggage and is careful not to be taken ill. For Mrs. Touchett those things constitute virtue; it's a blessing to be able to reduce it to its elements."

Madame Merle's own conversation, it will be perceived, was enriched with bold, free touches of criticism, which, even when they had a restrictive effect, never struck Isabel as ill-natured. It could n't occur to the girl for instance that Mrs. Touchett's accomplished guest was abusing her; and this for very good reasons. In the first place Isabel rose eagerly to the sense of her shades; in the second Madame Merle implied that there was a great deal more to say; and it was clear in the third that for a person to speak to one without ceremony of one's near relations was an agreeable sign of that person's intimacy with one's self. These signs of deep communion multiplied as the days elapsed, and there was none of which Isabel was more sensible than of her companion's preference for making Miss Archer herself a topic. Though she referred frequently to the incidents of her own career she never lingered upon them; she was as little of a gross egotist as she was of a flat gossip.

"I'm old and stale and faded," she said more than once; "I'm of no more interest than last week's newspaper. You're young and fresh and of to-day; you've the great thing — you've actuality. I once had it — we all have it for an hour. You, however, will have it for longer. Let us talk about you then; you can say nothing I shall not care to hear. It's a sign that I'm growing old — that I like to talk with younger people. I think it's a very pretty compensation. If we can't have youth within us we can have it outside, and I really think we see it and feel it better that way. Of course we must be in sympathy with it — that I shall always be. I don't know that I shall ever be ill-natured with old people — I hope not; there are certainly some old people I adore. But I shall never be anything but abject with the young; they touch me and appeal to me too much. I give you *carte blanche* then; you can even be impertinent if you like; I shall let it pass and horribly spoil you. I speak as if I were a hundred years old, you say? Well, I am, if you please; I was born before the French Revolution. Ah, my dear, *je viens de loin;* I belong to the old, old world. But it's not of that I want to talk; I want to talk about the new. You must tell me more about America; you never tell me enough. Here I've been since I was brought here as a helpless child, and it's ridiculous, or rather it's scandalous, how little I know about that splendid, dreadful, funny country — surely the greatest and drollest of them all. There are a great many of us like that in these parts, and I must say I think we're a wretched set of people. You should live in your own land; whatever it may be you have your natural place there. If we're not good Americans we're certainly poor Europeans; we've no natural place here. We're mere parasites, crawling over the surface; we have n't our feet in the soil. At least one can know it and not have illusions. A woman perhaps can get on; a woman, it seems to me, has no natural place anywhere; wherever she finds herself she has to remain on the surface and, more or less, to crawl. You protest, my dear? you're horrified? you declare you'll never crawl? It's very true that I don't see you crawling; you stand more upright than a good many poor creatures. Very good; on the whole, I don't think you'll crawl. But the men, the Americans; *je vous demande un peu*, what do they make of it over here? I don't envy them trying to arrange themselves. Look at poor Ralph Touchett: what sort of a figure do you call that? Fortunately he has a consumption; I say fortunately, because it gives him something to do. His consumption's his *carrière;* it's a kind of position. You can say: 'Oh, Mr. Touchett, he takes care of his lungs, he knows a great deal about climates.' But without that who would he be, what would he represent? 'Mr. Ralph Touchett: an American who lives in Europe.' That signifies absolutely nothing — it's impossible anything should signify less. 'He's very cultivated,' they say: 'he has a very pretty collection of old snuff-boxes.' The collection is all that's wanted to make it pitiful. I'm tired of the sound of the word; I think it's grotesque. With the poor old father it's different; he has his identity, and it's rather a massive one. He represents a great financial house, and that, in our day, is as good as anything else. For an American, at any rate, that will do very well. But I persist in thinking your cousin very lucky to have a chronic malady so long as he does n't die of it. It's much better than the snuff-boxes. If he were n't ill, you say, he'd do something? — he'd take his father's place in the house. My poor child, I doubt it; I don't think he's at all fond of the house. However, you know him better than I, though I used to know him rather well, and he may have the benefit of the doubt. The worst case, I think, is a friend of mine, a countryman of ours, who lives in Italy (where he also was brought before he knew better), and who is one of the most delightful men I know. Some day you must know him. I'll bring you together and then you'll see what I mean. He's Gilbert Osmond — he lives in Italy; that's all one can say about him or make of him. He's exceedingly clever, a man made to be distinguished; but, as I tell you, you exhaust the description when you say he's Mr. Osmond who lives *tout bêtement* in Italy. No career, no name, no position, no fortune, no past, no future, no anything. Oh yes, he paints, if you please — paints in water-colours; like me, only better than I. His painting's pretty bad; on the whole I'm rather glad of that. Fortunately he's very indolent, so indolent that it amounts to a sort of position. He can say, 'Oh, I do nothing; I'm too deadly lazy. You can do nothing to-day unless you get up at five o'clock in the morning.' In that way he becomes a sort of exception; you feel he might do something if he'd only rise early. He never speaks of his painting — to people at large; he's too clever for that. But he has a little girl — a dear little girl; he does speak of *her.* He's devoted to her, and if it were a career to be an excellent father he'd be very distinguished. But I'm afraid that's no better than the snuff-boxes; perhaps not even so good. Tell me what they do in America," pursued Madame Merle, who, it must be observed parenthetically, did not deliver herself all at once of these reflexions, which are presented in a cluster for the convenience of the reader. She talked of Florence, where Mr. Osmond lived and where Mrs. Touchett occupied a mediæval palace; she talked of Rome, where she herself had a little *pied-à-terre* with some rather good old damask. She talked of places, of people and even, as the phrase is, of "subjects"; and from time to time she talked of their kind old host and of the prospect of his recovery. From the first she had thought this prospect small, and Isabel had been struck with the positive, discriminating, competent way in which she took the measure of his remainder of life. One evening she announced definitely that he would n't live.

"Sir Matthew Hope told me so as plainly as was proper," she said; "standing there, near the fire, before dinner. He makes himself very agreeable, the great doctor. I don't mean his saying that has anything to do with it. But he says such things with great tact. I had told him I felt ill at my ease, staying here at such a time; it seemed to me so indiscreet — it was n't as if I could nurse. 'You must remain, you must remain,' he answered; 'your office will come later.' Was n't that a very delicate way of saying both that poor Mr. Touchett would go and that I might be of some use as a consoler? In fact, however, I shall not be of the slightest use. Your aunt will console herself; she, and she alone, knows just how much consolation she'll require. It would be a very delicate matter for another person to undertake to administer the dose. With your cousin it will be different; he'll miss his father immensely. But I should never presume to condole with Mr. Ralph; we're not on those terms." Madame Merle had alluded more than once to some undefined incongruity in her relations with Ralph Touchett; so Isabel took this occasion of asking her if they were not good friends.

"Perfectly, but he does n't like me."

"What have you done to him?"

"Nothing whatever. But one has no need of a reason for that."

"For not liking you? I think one has need of a very good reason."

"You're very kind. Be sure you have one ready for the day you begin."

"Begin to dislike you? I shall never begin."

"I hope not; because if you do you'll never end. That's the way with your cousin; he does n't get over it. It's an antipathy of nature — if I can call it that when it's all on his side. I've nothing whatever against him and don't bear him the least little grudge for not doing me justice. Justice is all I want. However, one feels that he's a gentleman and would never say anything underhand about one. *Cartes sur table*," Madame Merle subjoined in a moment, "I'm not afraid of him."

"I hope not indeed," said Isabel, who added something about his being the kindest creature living. She remembered, however, that on her first asking him about Madame Merle he had answered her in a manner which this lady might have thought injurious without being explicit. There was something between them, Isabel said to herself, but she said nothing more than this. If it were something of importance it should inspire respect; if it were not it was not worth her curiosity. With all her love of knowledge she had a natural shrinking from raising curtains and looking into unlighted corners. The love of knowledge coexisted in her mind with the finest capacity for ignorance.

But Madame Merle sometimes said things that startled her, made her raise her clear eyebrows at the time and think of the words afterwards. "I'd give a great deal to be your age again," she broke out once with a bitterness which, though diluted in her customary amplitude of ease, was imperfectly disguised by it. "If I could only begin again — if I could have my life before me!"

"Your life's before you yet," Isabel answered gently, for she was vaguely awe-struck.

"No; the best part's gone, and gone for nothing."

"Surely not for nothing," said Isabel.

"Why not — what have I got? Neither husband,

nor child, nor fortune, nor position, nor the traces of a beauty that I never had."

"You have many friends, dear lady."

"I'm not so sure!" cried Madame Merle.

"Ah, you're wrong. You have memories, graces, talents —"

But Madame Merle interrupted her. "What have my talents brought me? Nothing but the need of using them still, to get through the hours, the years, to cheat myself with some pretence of movement, of unconsciousness. As for my graces and memories the less said about them the better. You'll be my friend till you find a better use for your friendship."

"It will be for you to see that I don't then," said Isabel.

"Yes; I would make an effort to keep you." And her companion looked at her gravely. "When I say I should like to be your age I mean with your qualities — frank, generous, sincere like you. In that case I should have made something better of my life."

"What should you have liked to do that you've not done?"

Madame Merle took a sheet of music — she was seated at the piano and had abruptly wheeled about on the stool when she first spoke — and mechanically turned the leaves. "I'm very ambitious!" she at last replied.

"And your ambitions have not been satisfied? They must have been great."

"They *were* great. I should make myself ridiculous by talking of them."

Isabel wondered what they could have been —

whether Madame Merle had aspired to wear a crown. "I don't know what your idea of success may be, but you seem to me to have been successful. To me indeed you're a vivid image of success."

Madame Merle tossed away the music with a smile. "What's *your* idea of success?"

"You evidently think it must be a very tame one. It's to see some dream of one's youth come true."

"Ah," Madame Merle exclaimed, "that I've never seen! But my dreams were so great—so preposterous. Heaven forgive me, I'm dreaming now!" And she turned back to the piano and began grandly to play. On the morrow she said to Isabel that her definition of success had been very pretty, yet frightfully sad. Measured in that way, who had ever succeeded? The dreams of one's youth, why they were enchanting, they were divine! Who had ever seen such things come to pass?

"I myself—a few of them," Isabel ventured to answer.

"Already? They must have been dreams of yesterday."

"I began to dream very young," Isabel smiled.

"Ah, if you mean the aspirations of your childhood—that of having a pink sash and a doll that could close her eyes."

"No, I don't mean that."

"Or a young man with a fine moustache going down on his knees to you."

"No, nor that either," Isabel declared with still more emphasis.

Madame Merle appeared to note this eagerness.

"I suspect that's what you do mean. We've all had the young man with the moustache. He's the inevitable young man; he does n't count."

Isabel was silent a little but then spoke with extreme and characteristic inconsequence. "Why should n't he count? There are young men and young men."

"And yours was a paragon — is that what you mean?" asked her friend with a laugh. "If you've had the identical young man you dreamed of, then that was success, and I congratulate you with all my heart. Only in that case why did n't you fly with him to his castle in the Apennines?"

"He has no castle in the Apennines."

"What has he? An ugly brick house in Fortieth Street? Don't tell me that; I refuse to recognise that as an ideal."

"I don't care anything about his house," said Isabel.

"That's very crude of you. When you've lived as long as I you'll see that every human being has his shell and that you must take the shell into account. By the shell I mean the whole envelope of circumstances. There's no such thing as an isolated man or woman; we're each of us made up of some cluster of appurtenances. What shall we call our 'self'? Where does it begin? where does it end? It overflows into everything that belongs to us — and then it flows back again. I know a large part of myself is in the clothes I choose to wear. I've a great respect for *things!* One's self — for other people — is one's expression of one's self; and one's house, one's furniture, one's garments, the books one reads, the company one keeps — these things are all expressive."

This was very metaphysical; not more so, however, than several observations Madame Merle had already made. Isabel was fond of metaphysics, but was unable to accompany her friend into this bold analysis of the human personality. "I don't agree with you. I think just the other way. I don't know whether I succeed in expressing myself, but I know that nothing else expresses me. Nothing that belongs to me is any measure of me; everything's on the contrary a limit, a barrier, and a perfectly arbitrary one. Certainly the clothes which, as you say, I choose to wear, don't express me; and heaven forbid they should!"

"You dress very well," Madame Merle lightly interposed.

"Possibly; but I don't care to be judged by that. My clothes may express the dressmaker, but they don't express me. To begin with it's not my own choice that I wear them; they're imposed upon me by society."

"Should you prefer to go without them?" Madame Merle enquired in a tone which virtually terminated the discussion.

I am bound to confess, though it may cast some discredit on the sketch I have given of the youthful loyalty practised by our heroine toward this accomplished woman, that Isabel had said nothing whatever to her about Lord Warburton and had been equally reticent on the subject of Caspar Goodwood. She had not, however, concealed the fact that she had

had opportunities of marrying and had even let her friend know of how advantageous a kind they had been. Lord Warburton had left Lockleigh and was gone to Scotland, taking his sisters with him; and though he had written to Ralph more than once to ask about Mr. Touchett's health the girl was not liable to the embarrassment of such enquiries as, had he still been in the neighbourhood, he would probably have felt bound to make in person. He had excellent ways, but she felt sure that if he had come to Gardencourt he would have seen Madame Merle, and that if he had seen her he would have liked her and betrayed to her that he was in love with her young friend. It so happened that during this lady's previous visits to Gardencourt — each of them much shorter than the present — he had either not been at Lockleigh or had not called at Mr. Touchett's. Therefore, though she knew him by name as the great man of that county, she had no cause to suspect him as a suitor of Mrs. Touchett's freshly-imported niece.

"You 've plenty of time," she had said to Isabel in return for the mutilated confidences which our young woman made her and which did n't pretend to be perfect, though we have seen that at moments the girl had compunctions at having said so much. "I 'm glad you 've done nothing yet — that you have it still to do. It 's a very good thing for a girl to have refused a few good offers — so long of course as they are not the best she 's likely to have. Pardon me if my tone seems horribly corrupt; one must take the worldly view sometimes. Only don't keep on refusing for the sake of refusing. It 's a pleasant exercise of power; but accepting 's after all an exercise of power as well. There 's always the danger of refusing once too often. It was not the one I fell into — I did n't refuse often enough. You 're an exquisite creature, and I should like to see you married to a prime minister. But speaking strictly, you know, you 're not what is technically called a *parti*. You 're extremely good-looking and extremely clever; in yourself you 're quite exceptional. You appear to have the vaguest ideas about your earthly possessions; but from what I can make out you 're not embarrassed with an income. I wish you had a little money."

"I wish I had!" said Isabel, simply, apparently forgetting for the moment that her poverty had been a venial fault for two gallant gentlemen.

In spite of Sir Matthew Hope's benevolent recommendation Madame Merle did not remain to the end, as the issue of poor Mr. Touchett's malady had now come frankly to be designated. She was under pledges to other people which had at last to be redeemed, and she left Gardencourt with the understanding that she should in any event see Mrs. Touchett there again, or else in town, before quitting England. Her parting with Isabel was even more like the beginning of a friendship than their meeting had been. "I 'm going to six places in succession, but I shall see no one I like so well as you. They 'll all be old friends, however; one does n't make new friends at my age. I 've made a great exception for you. You must remember that and must think as well of me as possible. You must reward me by believing in me."

By way of answer Isabel kissed her, and, though

some women kiss with facility, there are kisses and kisses, and this embrace was satisfactory to Madame Merle. Our young lady, after this, was much alone; she saw her aunt and cousin only at meals, and discovered that of the hours during which Mrs. Touchett was invisible only a minor portion was now devoted to nursing her husband. She spent the rest in her own apartments, to which access was not allowed even to her niece, apparently occupied there with mysterious and inscrutable exercises. At table she was grave and silent; but her solemnity was not an attitude — Isabel could see it was a conviction. She wondered if her aunt repented of having taken her own way so much; but there was no visible evidence of this — no tears, no sighs, no exaggeration of a zeal always to its own sense adequate. Mrs. Touchett seemed simply to feel the need of thinking things over and summing them up; she had a little moral account-book — with columns unerringly ruled and a sharp steel clasp — which she kept with exemplary neatness. Uttered reflection had with her ever, at any rate, a practical ring. "If I had foreseen this I'd not have proposed your coming abroad now," she said to Isabel after Madame Merle had left the house. "I'd have waited and sent for you next year."

"So that perhaps I should never have known my uncle? It's a great happiness to me to have come now."

"That's very well. But it was not that you might know your uncle that I brought you to Europe" A perfectly veracious speech; but, as Isabel thought, not as perfectly timed. She had leisure to think of this and other matters. She took a solitary walk every day and spent vague hours in turning over books in the library. Among the subjects that engaged her attention were the adventures of her friend Miss Stackpole, with whom she was in regular correspondence. Isabel liked her friend's private epistolary style better than her public; that is she felt her public letters would have been excellent if they had not been printed. Henrietta's career, however, was not so successful as might have been wished even in the interest of her private felicity; that view of the inner life of Great Britain which she was so eager to take appeared to dance before her like an *ignis fatuus*. The invitation from Lady Pensil, for mysterious reasons, had never arrived; and poor Mr. Bantling himself, with all his friendly ingenuity, had been unable to explain so grave a dereliction on the part of a missive that had obviously been sent. He had evidently taken Henrietta's affairs much to heart, and believed that he owed her a set-off to this illusory visit to Bedfordshire. "He says he should think I would go to the Continent," Henrietta wrote; "and as he thinks of going there himself I suppose his advice is sincere. He wants to know why I don't take a view of French life; and it 's a fact that I want very much to see the new Republic. Mr. Bantling does n't care much about the Republic, but he thinks of going over to Paris anyway. I must say he 's quite as attentive as I could wish, and at least I shall have seen one polite Englishman. I keep telling Mr. Bantling that he ought to have been an American, and you should see how that pleases him. Whenever I say so he always breaks out with the same exclamation — 'Ah, but really, come now!'" A few days later she wrote that she had decided to go to Paris at the end of the week and that Mr. Bantling had promised to see her off — perhaps even would go as far as Dover with her. She would wait in Paris till Isabel should arrive, Henrietta added; speaking quite as if Isabel were to start on her continental journey alone and making no allusion to Mrs. Touchett. Bearing in mind his interest in their late companion, our heroine communicated several passages from this correspondence to Ralph, who followed with an emotion akin to suspense the career of the representative of the *Interviewer*.

"It seems to me she 's doing very well," he said, "going over to Paris with an ex-Lancer! If she wants something to write about she has only to describe that episode."

"It 's not conventional, certainly," Isabel answered; "but if you mean that — as far as Henrietta is concerned — it 's not perfectly innocent, you 're very much mistaken. You 'll never understand Henrietta."

"Pardon me, I understand her perfectly. I did n't at all at first, but now I 've the point of view. I 'm afraid, however, that Bantling has n't; he may have some surprises. Oh, I understand Henrietta as well as if I had made her!"

Isabel was by no means sure of this, but she abstained from expressing further doubt, for she was disposed in these days to extend a great charity to her cousin. One afternoon less than a week after Madame Merle's departure she was seated in the library with a volume to which her attention was not fastened.

She had placed herself in a deep window-bench, from which she looked out into the dull, damp park; and as the library stood at right angles to the entrance-front of the house she could see the doctor's brougham, which had been waiting for the last two hours before the door. She was struck with his remaining so long, but at last she saw him appear in the portico, stand a moment slowly drawing on his gloves and looking at the knees of his horse, and then get into the vehicle and roll away. Isabel kept her place for half an hour; there was a great stillness in the house. It was so great that when she at last heard a soft, slow step on the deep carpet of the room she was almost startled by the sound. She turned quickly away from the window and saw Ralph Touchett standing there with his hands still in his pockets, but with a face absolutely void of its usual latent smile. She got up and her movement and glance were a question.

"It's all over," said Ralph.

"Do you mean that my uncle ——?" And Isabel stopped.

"My dear father died an hour ago."

"Ah, my poor Ralph!" she gently wailed, putting out her two hands to him.

XX

Some fortnight after this Madame Merle drove up in a hansom cab to the house in Winchester Square. As she descended from her vehicle she observed, suspended between the dining-room windows, a large, neat, wooden tablet, on whose fresh black ground were inscribed in white paint the words — "This noble freehold mansion to be sold"; with the name of the agent to whom application should be made. "They certainly lose no time," said the visitor as, after sounding the big brass knocker, she waited to be admitted; "it 's a practical country!" And within the house, as she ascended to the drawing-room, she perceived numerous signs of abdication; pictures removed from the walls and placed upon sofas, windows undraped and floors laid bare. Mrs. Touchett presently received her and intimated in a few words that condolences might be taken for granted.

"I know what you 're going to say — he was a very good man. But I know it better than any one, because I gave him more chance to show it. In that I think I was a good wife." Mrs. Touchett added that at the end her husband apparently recognised this fact. "He has treated me most liberally," she said; "I won't say more liberally than I expected, because I did n't expect. You know that as a general thing I don't expect. But he chose, I presume, to recognise the fact that though I lived much abroad and mingled — you may say freely — in foreign life, I never exhibited the smallest preference for any one else."

"For any one but yourself," Madame Merle mentally observed; but the reflexion was perfectly inaudible.

"I never sacrificed my husband to another," Mrs. Touchett continued with her stout curtness.

"Oh no," thought Madame Merle; "you never did anything for another!"

There was a certain cynicism in these mute comments which demands an explanation; the more so as they are not in accord either with the view — somewhat superficial perhaps — that we have hitherto enjoyed of Madame Merle's character or with the literal facts of Mrs. Touchett's history; the more so, too, as Madame Merle had a well-founded conviction that her friend's last remark was not in the least to be construed as a side-thrust at herself. The truth is that the moment she had crossed the threshold she received an impression that Mr. Touchett's death had had subtle consequences and that these consequences had been profitable to a little circle of persons among whom she was not numbered. Of course it was an event which would naturally have consequences; her imagination had more than once rested upon this fact during her stay at Gardencourt. But it had been one thing to foresee such a matter mentally and another to stand among its massive records. The idea of a distribution of property — she would almost have said of spoils — just now pressed upon her senses and irritated her with a sense of exclusion. I am far from wishing to picture her as one of the hungry mouths or envious hearts of the general herd, but we have already learned of her having desires that had never been satisfied. If she had been questioned, she would of course have admitted — with a fine proud smile — that she had not the faintest claim to a share in Mr. Touchett's relics. "There was never anything in the world between us," she would have said. "There was never that, poor man!" — with a fillip of her thumb and her third finger. I hasten to add, moreover, that if she could n't at the present moment keep from quite perversely yearning she was careful not to betray herself. She had after all as much sympathy for Mrs. Touchett's gains as for her losses.

"He has left me this house," the newly-made widow said; "but of course I shall not live in it; I've a much better one in Florence. The will was opened only three days since, but I've already offered the house for sale. I've also a share in the bank; but I don't yet understand if I'm obliged to leave it there. If not I shall certainly take it out. Ralph, of course, has Gardencourt; but I'm not sure that he'll have means to keep up the place. He's naturally left very well off, but his father has given away an immense deal of money; there are bequests to a string of third cousins in Vermont. Ralph, however, is very fond of Gardencourt and would be quite capable of living there — in summer — with a maid-of-all-work and a gardener's boy. There's one remarkable clause in my husband's will," Mrs. Touchett added. "He has left my niece a fortune."

"A fortune!" Madame Merle softly repeated.

"Isabel steps into something like seventy thousand pounds."

Madame Merle's hands were clasped in her lap; at this she raised them, still clasped, and held them a moment against her bosom while her eyes, a little dilated, fixed themselves on those of her friend. "Ah," she cried, "the clever creature!"

Mrs. Touchett gave her a quick look. "What do you mean by that?"

For an instant Madame Merle's colour rose and she dropped her eyes. "It certainly is clever to achieve such results — without an effort!"

"There assuredly was no effort. Don't call it an achievement."

Madame Merle was seldom guilty of the awkwardness of retracting what she had said; her wisdom was shown rather in maintaining it and placing it in a favourable light. "My dear friend, Isabel would certainly not have had seventy thousand pounds left her if she had not been the most charming girl in the world. Her charm includes great cleverness."

"She never dreamed, I'm sure, of my husband's doing anything for her; and I never dreamed of it either, for he never spoke to me of his intention," Mrs. Touchett said. "She had no claim upon him whatever; it was no great recommendation to him that she was my niece. Whatever she achieved she achieved unconsciously."

"Ah," rejoined Madame Merle, "those are the greatest strokes!"

Mrs. Touchett reserved her opinion. "The girl's

fortunate; I don't deny that. But for the present she 's simply stupefied."

"Do you mean that she does n't know what to do with the money?"

"That, I think, she has hardly considered. She does n't know what to think about the matter at all. It has been as if a big gun were suddenly fired off behind her; she 's feeling herself to see if she be hurt. It 's but three days since she received a visit from the principal executor, who came in person, very gallantly, to notify her. He told me afterwards that when he had made his little speech she suddenly burst into tears. The money 's to remain in the affairs of the bank, and she 's to draw the interest."

Madame Merle shook her head with a wise and now quite benignant smile. "How very delicious! After she has done that two or three times she 'll get used to it." Then after a silence, "What does your son think of it?" she abruptly asked.

"He left England before the will was read — used up by his fatigue and anxiety and hurrying off to the south. He 's on his way to the Riviera and I 've not yet heard from him. But it 's not likely he 'll ever object to anything done by his father."

"Did n't you say his own share had been cut down?"

"Only at his wish. I know that he urged his father to do something for the people in America. He 's not in the least addicted to looking after number one."

"It depends upon whom he regards as number one!" said Madame Merle. And she remained thoughtful a moment, her eyes bent on the floor.

"Am I not to see your happy niece?" she asked at last as she raised them.

"You may see her; but you'll not be struck with her being happy. She has looked as solemn, these three days, as a Cimabue Madonna!" And Mrs. Touchett rang for a servant.

Isabel came in shortly after the footman had been sent to call her; and Madame Merle thought, as she appeared, that Mrs. Touchett's comparison had its force. The girl was pale and grave — an effect not mitigated by her deeper mourning; but the smile of her brightest moments came into her face as she saw Madame Merle, who went forward, laid her hand on our heroine's shoulder and, after looking at her a moment, kissed her as if she were returning the kiss she had received from her at Gardencourt. This was the only allusion the visitor, in her great good taste, made for the present to her young friend's inheritance.

Mrs. Touchett had no purpose of awaiting in London the sale of her house. After selecting from among its furniture the objects she wished to transport to her other abode, she left the rest of its contents to be disposed of by the auctioneer and took her departure for the Continent. She was of course accompanied on this journey by her niece, who now had plenty of leisure to measure and weigh and otherwise handle the windfall on which Madame Merle had covertly congratulated her. Isabel thought very often of the fact of her accession of means, looking at it in a dozen different lights; but we shall not now attempt to follow her train of thought or to explain exactly why her new consciousness was at first oppressive. This failure to rise to immediate joy was indeed but brief; the girl presently made up her mind that to be rich was a virtue because it was to be able to *do*, and that to do could only be sweet. It was the graceful contrary of the stupid side of weakness — especially the feminine variety. To be weak was, for a delicate young person, rather graceful, but, after all, as Isabel said to herself, there was a larger grace than that. Just now, it is true, there was not much to do — once she had sent off a cheque to Lily and another to poor Edith; but she was thankful for the quiet months which her mourning robes and her aunt's fresh widowhood compelled them to spend together. The acquisition of power made her serious; she scrutinised her power with a kind of tender ferocity, but was not eager to exercise it. She began to do so during a stay of some weeks which she eventually made with her aunt in Paris, though in ways that will inevitably present themselves as trivial. They were the ways most naturally imposed in a city in which the shops are the admiration of the world, and that were prescribed unreservedly by the guidance of Mrs. Touchett, who took a rigidly practical view of the transformation of her niece from a poor girl to a rich one. "Now that you're a young woman of fortune you must know how to play the part — I mean to play it well," she said to Isabel once for all; and she added that the girl's first duty was to have everything handsome. "You don't know how to take care of your things, but you must learn," she went on; this was Isabel's second duty. Isabel submitted, but for the present her imagination was not kindled; she longed for opportunities, but these were not the opportunities she meant.

Mrs. Touchett rarely changed her plans, and, having intended before her husband's death to spend a part of the winter in Paris, saw no reason to deprive herself — still less to deprive her companion — of this advantage. Though they would live in great retirement she might still present her niece, informally, to the little circle of her fellow countrymen dwelling upon the skirts of the Champs Elysées. With many of these amiable colonists Mrs. Touchett was intimate; she shared their expatriation, their convictions, their pastimes, their ennui. Isabel saw them arrive with a good deal of assiduity at her aunt's hotel, and pronounced on them with a trenchancy doubtless to be accounted for by the temporary exaltation of her sense of human duty. She made up her mind that their lives were, though luxurious, inane, and incurred some disfavour by expressing this view on bright Sunday afternoons, when the American absentees were engaged in calling on each other. Though her listeners passed for people kept exemplarily genial by their cooks and dressmakers, two or three of them thought her cleverness, which was generally admitted, inferior to that of the new theatrical pieces. "You all live here this way, but what does it lead to?" she was pleased to ask. "It does n't seem to lead to anything, and I should think you'd get very tired of it."

Mrs. Touchett thought the question worthy of

Henrietta Stackpole. The two ladies had found Henrietta in Paris, and Isabel constantly saw her; so that Mrs. Touchett had some reason for saying to herself that if her niece were not clever enough to originate almost anything, she might be suspected of having borrowed that style of remark from her journalistic friend. The first occasion on which Isabel had spoken was that of a visit paid by the two ladies to Mrs. Luce, an old friend of Mrs. Touchett's and the only person in Paris she now went to see. Mrs. Luce had been living in Paris since the days of Louis Philippe; she used to say jocosely that she was one of the generation of 1830 — a joke of which the point was not always taken. When it failed Mrs. Luce used to explain — "Oh yes, I 'm one of the romantics;" her French had never become quite perfect. She was always at home on Sunday afternoons and surrounded by sympathetic compatriots, usually the same. In fact she was at home at all times, and reproduced with wondrous truth in her well-cushioned little corner of the brilliant city, the domestic tone of her native Baltimore. This reduced Mr. Luce, her worthy husband, a tall, lean, grizzled, well-brushed gentleman who wore a gold eye-glass and carried his hat a little too much on the back of his head, to mere platonic praise of the "distractions" of Paris — they were his great word — since you would never have guessed from what cares he escaped to them. One of them was that he went every day to the American banker's, where he found a post-office that was almost as sociable and colloquial an institution as in an American country town. He passed an hour (in fine weather) in a chair in the Champs Elysées, and he dined uncommonly well at his own table, seated above a waxed floor which it was Mrs. Luce's happiness to believe had a finer polish than any other in the French capital. Occasionally he dined with a friend or two at the Café Anglais, where his talent for ordering a dinner was a source of felicity to his companions and an object of admiration even to the head-waiter of the establishment. These were his only known pastimes, but they had beguiled his hours for upwards of half a century, and they doubtless justified his frequent declaration that there was no place like Paris. In no other place, on these terms, could Mr. Luce flatter himself that he was enjoying life. There was nothing like Paris, but it must be confessed that Mr. Luce thought less highly of this scene of his dissipations than in earlier days. In the list of his resources his political reflections should not be omitted, for they were doubtless the animating principle of many hours that superficially seemed vacant. Like many of his fellow colonists Mr. Luce was a high — or rather a deep — conservative, and gave no countenance to the government lately established in France. He had no faith in its duration and would assure you from year to year that its end was close at hand. "They want to be kept down, sir, to be kept down; nothing but the strong hand — the iron heel — will do for them," he would frequently say of the French people; and his ideal of a fine showy clever rule was that of the superseded Empire. "Paris is much less attractive than in the days of the Emperor; *he* knew how to make a city pleasant," Mr. Luce had often remarked to Mrs. Touchett, who was quite of his own way of thinking and wished to know what one had crossed that odious Atlantic for but to get away from republics.

"Why, madam, sitting in the Champs Elysées, opposite to the Palace of Industry, I've seen the court-carriages from the Tuileries pass up and down as many as seven times a day. I remember one occasion when they went as high as nine. What do you see now? It's no use talking, the style's all gone. Napoleon knew what the French people want, and there'll be a dark cloud over Paris, *our* Paris, till they get the Empire back again."

Among Mrs. Luce's visitors on Sunday afternoons was a young man with whom Isabel had had a good deal of conversation and whom she found full of valuable knowledge. Mr. Edward Rosier — Ned Rosier as he was called — was native to New York and had been brought up in Paris, living there under the eye of his father who, as it happened, had been an early and intimate friend of the late Mr. Archer. Edward Rosier remembered Isabel as a little girl; it had been his father who came to the rescue of the small Archers at the inn at Neufchâtel (he was travelling that way with the boy and had stopped at the hotel by chance), after their *bonne* had gone off with the Russian prince and when Mr. Archer's whereabouts remained for some days a mystery. Isabel remembered perfectly the neat little male child whose hair smelt of a delicious cosmetic and who had a *bonne* all his own, warranted to lose sight of him under no provocation. Isabel took a walk with the pair beside the lake and thought little Edward as pretty as an angel — a comparison by no means conventional in her mind, for she had a very definite conception of a type of features which she supposed to be angelic and which her new friend perfectly illustrated. A small pink face surmounted by a blue velvet bonnet and set off by a stiff embroidered collar had become the countenance of her childish dreams; and she had firmly believed for some time afterwards that the heavenly hosts conversed among themselves in a queer little dialect of French-English, expressing the properest sentiments, as when Edward told her that he was "defended" by his *bonne* to go near the edge of the lake, and that one must always obey to one's *bonne*. Ned Rosier's English had improved; at least it exhibited in a less degree the French variation. His father was dead and his *bonne* dismissed, but the young man still conformed to the spirit of their teaching — he never went to the edge of the lake. There was still something agreeable to the nostrils about him and something not offensive to nobler organs. He was a very gentle and gracious youth, with what are called cultivated tastes — an acquaintance with old china, with good wine, with the bindings of books, with the *Almanach de Gotha*, with the best shops, the best hotels, the hours of railway-trains. He could order a dinner almost as well as Mr. Luce, and it was probable that as his experience accumulated he would be a worthy successor to that gentleman, whose rather grim politics he also advocated in a soft and innocent voice. He had some charming rooms in Paris, decorated with old Spanish altar-lace, the envy of his female friends, who declared that his chimney-piece was better draped than the high shoulders of many a duchess. He usually, however, spent a part of every winter at Pau, and had once passed a couple of months in the United States.

He took a great interest in Isabel and remembered perfectly the walk at Neufchâtel, when she would persist in going so near the edge. He seemed to recognise this same tendency in the subversive enquiry that I quoted a moment ago, and set himself to answer our heroine's question with greater urbanity than it perhaps deserved. "What does it lead to, Miss Archer? Why Paris leads everywhere. You can't go anywhere unless you come here first. Every one that comes to Europe has got to pass through. You don't mean it in that sense so much? You mean what good it does you? Well, how can you penetrate futurity? How can you tell what lies ahead? If it's a pleasant road I don't care where it leads. I like the road, Miss Archer; I like the dear old asphalte. You can't get tired of it — you can't if you try. You think you would, but you would n't; there's always something new and fresh. Take the Hôtel Drouot, now; they sometimes have three and four sales a week. Where can you get such things as you can here? In spite of all they say I maintain they're cheaper too, if you know the right places. I know plenty of places, but I keep them to myself.

I 'll tell you, if you like, as a particular favour; only you must n't tell any one else. Don't you go anywhere without asking me first; I want you to promise me that. As a general thing avoid the Boulevards; there 's very little to be done on the Boulevards. Speaking conscientiously — *sans blague* — I don't believe any one knows Paris better than I. You and Mrs. Touchett must come and breakfast with me some day, and I 'll show you my things; *je ne vous dis que ça!* There has been a great deal of talk about London of late; it 's the fashion to cry up London. But there 's nothing in it — you can't do anything in London. No Louis Quinze — nothing of the First Empire; nothing but their eternal Queen Anne. It 's good for one 's bed-room, Queen Anne — for one's washing-room; but it is n't proper for a *salon*. Do I spend my life at the auctioneer's ?" Mr. Rosier pursued in answer to another question of Isabel's. "Oh no; I have n't the means. I wish I had. You think I 'm a mere trifler; I can tell by the expression of your face — you 've got a wonderfully expressive face. I hope you don't mind my saying that; I mean it as a kind of warning. You think I ought to do something, and so do I, so long as you leave it vague. But when you come to the point you see you have to stop. I can't go home and be a shopkeeper. You think I 'm very well fitted ? Ah, Miss Archer, you overrate me. I can buy very well, but I can't sell; you should see when I sometimes try to get rid of my things. It takes much more ability to make other people buy than to buy yourself. When I think how clever they must be, the people who make *me* buy! Ah no; I could n't be a shopkeeper. I can't be a doctor; it's a repulsive business. I can't be a clergyman; I have n't got convictions. And then I can't pronounce the names right in the Bible. They're very difficult, in the Old Testament particularly. I can't be a lawyer; I don't understand — how do you call it? — the American *procédure*. Is there anything else? There's nothing for a gentleman in America. I should like to be a diplomatist; but American diplomacy — that 's not for gentlemen either. I'm sure if you had seen the last min—"

Henrietta Stackpole, who was often with her friend when Mr. Rosier, coming to pay his compliments late in the afternoon, expressed himself after the fashion I have sketched, usually interrupted the young man at this point and read him a lecture on the duties of the American citizen. She thought him most unnatural; he was worse than poor Ralph Touchett. Henrietta, however, was at this time more than ever addicted to fine criticism, for her conscience had been freshly alarmed as regards Isabel. She had not congratulated this young lady on her augmentations and begged to be excused from doing so.

"If Mr. Touchett had consulted me about leaving you the money," she frankly asserted, "I'd have said to him 'Never!'"

"I see," Isabel had answered. "You think it will prove a curse in disguise. Perhaps it will."

"Leave it to some one you care less for — that's what I should have said."

"To yourself for instance?" Isabel suggested

jocosely. And then, "Do you really believe it will ruin me?" she asked in quite another tone.

"I hope it won't ruin you; but it will certainly confirm your dangerous tendencies."

"Do you mean the love of luxury — of extravagance?"

"No, no," said Henrietta; "I mean your exposure on the moral side. I approve of luxury; I think we ought to be as elegant as possible. Look at the luxury of our western cities; I've seen nothing over here to compare with it. I hope you'll never become grossly sensual; but I'm not afraid of that. The peril for you is that you live too much in the world of your own dreams. You're not enough in contact with reality — with the toiling, striving, suffering, I may even say sinning, world that surrounds you. You're too fastidious; you've too many graceful illusions. Your newly-acquired thousands will shut you up more and more to the society of a few selfish and heartless people who will be interested in keeping them up."

Isabel's eyes expanded as she gazed at this lurid scene. "What are my illusions?" she asked. "I try so hard not to have any."

"Well," said Henrietta, "you think you can lead a romantic life, that you can live by pleasing yourself and pleasing others. You'll find you're mistaken. Whatever life you lead you must put your soul in it — to make any sort of success of it; and from the moment you do that it ceases to be romance, I assure you: it becomes grim reality! And you can't always please yourself; you must sometimes please other people. That, I admit, you 're very ready to do; but there 's another thing that 's still more important — you must often *dis*please others. You must always be ready for that — you must never shrink from it. That does n't suit you at all — you 're too fond of admiration, you like to be thought well of. You think we can escape disagreeable duties by taking romantic views — that 's your great illusion, my dear. But we can't. You must be prepared on many occasions in life to please no one at all — not even yourself."

Isabel shook her head sadly; she looked troubled and frightened. "This, for you, Henrietta," she said, "must be one of those occasions!"

It was certainly true that Miss Stackpole, during her visit to Paris, which had been professionally more remunerative than her English sojourn, had not been living in the world of dreams. Mr. Bantling, who had now returned to England, was her companion for the first four weeks of her stay; and about Mr. Bantling there was nothing dreamy. Isabel learned from her friend that the two had led a life of great personal intimacy and that this had been a peculiar advantage to Henrietta, owing to the gentleman's remarkable knowledge of Paris. He had explained everything, shown her everything, been her constant guide and interpreter. They had breakfasted together, dined together, gone to the theatre together, supped together, really in a manner quite lived together. He was a true friend, Henrietta more than once assured our heroine; and she had never supposed that she could like any

Englishman so well. Isabel could not have told you why, but she found something that ministered to mirth in the alliance the correspondent of the *Interviewer* had struck with Lady Pensil's brother; her amusement moreover subsisted in face of the fact that she thought it a credit to each of them. Isabel could n't rid herself of a suspicion that they were playing somehow at cross-purposes — that the simplicity of each had been entrapped. But this simplicity was on either side none the less honourable. It was as graceful on Henrietta's part to believe that Mr. Bantling took an interest in the diffusion of lively journalism and in consolidating the position of lady-correspondents as it was on the part of his companion to suppose that the cause of the *Interviewer* — a periodical of which he never formed a very definite conception — was, if subtly analysed (a task to which Mr. Bantling felt himself quite equal), but the cause of Miss Stackpole's need of demonstrative affection. Each of these groping celibates supplied at any rate a want of which the other was impatiently conscious. Mr. Bantling, who was of rather a slow and a discursive habit, relished a prompt, keen, positive woman, who charmed him by the influence of a shining, challenging eye and a kind of bandbox freshness, and who kindled a perception of raciness in a mind to which the usual fare of life seemed unsalted. Henrietta, on the other hand, enjoyed the society of a gentleman who appeared somehow, in his way, made, by expensive, roundabout, almost "quaint" processes, for her use, and whose leisured state, though generally indefensible, was a decided boon to a breathless mate, and who was furnished with an easy, traditional, though by no means exhaustive, answer to almost any social or practical question that could come up. She often found Mr. Bantling's answers very convenient, and in the press of catching the American post would largely and showily address them to publicity. It was to be feared that she was indeed drifting toward those abysses of sophistication as to which Isabel, wishing for a good-humoured retort, had warned her. There might be danger in store for Isabel; but it was scarcely to be hoped that Miss Stackpole, on her side, would find permanent rest in any adoption of the views of a class pledged to all the old abuses. Isabel continued to warn her good-humouredly; Lady Pensil's obliging brother was sometimes, on our heroine's lips, an object of irreverent and facetious allusion. Nothing, however, could exceed Henrietta's amiability on this point; she used to abound in the sense of Isabel's irony and to enumerate with elation the hours she had spent with this perfect man of the world — a term that had ceased to make with her, as previously, for opprobrium. Then, a few moments later, she would forget that they had been talking jocosely and would mention with impulsive earnestness some expedition she had enjoyed in his company. She would say: "Oh, I know all about Versailles; I went there with Mr. Bantling. I was bound to see it thoroughly — I warned him when we went out there that I was thorough: so we spent three days at the hotel and wandered all over the place. It was lovely weather — a kind of Indian summer, only not so good. We just lived in that park. Oh yes; you can't tell me anything about Versailles." Henrietta appeared to have made arrangements to meet her gallant friend during the spring in Italy.

XXI

Mrs. Touchett, before arriving in Paris, had fixed the day for her departure and by the middle of February had begun to travel southward. She interrupted her journey to pay a visit to her son, who at San Remo, on the Italian shore of the Mediterranean, had been spending a dull, bright winter beneath a slow-moving white umbrella. Isabel went with her aunt as a matter of course, though Mrs. Touchett, with homely, customary logic, had laid before her a pair of alternatives.

"Now, of course, you're completely your own mistress and are as free as the bird on the bough. I don't mean you were not so before, but you're at present on a different footing — property erects a kind of barrier. You can do a great many things if you're rich which would be severely criticised if you were poor. You can go and come, you can travel alone, you can have your own establishment: I mean of course if you'll take a companion — some decayed gentlewoman, with a darned cashmere and dyed hair, who paints on velvet. You don't think you'd like that? Of course you can do as you please; I only want you to understand how much you're at liberty. You might take Miss Stackpole as your *dame de compagnie;* she'd keep people off very well. I think, however, that it's a great deal better you should remain with me, in spite of there being no obligation. It's better for several reasons, quite apart from your liking it. I should n't think you 'd like it, but I recommend you to make the sacrifice. Of course whatever novelty there may have been at first in my society has quite passed away, and you see me as I am — a dull, obstinate, narrow-minded old woman."

"I don't think you're at all dull," Isabel had replied to this.

"But you do think I'm obstinate and narrow-minded? I told you so!" said Mrs. Touchett with much elation at being justified.

Isabel remained for the present with her aunt, because, in spite of eccentric impulses, she had a great regard for what was usually deemed decent, and a young gentlewoman without visible relations had always struck her as a flower without foliage. It was true that Mrs. Touchett's conversation had never again appeared so brilliant as that first afternoon in Albany, when she sat in her damp waterproof and sketched the opportunities that Europe would offer to a young person of taste. This, however, was in a great measure the girl's own fault; she had got a glimpse of her aunt's experience, and her imagination constantly anticipated the judgements and emotions of a woman who had very little of the same faculty. Apart from this, Mrs. Touchett had a great merit; she was as honest as a pair of compasses. There was a comfort in her stiffness and firmness; you knew exactly where to find her and were never liable to chance encounters and concussions. On her own ground she was perfectly present, but was never over-inquisitive as regards the territory of her neighbour.

Isabel came at last to have a kind of undemonstrable pity for her; there seemed something so dreary in the condition of a person whose nature had, as it were, so little surface — offered so limited a face to the accretions of human contact. Nothing tender, nothing sympathetic, had ever had a chance to fasten upon it — no wind-sown blossom, no familiar softening moss. Her offered, her passive extent, in other words, was about that of a knife-edge. Isabel had reason to believe none the less that as she advanced in life she made more of those concessions to the sense of something obscurely distinct from convenience — more of them than she independently exacted. She was learning to sacrifice consistency to considerations of that inferior order for which the excuse must be found in the particular case. It was not to the credit of her absolute rectitude that she should have gone the longest way round to Florence in order to spend a few weeks with her invalid son; since in former years it had been one of her most definite convictions that when Ralph wished to see her he was at liberty to remember that Palazzo Crescentini contained a large apartment known as the quarter of the signorino.

"I want to ask you something," Isabel said to this young man the day after her arrival at San Remo — "something I've thought more than once of asking you by letter, but that I've hesitated on the whole to write about. Face to face, nevertheless, my question seems easy enough. Did you know your father intended to leave me so much money?"

Ralph stretched his legs a little further than usual and gazed a little more fixedly at the Mediterranean.

"What does it matter, my dear Isabel, whether I knew? My father was very obstinate."

"So," said the girl, "you did know."

"Yes; he told me. We even talked it over a little."

"What did he do it for?" asked Isabel abruptly.

"Why, as a kind of compliment."

"A compliment on what?"

"On your so beautifully existing."

"He liked me too much," she presently declared.

"That's a way we all have."

"If I believed that I should be very unhappy. Fortunately I don't believe it. I want to be treated with justice; I want nothing but that."

"Very good. But you must remember that justice to a lovely being is after all a florid sort of sentiment."

"I'm not a lovely being. How can you say that, at the very moment when I'm asking such odious questions? I must seem to you delicate!"

"You seem to me troubled," said Ralph.

"I am troubled."

"About what?"

For a moment she answered nothing; then she broke out: "Do you think it good for me suddenly to be made so rich? Henrietta does n't."

"Oh, hang Henrietta!" said Ralph coarsely. "If you ask *me* I'm delighted at it."

"Is that why your father did it — for your amusement?

"I differ with Miss Stackpole," Ralph went on more gravely. "I think it very good for you to have means."

Isabel looked at him with serious eyes. "I wonder whether you know what's good for me — or whether you care."

"If I know depend upon it I care. Shall I tell you what it is? Not to torment yourself."

"Not to torment you, I suppose you mean."

"You can't do that; I'm proof. Take things more easily. Don't ask yourself so much whether this or that is good for you. Don't question your conscience so much — it will get out of tune like a strummed piano. Keep it for great occasions. Don't try so much to form your character — it's like trying to pull open a tight, tender young rose. Live as you like best, and your character will take care of itself. Most things are good for you; the exceptions are very rare, and a comfortable income's not one of them." Ralph paused, smiling; Isabel had listened quickly. "You've too much power of thought — above all too much conscience," Ralph added. "It's out of all reason, the number of things you think wrong. Put back your watch. Diet your fever. Spread your wings; rise above the ground. It's never wrong to do that."

She had listened eagerly, as I say; and it was her nature to understand quickly. "I wonder if you appreciate what you say. If you do, you take a great responsibility."

"You frighten me a little, but I think I'm right," said Ralph, persisting in cheer.

"All the same what you say is very true," Isabel pursued. "You could say nothing more true. I'm absorbed in myself — I look at life too much as a doctor's prescription. Why indeed should we perpetually be thinking whether things are good for us, as if we were patients lying in a hospital? Why should I be so afraid of not doing right? As if it mattered to the world whether I do right or wrong!"

"You're a capital person to advise," said Ralph; "you take the wind out of *my* sails!"

She looked at him as if she had not heard him — though she was following out the train of reflexion which he himself had kindled. "I try to care more about the world than about myself — but I always come back to myself. It's because I'm afraid." She stopped; her voice had trembled a little. "Yes, I'm afraid; I can't tell you. A large fortune means freedom, and I'm afraid of that. It's such a fine thing, and one should make such a good use of it. If one should n't one would be ashamed. And one must keep thinking; it's a constant effort. I'm not sure it's not a greater happiness to be powerless."

"For weak people I've no doubt it's a greater happiness. For weak people the effort not to be contemptible must be great."

"And how do you know I'm not weak?" Isabel asked.

"Ah," Ralph answered with a flush that the girl noticed, "if you are I'm awfully sold!"

The charm of the Mediterranean coast only deepened for our heroine on acquaintance, for it was the threshold of Italy, the gate of admirations. Italy, as yet imperfectly seen and felt, stretched before her as a land of promise, a land in which a love of the beautiful might be comforted by endless knowledge. Whenever she strolled upon the shore with her cousin

— and she was the companion of his daily walk — she looked across the sea, with longing eyes, to where she knew that Genoa lay. She was glad to pause, however, on the edge of this larger adventure; there was such a thrill even in the preliminary hovering. It affected her moreover as a peaceful interlude, as a hush of the drum and fife in a career which she had little warrant as yet for regarding as agitated, but which nevertheless she was constantly picturing to herself by the light of her hopes, her fears, her fancies, her ambitions, her predilections, and which reflected these subjective accidents in a manner sufficiently dramatic. Madame Merle had predicted to Mrs. Touchett that after their young friend had put her hand into her pocket half a dozen times she would be reconciled to the idea that it had been filled by a munificent uncle; and the event justified, as it had so often justified before, that lady's perspicacity. Ralph Touchett had praised his cousin for being morally inflammable, that is for being quick to take a hint that was meant as good advice. His advice had perhaps helped the matter; she had at any rate before leaving San Remo grown used to feeling rich. The consciousness in question found a proper place in rather a dense little group of ideas that she had about herself, and often it was by no means the least agreeable. It took perpetually for granted a thousand good intentions. She lost herself in a maze of visions; the fine things to be done by a rich, independent, generous girl who took a large human view of occasions and obligations were sublime in the mass. Her fortune therefore became to her mind a part of her better self; it gave her importance, gave her even, to her own imagination, a certain ideal beauty. What it did for her in the imagination of others is another affair, and on this point we must also touch in time. The visions I have just spoken of were mixed with other debates. Isabel liked better to think of the future than of the past; but at times, as she listened to the murmur of the Mediterranean waves, her glance took a backward flight. It rested upon two figures which, in spite of increasing distance, were still sufficiently salient; they were recognisable without difficulty as those of Caspar Goodwood and Lord Warburton. It was strange how quickly these images of energy had fallen into the background of our young lady's life. It was in her disposition at all times to lose faith in the reality of absent things; she could summon back her faith, in case of need, with an effort, but the effort was often painful even when the reality had been pleasant. The past was apt to look dead and its revival rather to show the livid light of a judgement-day. The girl moreover was not prone to take for granted that she herself lived in the mind of others — she had not the fatuity to believe she left indelible traces. She was capable of being wounded by the discovery that she had been forgotten; but of all liberties the one she herself found sweetest was the liberty to forget. She had not given her last shilling, sentimentally speaking, either to Caspar Goodwood or to Lord Warburton, and yet could n't but feel them appreciably in debt to her. She had of course reminded herself that she was to hear from Mr. Goodwood again; but this was not to be for another year and a half, and in that time a great many things might happen. She had indeed failed to say to herself that her American suitor might find some other girl more comfortable to woo; because, though it was certain many other girls would prove so, she had not the smallest belief that this merit would attract him. But she reflected that she herself might know the humiliation of change, might really, for that matter, come to the end of the things that were not Caspar (even though there appeared so many of them), and find rest in those very elements of his presence which struck her now as impediments to the finer respiration. It was conceivable that these impediments should some day prove a sort of blessing in disguise — a clear and quiet harbour enclosed by a brave granite breakwater. But that day could only come in its order, and she could n't wait for it with folded hands. That Lord Warburton should continue to cherish her image seemed to her more than a noble humility or an enlightened pride ought to wish to reckon with. She had so definitely undertaken to preserve no record of what had passed between them that a corresponding effort on his own part would be eminently just. This was not, as it may seem, merely a theory tinged with sarcasm. Isabel candidly believed that his lordship would, in the usual phrase, get over his disappointment. He had been deeply affected — this she believed, and she was still capable of deriving pleasure from the belief; but it was absurd that a man both so intelligent and so honourably dealt with should cultivate a scar out of proportion to any wound. Englishmen liked moreover to be comfortable, said

Isabel, and there could be little comfort for Lord Warburton, in the long run, in brooding over a self-sufficient American girl who had been but a casual acquaintance. She flattered herself that, should she hear from one day to another that he had married some young woman of his own country who had done more to deserve him, she should receive the news without a pang even of surprise. It would have proved that he believed she was firm — which was what she wished to seem to him. That alone was grateful to her pride.

XXII

On one of the first days of May, some six months after old Mr. Touchett's death, a small group that might have been described by a painter as composing well was gathered in one of the many rooms of an ancient villa crowning an olive-muffled hill outside of the Roman gate of Florence. The villa was a long, rather blank-looking structure, with the far-projecting roof which Tuscany loves and which, on the hills that encircle Florence, when considered from a distance, makes so harmonious a rectangle with the straight, dark, definite cypresses that usually rise in groups of three or four beside it. The house had a front upon a little grassy, empty, rural piazza which occupied a part of the hill-top; and this front, pierced with a few windows in irregular relations and furnished with a stone bench lengthily adjusted to the base of the structure and useful as a lounging-place to one or two persons wearing more or less of that air of undervalued merit which in Italy, for some reason or other, always gracefully invests any one who confidently assumes a perfectly passive attitude — this antique, solid, weather-worn, yet imposing front had a somewhat incommunicative character. It was the mask, not the face of the house. It had heavy lids, but no eyes; the house in reality looked another way — looked off behind, into splendid openness and the range of the afternoon light.

In that quarter the villa overhung the slope of its hill and the long valley of the Arno, hazy with Italian colour. It had a narrow garden, in the manner of a terrace, productive chiefly of tangles of wild roses and other old stone benches, mossy and sun-warmed. The parapet of the terrace was just the height to lean upon, and beneath it the ground declined into the vagueness of olive-crops and vineyards. It is not, however, with the outside of the place that we are concerned; on this bright morning of ripened spring its tenants had reason to prefer the shady side of the wall. The windows of the ground-floor, as you saw them from the piazza, were, in their noble proportions, extremely architectural; but their function seemed less to offer communication with the world than to defy the world to look in. They were massively cross-barred, and placed at such a height that curiosity, even on tiptoe, expired before it reached them. In an apartment lighted by a row of three of these jealous apertures — one of the several distinct apartments into which the villa was divided and which were mainly occupied by foreigners of random race long resident in Florence — a gentleman was seated in company with a young girl and two good sisters from a religious house. The room was, however, less sombre than our indications may have represented, for it had a wide, high door, which now stood open into the tangled garden behind; and the tall iron lattices admitted on occasion more than enough of the Italian sunshine. It was moreover a seat of ease, indeed of luxury, telling of arrangements subtly studied and refinements frankly proclaimed, and containing a variety of those faded hangings of damask and tapestry, those chests and cabinets of carved and time-polished oak, those angular specimens of pictorial art in frames as pedantically primitive, those perverse-looking relics of mediæval brass and pottery, of which Italy has long been the not quite exhausted storehouse. These things kept terms with articles of modern furniture in which large allowance had been made for a lounging generation; it was to be noticed that all the chairs were deep and well padded and that much space was occupied by a writing-table of which the ingenious perfection bore the stamp of London and the nineteenth century. There were books in profusion and magazines and newspapers, and a few small, odd, elaborate pictures, chiefly in water-colour. One of these productions stood on a drawing-room easel before which, at the moment we begin to be concerned with her, the young girl I have mentioned had placed herself. She was looking at the picture in silence.

Silence — absolute silence — had not fallen upon her companions; but their talk had an appearance of embarrassed continuity. The two good sisters had not settled themselves in their respective chairs; their attitude expressed a final reserve and their faces showed the glaze of prudence. They were plain, ample, mild-featured women, with a kind of business-like modesty to which the impersonal aspect of their stiffened linen and of the serge that draped them as if nailed on frames gave an advantage. One of them, a person of a certain age, in spectacles, with a fresh complexion and a full cheek, had a more discriminating manner than her colleague, as well as the responsibility of their errand, which apparently related to the young girl. This object of interest wore her hat — an ornament of extreme simplicity and not at variance with her plain muslin gown, too short for her years, though it must already have been "let out." The gentleman who might have been supposed to be entertaining the two nuns was perhaps conscious of the difficulties of his function, it being in its way as arduous to converse with the very meek as with the very mighty. At the same time he was clearly much occupied with their quiet charge, and while she turned her back to him his eyes rested gravely on her slim, small figure. He was a man of forty, with a high but well-shaped head, on which the hair, still dense, but prematurely grizzled, had been cropped close. He had a fine, narrow, extremely modelled and composed face, of which the only fault was just this effect of its running a trifle too much to points; an appearance to which the shape of the beard contributed not a little. This beard, cut in the manner of the portraits of the sixteenth century and surmounted by a fair moustache, of which the ends had a romantic upward flourish, gave its wearer a foreign, traditionary look and suggested that he was a gentleman who studied style. His conscious, curious eyes, however, eyes at once vague and penetrating, intelligent and hard, expressive of the observer as well as of the dreamer, would have assured you that he studied it only within well-chosen limits, and that in so far as he sought it he found it. You would have been much at a loss to determine his original clime and country; he had none of the superficial signs that usually render the answer to this question an insipidly easy one. If he had English blood in his veins it had probably received some French or Italian commixture; but he suggested, fine gold coin as he was, no stamp nor emblem of the common mintage that provides for general circulation; he was the elegant complicated medal struck off for a special occasion. He had a light, lean, rather languid-looking figure, and was apparently neither tall nor short. He was dressed as a man dresses who takes little other trouble about it than to have no vulgar things.

"Well, my dear, what do you think of it?" he asked of the young girl. He used the Italian tongue, and used it with perfect ease; but this would not have convinced you he was Italian.

The child turned her head earnestly to one side and the other. "It's very pretty, papa. Did you make it yourself?"

"Certainly I made it. Don't you think I'm clever?"

"Yes, papa, very clever; I also have learned to make pictures." And she turned round and showed a small, fair face painted with a fixed and intensely sweet smile.

"You should have brought me a specimen of your powers."

"I've brought a great many; they're in my trunk."

"She draws very — very carefully," the elder of the nuns remarked, speaking in French.

"I'm glad to hear it. Is it you who have instructed her?"

"Happily no," said the good sister, blushing a little. "*Ce n'est pas ma partie.* I teach nothing; I leave that to those who are wiser. We've an excellent drawing-master, Mr. — Mr. — what is his name?" she asked of her companion.

Her companion looked about at the carpet. "It's a German name," she said in Italian, as if it needed to be translated.

"Yes," the other went on, "he's a German, and we've had him many years."

The young girl, who was not heeding the conversation, had wandered away to the open door of the large room and stood looking into the garden. "And you, my sister, are French," said the gentleman.

"Yes, sir," the visitor gently replied. "I speak to the pupils in my own tongue. I know no other. But we have sisters of other countries — English, German, Irish. They all speak their proper language."

The gentleman gave a smile. "Has my daughter been under the care of one of the Irish ladies?" And then, as he saw that his visitors suspected a joke, though failing to understand it, "You're very complete," he instantly added.

"Oh, yes, we're complete. We've everything, and everything's of the best."

"We have gymnastics," the Italian sister ventured to remark. "But not dangerous."

"I hope not. Is that *your* branch?" A question which provoked much candid hilarity on the part of the two ladies; on the subsidence of which their entertainer, glancing at his daughter, remarked that she had grown.

"Yes, but I think she has finished. She'll remain — not big," said the French sister.

"I'm not sorry. I prefer women like books — very good and not too long. But I know," the gentleman said, "no particular reason why my child should be short."

The nun gave a temperate shrug, as if to intimate that such things might be beyond our knowledge. "She's in very good health; that's the best thing."

"Yes, she looks sound." And the young girl's father watched her a moment. "What do you see in the garden?" he asked in French.

"I see many flowers," she replied in a sweet, small voice and with an accent as good as his own.

"Yes, but not many good ones. However, such as they are, go out and gather some for *ces dames*."

The child turned to him with her smile heightened by pleasure. "May I, truly?"

"Ah, when I tell you," said her father.

The girl glanced at the elder of the nuns. "May I, truly, *ma mère?*"

"Obey monsieur your father, my child," said the sister, blushing again.

The child, satisfied with this authorisation, descended from the threshold and was presently lost to sight. "You don't spoil them," said her father gaily.

"For everything they must ask leave. That's our system. Leave is freely granted, but they must ask it."

"Oh, I don't quarrel with your system; I've no

doubt it's excellent. I sent you my daughter to see what you'd make of her. I had faith."

"One must have faith," the sister blandly rejoined, gazing through her spectacles.

"Well, has my faith been rewarded? What have you made of her?"

The sister dropped her eyes a moment. "A good Christian, monsieur."

Her host dropped his eyes as well; but it was probable that the movement had in each case a different spring. "Yes, and what else?"

He watched the lady from the convent, probably thinking she would say that a good Christian was everything; but for all her simplicity she was not so crude as that. "A charming young lady — a real little woman — a daughter in whom you will have nothing but contentment."

"She seems to me very *gentille*," said the father. "She's really pretty."

"She's perfect. She has no faults."

"She never had any as a child, and I'm glad you have given her none."

"We love her too much," said the spectacled sister with dignity. "And as for faults, how can we give what we have not? *Le couvent n'est pas comme le monde, monsieur*. She's our daughter, as you may say. We've had her since she was so small."

"Of all those we shall lose this year she's the one we shall miss most," the younger woman murmured deferentially.

"Ah, yes, we shall talk long of her," said the other. "We shall hold her up to the new ones." And at this the good sister appeared to find her spectacles dim; while her companion, after fumbling a moment, presently drew forth a pocket-handkerchief of durable texture.

"It's not certain you'll lose her; nothing's settled yet," their host rejoined quickly; not as if to anticipate their tears, but in the tone of a man saying what was most agreeable to himself.

"We should be very happy to believe that. Fifteen is very young to leave us."

"Oh," exclaimed the gentleman with more vivacity than he had yet used, "it is not I who wish to take her away. I wish you could keep her always!"

"Ah, monsieur," said the elder sister, smiling and getting up, "good as she is, she's made for the world. *Le monde y gagnera.*"

"If all the good people were hidden away in convents how would the world get on?" her companion softly enquired, rising also.

This was a question of a wider bearing than the good woman apparently supposed; and the lady in spectacles took a harmonising view by saying comfortably: "Fortunately there are good people everywhere."

"If you're going there will be two less here," her host remarked gallantly.

For this extravagant sally his simple visitors had no answer, and they simply looked at each other in decent deprecation; but their confusion was speedily covered by the return of the young girl with two large bunches of roses — one of them all white, the other red.

"I give you your choice, mamman Catherine," said the child. "It's only the colour that's different, mamman Justine; there are just as many roses in one bunch as in the other."

The two sisters turned to each other, smiling and hesitating, with "Which will you take?" and "No, it's for you to choose."

"I'll take the red, thank you," said mother Catherine in the spectacles. "I'm so red myself. They'll comfort us on our way back to Rome."

"Ah, they won't last," cried the young girl. "I wish I could give you something that would last!"

"You've given us a good memory of yourself, my daughter. That will last!"

"I wish nuns could wear pretty things. I would give you my blue beads," the child went on.

"And do you go back to Rome to-night?" her father enquired.

"Yes, we take the train again. We've so much to do *là-bas*."

"Are you not tired?"

"We are never tired."

"Ah, my sister, sometimes," murmured the junior votaress.

"Not to-day, at any rate. We have rested too well here. *Que Dieu vous garde, ma fille*."

Their host, while they exchanged kisses with his daughter, went forward to open the door through which they were to pass; but as he did so he gave a slight exclamation, and stood looking beyond. The door opened into a vaulted ante-chamber, as high as a chapel and paved with red tiles; and into this ante-chamber a lady had just been admitted by a servant, a lad in shabby livery, who was now ushering her toward the apartment in which our friends were grouped. The gentleman at the door, after dropping his exclamation, remained silent; in silence too the lady advanced. He gave her no further audible greeting and offered her no hand, but stood aside to let her pass into the saloon. At the threshold she hesitated. "Is there any one?" she asked.

"Some one you may see."

She went in and found herself confronted with the two nuns and their pupil, who was coming forward, between them, with a hand in the arm of each. At the sight of the new visitor they all paused, and the lady, who had also stopped, stood looking at them. The young girl gave a little soft cry: "Ah, Madame Merle!"

The visitor had been slightly startled, but her manner the next instant was none the less gracious. "Yes, it's Madame Merle, come to welcome you home." And she held out two hands to the girl, who immediately came up to her, presenting her forehead to be kissed. Madame Merle saluted this portion of her charming little person and then stood smiling at the two nuns. They acknowledged her smile with a decent obeisance, but permitted themselves no direct scrutiny of this imposing, brilliant woman, who seemed to bring in with her something of the radiance of the outer world.

"These ladies have brought my daughter home, and now they return to the convent," the gentleman explained.

"Ah, you go back to Rome? I've lately come from there. It's very lovely now," said Madame Merle.

The good sisters, standing with their hands folded into their sleeves, accepted this statement uncritically; and the master of the house asked his new visitor how long it was since she had left Rome. "She came to see me at the convent," said the young girl before the lady addressed had time to reply.

"I've been more than once, Pansy," Madame Merle declared. "Am I not your great friend in Rome?"

"I remember the last time best," said Pansy, "because you told me I should come away."

"Did you tell her that?" the child's father asked.

"I hardly remember. I told her what I thought would please her. I've been in Florence a week. I hoped you would come to see me."

"I should have done so if I had known you were there. One does n't know such things by inspiration — though I suppose one ought. You had better sit down."

These two speeches were made in a particular tone of voice — a tone half-lowered and carefully quiet, but as from habit rather than from any definite need. Madame Merle looked about her, choosing her seat. "You're going to the door with these women? Let me of course not interrupt the ceremony. *Je vous salue, mesdames,*" she added, in French, to the nuns, as if to dismiss them.

"This lady's a great friend of ours; you will have seen her at the convent," said their entertainer. "We've much faith in her judgement, and she'll help me to decide whether my daughter shall return to you at the end of the holidays."

"I hope you'll decide in our favour, madame," the sister in spectacles ventured to remark.

"That's Mr. Osmond's pleasantry; I decide nothing," said Madame Merle, but also as in pleasantry. "I believe you've a very good school, but Miss Osmond's friends must remember that she's very naturally meant for the world."

"That's what I've told monsieur," sister Catherine answered. "It's precisely to fit her for the world," she murmured, glancing at Pansy, who stood, at a little distance, attentive to Madame Merle's elegant apparel.

"Do you hear that, Pansy? You're very naturally meant for the world," said Pansy's father.

The child fixed him an instant with her pure young eyes. "Am I not meant for you, papa?"

Papa gave a quick, light laugh. "That does n't prevent it! I'm of the world, Pansy."

"Kindly permit us to retire," said sister Catherine. "Be good and wise and happy in any case, my daughter."

"I shall certainly come back and see you," Pansy returned, recommencing her embraces, which were presently interrupted by Madame Merle.

"Stay with me, dear child," she said, "while your father takes the good ladies to the door."

Pansy stared, disappointed, yet not protesting. She was evidently impregnated with the idea of submission, which was due to any one who took the tone of authority; and she was a passive spectator of the operation of her fate. "May I not see mamman Catherine get into the carriage?" she nevertheless asked very gently.

"It would please me better if you'd remain with me," said Madame Merle, while Mr. Osmond and his companions, who had bowed low again to the other visitor, passed into the ante-chamber.

"Oh yes, I'll stay," Pansy answered; and she stood near Madame Merle, surrendering her little hand, which this lady took. She stared out of the window; her eyes had filled with tears.

"I'm glad they've taught you to obey," said Madame Merle. "That's what good little girls should do."

"Oh yes, I obey very well," cried Pansy with soft eagerness, almost with boastfulness, as if she had been speaking of her piano-playing. And then she gave a faint, just audible sigh.

Madame Merle, holding her hand, drew it across her own fine palm and looked at it. The gaze was critical, but it found nothing to deprecate; the child's small hand was delicate and fair. "I hope they always see that you wear gloves," she said in a moment. "Little girls usually dislike them."

"I used to dislike them, but I like them now," the child made answer.

"Very good, I'll make you a present of a dozen."

"I thank you very much. What colours will they be?" Pansy demanded with interest.

Madame Merle meditated. "Useful colours."

"But very pretty?"

"Are you very fond of pretty things?"

"Yes; but—but not too fond," said Pansy with a trace of asceticism.

"Well, they won't be too pretty," Madame Merle returned with a laugh. She took the child's other hand and drew her nearer; after which, looking at her a moment, "Shall you miss mother Catherine?" she went on.

"Yes — when I think of her."

"Try then not to think of her. Perhaps some day," added Madame Merle, "you'll have another mother."

"I don't think that's necessary," Pansy said, repeating her little soft conciliatory sigh. "I had more than thirty mothers at the convent."

Her father's step sounded again in the antechamber, and Madame Merle got up, releasing the child. Mr. Osmond came in and closed the door; then, without looking at Madame Merle, he pushed one or two chairs back into their places. His visitor waited a moment for him to speak, watching him as he moved about. Then at last she said: "I hoped you'd have come to Rome. I thought it possible you'd have wished yourself to fetch Pansy away."

"That was a natural supposition; but I'm afraid it's not the first time I've acted in defiance of your calculations."

"Yes," said Madame Merle, "I think you very perverse."

Mr. Osmond busied himself for a moment in the room — there was plenty of space in it to move about — in the fashion of a man mechanically seeking pretexts for not giving an attention which may be embarrassing. Presently, however, he had exhausted his pretexts; there was nothing left for him—unless he took up a book—but to stand with his hands behind him looking at Pansy. "Why did n't you come and see the last of mamman Catherine?" he asked of her abruptly in French.

Pansy hesitated a moment, glancing at Madame Merle. "I asked her to stay with me," said this lady, who had seated herself again in another place.

"Ah, that was better," Osmond conceded. With which he dropped into a chair and sat looking at Madame Merle; bent forward a little, his elbows on the edge of the arms and his hands interlocked.

"She's going to give me some gloves," said Pansy.

"You need n't tell that to every one, my dear," Madame Merle observed.

"You're very kind to her," said Osmond. "She's supposed to have everything she needs."

"I should think she had had enough of the nuns."

"If we're going to discuss that matter she had better go out of the room."

"Let her stay," said Madame Merle. "We'll talk of something else."

"If you like I won't listen," Pansy suggested with an appearance of candour which imposed conviction.

"You may listen, charming child, because you won't understand," her father replied. The child sat down, deferentially, near the open door, within sight of the garden, into which she directed her innocent, wistful eyes; and Mr. Osmond went on irrelevantly, addressing himself to his other companion. "You're looking particularly well."

"I think I always look the same," said Madame Merle.

"You always *are* the same. You don't vary. You're a wonderful woman."

"Yes, I think I am."

"You sometimes change your mind, however. You told me on your return from England that you would n't leave Rome again for the present."

"I'm pleased that you remember so well what I say. That was my intention. But I've come to Florence to meet some friends who have lately arrived and as to whose movements I was at that time uncertain."

"That reason's characteristic. You're always doing something for your friends."

Madame Merle smiled straight at her host. "It's less characteristic than your comment upon it — which is perfectly insincere. I don't, however, make a crime of that," she added, "because if you don't believe what you say there's no reason *why* you should. I don't ruin myself for my friends; I don't deserve your praise. I care greatly for myself."

"Exactly; but yourself includes so many other selves — so much of every one else and of everything. I never knew a person whose life touched so many other lives."

"What do you call one's life?" asked Madame Merle. "One's appearance, one's movements, one's engagements, one's society?"

"I call *your* life your ambitions," said Osmond.

Madame Merle looked a moment at Pansy. "I wonder if she understands that," she murmured.

"You see she can't stay with us!" And Pansy's father gave rather a joyless smile. "Go into the garden, *mignonne*, and pluck a flower or two for Madame Merle," he went on in French.

"That's just what I wanted to do," Pansy exclaimed, rising with promptness and noiselessly departing. Her father followed her to the open door, stood a moment watching her, and then came back, but remained standing, or rather strolling to and fro, as if to cultivate a sense of freedom which in another attitude might be wanting.

"My ambitions are principally for you," said Madame Merle, looking up at him with a certain courage.

"That comes back to what I say. I'm part of your life — I and a thousand others. You're not selfish — I can't admit that. If you were selfish, what should I be? What epithet would properly describe me?"

"You're indolent. For me that's your worst fault."

"I'm afraid it's really my best."

"You don't care," said Madame Merle gravely.

"No; I don't think I care much. What sort of a fault do you call that? My indolence, at any rate, was one of the reasons I did n't go to Rome. But it was only one of them."

"It's not of importance — to me at least — that you did n't go; though I should have been glad to see you. I'm glad you're not in Rome now — which you might be, would probably be, if you had gone there a month ago. There's something I should like you to do at present in Florence."

"Please remember my indolence," said Osmond.

"I do remember it; but I beg you to forget it. In that way you'll have both the virtue and the reward. This is not a great labour, and it may prove a real interest. How long is it since you made a new acquaintance?"

"I don't think I've made any since I made yours."

"It's time then you should make another. There's a friend of mine I want you to know."

Mr. Osmond, in his walk, had gone back to the open door again and was looking at his daughter as she moved about in the intense sunshine. "What good will it do me?" he asked with a sort of genial crudity.

Madame Merle waited. "It will amuse you." There was nothing crude in this rejoinder; it had been thoroughly well considered.

"If you say that, you know, I believe it," said Osmond, coming toward her. "There are some points in which my confidence in you is complete. I'm perfectly aware, for instance, that you know good society from bad."

"Society is all bad."

"Pardon me. That is n't—the knowledge I impute to you—a common sort of wisdom. You've gained it in the right way—experimentally; you've compared an immense number of more or less impossible people with each other."

"Well, I invite you to profit by my knowledge."

"To profit? Are you very sure that I shall?"

"It's what I hope. It will depend on yourself. If I could only induce you to make an effort!"

"Ah, there you are! I knew something tiresome

was coming. What in the world — that's likely to turn up here — is worth an effort?"

Madame Merle flushed as with a wounded intention. "Don't be foolish, Osmond. No one knows better than you what *is* worth an effort. Haven't *I* seen you in old days?"

"I recognise some things. But they're none of them probable in this poor life."

"It's the effort that makes them probable," said Madame Merle.

"There's something in that. Who then is your friend?"

"The person I came to Florence to see. She's a niece of Mrs. Touchett, whom you'll not have forgotten."

"A niece? The word niece suggests youth and ignorance. I see what you're coming to."

"Yes, she's young — twenty-three years old. She's a great friend of mine. I met her for the first time in England, several months ago, and we struck up a grand alliance. I like her immensely, and I do what I don't do every day — I admire her. You'll do the same."

"Not if I can help it."

"Precisely. But you won't be able to help it."

"Is she beautiful, clever, rich, splendid, universally intelligent and unprecedentedly virtuous? It's only on those conditions that I care to make her acquaintance. You know I asked you some time ago never to speak to me of a creature who should n't correspond to that description. I know plenty of dingy people; I don't want to know any more."

"Miss Archer is n't dingy; she 's as bright as the morning. She corresponds to your description; it 's for that I wish you to know her. She fills all your requirements."

"More or less, of course."

"No; quite literally. She 's beautiful, accomplished, generous and, for an American, well-born. She 's also very clever and very amiable, and she has a handsome fortune."

Mr. Osmond listened to this in silence, appearing to turn it over in his mind with his eyes on his informant. "What do you want to do with her?" he asked at last.

"What you see. Put her in your way."

"Is n't she meant for something better than that?"

"I don't pretend to know what people are meant for," said Madame Merle. "I only know what I can do with them."

"I 'm sorry for Miss Archer!" Osmond declared.

Madame Merle got up. "If that 's a beginning of interest in her I take note of it."

The two stood there face to face; she settled her mantilla, looking down at it as she did so. "You 're looking very well," Osmond repeated still less relevantly than before. "You have some idea. You 're never so well as when you 've got an idea; they 're always becoming to you."

In the manner and tone of these two persons, on first meeting at any juncture, and especially when they met in the presence of others, was something indirect and circumspect, as if they had approached each other obliquely and addressed each other by implication. The effect of each appeared to be to intensify to an appreciable degree the self-consciousness of the other. Madame Merle of course carried off any embarrassment better than her friend; but even Madame Merle had not on this occasion the form she would have liked to have — the perfect self-possession she would have wished to wear for her host. The point to be made is, however, that at a certain moment the element between them, whatever it was, always levelled itself and left them more closely face to face than either ever was with any one else. This was what had happened now. They stood there knowing each other well and each on the whole willing to accept the satisfaction of knowing as a compensation for the inconvenience — whatever it might be — of being known. "I wish very much you were not so heartless," Madame Merle quietly said. "It has always been against you, and it will be against you now."

"I'm not so heartless as you think. Every now and then something touches me — as for instance your saying just now that your ambitions are for me. I don't understand it; I don't see how or why they should be. But it touches me, all the same."

"You'll probably understand it even less as time goes on. There are some things you'll never understand. There's no particular need you should."

"You, after all, are the most remarkable of women," said Osmond. "You have more in you than almost any one. I don't see why you think Mrs. Touchett's niece should matter very much to me, when — when ——" But he paused a moment.

"When I myself have mattered so little?"

"That of course is not what I meant to say. When I've known and appreciated such a woman as you."

"Isabel Archer's better than I," said Madame Merle.

Her companion gave a laugh. "How little you must think of her to say that!"

"Do you suppose I'm capable of jealousy? Please answer me that."

"With regard to me? No; on the whole I don't."

"Come and see me then, two days hence. I'm staying at Mrs. Touchett's — Palazzo Crescentini — and the girl will be there."

"Why did n't you ask me that at first simply, without speaking of the girl?" said Osmond. "You could have had her there at any rate."

Madame Merle looked at him in the manner of a woman whom no question he could ever put would find unprepared. "Do you wish to know why? Because I've spoken of you to her."

Osmond frowned and turned away. "I'd rather not know that." Then in a moment he pointed out the easel supporting the little water-colour drawing. "Have you seen what's there — my last?"

Madame Merle drew near and considered. "Is it the Venetian Alps — one of your last year's sketches?"

"Yes — but how you guess everything!"

She looked a moment longer, then turned away. "You know I don't care for your drawings."

"I know it, yet I'm always surprised at it. They're really so much better than most people's."

"That may very well be. But as the only thing

you do — well, it's so little. I should have liked you to do so many other things: those were my ambitions."

"Yes; you've told me many times — things that were impossible."

"Things that were impossible," said Madame Merle. And then in quite a different tone: "In itself your little picture's very good." She looked about the room — at the old cabinets, pictures, tapestries, surfaces of faded silk. "Your rooms at least are perfect. I'm struck with that afresh whenever I come back; I know none better anywhere. You understand this sort of thing as nobody anywhere does. You've such adorable taste."

"I'm sick of my adorable taste," said Gilbert Osmond.

"You must nevertheless let Miss Archer come and see it. I've told her about it."

"I don't object to showing my things — when people are not idiots."

"You do it delightfully. As cicerone of your museum you appear to particular advantage."

Mr. Osmond, in return for this compliment, simply looked at once colder and more attentive. "Did you say she was rich?"

"She has seventy thousand pounds."

"*En écus bien comptés?*"

"There's no doubt whatever about her fortune. I've seen it, as I may say."

"Satisfactory woman! — I mean *you*. And if I go to see her shall I see the mother?"

"The mother? She has none — nor father either."

"The aunt then — whom did you say? — Mrs. Touchett."

"I can easily keep her out of the way."

"I don't object to her," said Osmond; "I rather like Mrs. Touchett. She has a sort of old-fashioned character that 's passing away — a vivid identity. But that long jackanapes the son — is he about the place?"

"He 's there, but he won't trouble you."

"He 's a good deal of a donkey."

"I think you 're mistaken. He 's a very clever man. But he 's not fond of being about when I 'm there, because he does n't like me."

"What could be more asinine than that? Did you say she has looks?" Osmond went on.

"Yes; but I won't say it again, lest you should be disappointed in them. Come and make a beginning; that 's all I ask of you."

"A beginning of what?"

Madame Merle was silent a little. "I want you of course to marry her."

"The beginning of the end? Well, I 'll see for myself. Have you told her that?"

"For what do you take me? She 's not so coarse a piece of machinery — nor am I."

"Really," said Osmond after some meditation, "I don't understand your ambitions."

"I think you 'll understand this one after you 've seen Miss Archer. Suspend your judgement." Madame Merle, as she spoke, had drawn near the open door of the garden, where she stood a moment looking out. "Pansy has really grown pretty," she presently added.

"So it seemed to me."

"But she has had enough of the convent."

"I don't know," said Osmond. "I like what they 've made of her. It 's very charming."

"That 's not the convent. It 's the child's nature."

"It 's the combination, I think. She 's as pure as a pearl."

"Why does n't she come back with my flowers then?" Madame Merle asked. "She 's not in a hurry."

"We 'll go and get them."

"She does n't like me," the visitor murmured as she raised her parasol and they passed into the garden.

XXIII

MADAME MERLE, who had come to Florence on Mrs. Touchett's arrival at the invitation of this lady — Mrs. Touchett offering her for a month the hospitality of Palazzo Crescentini — the judicious Madame Merle spoke to Isabel afresh about Gilbert Osmond and expressed the hope she might know him; making, however, no such point of the matter as we have seen her do in recommending the girl herself to Mr. Osmond's attention. The reason of this was perhaps that Isabel offered no resistance whatever to Madame Merle's proposal. In Italy, as in England, the lady had a multitude of friends, both among the natives of the country and its heterogeneous visitors. She had mentioned to Isabel most of the people the girl would find it well to "meet" — of course, she said, Isabel could know whomever in the wide world she would — and had placed Mr. Osmond near the top of the list. He was an old friend of her own; she had known him these dozen years; he was one of the cleverest and most agreeable men — well, in Europe simply. He was altogether above the respectable average; quite another affair. He wasn't a professional charmer — far from it, and the effect he produced depended a good deal on the state of his nerves and his spirits. When not in the right mood he could fall as low as any one, saved only by his looking at such hours rather like a demoralised prince in exile. But if he cared or was interested or rightly challenged — just exactly rightly it had to be — then one felt his cleverness and his distinction. Those qualities did n't depend, in him, as in so many people, on his not committing or exposing himself. He had his perversities — which indeed Isabel would find to be the case with all the men really worth knowing — and did n't cause his light to shine equally for all persons. Madame Merle, however, thought she could undertake that for Isabel he would be brilliant. He was easily bored, too easily, and dull people always put him out; but a quick and cultivated girl like Isabel would give him a stimulus which was too absent from his life. At any rate he was a person not to miss. One should n't attempt to live in Italy without making a friend of Gilbert Osmond, who knew more about the country than any one except two or three German professors. And if they had more knowledge than he it was he who had most perception and taste — being artistic through and through. Isabel remembered that her friend had spoken of him during their plunge, at Gardencourt, into the deeps of talk, and wondered a little what was the nature of the tie binding these superior spirits. She felt that Madame Merle's ties always somehow had histories, and such an impression was part of the interest created by this inordinate woman. As regards her relations with Mr. Osmond, however, she hinted at nothing but a long-established calm friendship. Isabel said she should be happy to know a person who had enjoyed so high a confidence for so many years. "You ought to see a great many men," Madame Merle remarked; "you ought to see as many as possible, so as to get used to them."

"Used to them?" Isabel repeated with that solemn stare which sometimes seemed to proclaim her deficient in the sense of comedy. "Why, I'm not afraid of them — I'm as used to them as the cook to the butcher-boys."

"Used to them, I mean, so as to despise them. That's what one comes to with most of them. You'll pick out, for your society, the few whom you don't despise."

This was a note of cynicism that Madame Merle did n't often allow herself to sound; but Isabel was not alarmed, for she had never supposed that as one saw more of the world the sentiment of respect became the most active of one's emotions. It was excited, none the less, by the beautiful city of Florence, which pleased her not less than Madame Merle had promised; and if her unassisted perception had not been able to gauge its charms she had clever companions as priests to the mystery. She was in no want indeed of æsthetic illumination, for Ralph found it a joy that renewed his own early passion to act as cicerone to his eager young kinswoman. Madame Merle remained at home; she had seen the treasures of Florence again and again and had always something else to do. But she talked of all things with remarkable vividness of memory — she recalled the right-hand corner of the large Perugino and the position of the hands of the Saint Elizabeth in the picture next to it. She had her opinions as to the character of many famous works of art, differing often from Ralph with great sharpness and defending her interpretations with as much ingenuity as good-humour. Isabel listened to the discussions taking place between the two with a sense that she might derive much benefit from them and that they were among the advantages she could n't have enjoyed for instance in Albany. In the clear May mornings before the formal breakfast — this repast at Mrs. Touchett's was served at twelve o'clock — she wandered with her cousin through the narrow and sombre Florentine streets, resting a while in the thicker dusk of some historic church or the vaulted chambers of some dispeopled convent. She went to the galleries and palaces; she looked at the pictures and statues that had hitherto been great names to her, and exchanged for a knowledge which was sometimes a limitation a presentiment which proved usually to have been a blank. She performed all those acts of mental prostration in which, on a first visit to Italy, youth and enthusiasm so freely indulge; she felt her heart beat in the presence of immortal genius and knew the sweetness of rising tears in eyes to which faded fresco and darkened marble grew dim. But the return, every day, was even pleasanter than the going forth; the return into the wide, monumental court of the great house in which Mrs. Touchett, many years before, had established herself, and into the high, cool rooms where the carven rafters and pompous frescoes of the sixteenth century looked down on the familiar commodities of the age of advertisement. Mrs. Touchett inhabited an historic building in a narrow street whose very name recalled the strife of mediæval factions; and found compensation for the darkness of her frontage in the modicity of her rent and the brightness of a garden where nature itself looked as archaic as the rugged architecture of the palace and which cleared and scented the rooms in regular use. To live in such a place was, for Isabel, to hold to her ear all day a shell of the sea of the past. This vague eternal rumour kept her imagination awake.

Gilbert Osmond came to see Madame Merle, who presented him to the young lady lurking at the other side of the room. Isabel took on this occasion little part in the talk; she scarcely even smiled when the others turned to her invitingly; she sat there as if she had been at the play and had paid even a large sum for her place. Mrs. Touchett was not present, and these two had it, for the effect of brilliancy, all their own way. They talked of the Florentine, the Roman, the cosmopolite world, and might have been distinguished performers figuring for a charity. It all had the rich readiness that would have come from rehearsal. Madame Merle appealed to her as if she had been on the stage, but she could ignore any learnt cue without spoiling the scene — though of course she thus put dreadfully in the wrong the friend who had told Mr. Osmond she could be depended on. This was no matter for once; even if more had been involved she could have made no attempt to shine. There was something in the visitor that checked her and held her in suspense —

made it more important she should get an impression of him than that she should produce one herself. Besides, she had little skill in producing an impression which she knew to be expected: nothing could be happier, in general, than to seem dazzling, but she had a perverse unwillingness to glitter by arrangement. Mr. Osmond, to do him justice, had a well-bred air of expecting nothing, a quiet ease that covered everything, even the first show of his own wit. This was the more grateful as his face, his head, was sensitive; he was not handsome, but he was fine, as fine as one of the drawings in the long gallery above the bridge of the Uffizi. And his very voice was fine — the more strangely that, with its clearness, it yet somehow was n't sweet. This had had really to do with making her abstain from interference. His utterance was the vibration of glass, and if she had put out her finger she might have changed the pitch and spoiled the concert. Yet before he went she had to speak.

"Madame Merle," he said, "consents to come up to my hill-top some day next week and drink tea in my garden. It would give me much pleasure if you would come with her. It's thought rather pretty — there 's what they call a general view. My daughter too would be so glad — or rather, for she 's too young to have strong emotions, *I* should be so glad — so very glad." And Mr. Osmond paused with a slight air of embarrassment, leaving his sentence unfinished. "I should be so happy if you could know my daughter," he went on a moment afterwards.

Isabel replied that she should be delighted to see Miss Osmond and that if Madame Merle would show her the way to the hill-top she should be very grateful. Upon this assurance the visitor took his leave; after which Isabel fully expected her friend would scold her for having been so stupid. But to her surprise that lady, who indeed never fell into the mere matter-of-course, said to her in a few moments: "You were charming, my dear; you were just as one would have wished you. You're never disappointing."

A rebuke might possibly have been irritating, though it is much more probable that Isabel would have taken it in good part; but, strange to say, the words that Madame Merle actually used caused her the first feeling of displeasure she had known this ally to excite. "That's more than I intended," she answered coldly. "I'm under no obligation that I know of to charm Mr. Osmond."

Madame Merle perceptibly flushed, but we know it was not her habit to retract. "My dear child, I did n't speak for him, poor man; I spoke for yourself. It's not of course a question as to his liking you; it matters little whether he likes you or not! But I thought you liked *him*."

"I did," said Isabel honestly. "But I don't see what that matters either."

"Everything that concerns you matters to me," Madame Merle returned with her weary nobleness; "especially when at the same time another old friend's concerned."

Whatever Isabel's obligations may have been to

Mr. Osmond, it must be admitted that she found them sufficient to lead her to put to Ralph sundry questions about him. She thought Ralph's judgements distorted by his trials, but she flattered herself she had learned to make allowance for that.

"Do I know him?" said her cousin. "Oh, yes, I 'know' him; not well, but on the whole enough. I've never cultivated his society, and he apparently has never found mine indispensable to his happiness. Who is he, what is he? He's a vague, unexplained American who has been living these thirty years, or less, in Italy. Why do I call him unexplained? Only as a cover for my ignorance; I don't know his antecedents, his family, his origin. For all I do know he may be a prince in disguise; he rather looks like one, by the way — like a prince who has abdicated in a fit of fastidiousness and has been in a state of disgust ever since. He used to live in Rome; but of late years he has taken up his abode here; I remember hearing him say that Rome has grown vulgar. He has a great dread of vulgarity; that's his special line; he has n't any other that I know of. He lives on his income, which I suspect of not being vulgarly large. He's a poor but honest gentleman — that's what he calls himself. He married young and lost his wife, and I believe he has a daughter. He also has a sister, who's married to some small Count or other, of these parts; I remember meeting her of old. She's nicer than he, I should think, but rather impossible. I remember there used to be some stories about her. I don't think I recommend you to know her. But why don't you ask Madame Merle about these people? She knows them all much better than I."

"I ask you because I want your opinion as well as hers," said Isabel.

"A fig for my opinion! If you fall in love with Mr. Osmond what will you care for that?"

"Not much, probably. But meanwhile it has a certain importance. The more information one has about one's dangers the better."

"I don't agree to that — it may make them dangers. We know too much about people in these days; we hear too much. Our ears, our minds, our mouths, are stuffed with personalities. Don't mind anything any one tells you about any one else. Judge every one and everything for yourself."

"That's what I try to do," said Isabel; "but when you do that people call you conceited."

"You're not to mind them — that's precisely my argument; not to mind what they say about yourself any more than what they say about your friend or your enemy."

Isabel considered. "I think you're right; but there are some things I can't help minding: for instance when my friend's attacked or when I myself am praised."

"Of course you're always at liberty to judge the critic. Judge people as critics, however," Ralph added, "and you'll condemn them all!"

"I shall see Mr. Osmond for myself," said Isabel. "I've promised to pay him a visit."

"To pay him a visit?"

"To go and see his view, his pictures, his daughter

— I don't know exactly what. Madame Merle's to take me; she tells me a great many ladies call on him."

"Ah, with Madame Merle you may go anywhere, *de confiance*," said Ralph. "She knows none but the best people."

Isabel said no more about Mr. Osmond, but she presently remarked to her cousin that she was not satisfied with his tone about Madame Merle. "It seems to me you insinuate things about her. I don't know what you mean, but if you've any grounds for disliking her I think you should either mention them frankly or else say nothing at all."

Ralph, however, resented this charge with more apparent earnestness than he commonly used. "I speak of Madame Merle exactly as I speak *to* her: with an even exaggerated respect."

"Exaggerated, precisely. That's what I complain of."

"I do so because Madame Merle's merits are exaggerated."

"By whom, pray? By me? If so I do her a poor service."

"No, no; by herself."

"Ah, I protest!" Isabel earnestly cried. "If ever there was a woman who made small claims ——!"

"You put your finger on it," Ralph interrupted. "Her modesty's exaggerated. She has no business with small claims — she has a perfect right to make large ones."

"Her merits are large then. You contradict yourself."

"Her merits are immense," said Ralph. "She's indescribably blameless; a pathless desert of virtue; the only woman I know who never gives one a chance."

"A chance for what?"

"Well, say to call her a fool! She's the only woman I know who has but that one little fault."

Isabel turned away with impatience. "I don't understand you; you're too paradoxical for my plain mind."

"Let me explain. When I say she exaggerates I don't mean it in the vulgar sense — that she boasts, overstates, gives too fine an account of herself. I mean literally that she pushes the search for perfection too far — that her merits are in themselves overstrained. She's too good, too kind, too clever, too learned, too accomplished, too everything. She's too complete, in a word. I confess to you that she acts on my nerves and that I feel about her a good deal as that intensely human Athenian felt about Aristides the Just."

Isabel looked hard at her cousin; but the mocking spirit, if it lurked in his words, failed on this occasion to peep from his face. "Do you wish Madame Merle to be banished?"

"By no means. She's much too good company. I delight in Madame Merle," said Ralph Touchett simply.

"You're very odious, sir!" Isabel exclaimed. And then she asked him if he knew anything that was not to the honour of her brilliant friend.

"Nothing whatever. Don't you see that's just what I mean? On the character of every one else you may find some little black speck; if I were to take half an hour to it, some day, I've no doubt I should be able to find one on yours. For my own, of course, I'm spotted like a leopard. But on Madame Merle's nothing, nothing, nothing!"

"That's just what I think!" said Isabel with a toss of her head. "That is why I like her so much."

"She's a capital person for you to know. Since you wish to see the world you could n't have a better guide."

"I suppose you mean by that that she's worldly?"

"Worldly? No," said Ralph, "she's the great round world itself!"

It had certainly not, as Isabel for the moment took it into her head to believe, been a refinement of malice in him to say that he delighted in Madame Merle. Ralph Touchett took his refreshment wherever he could find it, and he would not have forgiven himself if he had been left wholly unbeguiled by such a mistress of the social art. There are deep-lying sympathies and antipathies, and it may have been that, in spite of the administered justice she enjoyed at his hands, her absence from his mother's house would not have made life barren to him. But Ralph Touchett had learned more or less inscrutably to attend, and there could have been nothing so "sustained" to attend to as the general performance of Madame Merle. He tasted her in sips, he let her stand, with an opportuneness she herself could not have surpassed. There were moments when he felt almost sorry for her; and these, oddly enough, were the moments when his kindness was least demonstrative. He was sure she had been yearningly ambitious and that what she had visibly accomplished was far below her secret measure. She had got herself into perfect training, but had won none of the prizes. She was always plain Madame Merle, the widow of a Swiss *négociant*, with a small income and a large acquaintance, who stayed with people a great deal and was almost as universally "liked" as some new volume of smooth twaddle. The contrast between this position and any one of some half-dozen others that he supposed to have at various moments engaged her hope had an element of the tragical. His mother thought he got on beautifully with their genial guest; to Mrs. Touchett's sense two persons who dealt so largely in too-ingenious theories of conduct — that is of their own — would have much in common. He had given due consideration to Isabel's intimacy with her eminent friend, having long since made up his mind that he could not, without opposition, keep his cousin to himself; and he made the best of it, as he had done of worse things. He believed it would take care of itself; it would n't last forever. Neither of these two superior persons knew the other as well as she supposed, and when each had made an important discovery or two there would be, if not a rupture, at least a relaxation. Meanwhile he was quite willing to admit that the conversation of the elder lady was an advantage to the younger, who had a great deal to learn and would doubtless learn it better from Madame Merle than from some other instructors of the young. It was not probable that Isabel would be injured.

XXIV

It would certainly have been hard to see what injury could arise to her from the visit she presently paid to Mr. Osmond's hill-top. Nothing could have been more charming than this occasion — a soft afternoon in the full maturity of the Tuscan spring. The companions drove out of the Roman Gate, beneath the enormous blank superstructure which crowns the fine clear arch of that portal and makes it nakedly impressive, and wound between high-walled lanes into which the wealth of blossoming orchards overdrooped and flung a fragrance, until they reached the small superurban piazza, of crooked shape, where the long brown wall of the villa occupied in part by Mr. Osmond formed a principal, or at least a very imposing, object. Isabel went with her friend through a wide, high court, where a clear shadow rested below and a pair of light-arched galleries, facing each other above, caught the upper sunshine upon their slim columns and the flowering plants in which they were dressed. There was something grave and strong in the place; it looked somehow as if, once you were in, you would need an act of energy to get out. For Isabel, however, there was of course as yet no thought of getting out, but only of advancing. Mr. Osmond met her in the cold ante-chamber — it was cold even in the month of May — and ushered her, with her conductress, into the apartment to which we have already been introduced. Madame Merle was in front, and while Isabel lingered a little, talking with him, she went forward familiarly and greeted two persons who were seated in the saloon. One of these was little Pansy, on whom she bestowed a kiss; the other was a lady whom Mr. Osmond indicated to Isabel as his sister, the Countess Gemini. "And that's my little girl," he said, "who has just come out of her convent."

Pansy had on a scant white dress, and her fair hair was neatly arranged in a net; she wore her small shoes tied sandal-fashion about her ankles. She made Isabel a little conventual curtsey and then came to be kissed. The Countess Gemini simply nodded without getting up: Isabel could see she was a woman of high fashion. She was thin and dark and not at all pretty, having features that suggested some tropical bird — a long beak-like nose, small, quickly-moving eyes and a mouth and chin that receded extremely. Her expression, however, thanks to various intensities of emphasis and wonder, of horror and joy, was not inhuman, and, as regards her appearance, it was plain she understood herself and made the most of her points. Her attire, voluminous and delicate, bristling with elegance, had the look of shimmering plumage, and her attitudes were as light and sudden as those of a creature who perched upon twigs. She had a great deal of manner; Isabel, who had never known any one with so much manner, immediately classed her as the most affected of women. She remembered that Ralph had not recommended her as an acquaintance; but she was ready to acknowledge that to a casual view the Countess Gemini revealed no depths.

Her demonstrations suggested the violent waving of some flag of general truce — white silk with fluttering streamers.

"You 'll believe I 'm glad to see you when I tell you it 's only because I knew you were to be here that I came myself. I don't come and see my brother — I make him come and see me. This hill of his is impossible — I don't see what possesses him. Really, Osmond, you 'll be the ruin of my horses some day, and if it hurts them you 'll have to give me another pair. I heard them wheezing to-day; I assure you I did. It 's very disagreeable to hear one's horses wheezing when one 's sitting in the carriage; it sounds too as if they were n't what they should be. But I 've always had good horses; whatever else I may have lacked I 've always managed that. My husband does n't know much, but I think he knows a horse. In general Italians don't, but my husband goes in, according to his poor light, for everything English. My horses are English — so it 's all the greater pity they should be ruined. I must tell you," she went on, directly addressing Isabel, "that Osmond does n't often invite me; I don't think he likes to have me. It was quite my own idea, coming to-day. I like to see new people, and I 'm sure you 're very new. But don't sit there; that chair 's not what it looks. There are some very good seats here, but there are also some horrors."

These remarks were delivered with a series of little jerks and pecks, of roulades of shrillness, and in an accent that was as some fond recall of good English, or rather of good American, in adversity.

"I don't like to have you, my dear?" said her brother. "I'm sure you're invaluable."

"I don't see any horrors anywhere," Isabel returned, looking about her. "Everything seems to me beautiful and precious."

"I've a few good things," Mr. Osmond allowed; "indeed I've nothing very bad. But I've not what I should have liked."

He stood there a little awkwardly, smiling and glancing about; his manner was an odd mixture of the detached and the involved. He seemed to hint that nothing but the right "values" was of any consequence. Isabel made a rapid induction: perfect simplicity was not the badge of his family. Even the little girl from the convent, who, in her prim white dress, with her small submissive face and her hands locked before her, stood there as if she were about to partake of her first communion, even Mr. Osmond's diminutive daughter had a kind of finish that was not entirely artless.

"You'd have liked a few things from the Uffizi and the Pitti — that's what you'd have liked," said Madame Merle.

"Poor Osmond, with his old curtains and crucifixes!" the Countess Gemini exclaimed: she appeared to call her brother only by his family-name. Her ejaculation had no particular object; she smiled at Isabel as she made it and looked at her from head to foot.

Her brother had not heard her; he seemed to be thinking what he could say to Isabel. "Won't you have some tea? — you must be very tired," he at last bethought himself of remarking.

"No indeed, I'm not tired; what have I done to tire me?" Isabel felt a certain need of being very direct, of pretending to nothing; there was something in the air, in her general impression of things — she could hardly have said what it was — that deprived her of all disposition to put herself forward. The place, the occasion, the combination of people, signified more than lay on the surface; she would try to understand — she would not simply utter graceful platitudes. Poor Isabel was doubtless not aware that many women would have uttered graceful platitudes to cover the working of their observation. It must be confessed that her pride was a trifle alarmed. A man she had heard spoken of in terms that excited interest and who was evidently capable of distinguishing himself, had invited her, a young lady not lavish of her favours, to come to his house. Now that she had done so the burden of the entertainment rested naturally on his wit. Isabel was not rendered less observant, and for the moment, we judge, she was not rendered more indulgent, by perceiving that Mr. Osmond carried his burden less complacently than might have been expected. "What a fool I was to have let myself so needlessly in—!" she could fancy his exclaiming to himself.

"You'll be tired when you go home, if he shows you all his bibelots and gives you a lecture on each," said the Countess Gemini.

"I'm not afraid of that; but if I'm tired I shall at least have learned something."

"Very little, I suspect. But my sister's dreadfully afraid of learning anything," said Mr. Osmond.

"Oh, I confess to that; I don't want to know anything more — I know too much already. The more you know the more unhappy you are."

"You should not undervalue knowledge before Pansy, who has not finished her education," Madame Merle interposed with a smile.

"Pansy will never know any harm," said the child's father. "Pansy 's a little convent-flower."

"Oh, the convents, the convents!" cried the Countess with a flutter of her ruffles. "Speak to me of the convents! You may learn anything there; I'm a convent-flower myself. I don't pretend to be good, but the nuns do. Don't you see what I mean?" she went on, appealing to Isabel.

Isabel was not sure she saw, and she answered that she was very bad at following arguments. The Countess then declared that she herself detested arguments, but that this was her brother's taste — he would always discuss. "For me," she said, "one should like a thing or one should n't; one can't like everything, of course. But one should n't attempt to reason it out — you never know where it may lead you. There are some very good feelings that may have bad reasons, don't you know? And then there are very bad feelings, sometimes, that have good reasons. Don't you see what I mean? I don't care anything about reasons, but I know what I like."

"Ah, that 's the great thing," said Isabel, smiling and suspecting that her acquaintance with this lightly-flitting personage would not lead to intellectual repose. If the Countess objected to argument Isabel at this moment had as little taste for it, and she put out her hand to Pansy with a pleasant sense that such a gesture committed her to nothing that would admit of a divergence of views. Gilbert Osmond apparently took a rather hopeless view of his sister's tone; he turned the conversation to another topic. He presently sat down on the other side of his daughter, who had shyly brushed Isabel's fingers with her own; but he ended by drawing her out of her chair and making her stand between his knees, leaning against him while he passed his arm round her slimness. The child fixed her eyes on Isabel with a still, disinterested gaze which seemed void of an intention, yet conscious of an attraction. Mr. Osmond talked of many things; Madame Merle had said he could be agreeable when he chose, and to-day, after a little, he appeared not only to have chosen but to have determined. Madame Merle and the Countess Gemini sat a little apart, conversing in the effortless manner of persons who knew each other well enough to take their ease; but every now and then Isabel heard the Countess, at something said by her companion, plunge into the latter's lucidity as a poodle splashes after a thrown stick. It was as if Madame Merle were seeing how far she would go. Mr. Osmond talked of Florence, of Italy, of the pleasure of living in that country and of the abatements to the pleasure. There were both satisfactions and drawbacks; the drawbacks were numerous; strangers were too apt to see such a world as all romantic. It met the case soothingly for the human, for the social failure — by which he meant the people who could n't "realise," as they said, on their sensibility:

they could keep it about them there, in their poverty, without ridicule, as you might keep an heirloom or an inconvenient entailed place that brought you in nothing. Thus there were advantages in living in the country which contained the greatest sum of beauty. Certain impressions you could get only there. Others, favourable to life, you never got, and you got some that were very bad. But from time to time you got one of a quality that made up for everything. Italy, all the same, had spoiled a great many people; he was even fatuous enough to believe at times that he himself might have been a better man if he had spent less of his life there. It made one idle and dilettantish and second-rate; it had no discipline for the character, did n't cultivate in you, otherwise expressed, the successful social and other "cheek" that flourished in Paris and London. "We're sweetly provincial," said Mr. Osmond, "and I'm perfectly aware that I myself am as rusty as a key that has no lock to fit it. It polishes me up a little to talk with you — not that I venture to pretend I can turn that very complicated lock I suspect your intellect of being! But you'll be going away before I've seen you three times, and I shall perhaps never see you after that. That's what it is to live in a country that people come to. When they're disagreeable here it's bad enough; when they're agreeable it's still worse. As soon as you like them they're off again! I've been deceived too often; I've ceased to form attachments, to permit myself to feel attractions. You mean to stay — to settle? That would be really comfortable. Ah yes, your aunt's a sort of guarantee; I believe she may be depended on. Oh, she's an old Florentine; I mean literally an old one; not a modern outsider. She's a contemporary of the Medici; she must have been present at the burning of Savonarola, and I'm not sure she did n't throw a handful of chips into the flame. Her face is very much like some faces in the early pictures; little, dry, definite faces that must have had a good deal of expression, but almost always the same one. Indeed I can show you her portrait in a fresco of Ghirlandaio's. I hope you don't object to my speaking that way of your aunt, eh? I've an idea you don't. Perhaps you think that's even worse. I assure you there's no want of respect in it, to either of you. You know I'm a particular admirer of Mrs. Touchett."

While Isabel's host exerted himself to entertain her in this somewhat confidential fashion she looked occasionally at Madame Merle, who met her eyes with an inattentive smile in which, on this occasion, there was no infelicitous intimation that our heroine appeared to advantage. Madame Merle eventually proposed to the Countess Gemini that they should go into the garden, and the Countess, rising and shaking out her feathers, began to rustle toward the door. "Poor Miss Archer!" she exclaimed, surveying the other group with expressive compassion. "She has been brought quite into the family."

"Miss Archer can certainly have nothing but sympathy for a family to which you belong," Mr. Osmond answered, with a laugh which, though it had something of a mocking ring, had also a finer patience.

"I don't know what you mean by that! I'm sure she'll see no harm in me but what you tell her. I'm better than he says, Miss Archer," the Countess went on. "I'm only rather an idiot and a bore. Is that all he has said? Ah then, you keep him in good-humour. Has he opened on one of his favourite subjects? I give you notice that there are two or three that he treats *à fond*. In that case you had better take off your bonnet."

"I don't think I know what Mr. Osmond's favourite subjects are," said Isabel, who had risen to her feet.

The Countess assumed for an instant an attitude of intense meditation, pressing one of her hands, with the finger-tips gathered together, to her forehead. "I'll tell you in a moment. One's Machiavelli; the other's Vittoria Colonna; the next is Metastasio."

"Ah, with me," said Madame Merle, passing her arm into the Countess Gemini's as if to guide her course to the garden, "Mr. Osmond's never so historical."

"Oh you," the Countess answered as they moved away, "you yourself are Machiavelli — you yourself are Vittoria Colonna!"

"We shall hear next that poor Madame Merle is Metastasio!" Gilbert Osmond resignedly sighed.

Isabel had got up on the assumption that they too were to go into the garden; but her host stood there with no apparent inclination to leave the room, his hands in the pockets of his jacket and his daughter, who had now locked her arm into one of his own, clinging to him and locking up while her eyes moved from his own face to Isabel's. Isabel waited, with a certain unuttered contentedness, to have her movements directed; she liked Mr. Osmond's talk, his company: she had what always gave her a very private thrill, the consciousness of a new relation. Through the open doors of the great room she saw Madame Merle and the Countess stroll across the fine grass of the garden; then she turned, and her eyes wandered over the things scattered about her. The understanding had been that Mr. Osmond should show her his treasures; his pictures and cabinets all looked like treasures. Isabel after a moment went toward one of the pictures to see it better; but just as she had done so he said to her abruptly: "Miss Archer, what do you think of my sister?"

She faced him with some surprise. "Ah, don't ask me that — I've seen your sister too little."

"Yes, you've seen her very little; but you must have observed that there is not a great deal of her to see. What do you think of our family tone?" he went on with his cool smile. "I should like to know how it strikes a fresh, unprejudiced mind. I know what you're going to say — you've had almost no observation of it. Of course this is only a glimpse. But just take notice, in future, if you have a chance. I sometimes think we've got into a rather bad way, living off here among things and people not our own, without responsibilities or attachments, with nothing to hold us together or keep us up; marrying foreigners, forming artificial tastes, playing tricks with our natural mission. Let me add, though, that I say that much more for myself than for my sister.

She's a very honest lady — more so than she seems. She's rather unhappy, and as she's not of a serious turn she does n't tend to show it tragically: she shows it comically instead. She has got a horrid husband, though I'm not sure she makes the best of him. Of course, however, a horrid husband's an awkward thing. Madame Merle gives her excellent advice, but it's a good deal like giving a child a dictionary to learn a language with. He can look out the words, but he can't put them together. My sister needs a grammar, but unfortunately she's not grammatical. Pardon my troubling you with these details; my sister was very right in saying you've been taken into the family. Let me take down that picture; you want more light."

He took down the picture, carried it toward the window, related some curious facts about it. She looked at the other works of art, and he gave her such further information as might appear most acceptable to a young lady making a call on a summer afternoon. His pictures, his medallions and tapestries were interesting; but after a while Isabel felt the owner much more so, and independently of them, thickly as they seemed to overhang him. He resembled no one she had ever seen; most of the people she knew might be divided into groups of half a dozen specimens. There were one or two exceptions to this; she could think for instance of no group that would contain her aunt Lydia. There were other people who were, relatively speaking, original — original, as one might say, by courtesy — such as Mr. Goodwood, as her cousin Ralph, as

Henrietta Stackpole, as Lord Warburton, as Madame Merle. But in essentials, when one came to look at them, these individuals belonged to types already present to her mind. Her mind contained no class offering a natural place to Mr. Osmond — he was a specimen apart. It was not that she recognised all these truths at the hour, but they were falling into order before her. For the moment she only said to herself that this "new relation" would perhaps prove her very most distinguished. Madame Merle had had that note of rarity, but what quite other power it immediately gained when sounded by a man! It was not so much what he said and did, but rather what he withheld, that marked him for her as by one of those signs of the highly curious that he was showing her on the underside of old plates and in the corner of sixteenth-century drawings: he indulged in no striking deflections from common usage, he was an original without being an eccentric. She had never met a person of so fine a grain. The peculiarity was physical, to begin with, and it extended to impalpabilities. His dense, delicate hair, his overdrawn, retouched features, his clear complexion, ripe without being coarse, the very evenness of the growth of his beard, and that light, smooth slenderness of structure which made the movement of a single one of his fingers produce the effect of an expressive gesture — these personal points struck our sensitive young woman as signs of quality, of intensity, somehow as promises of interest. He was certainly fastidious and critical; he was probably irritable. His sensibility had governed him — possibly governed him too much; it had made him impatient of vulgar troubles and had led him to live by himself, in a sorted, sifted, arranged world, thinking about art and beauty and history. He had consulted his taste in everything — his taste alone perhaps, as a sick man consciously incurable consults at last only his lawyer: that was what made him so different from every one else. Ralph had something of this same quality, this appearance of thinking that life was a matter of connoisseurship; but in Ralph it was an anomaly, a kind of humorous excrescence, whereas in Mr. Osmond it was the keynote, and everything was in harmony with it. She was certainly far from understanding him completely; his meaning was not at all times obvious. It was hard to see what he meant for instance by speaking of his provincial side — which was exactly the side she would have taken him most to lack. Was it a harmless paradox, intended to puzzle her? or was it the last refinement of high culture? She trusted she should learn in time; it would be very interesting to learn. If it was provincial to have that harmony, what then was the finish of the capital? And she could put this question in spite of so feeling her host a shy personage; since such shyness as his — the shyness of ticklish nerves and fine perceptions — was perfectly consistent with the best breeding. Indeed it was almost a proof of standards and touchstones other than the vulgar: he must be so sure the vulgar would be first on the ground. He was n't a man of easy assurance, who chatted and gossiped with the fluency of a superficial nature; he was critical of himself as well as of others, and, exacting a good deal of others, to think them agreeable, probably took a rather ironical view of what he himself offered: a proof into the bargain that he was not grossly conceited. If he had not been shy he would n't have effected that gradual, subtle, successful conversion of it to which she owed both what pleased her in him and what mystified her. If he had suddenly asked her what she thought of the Countess Gemini, that was doubtless a proof that he was interested in her; it could scarcely be as a help to knowledge of his own sister. That he should be so interested showed an enquiring mind; but it was a little singular he should sacrifice his fraternal feeling to his curiosity. This was the most eccentric thing he had done.

There were two other rooms, beyond the one in which she had been received, equally full of romantic objects, and in these apartments Isabel spent a quarter of an hour. Everything was in the last degree curious and precious, and Mr. Osmond continued to be the kindest of ciceroni as he led her from one fine piece to another and still held his little girl by the hand. His kindness almost surprised our young friend, who wondered why he should take so much trouble for her; and she was oppressed at last with the accumulation of beauty and knowledge to which she found herself introduced. There was enough for the present; she had ceased to attend to what he said; she listened to him with attentive eyes, but was not thinking of what he told her. He probably thought her quicker, cleverer in every way, more prepared, than she was. Madame Merle would have pleasantly exaggerated; which was a pity, because in the end he would be sure to find out, and then perhaps even her real intelligence would n't reconcile him to his mistake. A part of Isabel's fatigue came from the effort to appear as intelligent as she believed Madame Merle had described her, and from the fear (very unusual with her) of exposing — not her ignorance; for that she cared comparatively little — but her possible grossness of perception. It would have annoyed her to express a liking for something he, in his superior enlightenment, would think she ought n't to like; or to pass by something at which the truly initiated mind would arrest itself. She had no wish to fall into that grotesqueness — in which she had seen women (and it was a warning) serenely, yet ignobly, flounder. She was very careful therefore as to what she said, as to what she noticed or failed to notice; more careful than she had ever been before.

They came back into the first of the rooms, where the tea had been served; but as the two other ladies were still on the terrace, and as Isabel had not yet been made acquainted with the view, the paramount distinction of the place, Mr. Osmond directed her steps into the garden without more delay. Madame Merle and the Countess had had chairs brought out, and as the afternoon was lovely the Countess proposed they should take their tea in the open air. Pansy therefore was sent to bid the servant bring out the preparations. The sun had got low, the golden light took a deeper tone, and on the mountains and the plain that stretched beneath them the masses of purple shadow glowed as richly as the places that were still exposed. The scene had an extraordinary charm. The air was almost solemnly still, and the large expanse of the landscape, with its gardenlike culture and nobleness of outline, its teeming valley and delicately-fretted hills, its peculiarly human-looking touches of habitation, lay there in splendid harmony and classic grace. "You seem so well pleased that I think you can be trusted to come back," Osmond said as he led his companion to one of the angles of the terrace.

"I shall certainly come back," she returned, "in spite of what you say about its being bad to live in Italy. What was that you said about one's natural mission? I wonder if I should forsake my natural mission if I were to settle in Florence."

"A woman's natural mission is to be where she's most appreciated."

"The point's to find out where that is."

"Very true — she often wastes a great deal of time in the enquiry. People ought to make it very plain to her."

"Such a matter would have to be made very plain to me," smiled Isabel.

"I'm glad, at any rate, to hear you talk of settling. Madame Merle had given me an idea that you were of a rather roving disposition. I thought she spoke of your having some plan of going round the world."

"I'm rather ashamed of my plans; I make a new one every day."

"I don't see why you should be ashamed; it's the greatest of pleasures."

"It seems frivolous, I think," said Isabel. "One ought to choose something very deliberately, and be faithful to that."

"By that rule then, I've not been frivolous."

"Have you never made plans?"

"Yes, I made one years ago, and I'm acting on it to-day."

"It must have been a very pleasant one," Isabel permitted herself to observe.

"It was very simple. It was to be as quiet as possible."

"As quiet?" the girl repeated.

"Not to worry — not to strive nor struggle. To resign myself. To be content with little." He spoke these sentences slowly, with short pauses between, and his intelligent regard was fixed on his visitor's with the conscious air of a man who has brought himself to confess something.

"Do you call that simple?" she asked with mild irony.

"Yes, because it's negative."

"Has your life been negative?"

"Call it affirmative if you like. Only it has affirmed my indifference. Mind you, not my natural indifference — I *had* none. But my studied, my wilful renunciation."

She scarcely understood him; it seemed a question whether he were joking or not. Why should a man who struck her as having a great fund of reserve suddenly bring himself to be so confidential? This was his affair, however, and his confidences were interesting. "I don't see why you should have renounced," she said in a moment.

"Because I could do nothing. I had no prospects, I was poor, and I was not a man of genius. I had no talents even; I took my measure early in life. I was simply the most fastidious young gentleman living. There were two or three people in the world I envied — the Emperor of Russia, for instance, and the Sultan of Turkey! There were even moments when I envied the Pope of Rome — for the consideration he enjoys. I should have been delighted to be considered to that extent; but since that could n't be I did n't care for anything less, and I made up my mind not to go in for honours. The leanest gentleman can always consider himself, and fortunately I *was*, though lean, a gentleman. I could do nothing in Italy — I could n't even be an Italian patriot. To do that I should have had to get out of the country; and I was too fond of it to leave it, to say nothing of my being too well satisfied with it, on the whole, as it then was, to wish it altered. So I've passed a great many years here on that quiet plan I spoke of. I've not been at all unhappy. I don't mean to say I've cared for nothing; but the things I've cared for have been definite — limited. The events of my life have been absolutely unperceived by any one save myself; getting an old silver crucifix at a bargain (I've never bought anything dear, of course), or discovering, as I once did, a sketch by Correggio on a panel daubed over by some inspired idiot."

This would have been rather a dry account of Mr.

Osmond's career if Isabel had fully believed it; but her imagination supplied the human element which she was sure had not been wanting. His life had been mingled with other lives more than he admitted; naturally she could n't expect him to enter into this. For the present she abstained from provoking further revelations; to intimate that he had not told her everything would be more familiar and less considerate than she now desired to be — would in fact be uproariously vulgar. He had certainly told her quite enough. It was her present inclination, however, to express a measured sympathy for the success with which he had preserved his independence. "That's a very pleasant life," she said, "to renounce everything but Correggio!"

"Oh, I've made in my way a good thing of it. Don't imagine I'm whining about it. It's one's own fault if one is n't happy."

This was large; she kept down to something smaller. "Have you lived here always?"

"No, not always. I lived a long time at Naples, and many years in Rome. But I've been here a good while. Perhaps I shall have to change, however; to do something else. I've no longer myself to think of. My daughter's growing up and may very possibly not care so much for the Correggios and crucifixes as I. I shall have to do what's best for Pansy."

"Yes, do that," said Isabel. "She's such a dear little girl."

"Ah," cried Gilbert Osmond beautifully, "she's a little saint of heaven! She is my great happiness!"

XXV

WHILE this sufficiently intimate colloquy (prolonged for some time after we cease to follow it) went forward Madame Merle and her companion, breaking a silence of some duration, had begun to exchange remarks. They were sitting in an attitude of unexpressed expectancy; an attitude especially marked on the part of the Countess Gemini, who, being of a more nervous temperament than her friend, practised with less success the art of disguising impatience. What these ladies were waiting for would not have been apparent and was perhaps not very definite to their own minds. Madame Merle waited for Osmond to release their young friend from her *tête-à-tête*, and the Countess waited because Madame Merle did. The Countess, moreover, by waiting, found the time ripe for one of her pretty perversities. She might have desired for some minutes to place it. Her brother wandered with Isabel to the end of the garden, to which point her eyes followed them.

"My dear," she then observed to her companion, "you 'll excuse me if I don't congratulate you!"

"Very willingly, for I don't in the least know why you should."

"Have n't you a little plan that you think rather well of?" And the Countess nodded at the sequestered couple.

Madame Merle's eyes took the same direction; then

she looked serenely at her neighbour. "You know I never understand you very well," she smiled.

"No one can understand better than you when you wish. I see that just now you *don't* wish."

"You say things to me that no one else does," said Madame Merle gravely, yet without bitterness.

"You mean things you don't like? Does n't Osmond sometimes say such things?"

"What your brother says has a point."

"Yes, a poisoned one sometimes. If you mean that I'm not so clever as he you must n't think I shall suffer from your sense of our difference. But it will be much better that you should understand me."

"Why so?" asked Madame Merle. "To what will it conduce?"

"If I don't approve of your plan you ought to know it in order to appreciate the danger of my interfering with it."

Madame Merle looked as if she were ready to admit that there might be something in this; but in a moment she said quietly: "You think me more calculating than I am."

"It's not your calculating I think ill of; it's your calculating wrong. You've done so in this case."

"You must have made extensive calculations yourself to discover that."

"No, I've not had time. I've seen the girl but this once," said the Countess, "and the conviction has suddenly come to me. I like her very much."

"So do I," Madame Merle mentioned.

"You've a strange way of showing it."

"Surely I've given her the advantage of making your acquaintance."

"That indeed," piped the Countess, "is perhaps the best thing that could happen to her!"

Madame Merle said nothing for some time. The Countess's manner was odious, was really low; but it was an old story, and with her eyes upon the violet slope of Monte Morello she gave herself up to reflection. "My dear lady," she finally resumed, "I advise you not to agitate yourself. The matter you allude to concerns three persons much stronger of purpose than yourself."

"Three persons? You and Osmond of course. But is Miss Archer also very strong of purpose?"

"Quite as much so as we."

"Ah then," said the Countess radiantly, "if I convince her it's her interest to resist you she'll do so successfully!"

"Resist us? Why do you express yourself so coarsely? She's not exposed to compulsion or deception."

"I'm not sure of that. You're capable of anything, you and Osmond. I don't mean Osmond by himself, and I don't mean you by yourself. But together you're dangerous — like some chemical combination."

"You had better leave us alone then," smiled Madame Merle.

"I don't mean to touch you — but I shall talk to that girl."

"My poor Amy," Madame Merle murmured, "I don't see what has got into your head."

"I take an interest in her — that's what has got into my head. I like her."

Madame Merle hesitated a moment. "I don't think she likes you."

The Countess's bright little eyes expanded and her face was set in a grimace. "Ah, you *are* dangerous — even by yourself!"

"If you want her to like you don't abuse your brother to her," said Madame Merle.

"I don't suppose you pretend she has fallen in love with him in two interviews."

Madame Merle looked a moment at Isabel and at the master of the house. He was leaning against the parapet, facing her, his arms folded; and she at present was evidently not lost in the mere impersonal view, persistently as she gazed at it. As Madame Merle watched her she lowered her eyes; she was listening, possibly with a certain embarrassment, while she pressed the point of her parasol into the path. Madame Merle rose from her chair. "Yes, I think so!" she pronounced.

The shabby footboy, summoned by Pansy — he might, tarnished as to livery and quaint as to type, have issued from some stray sketch of old-time manners, been "put in" by the brush of a Longhi or a Goya — had come out with a small table and placed it on the grass, and then had gone back and fetched the tea-tray; after which he had again disappeared, to return with a couple of chairs. Pansy had watched these proceedings with the deepest interest, standing with her small hands folded together upon the front of her scanty frock; but she had not presumed to offer assistance. When the tea-table had been arranged, however, she gently approached her aunt.

"Do you think papa would object to my making the tea?"

The Countess looked at her with a deliberately critical gaze and without answering her question. "My poor niece," she said, "is that your best frock?"

"Ah no," Pansy answered, "it's just a little *toilette* for common occasions."

"Do you call it a common occasion when I come to see you? — to say nothing of Madame Merle and the pretty lady yonder."

Pansy reflected a moment, turning gravely from one of the persons mentioned to the other. Then her face broke into its perfect smile. "I have a pretty dress, but even that one's very simple. Why should I expose it beside your beautiful things?"

"Because it's the prettiest you have; for me you must always wear the prettiest. Please put it on the next time. It seems to me they don't dress you so well as they might."

The child sparingly stroked down her antiquated skirt. "It's a good little dress to make tea — don't you think? Don't you believe papa would allow me?"

"Impossible for me to say, my child," said the Countess. "For me, your father's ideas are unfathomable. Madame Merle understands them better. Ask *her*."

Madame Merle smiled with her usual grace. "It's a weighty question — let me think. It seems to me it would please your father to see a careful little daughter making his tea. It's the proper duty of the daughter of the house — when she grows up."

"So it seems to me, Madame Merle!" Pansy cried. "You shall see how well I'll make it. A spoonful for each." And she began to busy herself at the table.

"Two spoonfuls for me," said the Countess, who, with Madame Merle, remained for some moments watching her. "Listen to me, Pansy," the Countess resumed at last. "I should like to know what you think of your visitor."

"Ah, she's not mine — she's papa's," Pansy objected.

"Miss Archer came to see you as well," said Madame Merle.

"I'm very happy to hear that. She has been very polite to me."

"Do you like her then?" the Countess asked.

"She's charming — charming," Pansy repeated in her little neat conversational tone. "She pleases me thoroughly."

"And how do you think she pleases your father?"

"Ah really, Countess!" murmured Madame Merle dissuasively. "Go and call them to tea," she went on to the child.

"You'll see if they don't like it!" Pansy declared; and departed to summon the others, who had still lingered at the end of the terrace.

"If Miss Archer's to become her mother it's surely interesting to know if the child likes her," said the Countess.

"If your brother marries again it won't be for Pansy's sake," Madame Merle replied. "She'll soon be sixteen, and after that she'll begin to need a husband rather than a stepmother."

"And will you provide the husband as well?"

"I shall certainly take an interest in her marrying fortunately. I imagine you'll do the same."

"Indeed I shan't!" cried the Countess. "Why should I, of all women, set such a price on a husband?"

"You did n't marry fortunately; that's what I'm speaking of. When I say a husband I mean a good one."

"There are no good ones. Osmond won't be a good one."

Madame Merle closed her eyes a moment. "You're irritated just now; I don't know why," she presently said. "I don't think you'll really object either to your brother's or to your niece's marrying, when the time comes for them to do so; and as regards Pansy I'm confident that we shall some day have the pleasure of looking for a husband for her together. Your large acquaintance will be a great help."

"Yes, I'm irritated," the Countess answered. "You often irritate me. Your own coolness is fabulous. You're a strange woman."

"It's much better that we should always act together," Madame Merle went on.

"Do you mean that as a threat?" asked the Countess rising.

Madame Merle shook her head as for quiet amusement. "No indeed, you've not my coolness!"

Isabel and Mr. Osmond were now slowly coming toward them and Isabel had taken Pansy by the hand. "Do you pretend to believe he'd make her happy?" the Countess demanded.

"If he should marry Miss Archer I suppose he'd behave like a gentleman."

The Countess jerked herself into a succession of attitudes. "Do you mean as most gentlemen behave? That would be much to be thankful for! Of course Osmond's a gentleman; his own sister need n't be reminded of that. But does he think he can marry any girl he happens to pick out? Osmond's a gentleman, of course; but I must say I've *never*, no, no, never, seen any one of Osmond's pretensions! What they're all founded on is more than I can say. I'm his own sister; I might be supposed to know. Who is he, if you please? What has he ever done? If there had been anything particularly grand in his origin — if he were made of some superior clay — I presume I should have got some inkling of it. If there had been any great honours or splendours in the family I should certainly have made the most of them: they would have been quite in my line. But there's nothing, nothing, nothing. One's parents were charming people of course; but so were yours, I've no doubt. Every one's a charming person now-a-days. Even I'm a charming person; don't laugh, it has literally been said. As for Osmond, he has always appeared to believe that he's descended from the gods."

"You may say what you please," said Madame Merle, who had listened to this quick outbreak none the less attentively, we may believe, because her eye wandered away from the speaker and her hands busied themselves with adjusting the knots of ribbon on her dress. "You Osmonds are a fine race — your blood must flow from some very pure source. Your brother, like an intelligent man, has had the conviction of it if he has not had the proofs. You're modest about it, but you yourself are extremely distinguished. What do you say about your niece? The child's a little princess. Nevertheless," Madame Merle added, "it won't be an easy matter for Osmond to marry Miss Archer. Yet he can try."

"I hope she'll refuse him. It will take him down a little."

"We must n't forget that he is one of the cleverest of men."

"I've heard you say that before, but I have n't yet discovered what he has done."

"What he has done? He has done nothing that has had to be undone. And he has known how to wait."

"To wait for Miss Archer's money? How much of it is there?"

"That's not what I mean," said Madame Merle. "Miss Archer has seventy thousand pounds."

"Well, it's a pity she's so charming," the Countess declared. "To be sacrificed, any girl would do. She need n't be superior."

"If she were n't superior your brother would never look at her. He must have the best."

"Yes," returned the Countess as they went forward a little to meet the others, "he's very hard to satisfy. That makes me tremble for her happiness!"

XXVI

Gilbert Osmond came to see Isabel again; that is he came to Palazzo Crescentini. He had other friends there as well, and to Mrs. Touchett and Madame Merle he was always impartially civil; but the former of these ladies noted the fact that in the course of a fortnight he called five times, and compared it with another fact that she found no difficulty in remembering. Two visits a year had hitherto constituted his regular tribute to Mrs. Touchett's worth, and she had never observed him select for such visits those moments, of almost periodical recurrence, when Madame Merle was under her roof. It was not for Madame Merle that he came; these two were old friends and he never put himself out for her. He was not fond of Ralph — Ralph had told her so — and it was not supposable that Mr. Osmond had suddenly taken a fancy to her son. Ralph was imperturbable — Ralph had a kind of loose-fitting urbanity that wrapped him about like an ill-made overcoat, but of which he never divested himself; he thought Mr. Osmond very good company and was willing at any time to look at him in the light of hospitality. But he did n't flatter himself that the desire to repair a past injustice was the motive of their visitor's calls; he read the situation more clearly. Isabel was the attraction, and in all conscience a sufficient one. Osmond was a critic, a student of the exquisite, and it was natural he should be curious of so rare an apparition. So when his mother observed to him that it was plain what Mr. Osmond was thinking of, Ralph replied that he was quite of her opinion. Mrs. Touchett had from far back found a place on her scant list for this gentleman, though wondering dimly by what art and what process — so negative and so wise as they were — he had everywhere effectively imposed himself. As he had never been an importunate visitor he had had no chance to be offensive, and he was recommended to her by his appearance of being as well able to do without her as she was to do without him — a quality that always, oddly enough, affected her as providing ground for a relation with her. It gave her no satisfaction, however, to think that he had taken it into his head to marry her niece. Such an alliance, on Isabel's part, would have an air of almost morbid perversity. Mrs. Touchett easily remembered that the girl had refused an English peer; and that a young lady with whom Lord Warburton had not successfully wrestled should content herself with an obscure American dilettante, a middle-aged widower with an uncanny child and an ambiguous income, this answered to nothing in Mrs. Touchett's conception of success. She took, it will be observed, not the sentimental, but the political, view of matrimony — a view which has always had much to recommend it. "I trust she won't have the folly to listen to him," she said to her son; to which Ralph replied that Isabel's listening was one thing and Isabel's answering quite another. He knew she had listened to several parties, as his father would have said, but had made them listen in return; and he found much entertainment in the idea that in these few months of his knowing her he should observe a fresh suitor at her gate. She had wanted to see life, and fortune was serving her to her taste; a succession of fine gentlemen going down on their knees to her would do as well as anything else. Ralph looked forward to a fourth, a fifth, a tenth besieger; he had no conviction she would stop at a third. She would keep the gate ajar and open a parley; she would certainly not allow number three to come in. He expressed this view, somewhat after this fashion, to his mother, who looked at him as if he had been dancing a jig. He had such a fanciful, pictorial way of saying things that he might as well address her in the deaf-mute's alphabet.

"I don't think I know what you mean," she said; "you use too many figures of speech; I could never understand allegories. The two words in the language I most respect are Yes and No. If Isabel wants to marry Mr. Osmond she'll do so in spite of all your comparisons. Let her alone to find a fine one herself for anything she undertakes. I know very little about the young man in America; I don't think she spends much of her time in thinking of him, and I suspect he has got tired of waiting for her. There's nothing in life to prevent her marrying Mr. Osmond if she only looks at him in a certain way. That's all very well; no one approves more than I of one's pleasing one's self. But she takes her pleasure in such odd things; she's capable of marrying Mr.

Osmond for the beauty of his opinions or for his autograph of Michael Angelo. She wants to be disinterested: as if she were the only person who 's in danger of not being so! Will *he* be so disinterested when he has the spending of her money? That was her idea before your father's death, and it has acquired new charms for her since. She ought to marry some one of whose disinterestedness she shall herself be sure; and there would be no such proof of that as his having a fortune of his own."

"My dear mother, I 'm not afraid," Ralph answered. "She 's making fools of us all. She 'll please herself, of course; but she 'll do so by studying human nature at close quarters and yet retaining her liberty. She has started on an exploring expedition, and I don't think she 'll change her course, at the outset, at a signal from Gilbert Osmond. She may have slackened speed for an hour, but before we know it she 'll be steaming away again. Excuse another metaphor."

Mrs. Touchett excused it perhaps, but was not so much reassured as to withhold from Madame Merle the expression of her fears. "You who know everything," she said, "you must know this: whether that curious creature 's really making love to my niece."

"Gilbert Osmond?" Madame Merle widened her clear eyes and, with a full intelligence, "Heaven help us," she exclaimed, "that 's an idea!"

"Had n't it occurred to you?"

"You make me feel an idiot, but I confess it had n't. I wonder," she added, "if it has occurred to Isabel."

"Oh, I shall now ask her," said Mrs. Touchett.

Madame Merle reflected. "Don't put it into her head. The thing would be to ask Mr. Osmond."

"I can't do that," said Mrs. Touchett. "I won't have him enquire of me — as he perfectly may with that air of his, given Isabel's situation — what business it is of mine."

"I'll ask him myself," Madame Merle bravely declared.

"But what business — for *him* — is it of yours?"

"It's being none whatever is just why I can afford to speak. It's so much less my business than any one's else that he can put me off with anything he chooses. But it will be by the way he does this that I shall know."

"Pray let me hear then," said Mrs. Touchett, "of the fruits of your penetration. If I can't speak to him, however, at least I can speak to Isabel."

Her companion sounded at this the note of warning. "Don't be too quick with her. Don't inflame her imagination."

"I never did anything in life to any one's imagination. But I'm always sure of her doing something — well, not of *my* kind."

"No, you would n't like this," Madame Merle observed without the point of interrogation.

"Why in the world should I, pray? Mr. Osmond has nothing the least solid to offer."

Again Madame Merle was silent while her thoughtful smile drew up her mouth even more charmingly than usual toward the left corner. "Let us distinguish. Gilbert Osmond's certainly not the first comer. He's a man who in favourable conditions might very well make a great impression. He has made a great impression, to my knowledge, more than once."

"Don't tell me about his probably quite cold-blooded love-affairs; they're nothing to me!" Mrs. Touchett cried. "What you say's precisely why I wish he would cease his visits. He has nothing in the world that I know of but a dozen or two of early masters and a more or less pert little daughter."

"The early masters are now worth a good deal of money," said Madame Merle, "and the daughter's a very young and very innocent and very harmless person."

"In other words she's an insipid little chit. Is that what you mean? Having no fortune she can't hope to marry as they marry here; so that Isabel will have to furnish her either with a maintenance or with a dowry."

"Isabel probably would n't object to being kind to her. I think she likes the poor child."

"Another reason then for Mr. Osmond's stopping at home! Otherwise, a week hence, we shall have my niece arriving at the conviction that her mission in life's to prove that a stepmother may sacrifice herself — and that, to prove it, she must first become one."

"She would make a charming stepmother," smiled Madame Merle; "but I quite agree with you that she had better not decide upon her mission too hastily. Changing the form of one's mission's almost as difficult as changing the shape of one's nose: there they are, each, in the middle of one's face and one's character — one has to begin too far back. But I'll investigate and report to you."

All this went on quite over Isabel's head; she had no suspicions that her relations with Mr. Osmond were being discussed. Madame Merle had said nothing to put her on her guard; she alluded no more pointedly to him than to the other gentlemen of Florence, native and foreign, who now arrived in considerable numbers to pay their respects to Miss Archer's aunt. Isabel thought him interesting — she came back to that; she liked so to think of him. She had carried away an image from her visit to his hill-top which her subsequent knowledge of him did nothing to efface and which put on for her a particular harmony with other supposed and divined things, histories within histories: the image of a quiet, clever, sensitive, distinguished man, strolling on a moss-grown terrace above the sweet Val d'Arno and holding by the hand a little girl whose bell-like clearness gave a new grace to childhood. The picture had no flourishes, but she liked its lowness of tone and the atmosphere of summer twilight that pervaded it. It spoke of the kind of personal issue that touched her most nearly; of the choice between objects, subjects, contacts — what might she call them? — of a thin and those of a rich association; of a lonely, studious life in a lovely land; of an old sorrow that sometimes ached to-day; of a feeling of pride that was perhaps exaggerated, but that had an element of nobleness; of a care for beauty and perfection so natural and so cultivated together that the career appeared to stretch beneath it in the disposed vistas and with the ranges of steps and terraces and fountains of a formal Italian garden — allowing only for arid places freshened by the natural dews of a quaint half-anxious, half-helpless fatherhood. At Palazzo Crescentini Mr. Osmond's manner remained the same; diffident at first — oh self-conscious beyond doubt! and full of the effort (visible only to a sympathetic eye) to overcome this disadvantage; an effort which usually resulted in a great deal of easy, lively, very positive, rather aggressive, always suggestive talk. Mr. Osmond's talk was not injured by the indication of an eagerness to shine; Isabel found no difficulty in believing that a person was sincere who had so many of the signs of strong conviction — as for instance an explicit and graceful appreciation of anything that might be said on his own side of the question, said perhaps by Miss Archer in especial. What continued to please this young woman was that while he talked so for amusement he did n't talk, as she had heard people, for "effect." He uttered his ideas as if, odd as they often appeared, he were used to them and had lived with them; old polished knobs and heads and handles, of precious substance, that could be fitted if necessary to new walking-sticks — not switches plucked in destitution from the common tree and then too elegantly waved about. One day he brought his small daughter with him, and she rejoiced to renew acquaintance with the child, who, as she presented her forehead to be kissed by every member of the circle, reminded her vividly of an *ingénue* in a French play. Isabel had never seen a little person of this pattern; American girls were very different — different too were the maidens of England. Pansy was so formed and finished for her tiny place in the world, and yet in imagination, as one could see, so innocent and infantine. She sat on the sofa by Isabel; she wore a small grenadine mantle and a pair of the useful gloves that Madame Merle had given her — little grey gloves with a single button. She was like a sheet of blank paper — the ideal *jeune fille* of foreign fiction. Isabel hoped that so fair and smooth a page would be covered with an edifying text.

The Countess Gemini also came to call upon her, but the Countess was quite another affair. She was by no means a blank sheet; she had been written over in a variety of hands, and Mrs. Touchett, who felt by no means honoured by her visit, pronounced that a number of unmistakeable blots were to be seen upon her surface. The Countess gave rise indeed to some discussion between the mistress of the house and the visitor from Rome, in which Madame Merle (who was not such a fool as to irritate people by always agreeing with them) availed herself felicitously enough of that large licence of dissent which her hostess permitted as freely as she practised it. Mrs. Touchett had declared it a piece of audacity that this highly compromised character should have presented herself at such a time of day at the door of a house in which she was esteemed so little as she must long have known herself to be at Palazzo Crescentini. Isabel had been made acquainted with the estimate prevailing under that roof: it represented Mr. Osmond's sister as a lady who had so mismanaged her improprieties that they had ceased to hang together at all — which was at the least what one asked of such matters — and had become the mere floating fragments of a wrecked renown, incommoding social circulation. She had been married by her mother — a more administrative person, with an appreciation of foreign titles which the daughter, to do her justice, had probably by this time thrown off — to an Italian nobleman who had perhaps given her some excuse for attempting to quench the consciousness of outrage. The Countess, however, had consoled herself outrageously, and the list of her excuses had now lost itself in the labyrinth of her adventures. Mrs. Touchett had never consented to receive her, though the Countess had made overtures of old. Florence was not an austere city; but, as Mrs. Touchett said, she had to draw the line somewhere.

Madame Merle defended the luckless lady with a great deal of zeal and wit. She could n't see why Mrs. Touchett should make a scapegoat of a woman who had really done no harm, who had only done good in the wrong way. One must certainly draw the line, but while one was about it one should draw it straight: it was a very crooked chalk-mark that would exclude the Countess Gemini. In that case Mrs. Touchett had better shut up her house; this perhaps would be the best course so long as she remained in Florence. One must be fair and not make arbitrary differences: the Countess had doubtless been imprudent, she had not been so clever as other women. She was a good creature, not clever at all; but since when had that been a ground of exclusion from the best society? For ever so long now one had heard nothing about her, and there could be no better proof of her having renounced the error of her ways than her desire to become a member of Mrs. Touchett's circle. Isabel could contribute nothing to this interesting dispute, not even a patient attention; she contented herself with having given a friendly welcome to the unfortunate lady, who, whatever her defects, had at least the merit of being Mr. Osmond's sister. As she liked the brother Isabel thought it proper to try and like the sister: in spite of the growing complexity of things she was still capable of these primitive sequences. She had not received the happiest impression of the Countess on meeting her at the villa, but was thankful for an opportunity to repair the accident. Had not Mr. Osmond remarked that she was a respectable person? To have proceeded from Gilbert Osmond this was a crude proposition, but Madame Merle bestowed upon it a certain improving polish. She told Isabel more about the poor Countess than Mr. Osmond had done, and related the history of her marriage and its consequences. The Count was a member of an ancient Tuscan family, but of such small estate that he had been glad to accept Amy Osmond, in spite of the questionable beauty which had yet not hampered her career, with the modest dowry her mother was able to offer — a sum about equivalent to that which had already formed her brother's share of their patrimony. Count Gemini since then, however, had inherited money, and now they were well enough off, as Italians went, though Amy was horribly extravagant. The Count was a low-lived brute; he had given his wife every pretext. She had no children; she had lost three within a year of their birth. Her mother, who had bristled with pretensions to elegant learning and published descriptive poems and corresponded on Italian subjects with the English weekly journals, her mother had died three years after the Countess's marriage, the father, lost in the grey American dawn of the situation, but reputed originally rich and wild, having died much earlier. One could see this in Gilbert Osmond, Madame Merle held — see that he had been brought up by a woman; though, to do him justice, one would suppose it had been by a more sensible woman than the American Corinne, as Mrs. Osmond had liked to be called. She had brought her children to Italy after her husband's death, and Mrs. Touchett remembered her during the year that followed her arrival. She thought her a horrible snob; but this was an irregularity of judgement on Mrs. Touchett's part, for she, like Mrs. Osmond, approved of political marriages. The Countess was very good company and not really the featherhead she seemed; all one had to do with her was to observe the simple condition of not believing a word she said. Madame Merle had always made the best of her for her brother's sake; he appreciated any kindness shown to Amy, because (if it had to be confessed for him) he rather felt she let down their common name. Naturally he could n't like her style, her shrillness, her egotism, her violations of taste and above all of truth: she acted badly on his nerves, she was not *his* sort of woman. What was his sort of woman? Oh, the very opposite of the Countess, a woman to whom the truth should be habitually sacred. Isabel was unable to estimate the number of times her visitor had, in half an hour, profaned it: the Countess indeed had given her an impression of rather silly sincerity. She had talked almost exclusively about herself; how much she should like to know Miss Archer; how thankful she should be for a real friend; how base the people in Florence were; how tired she was of the place; how much she should like to live somewhere else — in Paris, in London, in Washington; how impossible it was to get anything nice to wear in Italy except a little old lace; how dear the world was growing everywhere; what a life of suffering and privation she had led. Madame Merle listened with interest to Isabel's account of this passage, but she had not needed it to feel exempt from anxiety. On the whole she was not afraid of the Countess, and she could afford to do what was altogether best — not to appear so.

Isabel had meanwhile another visitor, whom it was not, even behind her back, so easy a matter to patronise. Henrietta Stackpole, who had left Paris after Mrs. Touchett's departure for San Remo and had worked her way down, as she said, through the cities of North Italy, reached the banks of the Arno about the middle of May. Madame Merle surveyed her with a single glance, took her in from head to foot, and after a pang of despair determined to endure her. She determined indeed to delight in her. She might n't be inhaled as a rose, but she might be grasped as a nettle. Madame Merle genially squeezed her into insignificance, and Isabel felt that in foreseeing this liberality she had done justice to her friend's intelligence. Henrietta's arrival had been announced by Mr. Bantling, who, coming down from Nice while she was at Venice, and expecting to find her in Florence, which she had not yet reached, called at Palazzo Crescentini to express his disappointment. Henrietta's own advent occurred two days later and produced in Mr. Bantling an emotion amply accounted for by the fact that he had not seen her since the termination of the episode at Versailles. The humorous view of his situation was generally taken, but it was uttered only by Ralph Touchett, who, in the privacy of his own apartment, when Bantling smoked a cigar there, indulged in goodness knew what strong comedy on the subject of the all-judging one and her British backer. This gentleman took the joke in perfectly good part and candidly confessed that he regarded the affair as a positive intellectual adventure. He liked Miss Stackpole extremely; he thought she had a wonderful head on her shoulders, and found great comfort in the society of a woman who was not perpetually thinking about what would be said and how what she did, how what *they* did — and they had done things! — would look. Miss Stackpole never cared how anything looked, and, if she did n't care, pray why should he? But his curiosity had been roused; he wanted awfully to see if she ever *would* care. He was prepared to go as far as she — he did n't see why he should break down first.

Henrietta showed no signs of breaking down. Her prospects had brightened on her leaving England, and she was now in the full enjoyment of her copious resources. She had indeed been obliged to sacrifice her hopes with regard to the inner life; the social question, on the Continent, bristled with difficulties even more numerous than those she had encountered in England. But on the Continent there was the outer life, which was palpable and visible at every turn, and more easily convertible to literary uses than the customs of those opaque islanders. Out of doors in foreign lands, as she ingeniously remarked, one seemed to see the right side of the tapestry; out of doors in England one seemed to see the wrong side, which gave one no notion of the figure. The admission costs her historian a pang, but Henrietta, despairing of more occult things, was now paying much attention to the outer life. She had been studying it for two months at Venice, from which city she sent to the *Interviewer* a conscientious account of the gondolas, the Piazza, the Bridge of Sighs, the pigeons and the young boatman who chanted Tasso. The *Interviewer* was perhaps disappointed, but Henrietta was at least seeing Europe. Her present purpose was to get down to Rome before the malaria should come on — she apparently supposed that it began on a fixed day; and with this design she was to spend at present but few days in Florence. Mr. Bantling was to go with her to Rome, and she pointed out to Isabel that as he had been there before, as he was a military man and as he had had a classical education — he had been bred at Eton, where they study nothing but

Latin and Whyte-Melville, said Miss Stackpole — he would be a most useful companion in the city of the Cæsars. At this juncture Ralph had the happy idea of proposing to Isabel that she also, under his own escort, should make a pilgrimage to Rome. She expected to pass a portion of the next winter there — that was very well; but meantime there was no harm in surveying the field. There were ten days left of the beautiful month of May — the most precious month of all to the true Rome-lover. Isabel would become a Rome-lover; that was a foregone conclusion. She was provided with a trusty companion of her own sex, whose society, thanks to the fact of other calls on this lady's attention, would probably not be oppressive. Madame Merle would remain with Mrs. Touchett; she had left Rome for the summer and would n't care to return. She professed herself delighted to be left at peace in Florence; she had locked up her apartment and sent her cook home to Palestrina. She urged Isabel, however, to assent to Ralph's proposal, and assured her that a good introduction to Rome was not a thing to be despised. Isabel in truth needed no urgjng, and the party of four arranged its little journey. Mrs. Touchett, on this occasion, had resigned herself to the absence of a duenna; we have seen that she now inclined to the belief that her niece should stand alone. One of Isabel's preparations consisted of her seeing Gilbert Osmond before she started and mentioning her intention to him.

"I should like to be in Rome with you," he commented. "I should like to see you on that wonderful ground."

She scarcely faltered. "You might come then."

"But you 'll have a lot of people with you."

"Ah," Isabel admitted, "of course I shall not be alone."

For a moment he said nothing more. "You 'll like it," he went on at last. "They 've spoiled it, but you 'll rave about it."

"Ought I to dislike it because, poor old dear — the Niobe of Nations, you know — it has been spoiled?" she asked.

"No, I think not. It has been spoiled so often," he smiled. "If I were to go, what should I do with my little girl?"

"Can't you leave her at the villa?"

"I don't know that I like that — though there 's a very good old woman who looks after her. I can 't afford a governess."

"Bring her with you then," said Isabel promptly.

Mr. Osmond looked grave. "She has been in Rome all winter, at her convent; and she 's too young to make journeys of pleasure."

"You don't like bringing her forward?" Isabel enquired.

"No, I think young girls should be kept out of the world."

"I was brought up on a different system."

"You? Oh, with you it succeeded, because you — you were exceptional."

"I don't see why," said Isabel, who, however, was not sure there was not some truth in the speech.

Mr. Osmond did n't explain; he simply went on: "If I thought it would make her resemble you to join a social group in Rome I'd take her there to-morrow."

"Don't make her resemble me," said Isabel. "Keep her like herself."

"I might send her to my sister," Mr. Osmond observed. He had almost the air of asking advice; he seemed to like to talk over his domestic matters with Miss Archer.

"Yes," she concurred; "I think that would n't do much towards making her resemble me!"

After she had left Florence Gilbert Osmond met Madame Merle at the Countess Gemini's. There were other people present; the Countess's drawing-room was usually well filled, and the talk had been general, but after a while Osmond left his place and came and sat on an ottoman half-behind, half-beside Madame Merle's chair. "She wants me to go to Rome with her," he remarked in a low voice.

"To go with her?"

"To be there while she's there. She proposed it."

"I suppose you mean that you proposed it and she assented."

"Of course I gave her a chance. But she's encouraging — she's very encouraging."

"I rejoice to hear it — but don't cry victory too soon. Of course you'll go to Rome."

"Ah," said Osmond, "it makes one work, this idea of yours!"

"Don't pretend you don't enjoy it — you're very ungrateful. You've not been so well occupied these many years."

"The way you take it 's beautiful," said Osmond. "I ought to be grateful for that."

"Not too much so, however," Madame Merle answered. She talked with her usual smile, leaning back in her chair and looking round the room. "You 've made a very good impression, and I 've seen for myself that you 've received one. You 've not come to Mrs. Touchett's seven times to oblige me."

"The girl 's not disagreeable," Osmond quietly conceded.

Madame Merle dropped her eye on him a moment, during which her lips closed with a certain firmness. "Is that all you can find to say about that fine creature?"

"All? Is n't it enough? Of how many people have you heard me say more?"

She made no answer to this, but still presented her talkative grace to the room. "You 're unfathomable," she murmured at last. "I 'm frightened at the abyss into which I shall have cast her."

He took it almost gaily. "You can't draw back — you 've gone too far."

"Very good; but you must do the rest yourself."

"I shall do it," said Gilbert Osmond.

Madame Merle remained silent and he changed his place again; but when she rose to go he also took leave. Mrs. Touchett's victoria was awaiting her guest in the court, and after he had helped his friend into it he stood there detaining her. "You 're very indiscreet," she said rather wearily; "you should n't have moved when I did."

He had taken off his hat; he passed his hand over

his forehead. "I always forget; I'm out of the habit."

"You're quite unfathomable," she repeated, glancing up at the windows of the house, a modern structure in the new part of the town.

He paid no heed to this remark, but spoke in his own sense. "She's really very charming. I've scarcely known any one more graceful."

"It does me good to hear you say that. The better you like her the better for me."

"I like her very much. She's all you described her, and into the bargain capable, I feel, of great devotion. She has only one fault."

"What's that?"

"Too many ideas."

"I warned you she was clever."

"Fortunately they're very bad ones," said Osmond.

"Why is that fortunate?"

"*Dame*, if they must be sacrificed!"

Madame Merle leaned back, looking straight before her; then she spoke to the coachman. But her friend again detained her. "If I go to Rome what shall I do with Pansy?"

"I'll go and see her," said Madame Merle.

XXVII

I MAY not attempt to report in its fulness our young woman's response to the deep appeal of Rome, to analyse her feelings as she trod the pavement of the Forum or to number her pulsations as she crossed the threshold of Saint Peter's. It is enough to say that her impression was such as might have been expected of a person of her freshness and her eagerness. She had always been fond of history, and here was history in the stones of the street and the atoms of the sunshine. She had an imagination that kindled at the mention of great deeds, and wherever she turned some great deed had been acted. These things strongly moved her, but moved her all inwardly. It seemed to her companions that she talked less than usual, and Ralph Touchett, when he appeared to be looking listlessly and awkwardly over her head, was really dropping on her an intensity of observation. By her own measure she was very happy; she would even have been willing to take these hours for the happiest she was ever to know. The sense of the terrible human past was heavy to her, but that of something altogether contemporary would suddenly give it wings that it could wave in the blue. Her consciousness was so mixed that she scarcely knew where the different parts of it would lead her, and she went about in a repressed ecstasy of contemplation, seeing often in the things she looked at a great deal more than was there, and yet not seeing many of the items enumerated in her Murray. Rome, as Ralph said, confessed to the psychological moment. The herd of reëchoing tourists had departed and most of the solemn places had relapsed into solemnity. The sky was a blaze of blue, and the plash of the fountains in their mossy niches had lost its chill and doubled its music. On the corners of the warm, bright streets one stumbled on bundles of flowers. Our friends had gone one afternoon — it was the third of their stay — to look at the latest excavations in the Forum, these labours having been for some time previous largely extended. They had descended from the modern street to the level of the Sacred Way, along which they wandered with a reverence of step which was not the same on the part of each. Henrietta Stackpole was struck with the fact that ancient Rome had been paved a good deal like New York, and even found an analogy between the deep chariot-ruts traceable in the antique street and the overjangled iron grooves which express the intensity of American life. The sun had begun to sink, the air was a golden haze, and the long shadows of broken column and vague pedestal leaned across the field of ruin. Henrietta wandered away with Mr. Bantling, whom it was apparently delightful to her to hear speak of Julius Cæsar as a "cheeky old boy," and Ralph addressed such elucidations as he was prepared to offer to the attentive ear of our heroine. One of the humble archæologists who hover about the place had put himself at the disposal of the two, and repeated his lesson with a fluency which the decline of the season had done nothing to impair. A process of digging was on view in a remote corner of the Forum, and he presently remarked that if it should please the *signori* to go and watch it a little they might see something of interest. The proposal commended itself more to Ralph than to Isabel, weary with much wandering; so that she admonished her companion to satisfy his curiosity while she patiently awaited his return. The hour and the place were much to her taste — she should enjoy being briefly alone. Ralph accordingly went off with the cicerone while Isabel sat down on a prostrate column near the foundations of the Capitol. She wanted a short solitude, but she was not long to enjoy it. Keen as was her interest in the rugged relics of the Roman past that lay scattered about her and in which the corrosion of centuries had still left so much of individual life, her thoughts, after resting a while on these things, had wandered, by a concatenation of stages it might require some subtlety to trace, to regions and objects charged with a more active appeal. From the Roman past to Isabel Archer's future was a long stride, but her imagination had taken it in a single flight and now hovered in slow circles over the nearer and richer field. She was so absorbed in her thoughts, as she bent her eyes upon a row of cracked but not dislocated slabs covering the ground at her feet, that she had not heard the sound of approaching footsteps before a shadow was thrown across the line of her vision. She looked up and saw a gentleman — a gentleman who was not Ralph come back to say that the excavations were a bore. This personage was startled as she was startled; he stood there baring his head to her perceptibly pale surprise.

"Lord Warburton!" Isabel exclaimed as she rose.

"I had no idea it was you. I turned that corner and came upon you."

She looked about her to explain. "I 'm alone, but my companions have just left me. My cousin 's gone to look at the work over there."

"Ah yes; I see." And Lord Warburton's eyes wandered vaguely in the direction she had indicated. He stood firmly before her now; he had recovered his balance and seemed to wish to show it, though very kindly. "Don't let me disturb you," he went on, looking at her dejected pillar. "I 'm afraid you 're tired."

"Yes, I 'm rather tired." She hesitated a moment, but sat down again. "Don't let me interrupt *you*," she added.

"Oh dear, I 'm quite alone, I 've nothing on earth to do. I had no idea you were in Rome. I 've just come from the East. I 'm only passing through."

"You 've been making a long journey," said Isabel, who had learned from Ralph that Lord Warburton was absent from England.

"Yes, I came abroad for six months — soon after I saw you last. I 've been in Turkey and Asia Minor; I came the other day from Athens." He managed not to be awkward, but he was n't easy, and after a longer look at the girl he came down to nature. "Do you wish me to leave you, or will you let me stay a little?"

She took it all humanely. "I don't wish you to

leave me, Lord Warburton; I'm very glad to see you."

"Thank you for saying that. May I sit down?"

The fluted shaft on which she had taken her seat would have afforded a resting-place to several persons, and there was plenty of room even for a highly-developed Englishman. This fine specimen of that great class seated himself near our young lady, and in the course of five minutes he had asked her several questions, taken rather at random and to which, as he put some of them twice over, he apparently somewhat missed catching the answer; had given her too some information about himself which was not wasted upon her calmer feminine sense. He repeated more than once that he had not expected to meet her, and it was evident that the encounter touched him in a way that would have made preparation advisable. He began abruptly to pass from the impunity of things to their solemnity, and from their being delightful to their being impossible. He was splendidly sunburnt; even his multitudinous beard had been burnished by the fire of Asia. He was dressed in the loose-fitting, heterogeneous garments in which the English traveller in foreign lands is wont to consult his comfort and affirm his nationality; and with his pleasant steady eyes, his bronzed complexion, fresh beneath its seasoning, his manly figure, his minimising manner and his general air of being a gentleman and an explorer, he was such a representative of the British race as need not in any clime have been disavowed by those who have a kindness for it. Isabel noted these things and was glad she had always liked him. He had kept, evidently in spite of shocks, every one of his merits — properties these partaking of the essence of great decent houses, as one might put it; resembling their innermost fixtures and ornaments, not subject to vulgar shifting and removable only by some whole break-up. They talked of the matters naturally in order; her uncle's death, Ralph's state of health, the way she had passed her winter, her visit to Rome, her return to Florence, her plans for the summer, the hotel she was staying at; and then of Lord Warburton's own adventures, movements, intentions, impressions and present domicile. At last there was a silence, and it said so much more than either had said that it scarce needed his final words. "I 've written to you several times."

"Written to me? I 've never had your letters."

"I never sent them. I burned them up."

"Ah," laughed Isabel, "it was better that you should do that than I!"

"I thought you would n't care for them," he went on with a simplicity that touched her. "It seemed to me that after all I had no right to trouble you with letters."

"I should have been very glad to have news of you. You know how I hoped that — that —" But she stopped; there would be such a flatness in the utterance of her thought.

"I know what you 're going to say. You hoped we should always remain good friends." This formula, as Lord Warburton uttered it, was certainly flat enough; but then he was interested in making it appear so.

She found herself reduced simply to "Please don't talk of all that"; a speech which hardly struck her as improvement on the other.

"It's a small consolation to allow me!" her companion exclaimed with force.

"I can't pretend to console you," said the girl, who, all still as she sat there, threw herself back with a sort of inward triumph on the answer that had satisfied him so little six months before. He was pleasant, he was powerful, he was gallant; there was no better man than he. But her answer remained.

"It's very well you don't try to console me; it would n't be in your power," she heard him say through the medium of her strange elation.

"I hoped we should meet again, because I had no fear you would attempt to make me feel I had wronged you. But when you do that — the pain's greater than the pleasure." And she got up with a small conscious majesty, looking for her companions.

"I don't want to make you feel that; of course I can't say that. I only just want you to know one or two things — in fairness to myself, as it were. I won't return to the subject again. I felt very strongly what I expressed to you last year; I could n't think of anything else. I tried to forget — energetically, systematically. I tried to take an interest in somebody else. I tell you this because I want you to know I did my duty. I did n't succeed. It was for the same purpose I went abroad — as far away as possible. They say travelling distracts the mind, but it did n't distract mine. I've thought of you perpetually, ever since I last saw you. I'm exactly the same. I love you just as much, and everything I said to you then is just as true. This instant at which I speak to you shows me again exactly how, to my great misfortune, you just insuperably *charm* me. There — I can't say less. I don't mean, however, to insist; it 's only for a moment. I may add that when I came upon you a few minutes since, without the smallest idea of seeing you, I was, upon my honour, in the very act of wishing I knew where you were." He had recovered his self-control, and while he spoke it became complete. He might have been addressing a small committee — making all quietly and clearly a statement of importance; aided by an occasional look at a paper of notes concealed in his hat, which he had not again put on. And the committee, assuredly, would have felt the point proved.

"I 've often thought of you, Lord Warburton," Isabel answered. "You may be sure I shall always do that." And she added in a tone of which she tried to keep up the kindness and keep down the meaning: "There 's no harm in that on either side."

They walked along together, and she was prompt to ask about his sisters and request him to let them know she had done so. He made for the moment no further reference to their great question, but dipped again into shallower and safer waters. But he wished to know when she was to leave Rome, and on her mentioning the limit of her stay declared he was glad it was still so distant.

"Why do you say that if you yourself are only passing through?" she enquired with some anxiety.

"Ah, when I said I was passing through I did n't

mean that one would treat Rome as if it were Clapham Junction. To pass through Rome is to stop a week or two."

"Say frankly that you mean to stay as long as I do!"

His flushed smile, for a little, seemed to sound her. "You won't like that. You're afraid you'll see too much of me."

"It does n't matter what I like. I certainly can't expect you to leave this delightful place on my account. But I confess I'm afraid of you."

"Afraid I'll begin again? I promise to be very careful."

They had gradually stopped and they stood a moment face to face. "Poor Lord Warburton!" she said with a compassion intended to be good for both of them.

"Poor Lord Warburton indeed! But I'll be careful."

"You may be unhappy, but you shall not make *me* so. That I can't allow."

"If I believed I could make you unhappy I think I should try it." At this she walked in advance and he also proceeded. "I'll never say a word to displease you."

"Very good. If you do, our friendship's at an end."

"Perhaps some day — after a while — you'll give me leave."

"Give you leave to make me unhappy?"

He hesitated. "To tell you again —" But he checked himself. "I'll keep it down. I'll keep it down always."

Ralph Touchett had been joined in his visit to the excavation by Miss Stackpole and her attendant, and these three now emerged from among the mounds of earth and stone collected round the aperture and came into sight of Isabel and her companion. Poor Ralph hailed his friend with joy qualified by wonder, and Henrietta exclaimed in a high voice "Gracious, there's that lord!" Ralph and his English neighbour greeted with the austerity with which, after long separations, English neighbours greet, and Miss Stackpole rested her large intellectual gaze upon the sunburnt traveller. But she soon established her relation to the crisis. "I don't suppose you remember me, sir."

"Indeed I do remember you," said Lord Warburton. "I asked you to come and see me, and you never came."

"I don't go everywhere I'm asked," Miss Stackpole answered coldly.

"Ah well, I won't ask you again," laughed the master of Lockleigh.

"If you do I'll go; so be sure!"

Lord Warburton, for all his hilarity, seemed sure enough. Mr. Bantling had stood by without claiming a recognition, but he now took occasion to nod to his lordship, who answered him with a friendly "Oh, you here, Bantling?" and a hand-shake.

"Well," said Henrietta, "I did n't know you knew him!"

"I guess you don't know every one I know," Mr. Bantling rejoined facetiously.

"I thought that when an Englishman knew a lord he always told you."

"Ah, I'm afraid Bantling was ashamed of me," Lord Warburton laughed again. Isabel took pleasure in that note; she gave a small sigh of relief as they kept their course homeward.

The next day was Sunday; she spent her morning over two long letters — one to her sister Lily, the other to Madame Merle; but in neither of these epistles did she mention the fact that a rejected suitor had threatened her with another appeal. Of a Sunday afternoon all good Romans (and the best Romans are often the northern barbarians) follow the custom of going to vespers at Saint Peter's; and it had been agreed among our friends that they would drive together to the great church. After lunch, an hour before the carriage came, Lord Warburton presented himself at the Hôtel de Paris and paid a visit to the two ladies, Ralph Touchett and Mr. Bantling having gone out together. The visitor seemed to have wished to give Isabel a proof of his intention to keep the promise made her the evening before; he was both discreet and frank — not even dumbly importunate or remotely intense. He thus left her to judge what a mere good friend he could be. He talked about his travels, about Persia, about Turkey, and when Miss Stackpole asked him whether it would "pay" for her to visit those countries assured her they offered a great field to female enterprise. Isabel did him justice, but she wondered what his purpose was and what he expected to gain even by proving the superior strain of his sincerity. If he expected to melt her by showing what a good fellow he was, he might spare himself the trouble. She knew the superior strain of everything about him, and nothing he could now do was required to light the view. Moreover his being in Rome at all affected her as a complication of the wrong sort — she liked so complications of the right. Nevertheless, when, on bringing his call to a close, he said he too should be at Saint Peter's and should look out for her and her friends, she was obliged to reply that he must follow his convenience.

In the church, as she strolled over its tesselated acres, he was the first person she encountered. She had not been one of the superior tourists who are "disappointed" in Saint Peter's and find it smaller than its fame; the first time she passed beneath the huge leathern curtain that strains and bangs at the entrance, the first time she found herself beneath the far-arching dome and saw the light drizzle down through the air thickened with incense and with the reflections of marble and gilt, of mosaic and bronze, her conception of greatness rose and dizzily rose. After this it never lacked space to soar. She gazed and wondered like a child or a peasant, she paid her silent tribute to the seated sublime. Lord Warburton walked beside her and talked of Saint Sophia of Constantinople; she feared for instance that he would end by calling attention to his exemplary conduct. The service had not yet begun, but at Saint Peter's there is much to observe, and as there is something almost profane in the vastness of the place, which seems meant as much for physical as for spiritual exercise, the different figures and groups, the mingled worshippers and spectators, may follow their various intentions without conflict or scandal. In that splendid immensity individual indiscretion carries but a short distance. Isabel and her companions, however, were guilty of none; for though Henrietta was obliged in candour to declare that Michael Angelo's dome suffered by comparison with that of the Capitol at Washington, she addressed her protest chiefly to Mr. Bantling's ear and reserved it in its more accentuated form for the columns of the *Interviewer*. Isabel made the circuit of the church with his lordship, and as they drew near the choir on the left of the entrance the voices of the Pope's singers were borne to them over the heads of the large number of persons clustered outside the doors. They paused a while on the skirts of this crowd, composed in equal measure of Roman cockneys and inquisitive strangers, and while they stood there the sacred concert went forward. Ralph, with Henrietta and Mr. Bantling, was apparently within, where Isabel, looking beyond the dense group in front of her, saw the afternoon light, silvered by clouds of incense that seemed to mingle with the splendid chant, slope through the embossed recesses of high windows. After a while the singing stopped and then Lord Warburton seemed disposed to move off with her. Isabel could only accompany him; whereupon she found herself confronted with Gilbert Osmond, who appeared to have been standing at a short distance behind her. He now approached with all the forms — he appeared to have multiplied them on this occasion to suit the place.

"So you decided to come?" she said as she put out her hand.

"Yes, I came last night and called this afternoon at your hotel. They told me you had come here, and I looked about for you."

"The others are inside," she decided to say.

"I did n't come for the others," he promptly returned.

She looked away; Lord Warburton was watching them; perhaps he had heard this. Suddenly she remembered it to be just what he had said to her the morning he came to Gardencourt to ask her to marry him. Mr. Osmond's words had brought the colour to her cheek, and this reminiscence had not the effect of dispelling it. She repaired any betrayal by mentioning to each companion the name of the other, and fortunately at this moment Mr. Bantling emerged from the choir, cleaving the crowd with British valour and followed by Miss Stackpole and Ralph Touchett. I say fortunately, but this is perhaps a superficial view of the matter; since on perceiving the gentleman from Florence Ralph Touchett appeared to take the case as not committing him to joy. He did n't hang back, however, from civility, and presently observed to Isabel, with due benevolence, that she would soon have all her friends about her. Miss Stackpole had met Mr. Osmond in Florence, but she had already found occasion to say to Isabel that she liked him no better than her other admirers — than Mr. Touchett and Lord Warburton, and even than little Mr. Rosier in Paris. "I don't know what it's in you," she had been pleased to remark, "but for a nice girl you do attract the most unnatural people. Mr. Goodwood 's the only one I 've any respect for, and he's just the one you don't appreciate."

"What's your opinion of Saint Peter's?" Mr. Osmond was meanwhile enquiring of our young lady.

"It's very large and very bright," she contented herself with replying.

"It's too large; it makes one feel like an atom."

"Is n't that the right way to feel in the greatest of human temples?" she asked with rather a liking for her phrase.

"I suppose it's the right way to feel everywhere, when one *is* nobody. But I like it in a church as little as anywhere else."

"You ought indeed to be a Pope!" Isabel exclaimed, remembering something he had referred to in Florence.

"Ah, I should have enjoyed that!" said Gilbert Osmond.

Lord Warburton meanwhile had joined Ralph Touchett, and the two strolled away together. "Who's the fellow speaking to Miss Archer?" his lordship demanded.

"His name's Gilbert Osmond — he lives in Florence," Ralph said.

"What is he besides?"

"Nothing at all. Oh yes, he's an American; but one forgets that — he's so little of one."

"Has he known Miss Archer long?"

"Three or four weeks."

"Does she like him?"

"She's trying to find out."

"And will she?"

"Find out — ?" Ralph asked.

"Will she like him ?"

"Do you mean will she accept him ?"

"Yes," said Lord Warburton after an instant; "I suppose that 's what I horribly mean."

"Perhaps not if one does nothing to prevent it," Ralph replied.

His lordship stared a moment, but apprehended. "Then we must be perfectly quiet ?"

"As quiet as the grave. And only on the chance!" Ralph added.

"The chance she may ?"

"The chance she may not ?"

Lord Warburton took this at first in silence, but he spoke again. "Is he awfully clever ?"

"Awfully," said Ralph.

His companion thought. "And what else ?"

"What more do you want ?" Ralph groaned.

"Do you mean what more does *she?*"

Ralph took him by the arm to turn him: they had to rejoin the others. "She wants nothing that *we* can give her."

"Ah well, if she won't have You —!" said his lordship handsomely as they went.

END OF VOLUME I